RIVEN EMPIRE

KAVORA
SHAVHALLA
VIHAARA FOREST
TARSI
VALMANDI
JAKHAT
MAYUKA RIVER
ADRATI RIVER
CHATANDA
SHARMOK
HAYATHU
SULAR DESERT

OSELIEN
HARI
LIBERA
DEVEAURAL
MALFRAM
ATREA
N
ERYTHYR

ALSO BY T. A. HERNANDEZ

THE CURSE OF SHAVHALLA TRILOGY

Tethered Spirits
Revenant Prince
Riven Empire

THE SECRETS OF PEACE TRILOGY

Secrets of PEACE
Renegades of PEACE
Survivors of PEACE

OTHER WORKS

Calico Thunder Rides Again
Whispers of Shadow and Starlight

RIVEN EMPIRE

T. A. HERNANDEZ

This book contains varying degrees of the following:
Mild language, violence, depictions of death, references to self-harm and suicidal ideation, exploration of trauma and mental illness, discrimination, torture, and imprisonment. Please read safely and responsibly.

RIVEN EMPIRE

Cover art and design by T. A. Hernandez

ISBN: 9781734033038

THE STORY SO FAR

Tethered Spirits

A MAN NAMED AMAR TRAVELS THE KAVORAN EMPIRE WITH TWO companions, a musician named Mitul and a Sularan warrior named Saya. Together, they seek answers about Amar's mysterious immortality, which allows him to return to life each time he is killed…but without any of his previous memories. They enlist the help of a girl named Kesari and the Spirit Tarja she is Bonded to, a fiery being named Lucian.

Meanwhile, orphaned refugee Aleida and her white dragon Spirit Tarja, Valkyra, pursue Amar, believing his immortality could save Aleida's brother Tyrus from a fatal illness. They attack Amar and his companions, and Amar dies while Aleida escapes.

Amar's body is taken to the home of Tamaya Takhar, a Tarja who may have answers about Amar's immortality. While there, Kesari asks Tamaya to break her Bond with Lucian. Tamaya refuses and urges Kesari not to pursue this.

When Amar returns to life the next morning, he has no recollection of who he is or anything that happened previously. Tamaya suggests that Amar may be cursed, and she encourages him to seek help from a powerful Atrean Tarja named Jameson. The group sets off for Atrea together.

Having recovered from her injuries, Aleida breaks into Tamaya's home and interrogates her about Amar and the others, even going so far as to torture the old woman. From there, she follows Amar's trail through Kavora. At one point she is arrested, but Valkyra arranges her escape with the help of Magistrate Ashaya. Aleida is disturbed by Valkyra's connection to Ashaya, who is a known friend of Nandini Kumar, the woman responsible for the invasion of Aleida's homeland.

Saya leads Amar and the others through the Sular desert. Through a rite of passage known as haseph, she hopes to strengthen her people's ability to defend and preserve their way of life using the same curse that has made Amar immortal.

Aleida and Valkyra visit the town of Chatanda, where Tyrus lives under the care of a healer named Hasan. Hasan advises Aleida to stay so she can be with Tyrus in his final days, but Aleida leaves to continue hunting Amar.

Kesari leads Amar and the others to her home city, where they visit the Wizard Jameson. He agrees to try restoring Amar's memories. Kesari experiences disturbing flashbacks and a panic attack related to an accident caused by her magic, which resulted in many deaths, including her older brother's. She ran away, vowing to never use her magic again. She decides to visit her family, who welcome her with open arms.

Several days later, Kesari and Lucian assist Jameson as he performs the spell that will restore Amar's memories. Through this process they learn that Amar's curse is connected to Shavhalla, an ancient city now in ruins and said to be haunted. Kesari decides to accompany Amar and the others to Shavhalla. They depart by ship.

Aleida finds Jameson, who reveals that Amar has gone to Shavhalla. Aleida and Valkyra hire a ship of their own and bring Jameson along as a guide. When their ship catches up to Amar's, a naval battle ensues. Amar and his companions are victorious and sail on. Aleida, Valkyra, and Jameson abandon ship, make their way to shore, and continue their journey on foot.

Amar and the others make landfall and travel through the forest to the haunted ruins of Shavhalla. At the palace, Amar remembers how he was cursed.

Six hundred years prior, Amar was prince of Shavhalla and son of a cruel warlord. The warlord conquered, stole from, and enslaved many people, including a young woman named Mahati. Mahati went to Shavhalla hoping to curse the warlord but instead found Amar. Out of time and options, she cursed him in his father's place, binding his soul to the physical world until he can atone for the atrocities of war.

Amar tells the others about this realization, and they seek more information in the palace records room. There Saya discovers what she has been looking for—a journal describing Amar's curse and potentially the means to replicate it.

Valkyra scouts ahead for Amar and the others, leaving Aleida alone with Jameson. He tells her what he knows of Nandini Kumar's demise, suggesting she may not have been killed properly and instead became a Spirit Tarja. He reads a letter Aleida had previously received from Hasan, which reveals that Tyrus has passed away. Aleida realizes Valkyra is actually the spirit of Nandini Kumar. When Valkyra returns, she confronts her, and Valkyra severs the Bond between them. As Aleida fades into unconsciousness, she witnesses Valkyra forcing a new Bond with Jameson.

Amar finds Mahati's bones in a cell and determines she must have used the last of her life to fuel the curse that now lays over Shavhalla. He gathers her remains and lays her to rest. The curse over the city is broken, but Amar's curse remains intact.

Amar and his friends find Aleida unconscious. When she wakes, she pleads with them to help her defeat Valkyra. Killing Jameson would be the easiest way to do this, but Kesari and Amar do not want to harm the wizard and insist on trying to trap Valkyra instead. They continue through the forest without any sign of the pair. When they stop to rest, Amar translates records Saya took from Shavhalla.

The following night, Valkyra attacks using Jameson as her puppet. A fight ensues. Valkyra gains the upper hand. In exchange for his friends' safety, Amar offers to go with her. She puts the others to sleep before taking Amar deeper into the forest. She forces Jameson to stab Amar, then severs her Bond with him. Jameson dies.

Amar realizes Valkyra intends to make a Bond with him, which would allow her to share his immortality. He knows he's dying and will come back to life without his memories, at which point Valkyra could manipulate him into killing his own friends. He manages to ingest a magic-inhibiting fungus called daravak before he dies, hoping this will buy his friends some time.

Kesari and the others regain consciousness the following morning. They find Jameson's body, as well as a pool of blood they realize is Amar's. They decide to split up. Mitul and Aleida will search for Amar and determine what Valkyra's plans are. Saya will go to Hayathu to finish her haseph. Afterward, she, Kesari, and Lucian will travel to Atrea to recover Jameson's research so they can restore Amar's memories again.

In the final scene, a young man named Savir travels to Valmandi. He doesn't remember his past, but he's been told he is Prince Savir, long-lost heir to the Kavoran throne. He formed a Bond with his Tarja guardian, Valkyra, who died when they were attacked on the road. They both hope Savir's memories will return, but if not, Valkyra reassures Savir that he needn't worry. She has planned for everything…

Revenant Prince

AMAR NOW BELIEVES HIMSELF TO BE SAVIR, LOST PRINCE AND rightful heir to the imperial throne. With Valkyra, he travels to Valmandi to reclaim his birthright. When they reach the city, Savir eavesdrops on a secret meeting between Valkyra and Magistrate Ashaya, an advisor on Valmandi's royal council. Afterward, Ashaya presents Savir to King Bhajan and Queen Indira, his maternal grandparents, along with evidence that he is the true prince. King Bhajan immediately begins working to put Savir on the throne, demanding that the current empress, Dashiva, step down.

Meanwhile, Aleida and Mitul travel to Jakhat, where they hope to find information about Amar. Mitul builds up a reputation as a musical performer, which grants him access to higher social circles within the city. Aleida works as a servant. Her trust for Mitul grows as he consistently treats her with kindness. One evening, he introduces her to his former romantic partner, Kamaal Ruman, a famed artist and Aleida's idol. Kamaal encourages Aleida to continue pursuing her art, which she has been discouraged about due to physical limitations brought on by the severing of her Bond with Valkyra.

Kesari, Lucian, and Saya reach Hayathu, and Saya presents the records she took from Shavhalla to complete her haseph. Her offering is accepted, but the council decides not to use the knowledge those records contain, fearing the consequences of bringing curses back to the world. Saya's outcast uncle Zefar disagrees with this decision, attempts to steal the records, and is banished.

Savir visits Jakhat at Empress Dashiva's invitation. There he also meets her daughter Jasala. Ashaya presents evidence regarding Savir's identity and claim to the throne, but Dashiva remains skeptical. Some time later, Ashaya takes Savir to meet with Muraka, the general of Jakhat's Tarja army. Ashaya attempts to convince Muraka to side with Savir and Valmandi in the conflict that is sure to come, but she won't commit. Afterward, Savir overhears Valkyra and Ashaya discussing the encounter. Valkyra believes she can personally persuade Muraka to agree to their plan.

Upon learning that Prince Savir may be Amar, Aleida and Mitul enlist Kamaal's help in confirming this. Mitul worries for Amar given the manipulation he is under. Kamaal is able to soothe him, and the two begin to rekindle their romance. Aleida finds comfort in seeing them happy together and allows herself to form attachments to them in a way she hasn't connected with anyone since her parents died.

Kesari and her companions continue to Atrea. With some help from Kesari's sister Navya and her dubious friends, they are able to retrieve the research they need. Kesari and Navya make amends before Kesari departs again.

Empress Dashiva tells Savir she does not believe him to be the rightful heir to the throne and thus refuses to abdicate. Valkyra assures Savir that he did his best to prevent a conflict, but now it is time for him to take a stand. Savir remains uncertain as he prepares to return home to Valmandi.

While travelling to Valmandi to reunite with their friends, Kesari, Lucian, and Saya stop in Hayathu again. They learn Zefar has stolen the Shavhallan records and disappeared. Saya's mother asks her to do what she can to retrieve them.

With Savir's departure from Jakhat, Mitul and Aleida decide it is time to set out for Valmandi themselves, where they plan to meet up with Kesari and the others. Mitul asks Kamaal to come with him, but he declines. They set out anyway. In his heartbreak, Mitul withdraws, leaving Aleida feeling panicked and alone. When Kesari and the others fail to arrive on schedule, she takes matters into her own hands, sneaking into Savir's room at the palace. She is discovered and arrested.

Kesari and the others reunite with Mitul, who informs them Aleida has gone missing. Lucian tracks her down in a cell, and they plan to free her. At the same time, Savir learns someone was arrested sneaking into his room and that Valkyra hid this information from him. He insists on going to question the intruder himself as he no longer trusts Valkyra to tell him the truth.

While attempting to sneak Aleida out of her cell, Kesari, Lucian, and Mitul are confronted by Amar. Amar shoots Mitul, and Kesari takes mesala to enhance her magic and get her friends to safely. Pursued by guards, they take refuge in a temple, where Kesari works with healers to save Mitul's life. Saya arrives with Kamaal, who came to the city looking for Mitul after realizing it was a mistake to let him go. Kamaal is able to lead them all to safety at his sister's house, where they recover and make plans to get Amar out of Valkyra's clutches.

Back at the palace, Savir questions Valkyra about the strangers who seemed to know him. She refuses to answer his questions. Before he can press her further, he is informed that Jakhat's forces are on the move. Valkyra avoids him for the next several days as preparations for battle are made.

Saya finds Zefar and forces him to give up the Shavhallan records, but he has already turned over parts of it to the Valmandi royal council. With Jameson's research, Kesari recreates the spell that can restore Amar's memories. She imbues Amar's journal with this magic, and Kamaal is able to get it to him at the palace.

Savir hides the journal away, not wanting Valkyra to discover him reading it. He and King Bhajan ride out to Valmandi's military encampment and prepare to meet Jakhat's forces in battle. While there, a message from Ashaya arrives, stating that Savir's attackers from the guardhouse have been found. Valkyra flies off to join Ashaya. Savir reads the journal. By the time he finishes, Jakhat's forces have arrived and the battle begins.

Kesari and the others are attacked by Magistrate Ashaya and additional enemies. Zefar sacrifices himself to allow Kesari time to burn the Shavhallan records, but she has a single page saved inside her pocket. Kesari manages to wound Ashaya before he flees. Aleida attempts to capture Valkyra but fails. Saya decides to leave the group to return Zefar's body home and inform her people of what has happened.

As the battle between Valmandi and Jakhat intensifies, Savir begins to remember his true past. He realizes he isn't the prince after all, and he frantically tries to call for an end to the fighting. In his distraction, he is wounded, and his personal guard, Tarik, ushers him away from the fight. When Amar continues raving, Tarik uses magic to sedate him.

Amar comes to and finds King Bhajan at his bedside. He immediately wants to tell him everything. However, Valkyra is also there, and Amar can't risk letting on what he knows. For now, he will have to continue playing the role of Prince Savir.

Part I

Flight from a Gilded Cage

AMAR

ARE THEY SAFE?

That question rattled around Amar's head like dice in a cup, a clamor he knew would not end until he finally reunited with his friends. They were being hunted, and it was his fault, and he wanted nothing more than to protect them.

But for now, they'd proven capable of protecting themselves. Before any reunion could happen, there was something more important he needed to do.

He tugged at the cuffs of his jacket and stepped up to the flap of his tent, mentally readying himself for what was to come. Valkyra hadn't left him alone for more than an hour the day prior, but she'd flown off early this morning to check in with Ashaya. With the dragon gone, he had a rare opportunity to speak to King Bhajan alone, and he needed to take advantage of that.

He stepped outside, squinting a little against the sun. Tarik gave him a curt nod, his dark eyes as hard and stern as ever beneath thick brows. "Good morning."

Amar tried not to read too much into the lack of formal address in the guard's greeting. Tarik had only recently decided to acknowledge him as *Prince* Savir. Amar shouting that he *wasn't* the prince in the middle of a battlefield was sure to have raised the man's old suspicions. But it didn't matter. Amar just needed to talk to Bhajan, and then they could start setting everything right.

Even if that meant the king was going to have him arrested and executed for treason.

He set off for the healer's tent where Bhajan had taken to visiting injured soldiers. Looking around the camp, it was hard to believe their battle with Jakhat's forces had ended only the night before last. Everything felt different now, and not only because Amar had started that battle believing himself to be an entirely different person. Burial parties still labored to collect the dead and lay them to rest in graves opened by Tarja magic. Any wounded who could be safely moved were taken to healing centers in Valmandi to complete their recovery. A crew of additional Tarja healers had arrived yesterday morning to care for those still too injured to move, and the pained cries that had initially haunted the camp were now mercifully absent.

Perhaps the strangest change of all was the presence of dozens of new Spirit Tarja hovering around the outskirts of the camp. They weren't as visible now as they were at night, but in their unbonded human forms, they emanated a faint, blue glow that made them hard to miss. Many of the spirits had already departed, choosing to spend their last hours with loved ones before fading away into whatever afterlife came next. Others would seek out willing Bond partners elsewhere, but dozens more remained. They kept a respectful distance, closely monitored by the scholars who had come not only to observe and study but to ensure that any Bonds made were well-informed and ethically consented to by both parties involved.

Some of these Bonds had already been forged, and the new Tarja gathered to test their magic and show off the various forms their Spirit Tarja had taken. Most were inanimate objects. Books were particularly useful as they allowed for some type of communication through the written words on the page. More complex abilities such as maintaining a speaking voice or an independently moving form required a greater level of power and skill from the Spirit Tarja, and Amar had only seen a few of these so far—a swirling cloud of smoke, a butterfly, the talking skull of a bird.

It gave him a new appreciation for Lucian, who had cleverly and skillfully taken a form that allowed him to maintain both his voice and his mobility without the power needed for a larger or more complicated form—an animal, for instance. It also renewed a healthy sense of caution regarding Valkyra, who had been powerful enough to become a small, talking dragon.

Amar reached the large healing tent and swept open the entry with his arm. With so few people inside, he should have been able to spot Bhajan quickly, but the king was nowhere to be seen. Amar exited the tent and spoke to Tarik, who still trailed dutifully behind him. "Where is the—my grandfather?"

A tiny hesitation, barely a slip at all. But he couldn't afford such slips around Tarik, and certainly not around Valkyra. *I am still Prince Savir.*

"He left early this morning," Tarik said. "I thought you knew."

"He didn't tell me."

"Probably didn't want to wake you. There was an urgent message last night from Advisor Khatri. He wanted to review it with the rest of the council."

Amar swallowed the curses that jumped to the tip of his tongue. If Bhajan had returned to Valmandi, it would be at least another day before he could speak to him. By then, Valkyra would be back, constantly perched on Amar's shoulder or lurking around some corner with Ashaya.

"Savir?" Tarik asked in a concerned tone, probably noting the deep furrows that had formed between Amar's brows.

"What was the message?" he asked.

"Jakhat's armies are moving on Chatanda and the southern farmlands. The forces we routed are already making their way east to join a smaller contingent stationed there."

This time, Amar let his curses out in a quiet hiss. The nobles of that region had remained neutral in Kavora's civil war thus far, with farmers and merchants continuing to sell their crops to both sides as if nothing had changed. There had been an unspoken understanding between Jakhat and Valmandi that permitting the region's neutrality benefited everyone, particularly Kavora's innocent citizens unwillingly swept up in this conflict. If Dashiva was willing to take the region for herself and cut off Valmandi, its allies, and their people from a vital food source, she was condemning those same innocents to starvation. And the longer this war continued, the harsher the impact would be.

"This has to stop."

"We all knew what might happen when it started." The harsh edge in Tarik's voice sounded like an accusation.

Whatever misgivings the guard held toward him, Amar would have to deal with them later. "My grandfather wouldn't have left without telling me anything. He must have left something—a letter, a message. Did he tell you what he wanted me to do?"

"No. Are you sure he didn't leave a note in your tent?"

Amar hadn't noticed, but he'd been too fixated on other concerns to pay much attention to his surroundings. He made his way back to the tent he and Bhajan had shared. A quick scan revealed a plain, folded sheet of paper sticking out from beneath his helmet—the helmet Bhajan had directed him to wear at all times when walking about the camp. An overly-cautious but caring safety measure to protect the grandson for whom he'd risked everything.

Amar snatched up the page and unfolded it, his eyes skimming over the king's neat handwriting. Bhajan made a brief mention of Khatri's message—nothing as specific as what Tarik had told him—and announced he was returning to Valmandi. Savir was to join him as soon as possible, if he was feeling up to the journey with his injury. A few mid-ranking officers had already been charged with overseeing the rest of the camp's breakdown and the troops' return to the city.

Amar tucked the note into his pocket. His injury was of little concern thanks to the Tarja healer who had attended to him; he could make it to Valmandi by this evening if he left now and rode hard. He might even catch the end of the council meeting, and perhaps afterward, he could find an opportunity to speak to Bhajan in private.

With haste, he gathered his most important belongings and stuffed them into a satchel. His old journal was already tucked inside, wrapped in a spare tunic and buried beneath another change of clothes. As he buckled his flintlock pistol around his waist, he felt suddenly naked without the weight of his old sword on his opposite hip. It was the only thing he'd owned from his original life, before the curse. What had become of it? Had one of the others picked it up, or was it still lying in the forest somewhere near Shavhalla?

Perhaps his friends could answer that, along with the dozens of other questions he had. They were out there somewhere, and he knew they must still be trying to make contact with him, like they had with Kamaal and the journal.

A flame burned in a lantern next to his bed, and he gave it a hopeful look as he picked it up, searching for a familiar face.

"Lucian?" he whispered.

The fire flickered a little, but there was no answer, no crackling laugh or jagged grin in the orange glow. For now, Amar was on his own.

He sighed, opened the lantern door, and blew out the flame in a quick puff.

KESARI

KESARI WAS IN THE PROCESS OF SETTING A MAGICAL ALARM WHEN A sudden noise drew her attention. She tensed at the loud rustling in the trees ahead and exchanged a quick glance with Lucian. The fiery Spirit Tarja drifted forward a few paces, and Kesari watched, half expecting a soldier or assassin to attack. Or perhaps it would be a flash of white feathers—clear confirmation that Valkyra had managed to track them down.

Worse yet, perhaps there would be nothing at all, and they'd be left to torment themselves wondering whether the sound had been merely coincidence or some unseen trap yet to spring.

When another branch rustled, Kesari conjured fire in her palm, ready to hurl it at the enemy. Defending herself and the others was all up to her now. Saya was gone, and Aleida, Mitul, and Kamaal weren't exactly warriors. Neither was she, but at least she had her magic. She just had to find enough courage to face whatever threats hunted them.

A shadow moved. Kesari clenched her jaw and squinted harder. And there, from the trees, something emerged. Her heart jumped into her throat.

It was only a deer.

She released a breath and extinguished her fire in a closed fist. Her pulse settled back into its natural rhythm as she returned her attention to her magical alarm.

"Almost scared me to death," Lucian said with a wink, but his soft chuckle prickled with an undercurrent of tension. They'd all been on edge since fleeing the house where they'd been attacked two days ago. They'd been travelling almost nonstop, pushing Kamaal's horses and wagon hard over rough terrain that was decidedly unsuitable for such a journey this time of year. Rain turned the road to a mess of slick mud and puddles that froze solid overnight. They'd found a spot yesterday where they could camp and hide out for a little while, but they needed to secure it, especially since Lucian was their best lookout and he was leaving as soon as the task was finished.

"You'll need to redo that section," he said, drifting closer to the ground to inspect her work. "Channel a little more altma into it."

Kesari did as instructed, strengthening the barely visible thread of altma she'd stretched across the forest floor. Should anyone walk through it, a shriek would sound and a plume of light would shoot into the sky, alerting Kesari and her friends of danger. Once she and Lucian were both satisfied with the alarm, she continued on to the next section of their perimeter.

It was slow work and not particularly challenging, which allowed Kesari's mind to wander a little as she went along. Mostly, her thoughts jumped to dire scenarios in which she and the others were surrounded by enemies, but Lucian was gone and couldn't help her. She found herself wishing again that Saya was still here and that Zefar was still alive.

If only she'd been able to save him.

"How long will it take you to get back to Amar?" she asked Lucian.

"Not long," he replied. "We didn't exactly take the easiest path here, did we? I can fly back much quicker without you all holding me up." He gave her a teasing smile when he said this, probably trying to be reassuring, but it didn't help much. When she didn't respond, he sighed. "Look, I know the timing is awful, but what better choice do we have? I have to find out what's going on. We can't decide what to do next until we know how Amar's doing and whether or not he's remembered."

"I know." He was right; he always was. But she still hated it. The new thread of altma she was trying to form fizzled in her fingers like smoke—hardly a reassuring sign.

"I'll be back as soon as I can. You're all going to be fine."

"You don't know that."

"I do. I doubt anyone will find you all the way out here, and even if they do, you can handle it."

Kesari scowled down at the alarm still refusing to take shape, and she threw her hands up. "I can't handle *anything*. Look at this!"

Lucian came to hover directly in front of her, his black-void eyes gazing straight into hers. "Kes, look at me. Just take a breath."

She hated that he was right about that, too. She didn't *want* to take a breath. She wanted to scream. But that wasn't going to make things any better.

Lucian grew a little bigger, and she inhaled deeply, then exhaled slow when he shrunk back down. They did it again and again, a familiar exercise, and still one that anchored her in moments like this when everything inside her was a swirling mess.

"Talk to me," Lucian said. "What are you thinking?"

"I'm thinking that I *hate* this," she said, the anger scalding the back of her throat like a burning coal. "I'm upset that Saya's gone, and I think maybe it's my fault because I couldn't save Zefar. But that's stupid, because I did everything I could—I *know* that—but it wasn't good enough, and it's not fair. Now she's gone, and you're leaving, and I'm…" The hot, rapid fury burned out of her in a sudden whoosh, and her voice trembled. "I'm scared, Lucian," she whispered. "What if something else happens, and I can't protect them?"

He drew a little closer. "That's not your burden to bear alone. You protect *each other*. They might not have your power, but they're not completely defenseless. Don't you remember when we left Shavhalla, how Aleida attacked Jameson with Amar's sword? I wouldn't want to take her on. Would you?"

He was half teasing again, but this time, it almost worked. Kesari blinked away her tears and gave him a watery smile. "I guess not."

"This is part of why we need Amar back," Lucian said, sobering a little. "He can help us protect each other. Better yet, once we have him, we can leave Valmandi far behind us and go somewhere safer until we figure out how to rid ourselves of Valkyra."

"I know," she sighed. "You have to go to him."

"Only for a little while."

"A little while." She could handle that. She *would.* With another deep breath, she went back to setting her alarms.

"You're right about Zefar, too," Lucian said. "You *did* do everything you could. You were perfect. What happened to him was beyond your control—beyond any Tarja's control, if they'd been in your shoes."

She nodded. Once, she might not have believed him, too consumed by self-doubt and the pain of past mistakes to trust her own judgment. There would probably always be a part of her that wondered if she could have done something different, something better. She also recognized that she'd made the best choices she knew how to make in that situation. It hadn't been enough to save Zefar, but it was a far cry better than what she could have done—what she would have even *considered* doing—just a year before. That growth mattered, not only for herself but for the people she cared about and wanted to defend.

She glanced over at Lucian. Hard to believe how far they'd *both* come in a year. Back then, she'd been willing to do just about anything to get rid of her magic, even if it meant getting rid of him. She'd rationalized it away with the argument that it was her life, after all, and he'd already had his chance to live. That was what he'd told her himself, always willing to support whatever she wanted and needed. Now, she couldn't imagine life without him, and it shamed her to think that she'd ever considered breaking their Bond.

He beamed at her as she finished setting the alarms in the final section of their perimeter. "Good! Very good. Now you're all safe as can be."

"Thank you, Lucian."

"Oh, I didn't do much."

"No, I mean…you know." She shrugged. "For everything."

His grin flickered a little, the way it usually did when he was about to make some quip. Instead, he only said, "You're welcome, Kes. Now come on. The others will be starting to wonder what's taking so long."

They made their way back to the tiny clearing where their friends waited. The makeshift shelter they'd been working on was now complete, and they all huddled beneath it to shield themselves from the misty drizzle that was starting up. Mitul and Kamaal shared a blanket, and Aleida sat close by, hunched over with her sketchbook in her lap and a stick of charcoal in her hand. The horses were tethered to a nearby tree, and Kamaal's wagon had been concealed using branches and brush gathered from the forest floor.

"Oh good, you're back!" Kamaal said, beckoning Lucian closer. "Bring those flames over here, if you don't mind."

They'd cleared a hole in the ground for a campfire to prevent it from being easily seen at a distance. Unfortunately, all the wood they could find was too wet to burn, and Kesari found it surprisingly difficult and tedious to pull the moisture out with her magic. Lucian's flames required no fuel, and his warmth was a welcome comfort, though it was doomed to be short-lived today.

"Ah, that's better," Mitul said, scooting closer to the edge of the pit as Lucian expanded to fill it. "Thank you. I take it you both finished setting up those security measures you were talking about?"

Kesari nodded and tried to project as much confidence as Saya would have if she were here. "We should be safe enough until Lucian gets back. He won't be gone long."

"Not long at all," he confirmed. "I'll check on Amar and try to return here with news by tomorrow morning."

"Tomorrow morning," Kamaal said with a crestfallen look. "I'll be frozen solid by then."

Mitul pulled the blanket a little more snugly around them both. "I'll keep you warm."

"Well, I'm obviously not going to say 'no' to that, but I will miss the fire."

"It's not even that cold," Aleida muttered, barely looking up from her sketch. "You're being a baby."

Mitul laughed, but Kamaal's jaw dropped in mock indignation. "A *baby*? I'm old enough to be your father. Have some respect for your elders. It's not my fault I wasn't built for traipsing through the forest and camping in the winter cold." He looked over at Mitul with a wink. "Not that there's anywhere else I'd rather be, of course."

Aleida rolled her eyes, but the corners of her mouth lifted in a smile as she went back to her drawing.

"I should get going," Lucian said, shrinking back down to his usual size and drifting up from the pit.

"No, not yet!" Kamaal protested. "Please, I was just starting to feel my toes again."

"I'm sure you'll survive," Lucian said flatly. "And the sooner I go, the sooner I can get back."

The man shifted a little closer against Mitul's side. "Oh, all right. Go on then."

Kesari threw her own blanket over her shoulders and followed Lucian some distance away from the others. "Please don't get caught and captured by Valkyra or that magistrate."

He grinned. "Oh, I'm far too clever for that, and we both know it."

She laughed. Whenever she started to lose her own confidence, she knew she could lean on his. He certainly had enough for the both of them. "I'll see you soon."

"See you soon. You'll be all right."

"I will."

He darted up into the sky, and Kesari watched until he disappeared from view. She returned to the others with her head held high, hoping that if she projected enough strength and bravery, it would start to feel more real.

We'll be all right.

AMAR

AMAR AND TARIK RODE THROUGH THE VALMANDI CITY GATES LATE in the afternoon, their horses breathing hard and sending cloudy puffs into the cold winter air. At the palace, they handed the reins off to a pair of stablehands and went inside, making their way up the stairs and down the hallway to the council chambers. As expected, the king was already in a meeting with his advisors.

All stood and bowed when Amar entered, and a few words of congratulations were offered for his part in their victorious battle. Amar accepted these as graciously as he could, plastering on a smile despite the uncomfortable churning in his stomach. Hundreds of soldiers were dead as a result of that battle, fought for a lie he'd unwillingly perpetuated. He took no pleasure in such a victory.

As he settled into his chair, Valkyra hopped from Ashaya's shoulder and fluttered over to Amar's. A few of the others chuckled at this, and Chayani Sha, the Advisor of Magic, cooed at the little white dragon. "Oh, look how sweet she is. She must have missed you."

Amar resisted the urge to clench his jaw and instead reached up to scratch Valkyra under the chin. She leaned into the gesture like a cat seeking more affection. He didn't recoil, though he certainly wanted to.

I am Prince Savir, and she is only my beloved pet. What convincing actors they both were.

"I'm so sorry to interrupt," he said. "Please, carry on."

"We were discussing the status of the southern farmlands," King Bhajan said. "You heard the news?"

"Only that Jakhat is moving to take them."

Bhajan nodded. "We can't afford to send a force to stop them—not without leaving ourselves vulnerable here. Even if we could, it's likely too late. They were already moving to take the region while we were busy fending off their attack. But we might have a different solution, which Advisor Sha was just getting to."

Chayani Sha extended a graceful hand toward Magistrate Ashaya on her left. "Yes, but first, I'd like to hear an update from the magistrate. Last I heard, you were recovering the Shavhallan records from that Sularan outcast."

Ashaya pulled the billowing sleeves of his robes over his hands, but not before Amar caught a glimpse of the bandages wrapped around them. Injuries sustained during his fight with Amar's friends, no doubt. He found a smug sense of delight in the grimace that passed over the man's face.

"Unfortunately, we were unsuccessful," the magistrate said. "We discovered the Sularan to be working with a larger group, including the same individuals who attacked Prince Savir some time ago. They were well-armed, and that Tarja girl was with them."

Lord Vasu raised an eyebrow. "A girl who is little more than a child, as I hear it."

Valkyra growled her irritation against Amar's ear.

Ashaya sat up a little taller and leveled his gaze at Vasu. "A girl with power that is not to be underestimated. Would you care to go after her yourself next time and see if you fare any better?"

Amar kept his expression carefully neutral, but a swell of warmth had him cheering on the inside. Kesari had certainly made an impression. He'd underestimated her himself on multiple occasions, but it seemed she'd only grown in skill and strength during his time playing prince.

Chayani Sha cleared her throat loudly before the tension between

Vasu and Ashaya could escalate further. "What about the records? You didn't recover them, so where are they now?"

"Destroyed," the magistrate snapped. "The girl burned them."

Murmurs of dismay rippled around the table, and though Amar was as surprised as the rest, he didn't share their disappointment. The less the world knew about creating curses, the better.

"That does complicate what I was hoping to propose," Advisor Sha said. "Our Tarja scholars are still studying what we've already obtained from those records. Their progress seems promising. Given a little more time, they might be able to develop a curse to use against Jakhat and shift this war undeniably in our favor."

This time, Amar couldn't contain his emotion. "Curses were outlawed centuries ago for good reason," he blurted out. Valkyra's claws pricked against his shoulder, but he ignored her and pressed on. "Bringing them back may serve us now, but what will happen in the future? A curse could just as easily be used against us. Or worse, against innocent people."

"We won't get a chance at *any* future if we don't win this war," Advisor Sha argued.

Amar shook his head. He was a man without status in a room full of people he had no right to even be speaking to, but as long as they believed he held some power, he would wield it for whatever good he could accomplish. With force, if necessary.

He slammed his hands down on the table and stood up. "I won't have such dangerous magic used against my own people! Jakhat's forces may be our enemy now, but that won't always be the case. If you mean to put me on the throne, we *have* to consider the impact today's actions will have later on."

Some of the advisors blinked in stunned silence while others exchanged looks with one another. It was the first time Amar had spoken so forcefully in one of these meetings, and for a few seconds, he feared he'd gone too far.

Then King Bhajan gave him a nod. "Prince Savir is right. So little is known about curses, and we can't predict the consequences that may follow. We should keep studying whatever information we have. Even if we do find a way to create a curse, we should only do so as a last resort, after much careful deliberation."

The fact that it was even still an option unsettled Amar, but at least a more cautious approach would buy him some time. Hopefully he wouldn't need much, and this war would be over before a functional curse could even be realistically considered.

"What became of the Sularan mercenary?" General Khan asked.

"He's dead," Ashaya replied. "I killed him."

Amar had known that already, but the reminder made him think of Saya, and he lamented whatever suffering she'd felt over Zefar's death. As obnoxious as the man was, he'd been a mentor to her, and the bond between them was an important one, even if Amar didn't fully understand it.

"It would have been better to bring him back here alive," General Khan chided. "He might have had useful information. Still, with him dead and the records destroyed, I see no reason why we should uphold our end of the agreement we had with him."

Amar stiffened. He didn't like where this was going.

"We still don't have Jakhat's numbers," the general went on, "but our Tarja forces remain strong. In fact, we've had dozens join our ranks in the last two days, newly Bonded with the spirits of those we lost in the battle. We could strengthen our forces even more with mesala."

"We can't afford to fight the Sularans *and* Jakhat," Amar barked. "Or do you think they'll simply allow us to walk in and take what we want?"

"We'd have to be clever about it," General Khan replied with a shrug that was far too casual for Amar's liking. "But I do think the benefits far outweigh the risks."

Clearly a conflict with the Sularans wasn't enough to dissuade him, and he'd never cared about the ethics of stealing from their desert neighbors. Amar tried a different approach. "Mesala isn't a solution if our soldiers can't even use it to fight. You remember the daravak they used to incapacitate so many of our Tarja during battle."

"We'll be better prepared next time."

"I think Prince Savir is right on this," Lord Vasu cut in. "Our forces are already spread thin, and the Sularans will still be watching their borders carefully. We can't risk angering them further and splitting our defenses."

"Last I checked, you were not a military strategist, Lord Vasu," Khan said evenly.

"Nor are you aware of the delicate balance in our diplomatic relations with all of Erythyr. This plan of yours is ill-advised. It will destroy any hope we have of maintaining peace with the Sularans."

"I appreciate your concerns, Lord Vasu," King Bhajan said, putting a definitive end to their squabbling. "But if this battle has proven anything, it's that we're going to need all the resources at our disposal. Our Tarja scholars will continue their study of curses, and we'll send a few small groups into the desert to harvest mesala. *Discreetly.*"

"A wise plan, Your Majesty," Khan replied.

No. No, it was decidedly *not* a wise plan, and Amar felt compelled to protest. "I don't think—"

Bhajan cut him off immediately, as if he'd been expecting such pushback. "I've made my decision. We can reevaluate the situation at a later time, but for now, this is how we'll proceed."

The hard set of his jaw made clear that no amount of arguing was going to change his mind. Amar could only hope he'd call off the plan once he learned the truth.

"What about the southern farmlands?" the Advisor of Coin asked. "Are we just going to let Jakhat cut off our food supply?"

"For now," Bhajan said. "We don't have the strength or the numbers to fight them for it. Not yet, anyway." He gave a nod to the Advisor of Grain. "We might have to tighten our belts, but we should be all right for a little while. I've been informed that we have enough food stores to feed our people through the rest of winter and into spring, if we're careful."

"That doesn't sound like much of a long-term strategy."

"It's not, which is why we need to prioritize winning this war as soon as possible." He sounded completely assured that they could and would do exactly that.

"Agreed," Advisor Sha replied. "The mesala and our research into curses will help in taking back that region, but both will take time—time it seems we don't have. Judging by the look on your face, I assume you have another plan to see Savir crowned even sooner."

"I do." The king's eyes sparked with sly cunning as he looked between Amar and General Khan. "We have a powerful ally among Jakhat's military ranks—someone willing to help us take control from within."

So much had happened since the last time Amar had given General Muraka any thought that it took him a few seconds to remember who Bhajan was referring to. A flicker of memory came to his mind from the night he'd met with her while staying in Jakhat—the muffled conversation he'd heard between Valkyra and Ashaya after that meeting.

You may need to pay her a visit yourself.

I can do that. She'll fall in line soon enough.

Did that mean Valkyra had actually talked to Muraka herself? Was that the only reason the general had ultimately agreed to help Valmandi—not out of loyalty to Savir or the late Emperor Akraja, but out of loyalty to *Valkyra*? Nandini Kumar undoubtedly would have had connections to Kavora's elite, including the general of Jakhat's Tarja army. Perhaps there had been some preexisting rapport between them that ultimately elicited Muraka's assistance.

The more he pulled on the thread of Valkyra's plot, the deeper the scheme went, and the more connected pieces he found. It was like an enormous spider's web, and as much as he wanted to tear the whole thing apart in one fell swoop, any misstep could alert her and cause her to react accordingly.

That was not something he could afford to risk.

The council's conversation had shifted to discussions of a takeover—one to be executed with General Muraka's cooperation. There were still too many unknown pieces to put any solid plans into motion, but Khatri had spies due to report soon regarding the state of affairs in Jakhat and other important areas. That information should give them a better idea of where to start. Much to Amar's dismay, the whole council seemed keen to set the plot in motion as soon as possible. By the time the meeting ended, all he could think about was how badly he needed to put an end to this before things got any worse.

He'd hoped Valkyra would want to talk to Ashaya, thus giving Amar an opportunity to speak to Bhajan alone. However, she remained firmly planted on his shoulder, and all he could do was make his way to his room with Tarik walking dutifully beside him. Night had fallen, and lanterns illuminated the palace halls. Most were the kind lit by magic, orbs of light that would die in a few hours without a Tarja to power them. A few held flickering flames, and Amar kept each one in the corner of his vision as he passed, hoping to see a face there. Once, he was almost sure he did. It winked—or so he thought—and he blinked back. He didn't dare give any further indication that he might be interested in the fire. He wasn't even sure of what he'd seen.

When they were secluded in the privacy of his room, Valkyra finally spoke. "You were quite vocal in there today, Your Highness."

"Should I not have been?" he snapped back before he could stop himself.

"It's merely an observation," she replied, her eyes narrowing slightly. "No need to get defensive."

He swallowed his annoyance and tried to play it off as something else. "I'm sorry. I'm tired. Overwhelmed."

"As anyone in your position would be. It's good to see you take such an interest in the affairs of this country. You'll soon be its ruler, after all. But if I might offer a word of advice, as someone who cares for you." She brushed her silky tail over the back of his neck and draped it around his shoulder.

Amar suppressed a shudder and nodded stiffly.

"A softer approach is often better than a sharp one," she said. "Your advisors are there to help you and offer suggestions. You won't like all of their ideas, but you do need to hear them out so you can decide what's best. They won't be willing to share their thoughts if you knock them down so harshly."

He held back a scoff. She wanted him to lead and to rule, but she didn't want him rising so high in confidence that he forgot who was *really* in charge. She wanted him to maintain an image of strength, but still remain soft and pliable enough that she could pull his strings to weave her own plots.

So far, she'd done exactly that, and without knowing any better, he had *let* her.

It made him so angry he wanted to *do* something about it, maybe even something reckless. He could use his magic to confine her right now, then lock her away somewhere while he confessed to Bhajan everything that had happened. They'd figure out a way to end this war peacefully, and after that, he could go to his friends and finally focus on breaking his curse.

But he was too old and too jaded to believe anything would play out so simply, especially where her schemes were concerned. He needed to think this through, come up with a solid plan.

"You should get some rest," Valkyra suggested when Amar's silence lingered. "I'm going to speak with Ashaya, but I'll be back in a few minutes. Leave the window open."

"Talk to him about what?" he asked, striding over to open the window for her.

He half expected her to deflect the question by telling him it was none of his concern, like she had so many times before. Instead, it seemed all his frustration with her for keeping secrets had finally sunk in, because this time, she gave him a real answer. "He was supposed to hire more people to track down your attackers. I want to get an update on the situation."

"Good," Amar said—the opposite of what he felt. He watched her fly away until she disappeared from view. A few minutes alone weren't enough to have any kind of real conversation with Bhajan, but perhaps he could make even better use of his time while Valkyra was away.

Quickly, he went to the door and spoke to the night guard posted outside. "Would you mind fetching me another blanket? It's a bit cold in here. Thank you!"

He closed the door before the man could suggest he call for a servant. After a few seconds, he heard the muffled *thump thump* of booted feet retreating down the hall. When the sound faded, he eased the door open, slipped out, and walked back to the lantern that had caught his attention earlier.

"Lucian?" he whispered as he approached, looking around to make sure no one was around to hear. "Are you there?"

"Finally," replied a crackling voice, and Lucian's face materialized inside the lantern. A devilish grin split through his orange flames. "It's good to see you again, Amar."

His heart leapt with a renewed sense of hope. "You too. But I don't have much time. How are the others? Are they safe?"

"Everyone is alive and well, though their safety is less certain. I didn't want to leave them, but I needed to check in on you so we could start planning your escape. And theirs."

"You're all waiting for me?"

"Of course we are."

He should have known. Mitul never would have left him here, and time and again, they'd all proven their loyalty and their care for him. Still, the solid reassurance that he wasn't alone—that he'd never really been alone—was enough to pierce straight through the cynicism that had long since calcified around his old, calloused heart. It simultaneously filled him with affection and drove him mad that they'd put themselves in so much danger for his sake.

"I think I can get us out of here without you being spotted," Lucian said. "We'll have to be careful. How much time do you think you have before Valkyra comes looking for you?"

"No. You have to leave me. Get the others somewhere safe, and—"

"What are you talking about? No one's leaving you, Amar—not after everything we went through trying to bring your memories back."

"And I'm grateful for that, truly. But I can't go yet."

His dark eyes narrowed. "Why not? I don't see Valkyra around. You could come with me right now. There's a room down the hall with a big window, and the stables are a quick walk from there. You can just—"

"I *can't*, Lucian. Not after the mess I've made." His brows furrowed in frustration. "I'm supposed to be atoning for my father's wars, remember? All I've done so far is repeat his mistakes. I can't simply walk away from this. I won't."

"You didn't know what you were doing."

"No, but someone has to take responsibility for fixing things. I have to at least talk to King Bhajan and explain what happened. Hopefully he'll understand, and we can put an end to the fighting."

"You expect him to *understand*?" Lucian scoffed. "He'll lock you away. He'll have you executed for treason."

"Maybe so, but what does that matter? Even if he kills me, I won't stay dead. At least that way, he'll know I'm telling the truth. I owe him an explanation, and I owe *everyone* my best efforts to set things right."

"What about us? Me and Kes, the others? Don't you owe *us* something, too?" His voice was more somber than Amar had ever heard it, and it wrenched at a crack in his heart.

"I'll talk to Bhajan as soon as I can. Tomorrow, if I can get away from Valkyra long enough to make it happen. Come back then, and we can figure out what to do next. That's the best I can offer right now."

"You put yourself at risk every second you stay here. The others, too."

"I know. They should get as far away from here as they can. There are people looking for them. You can warn them, at least."

Lucian let out a long hiss might have been a sigh. "Fine. I'll be back tomorrow. For all our sakes, I hope you have a better plan by then."

"I will. Thank you, and I'm sorry."

"You don't need to apologize for doing what you think is right. I just worry. For Kes. For all of them."

"So do I." He gave the Spirit Tarja a final nod and made his way back to his room. He beat Valkyra there by only a couple of minutes—a small reminder of the precarious position he was in, and how badly he needed to get himself out of it.

ALEIDA

ALEIDA WOKE THE NEXT MORNING BEFORE ANYONE ELSE, HER body stiff from the cold. With no hope of being able to go back to sleep, she made a new fire to replace the one that had burned out. It would have been easier if she still had her magic, and she could have woken Kesari to make quick work of it, but she suspected the younger girl had stayed up later than any of them. Besides, she needed something to keep herself busy. All this waiting had her insides bubbling like a pot of hot water. If she didn't keep the tension at a manageable simmer, it would boil over and spill out.

Once the fire was going, she went to Kamaal's wagon to see what she could find for breakfast. Most of his paints, canvases, and other supplies had been left behind at his sister's house, and the food they'd taken from the cellar was in disarray. Maybe she could organize things later—anything to keep her busy before the all-too-familiar pull of helplessness took over.

There was nothing she could do about Valkyra or Amar right now, she reminded herself yet again. Or rather, she was doing everything she could. They had to be patient, at least until Lucian returned with news. But she hated this feeling—that bubbling restlessness, the tug urging her to do something, the prodding insistence that doing *anything* had to be better than doing nothing.

She'd learned the hard way to be more careful about following through with those impulses. If she hadn't been so hell-bent on doing something about Valkyra, she wouldn't have been arrested in the palace, and Mitul wouldn't have been shot trying to rescue her. If she hadn't been so convinced she had to do something to save Tyrus, she might have listened to Hasan's advice and stayed to comfort her brother in his final days.

As much as she hated it, doing nothing sometimes was the best option, but that certainly didn't make it easy.

She grabbed some ingredients from the back of the wagon and returned to the fire. The cookware Mitul had been hauling all over Erythyr for years sat upside down on a nearby rock where they'd left it to dry, and she used a thick branch to hang a shallow pot over the fire. Before too long, she had a simple but aromatic rice and lentil stew cooking, which she stirred occasionally to keep it from burning at the bottom.

"Smells good," Kamaal said from behind her, and she startled a little at the sound of his voice. She hadn't heard him get up, but he came to sit beside her now with a blanket wrapped around his shoulders. Kesari and Mitul still lay under their makeshift shelter of branches, dozing peacefully.

"Can I help with anything?" the artist asked.

Aleida shrugged. "I was going to make some more flatbread. I can't do it as well as you, though. Mine always turns out dry and salty."

"I can show you, if you'd like."

She nodded, and he went to the wagon to retrieve the ingredients they'd need, along with a bowl for mixing.

"Honey?" Aleida glanced at the little jar of amber liquid. She'd never used it when she made flatbread.

He winked. "That's the secret ingredient, plus a little saffron in the water. We'll have to go without that, though. I didn't think to grab any spices when we left."

"Mitul might have some. Check in his bag. He keeps a bunch of seasonings in a small wooden box."

"Ah, so you weren't subjected to endless days of bland and flavorless fare on the road?" He rose and went to search through Mitul's satchel.

"Not since I started traveling with him." She wasn't a particularly skilled cook herself, and she hadn't ever cared enough to make the effort to improve. She'd gone hungry too many days to think of food as much more than a necessity. What it tasted like didn't matter as much as whether there was enough of it.

"Here it is." Kamaal returned with Mitul's wooden box in hand. He pulled the lid open to reveal several smaller compartments containing various spices. Most were growing empty, but he did find some saffron threads and added these to the cup of water heating near the edge of the fire pit.

He showed her how to mix the dough, making a depression in the dry ingredients to add the water, oil, and a generous spoonful of honey. They divided it up into equal parts and stretched each one into a circle, then laid them in a pan to cook. Aleida continued to stir her pot of stew. Kamaal flipped the bread and switched each finished piece out with a new doughy one, chattering to her all the while. The calm, easy ritual of it was almost enough to make Aleida feel she was safe at home rather than camping out in the forest hoping assassins wouldn't find them.

Almost.

Their conversation lapsed, and when Aleida made no effort to fill the silence, Kamaal nudged her in the shoulder. "You're more quiet than usual this morning. Something on your mind?"

She shrugged. "Not really. I'm trying not to think about anything too much."

He gave a little chuckle. "That must be difficult. Seems like every time *I* try not to think about something, it ends up being all I can think about."

She grunted in agreement.

"You're a little like me, I think," he said. "It's hard to sit still, hard to wait. I can see your agitation."

She scowled. "I'm not going to run off again and do something stupid, if that's what you're worried about. Did Mitul ask you to talk to me? You can trust me, all right? I know I messed up before, but you don't need to—"

"Hey there, slow down." He met her gaze with warm, gentle eyes. "I'm not worried about that. I trust you."

Some of the tension in her shoulders eased, and she picked up a hot piece of flatbread to chew on. She didn't argue with him aloud, but to be fair, why should *any* of them trust her? She'd been more of a hindrance to them than a help, especially considering all she'd done before joining up with them. Kamaal hadn't been around for that part; trust was easy for him to claim. The others might not extend it so freely, and she couldn't blame them.

Her father had always said trust was a road, not a river. It went in both directions. She was almost surprised by how much she wanted Kamaal's trust, and how relieved she felt when he offered it. But did she trust him—or any of them—at the same level?

For Mitul and Kamaal, the answer was easy. Of course she did. With the others…she wasn't as certain. She didn't yet know them well enough, and where their goals had once seemed unified, now things were shifting. They only wanted Amar back. Aleida wanted to end Valkyra. Those two objectives were not necessarily the same thing. With enough time, enough change, their goals might not remain aligned.

"Did Mitul ever tell you how I ended up with him?" she asked.

"His side of it," Kamaal said. "But I imagine you have your own side to tell, if you want to."

"You know enough, then," she said, unable to voice the details aloud. It all went back to Tyrus, and she couldn't even speak his name without a flood of tears behind it. "I need to make Valkyra pay for everything she's done to me. I need to stop her from hurting anyone ever again. But the others—and you—you only want to help Amar. And I understand that, I really do. If he was my brother or my friend, I'd want the same. But…"

She struggled to put her thoughts into words, and the only thing she could come up with made her sound like a monster. Because if it came right down to it, she would sacrifice Amar to kill Valkyra. If he broke his curse, and the only way to get rid of her was to kill him, she wouldn't even hesitate.

"I just want her gone," she said at last. "Whatever it takes. I *hate* her, Kamaal. I hate her so much, it's all I can think about sometimes. Does that make me a terrible person?"

"Of course not," he said, without hesitation or any shred of doubt.

"You're human, like the rest of us. It's not your feelings that make you the kind of person you are, but what you choose to do with them."

"You mean like running off and getting myself arrested," she murmured. "Mitul could have died."

"Which is why I trust you won't do something like that again." He smiled at her kindly. "Mistakes happen. You're smart enough to learn from yours. And whatever your motivations were before, I'd wager the people here are more important to you now than revenge."

Aleida hunched her shoulders. He was putting far too much faith in her. "I wouldn't make that bet."

"Oh, come on. Mitul is, at least. Maybe not the rest of us, but—"

"And you," she said, quiet but sure.

He nudged his shoulder against hers. "See? You're stuck with us then, like it or not. And we're stuck with you. For what it's worth, I doubt Amar will be content to let Valkyra off easy for all she's done. He'll want revenge, too, and I think we can all agree she needs to be stopped. It's all about the timing, and making sure we live long enough to make it happen."

She sighed. That level of patience was always going to be the part she had trouble with.

They finished their cooking, and Kamaal helped her lift the pot of stew out of the pit. Within a few minutes, Kesari and Mitul had roused themselves, too, and they all ate together while they warmed themselves around the fire.

They were still eating when Lucian returned. Kesari waved to him in greeting, and he floated down to hover in their midst. "Amar's remembered."

Mitul's entire demeanor transformed with that simple statement. He grabbed Kamaal by the arm and shook him a little as if to make sure he'd heard. "He's remembered!" he repeated, all buoyant energy and smiling optimism. "So where is he? He's coming here, right?"

"Not yet," Lucian said, and he relayed the conversation he'd had with Amar at the palace. Their meeting had been brief, and the details were scant, but it seemed Amar felt an obligation to stop Kavora's civil war before he went anywhere. Aleida agreed with that sentiment wholeheartedly.

Worry was settling back into the creases between Mitul's brows, and Aleida tried to offer what comfort she could. "The important thing is that he knows who he really is. Valkyra can't manipulate him anymore."

"I'm going back for him today," Lucian said. "He's supposed to be talking to King Bhajan, and after that, we can make a better plan. I only came to give you the news and deliver a warning. Valkyra and that magistrate have hired more hunters to look for us. You should find a place to hide, preferably far away from here. Wait for Amar and I to come back if you must, but if we haven't returned by tomorrow night, you should go."

"We're as safe here as anywhere," Mitul said. "And we can't just leave without him."

"Or you," Kesari added. "How will you find us again?"

"That's not as important as your safety." Lucian's voice was more stern than usual. "None of us want to leave anyone behind, but if that's what we have to do to stay safe, so be it." He drifted to hover directly in front of Kesari. "Promise me. If we're not back before tomorrow night, you'll go."

She hesitated, looking between the rest of her companions for reassurance. Aleida nodded, and after some reluctance, so did Mitul. Once he'd agreed, Kamaal nodded, too.

"I promise," Kesari said.

"We'll head east, toward Pahari," Mitul said. "You can find us there, if not before."

"Good," Lucian said. "I'll do what I can to get him out as soon as possible." Then he was off again, flying up above the trees and out of sight. Aleida watched him go, hoping the next time they saw him, it would be with Amar and better news.

AMAR

AMAR WATCHED VALKYRA FLY OUT HIS WINDOW AND DOWN TO THE courtyard, the golden glint of afternoon sunlight catching the tops of her wings. She was off to visit a Tarja academy with Magistrate Ashaya and Advisor Sha, and he didn't expect her to return for at least a few hours. Finally, he had the opportunity he'd been waiting for.

He washed up quickly and dressed himself, then ran a comb through his hair to tidy it as best he could. It was getting too long again, falling in shaggy waves around his ears and skimming the top of his collar. His crown might have helped to hold it out of his eyes a little better, but he couldn't bring himself to wear the thing—not if he didn't have to. He left it hanging unceremoniously from one bedpost and exited the room.

"Good morning," he said to Tarik.

The man nodded back, falling in beside him as he strode to the dining hall for breakfast. Half the time, Bhajan skipped the meal in favor of strategy meetings and talks with allies. Amar was relieved to see him at the table this morning, seated beside Indira and already half-finished with his plate.

"Savir!" The queen's eyes brightened with her warm greeting. They'd not had a chance to say more than a few words to each other since his return from the battlefield, and she'd obviously missed her grandson. The truth he needed to deliver seemed especially cruel here in the presence of her affection. It couldn't be helped, but both monarchs were soon likely to feel they were losing their grandson all over again.

"Hello," he said, trying not to let his own unease cloud the cheery greeting. He sat in the chair pulled out for him by a waiting servant and turned to Bhajan. "I was hoping you might have some time to talk with me this morning."

The king wiped his mouth with a napkin. "Of course, but it will have to be later. I'm already overdue to meet with a few delegates from the eastern provinces, and Lord Vasu will have my head if I keep them waiting any longer."

As important as his own conversation with the king was, Amar couldn't think of a reasonable argument that wouldn't raise more questions. "That's fine. But it's important. I'd appreciate it you could make the time as soon as you're done."

Bhajan pushed his chair away from the table and clapped a hand over Amar's shoulder as he passed. "I'll come find you. It shouldn't be long."

"I'll be in my room."

"Is it anything I can help you with, dear?" Indira asked as the heavy doors thudded shut behind Bhajan.

Kings and queens had equal status in Valmandi, but Indira had always seemed content to let her husband take the lead in ruling. Amar knew he often sought her opinion before making any major decisions, but ultimately, Bhajan was the one who had final say. He had to be the first to know.

"Thank you, but no," he replied.

She proceeded to talk to him as if this were any ordinary morning. Amar let her, his only contributions to the conversation being the occasional nod or a reflection of whatever she'd said. Once he finished eating and found an opportunity to politely excuse himself, he returned to his room. Lucian was due to make an appearance today, and he glanced at the lantern on his bedside table, half-expecting to see the Spirit Tarja inside. It remained unlit and empty, and King Bhajan hadn't arrived yet, either. But it hadn't been very long. As impatient as he was, Amar could wait a little while.

That wait ended up being more than an hour, by which point he had grown quite restless. There was still some time before Valkyra could be expected back, but this wasn't going to be an easy conversation or a straightforward one, and he wanted as much time as he could get. He was about to go looking for the king when a knock sounded from the door. He hurried over to open it, and there at last was Bhajan.

"Come in." Amar stood aside to let him through.

The king gave his arm a pat as he walked by. "I'm sorry, my boy, I got caught up talking to Khatri after the meeting. You know how she is, slipping out of the shadows when you least expect it, and always with some urgent information that needs to be discussed immediately. She received word from General Muraka—an update on troop movements in the southern farmlands and the state of Jakhat's defenses. It was better news than I could have hoped."

"Your Majesty—" Amar began, then decided a more personal approach might be the best way to grab the king's attention. "Grandfather, please sit, I—"

Bhajan waved a hand dismissively and sat at the small table where Amar sometimes played samud with the queen. "Yes, yes, you had something important to discuss. But you'll want to hear this Savir, I promise. It could mean an even swifter end to the war than we planned."

Amar couldn't help being intrigued by that. He took the chair across from Bhajan, his back to the window, and listened more intently as the king continued.

"Muraka's still willing to head an uprising from within the palace," he said, lips rising in a confident and conspiratorial smile. "The details would all have to be worked out, of course, but if we could take Dashiva down from the inside, think how much simpler everything would be."

"There's still Princess Jasala," Amar said.

"We'd take care of her too, of course. Don't look at me like that, I didn't mean we'd *kill* the young lady. She'd serve us far better alive than dead." He leaned forward, gesturing with his hands as he spoke. "Once we've taken out Dashiva and her supporters, we could easily get the princess to sign a decree renouncing her claim and throwing her support to you. Don't you see, Savir? *This* is how we win the war. We may not have the numbers, but we don't need them. Half of Jakhat's armies are in the south, focused on taking control of the region. The city has never been less defended, and with General Muraka's help and the right plan, we could end this war in a single day."

Dismay chilled Amar's blood, not only at such a callous description of the plot but because of how close he'd come to following through with it. If his friends hadn't found a way to restore his memories, or if they'd been even a week later in doing so, he might be agreeing with Bhajan wholeheartedly right now. Valkyra certainly would have been delighted by this plan.

Come to think of it, Valkyra had probably orchestrated at least some part of it herself, especially given what Amar now suspected about her connection to Muraka.

Bhajan was still speaking, but Amar found he'd missed the last few sentences. More schemes and grand designs for victory, no doubt. All Amar could think of was how many more people would die along the path to that victory, and what repercussions would follow. He could stop all of that now if he could make Bhajan understand the truth.

The king leaned in a little closer, clasping his hands together on the table. He was more somber now, far less animated than he'd been a few seconds before. "I know this isn't what you wanted, Savir. You've always struggled to accept this fight. It shows you have a good heart, and someday your people will love you for that."

Amar's mouth went dry. Centuries ago, he'd dreamed of becoming a king beloved by his people. Now the idea made him sick. He wasn't suited for power—not on that level. He wasn't sure anyone really was.

"You'll be a good ruler," Bhajan continued. "A kind ruler, one who strives to do the right thing and values fairness more than power. Skies know the world could use more of that. But first, we have to get you on that throne and secure what's rightfully yours."

Amar swallowed. There would never be a better time to tell him than now. "What if it's not rightfully mine, though?"

The king's brows furrowed. "What? Of course it's yours. Emperor Akraja was your father. You were named his heir at birth. You—"

"None of that is true. I'm no one."

For half a second, Bhajan's confident demeanor shifted. When he spoke, he sounded uncharacteristically flustered. "Well—just because you weren't raised here in the palace doesn't mean you're *no one.* That's still my noble blood in your veins, and your father's, your mother's."

Amar ignored the nausea in his stomach, the pounding in his skull. "No, it's not. I'm sorry. You were deceived. *I* deceived you. I'm not Prince Savir. I—"

"Stop!" Bhajan bellowed, slamming both hands down on the little table so hard it shook. His eyes were as hard and cold as Amar had ever seen them. "Not another word."

But Amar couldn't stop. He had to tell the king everything. It was the only way to end this. He still needed to—

The hair on the back of his head rippled with a gentle gust of air. With a brush of feathers and silky fur, Valkyra alighted on his shoulder. She'd entered as silently as a ghost, and Amar had no way of knowing how long she'd been lingering outside. His palms began to sweat, and a tiny shiver thrummed over his skin.

What had she heard? What did she know? What did she suspect?

He backtracked, trying to mitigate the damage of what he'd just said. "I don't want the throne. It's not worth all this fighting. Let Dashiva keep her power. Surrender before things get any worse."

"Enough!" Bhajan hissed sharply, rising to stare down at Amar. The muscles in his neck were as tight as a drawn bowstring, and a few flecks of spittle clung to his mustache. Amar had never seen him so angry, like a wolf trapped in a corner and ready to bite anyone who came too close, even if they meant to free him.

"I know it's not what you want to hear," he said, keeping his voice as calm and steady as he could. "But you have to listen. This can't continue."

"Let me make something very clear to you," the king growled. "It is far too late for any of us to back down. It was too late the moment you stepped into this palace to present yourself and your claim. What did you think would happen? Power is neither won nor given up without a fight."

"I didn't think it would go this far," Amar said. There was more he wanted—needed—to say, but Bhajan was not responding at all the way he'd hoped, and with Valkyra on his shoulder, he needed to be careful. It was looking more and more like he'd have to make a quick escape at some point. "I'm sorry. I don't want the throne—not if this is what it costs."

Bhajan took a step back, clenching and unclenching his fists like he was trying to refrain from striking Amar. "I don't *care* what you want. My only child is dead, and her murderer remains in power. I will see her deposed no matter what it takes. Whatever your life was before this, you *are* the prince we need now, and this war has been a long time coming."

Amar's eyes narrowed. It seemed Bhajan *had* heard what he'd said about not being the rightful heir. He understood, had maybe even suspected it already.

He just didn't care.

"If you don't end this, the fighting could last months!" Amar said. "How many more will die before you give this up?"

"As many as it takes!" Bhajan's nostrils flared. "Their blood is not on *my* hands. Dashiva has had every opportunity to surrender, yet she refuses. Lay your accusations at her feet."

Amar shook his head and made one last effort to appeal to the man who had cared for him as if he truly were his grandson, even if both of them now knew better. He pushed his chair back and knelt, bowing so low that Valkyra had to scamper back between his shoulder blades to avoid being dumped onto the floor. "Your Majesty, I'm begging you, not as Prince Savir but as one of your subjects. *Please* end this."

Bhajan said nothing for several seconds, and Amar remained where he was, staring at the man's feet rather than his face. He had to understand. He had to see what a terrible idea this was, that no revenge or justice was worth the cost of hundreds or thousands of lives.

"Emperors do not beg," the king said at last, his tone even and dangerous. "You should get up before you become too accustomed to kneeling."

Amar set his jaw and rose slowly. He faced Bhajan with square shoulders and Valkyra's claws hooked against his skin.

"You're only a boy," Bhajan said. "A soft, scared boy who hasn't yet found the will to fight for his place in the world. Fortunately, you're surrounded by stronger, wiser elders who will pave the way for you to rule. All you have to do is stand aside and not get in our way."

A soft, scared boy, with elders aplenty to guide him. If only Bhajan fully understood the truth. Amar might have laughed if he weren't so disappointed by the king's unwillingness to listen.

The man marched past him and out the door. It slammed shut, and Amar sucked in a deep breath.

Now, to deal with his other problem.

Valkyra's voice was as sharp as a steel blade in his ear. "We need to talk, *Your Highness.*"

AMAR

Amar turned around slowly, watching as Valkyra jumped from his shoulder onto the top of a mirror in one corner of the room. She perched there, looming above him with narrowed silver eyes.

I am Prince Savir.

She was obviously displeased with him, but there was a chance she hadn't overheard everything. If he was careful, maybe he could still maintain this facade long enough to plan his escape.

"What was that about?" she asked, an icy undertone chilling each word.

He crossed his arms. As Savir, he'd never been particularly enthusiastic about this war. She shouldn't have been surprised to find him voicing those same concerns to Bhajan. "I don't want to keep fighting. I don't want the throne if it means more people are going to die. I never should have let you talk me into this in the first place."

"Yes, you certainly made a good argument for surrender," she said, her tail lashing through the air behind her. "What else was it you said…that you're *not* Prince Savir? Now where would you have gotten an idea like that?"

The question almost sounded sincere, all syrupy sweet with the concern of a mother wanting to lay her child's fears to rest. Amar's skin prickled with the sensation of a thousand tiny spiders crawling over him.

She *knew.*

His time was up. She watched him, still waiting for an answer or perhaps deciding how to proceed. He needed to act quickly. The window was still open, and if he didn't contain her, she'd fly off to tell Ashaya what had happened, and Amar might be killed before he could escape the palace. He didn't trust his magic enough to attempt a barrier, but perhaps there was some other way.

His eyes went to the reflection in the mirror. Inside the lamp at his bedside table, a tiny flame glowed—one he was certain hadn't been there before.

Lucian. It had to be. And there on the bed…yes, that might work.

He stared directly at the fire's reflection for a moment, hoping the Spirit Tarja would notice and take the hint. Then, before Valkyra could make a move, he spun and lunged for the bed.

The dragon launched herself at the window, wings spread to their full span. Amar seized the heavy woolen blanket at the end of the bed, meaning to throw it over her and stop her mid-flight. But he was too late. Escape was merely a wing-flap away.

A wall of fire rose up to cover the entire window in a sudden *whoosh.* Though Lucian's flames couldn't hurt her, Valkyra shrieked and twisted away on instinct. She immediately wheeled back around, but the hesitation was enough opportunity for Amar. He threw the blanket over her and leapt after it, throwing himself atop her squirming body and gathering the fabric's edges beneath them both.

"What now?" Lucian asked, shrinking back to his usual size.

Amar wasn't sure. He frantically scanned the room for some means of containing her. Keeping a firm hold on the roiling bundle in his arms, he scooted over to a wood chest with heavy latches.

Valkyra was screeching like some wounded, wild animal, her words mostly unintelligible. As Amar moved to undo a latch, one clawed foreleg tore through the blanket. She opened a painful gash along his arm, but he didn't let go. He dumped the entire bundle unceremoniously into the trunk, shut the lid, and sat on it with an exhausted huff. She was far stronger than she had any right to be, given how small and fragile she looked.

"Is everything all right in there?" came Tarik's voice from the other side of the door. It was only then that Amar registered some of the sounds he'd heard during the struggle as knocking.

"I'm fine!" He secured the latches and checked them again to make sure they were tight. A muffled snarl and several thuds came from the trunk.

"Can I…help you with anything?" Tarik didn't sound convinced by Amar's reassurances.

"No, thank you. Everything's fine." He grabbed the rest of his pillows and blankets from the bed to heap around and on top of Valkyra's makeshift prison. Her screeching grew more muffled with each added layer. As a final precaution, he even managed to haul his mattress over and leaned it against the whole plush pile. Then he stood back to examine his work, clutching the gash across his forearm with his opposite hand as blood dripped onto the carpet.

"We're leaving now, right?" Lucian asked quietly.

Amar didn't see what other choice there was. Skies, what a mess! Everything that could have gone wrong today had, and even his one success—locking Valkyra inside that trunk—wasn't going to last. He couldn't haul it out of the palace without raising any suspicions, and he didn't dare open it again now that she was locked inside. Knowing her, she was already prepared to escape the second she was given the opportunity. She'd have to stay here, and he needed to leave. Hopefully, he could get far enough away that she wouldn't find him, at least not for a while.

Quickly, he tore off his bloodied shirt and wrapped it around his injury. After donning something more casual, he threw a cloak over the top and grabbed his satchel from the armoire. His journal and a few other personal belongings were still inside. Then he belted on his pistol and cartridge pouch, along with the empty scabbard that should have held his Shavhallan sword.

"Savir?" Tarik's voice called again, followed by a harder knock.

"Is he going to be a problem?" Lucian hissed.

"Probably," Amar muttered, then called out to the guard sharply "What is it?"

"The commotion in your room—I really must insist on coming in. Just to make sure everything's all right."

So much for sneaking out quietly and without notice. Before the man could come bursting in on his own, Amar strode to the door and flung it open. "I'm fine. See? There's no problem."

Tarik, a full head taller than Amar, easily peered over him and into the room. Concern knotted his features, and he started to reach for the sword at his waist. "What happened in there?"

Amar stepped out into the hall, putting himself nearly chest-to-chest with the man, and pulled the door forcefully shut behind him. Lucian would find some other way out and rejoin him when he could. "You saw the state my grandfather was in when he left?" he asked.

"Yes," Tarik admitted. "I overheard...well, it sounded like things were tense."

Amar inhaled a deep breath and put on his best impression of a petulant teenager trying to play grown-up. "I'm having a very bad day, Tarik, in case you couldn't tell. I got a bit carried away after our argument. I'll put everything back where it belongs, but later. Right now, I really need some fresh air. I'm going for a ride."

"At least let me come with you, then," Tarik said.

It was far less argument that Amar had expected from him, and though a chaperone was the last thing he wanted, getting out of the palace and away from the city was his most pressing concern. He could figure out how to ditch the guard afterward.

"Fine. Come on, then."

Less than a half hour later, Amar and Tarik were approaching the city gates on horseback, and Amar had formulated what he thought was a decent plan for getting rid of his escort. He'd caught sight of Lucian here and there as they made their way through the city—a flash of orange in a lantern, a small but bright glint against the blue sky when he looked up. The Spirit Tarja was doing well not to make himself known to Tarik, but the reassurance that he was still close by helped bring Amar's stress back down to a manageable level after his tussle with Valkyra.

It was a slow day at the checkpoint; not many people wanted to leave the safety of the city walls so soon after the battle, even if Jakhat's forces had been driven off. Amar flashed his signet ring to the guard on duty, who gave him a surprised look but allowed both him and Tarik to pass without question. Once they'd crossed beyond the shadow of the wall, Amar kicked his horse into a trot.

Tarik did the same. "We'll stick to the main road," he said, not a question but a command. "And we can't go very far, just to be safe."

"But *you're* here," Amar replied with only a little sarcasm. "What could I possibly have to worry about?" Before Tarik could argue, he nudged his horse into a gallop.

A narrow path branched off from the main road, and he tugged the reins in that direction, listening for the sound of hooves behind him as he broke through the tree line of the forest. Tarik drew closer and closer, calling out for him to slow. Amar did…but not before he'd ridden a fair distance into the trees and out of sight of the city walls, far enough to spring his trap and allow himself time to get away.

Tarik hissed a stream of curses as he pulled back the reins to slow his mount. "You can't be taking off like that," he said with a glare in Amar's direction. "If you're not going to behave safely and responsibly, I'll knock you out and drag you back to the palace."

"Sorry," Amar replied, doing his best to sound chastised. "Just needed a taste of freedom."

"Freedom," the guard huffed, but he didn't sound quite as upset as before. "Well, I suppose you haven't had very much of that lately, what with the battle and your other duties."

Amar shrugged. "Comes with being prince, I guess."

"We all have our cages. Be glad yours is a gilded one where the songs you sing matter and your life is deemed valuable enough to be protected."

Amar couldn't help the humorless little chuckle that escaped him. Skies bless the old guard and all the shrewd wisdom he possessed. He'd seen straight through at least a portion of Valkyra's deceit from the beginning, never fully believing that Amar was the real Prince Savir. It was a shame he couldn't explain to Tarik how right he'd been from the start, but he'd realize that on his own soon enough. Especially after Amar pulled the same trick Tarik once had while they were sparring in the courtyard.

Swords and guns aren't the only weapons at an enemy's disposal. You can't always know who you're really fighting.

The path grew narrow, and Amar let Tarik take the lead. With careful focus, he channeled his altma, but the level of power and control he had over it wavered and weakened. He still didn't know how to use his magic very well, and he was just as likely to hurt himself as he was to incapacitate Tarik. Or Tarik could overpower him, and all chances of escape would be gone.

But he had no better options. It was this, or try to make a run for it, and that was even less likely to be successful.

What was it Lucian was always telling Kesari? *Breathe, just breathe.* A simple directive, but it seemed to help. The energy within Amar steadied itself enough for him to regain some control, and he made his move.

A single tendril of lightning shot from his raised palm. Tarik barely had time to glance over his shoulder before the bolt struck him square in the back. At the same instant, both horses whinnied in fear and threw their riders. Amar landed hard on his side and scrambled to his feet. Tarik lay on the ground several paces up the path, his body slumped and motionless.

Shit. Was he dead? He couldn't be dead. Amar hadn't put enough altma into that attack to kill anyone. Or at least, he hadn't meant to.

He hurried to the man's side and let out a breath of relief when he felt the pulse at his neck. Not dead, but unconscious. As for what state he might be in when he came to…well, Amar couldn't worry about that. He had to put as much distance between himself and the city as he could right now, and he needed to find his friends.

"Lucian?" he asked the empty air. "A little help?"

A glint no bigger than a single spark materialized in the shadows ahead. It flew closer, expanding until Lucian's face appeared in the hovering fireball. "Oh, I don't think you need my help at all. You took care of that problem fine all on your own." One eye flickered out in a quick wink. "Come on. I know some people who are very anxious to see you."

AMAR

"THEY'RE LIKELY GONE ALREADY," LUCIAN SAID AS HE LED AMAR deeper into the forest. They'd left the path some time ago. With night already fallen and Lucian keeping himself small to reduce their visibility, it was hard to see more than a few steps ahead. "In fact," the Spirit Tarja continued, "I'm going to be very grumpy if they're still lurking around here. I told them they needed to leave tonight if I hadn't returned yet."

"Where would they have gone?" Amar asked.

"East. Headed to Pahari with the idea things might be safer there, farther away from Valkyra and the war."

Amar nodded approvingly. It was a good plan. The worst of the conflict hadn't fully bled into the eastern parts of the country, so far away from Jakhat and Valmandi. Of course he wanted to see the others, but more than that, he wanted them safe. Amar himself couldn't leave—not yet. Nor could he in good conscience expect the others to stay with him. Given the way things had played out with Bhajan, he knew exactly where he needed to go next.

It wasn't to Pahari, and it certainly wouldn't be safe.

"Hey," Lucian called. "Did you get lost back there?"

Amar realized he'd lagged behind when the Spirit Tarja drifted out from the shadows ahead. "Sorry. Just thinking. Maybe you should go on, let the others know what happened and make sure they get to Pahari safely."

"Why would I do that?" Lucian asked. "And why are you telling me like this is where we say goodbye?"

"I think it needs to be. I can't go to Pahari. I—"

"I'm going to stop you right there and insist you come with me. The spot where we camped isn't much farther. If they're already gone, you can tell me what your plan is once we get there, and then I'll decide whether or not I'm willing to go along with it."

Amar shrugged in resignation and continued traipsing through the trees after Lucian. He wasn't sure which he hoped for more: that he'd find his friends waiting, or that he wouldn't because they were already on their way to safety.

"Watch out right here," Lucian said, hovering at knee level. "It's one of Kesari's alarms. See the thread?"

Amar looked closer, and a thin line of silver caught the light. It would have been imperceptible in the dark—an effective warning should anyone get close or try to sneak up on them. He carefully stepped over the tendril of altma and kept going, slower now, with Lucian guiding him to avoid a few more alarms as they went along.

"There, that should be the last of them," the Spirit Tarja said. "Come on. Almost there."

A few minutes later, Amar heard voices and movement. His heart rate spiked with a sudden thrill. He *knew* those voices, and while he wasn't entirely surprised to hear them, he was certainly excited.

Lucian turned back to grin at him. "They're still here, the damn fools." There was more affection in his crackling voice than frustration. Floating ahead several paces, he called out, "Kesari, I'm home."

Amar stumbled along after him, every nerve abuzz with a glow like starlight. Now that he could hear them and knew they were close, he needed to *see* them, but his feet couldn't seem to move as fast as he wanted.

A single figure stepped into view. Kesari appeared to have grown taller since the last time Amar had seen her, or perhaps it was something new in the way she carried herself. Confidence, perhaps. She looked happier, too, all smiles and jaunty energy as she danced around Lucian in the dark. She'd traded her worn Atrean seafaring coat for a cloak of Kavoran make, and she hadn't yet noticed Amar's presence.

Lucian grew a little bigger and hovered in front of her face like a scolding parent. "I seem to remember agreeing you'd all leave if I wasn't back by tonight."

"It's still tonight," she replied cheerfully. "It didn't seem like a good idea, trying to navigate the forest in the dark. We decided to give you until—" Her gaze fell on Amar, and she lifted both hands to her mouth. "Oh! Amar, it's you!"

"Hello, Kes," he said and took another tentative step forward.

Without hesitation, she embraced him, squeezing tight. He hugged her back, his chin resting against the top of her head.

"You remembered?" she asked. "Everything? It worked?"

He pulled back with his hands on her shoulders and looked her in the eye. "It worked perfectly. That was you?"

She nodded.

"Then I owe you everything. Thank you."

Three more figures stepped into view, but Amar's mind only fully registered one of them. Mitul, alive and whole. They met in two matched strides and threw their arms around each other. The strength of the musician's hold on him was a powerful reassurance that Amar's gunshot hadn't left him permanently weakened.

"You're back," Mitul said with a laugh. Amar hadn't realized how much he'd missed that sound until now. He'd come so close to silencing it forever.

His throat tightened, and he released his brother to step back and get a better look at him. Something in him needed to make sure, needed more evidence that he hadn't done any lasting damage. His eyes immediately went to Mitul's chest, and a flash of memory from the guardhouse struck him full force. Even now, he half expected to see blood spreading across the man's tunic.

"I shot you," he said, the words strained with overwhelming emotion. His eyes burned and his sight blurred. Skies, what was wrong with him? He'd known he would find Mitul alive and well before he even got here. Still, knowing that and seeing it for himself were two very different things. The odd mixture of relief and guilt was almost more than he could bear. "I'm so sorry, Mitul."

The man pulled Amar into another hug and patted his back. "You didn't know. And I'm fine, I promise. Kes put me back together as good as new."

Amar released Mitul and gave the girl a grateful look. "I owe you for that, too."

She looked away bashfully. "I was just glad I could do something."

"The important thing is you're back," Mitul said, laughing again, his eyes brimming with tears. "You're back! I can't believe it."

"All right, love." Kamaal stepped forward to put an arm around Mitul's waist. "Maybe come sit down for a minute, yes? You're still supposed to be taking things easy." He gave Amar a wink. "Happy to have you back."

Amar tried not to let his concern show as he eyed Mitul more carefully. He did seem to be breathing a little harder than he should have been, especially considering he hadn't done anything strenuous.

"Stop looking at me like that," Mitul said. "I said I'm fine, and I meant it. Still recovering a little, that's all."

"You said you were as good as new." Amar came around to his other side as Kamaal led him to a small lean-to nearby.

"And I will be. Isn't that right, Lucian?"

"In time. But you really do need to get all the rest you can."

"How boring," he grumbled.

They arranged themselves around a deep pit where a small fire burned. Aleida watched Amar with all the intensity of a wolf cornered by a hunter but kept her distance and didn't say anything to him. She seemed to relax a little after sitting next to Kamaal.

Amar looked around at them all, the scene so drastically different from where he'd been this morning that he almost felt he was in a dream. How many nights had they spent on the road exactly like this, gathered around a fire together at the end of a long day's travel? Kamaal and Aleida were new additions to the scene, at least for Amar, and Saya was missing. But it still felt so familiar, so comfortable. Even if it was only temporary and he parted ways with the others after tonight, he was glad he got to experience this one last time.

Kesari came close to take a look at his wounded arm, which had long since bled through his shirt. "I can heal that for you, if you want." She said it so easily, with none of the hesitation the idea of using her magic had previously elicited.

"That would be nice. Thank you."

She gently laid her hands over his skin, and though the pain had already eased to a tolerable level, Amar felt an immediate improvement as her magic did its work.

"How did you get out?" Mitul asked.

"First, when did you get your memories back?" Kesari added.

"Yes, start there. Tell us everything."

He recounted the events of the last few days as quickly as he could, starting with the battle and the dreadful realization of who he was and what that meant in the context of all that had happened since his arrival in Valmandi. Then he told of his conversation with Bhajan and subsequent escape from the palace—and from Tarik, who really hadn't deserved to be left alone and unconscious in the middle of the forest. Amar hoped the man wouldn't be in too much trouble when he returned to Bhajan.

"So what happens now?" Kesari asked when he'd finished his account.

"We lie low," Mitul said. "Get away from here and avoid being found. With Prince Savir missing, they can't very well keep the war going, can they?"

Amar opened his mouth to reply that this wasn't necessarily true, but Kamaal spoke first. "They'll be looking for him. Even if no one else knows what really happened or why he ran, Valkyra does. And it seems she has Magistrate Ashaya on puppet strings ready to do whatever she asks."

"They've probably already sent people out looking for Amar," Lucian added. "It's going to be hard for us to lie low with everyone searching for Prince Savir, not to mention whoever Valkyra has already sent after us. We'll have to move slow, scout ahead for trouble, keep away from civilization as much as possible. But we can still reach Pahari in a few weeks, maybe sail to Atrea or even Oselien after that."

The others nodded in agreement, and Amar decided he had better put an end to those plans before they set their hearts on them. "This war isn't going to end simply because I'm gone," he said. "In fact, I doubt the king will let the news get out, if he can help it. It would complicate everything, and he's determined to finish this fight with Jakhat no matter what." As his conversation with Bhajan had made clear, from the king's perspective, this was never about Prince Savir being the rightful heir. Rather, that was the excuse he needed to set things in motion. His true motive was to punish Empress Dashiva for allegedly killing his daughter.

"You can't change that, Amar," Mitul said gently. "You tried talking to King Bhajan. It's not your fault he wouldn't listen."

"I *barely* got a chance to talk to him. It wasn't enough. I can't stop there, though. I have to try something else."

"The king can't keep your departure a secret forever. You *leaving* is the best way to stop the fighting."

"Eventually," Aleida said. It was the first time she'd spoken all night. "*Eventually*, the fighting will stop. But until then? Amar's right. The war will keep going, at least for a while. People will suffer."

Mitul shook his head and turned back to Amar. "And what happens if Valkyra finds you? If she has assassins kill us all and then drags you back to Valmandi to be her pawn again? You can't give her that chance."

"I can't just run away!" Amar said. Why was Mitul fighting him on this? Why didn't he understand? "I'm not asking you to come with me. Any of you. In fact, I think I'd be happier knowing you were far away and out of danger. But I can't go with you to Pahari, or Oselien, or Atrea, or anywhere else."

"Then where will you go?" Lucian asked.

"Jakhat. If Bhajan isn't willing to stop this, maybe the empress will be."

ALEIDA

KAMAAL INHALED A GASP THAT NEARLY MATCHED MITUL'S. ALEIDA could understand their surprise—this wasn't at all what they'd planned for when Amar finally returned to them—but a mere second of consideration was all it took for her to see the sense in his words. The quickest way to end Kavora's civil war was through the rulers in charge of it. He'd tried with one. Now it was time to try with the other.

"You *can't*," Mitul said. "There are hundreds of soldiers between here and Jakhat. We'll never make it through unseen."

"*We* aren't going. Only me. There's no reason for the rest of you to put your lives at risk."

Aleida would have protested that statement herself if Mitul didn't beat her to it. "Out of the question," he said. "You barely came back to us, and getting you here was no easy feat. I'm not about to let you go running off alone."

Amar shook his head. "I don't want to put any of *you* in danger, either. Skies, you're still recovering from when I *shot* you. You should go to Pahari. Kes and Lucian can take you. You'll be safe."

"And what would be the point of that?" Mitul sat a little taller and looped his arm through Kamaal's as if he were anchoring himself. "I'd just be worried about whether or not *you* were still safe. What terrible predicament will you end up in if you die and lose your memories again? That's the whole reason I didn't let you go off into the world on your own the first time."

"It's not your responsibility to worry about me!"

"We're family, Amar. Like it or not, worrying about each other comes with the territory. And I was right to worry, wasn't I? Look at everything that's happened. You absolutely cannot go to Jakhat alone."

Amar let out an exasperated sigh. "I can't ask you to come with me."

"You don't have to ask," Kesari said. "We're with you anyway."

Aleida nodded. "Valkyra's caused enough damage already, and ending the war means spoiling her plans and ruining some small part of her life like she ruined mine. I'm coming with you."

"But breaking the curse will also ruin her plans, won't it?" Mitul said. "Why don't we focus on that?"

"Atonement," Amar said. "Atonement for the atrocities of war—that's what it's going to take to break my curse. Running away from the war *I* started is exactly the opposite of that, don't you think? People are *dying* because of me."

"They're dying because of Valkyra. This isn't your fault."

"That doesn't change the fact that I'm a big part of why this whole conflict started."

"You don't even know if the empress will listen to you." Mitul's voice was harsher than Aleida had ever heard it. "Why should she? You're the enemy. And even if you *can* make her listen, your story isn't an easy one to swallow. She may not believe you."

Amar shrugged. "Since you're all set on coming along, I suppose you'll have to vouch for me."

"I'm not sure that will do much good," Lucian mused unhelpfully, and Kesari cut him a glare. "What? It's true. We're nobody to her."

"So what?" Aleida snapped. She was tired of talking in circles about this. There was only one right choice, and she couldn't see why any of them were still debating it. "Amar's right. If there's even a chance for us to end this, we have to try."

He gave her an appreciative nod, and a tiny thread of camaraderie seemed to spool out between them.

"They've named Prince Savir a traitor to the empire." Mitul spoke the words with a solemn weight, like it was his last chance to convince them. Aleida wanted to grab him by the shoulders and shake him back to his senses. Why was he so adamant about this? "The second you reach the palace," he went on, "they'll kill you."

Amar shrugged one shoulder, his expression nonchalant. "Not right away. I expect Dashiva will want to make a spectacle of it. All I have to do is talk to her before the execution. And if she kills me anyway, well...when I come back to life, that will certainly give my story some credibility."

It was a dark thought, but he wasn't wrong.

Mitul, however, didn't seem comforted by this fact. Instead, he was visibly more upset than before, every line of his body rigid. The expression he wore was one Aleida recognized well enough, not from seeing it on his features but from having it reflected back at her in the mirror many times in the last several years. Drawn brows, cold eyes, tight mouth—something that was equal parts hurt and anger and dismay.

He pulled his arm free from Kamaal's and stood up. "I can't have this conversation right now." His voice was careful and measured, perfectly controlled except for the slightest gravel in the back of his throat. "I'm glad you're back, but I need some space." He turned on his heel and walked away from the group, disappearing into the darkness of the surrounding forest.

Aleida frowned as she watched him go. Mitul always knew exactly what to say. Was he really so angry he couldn't continue the conversation for fear of saying something he'd regret? But why? He had to see the sense in Amar's plan and appreciate the desire to avoid further harm.

Kamaal was the first to fill the awkward silence left by his departure. "You really are an ass sometimes, you know that?"

Amar leaned back with his arms crossed. "What? I'm only saying what's true."

"It's the *way* you say it. You don't have to be so callous."

"I have to do this. I won't be turned away just because it might be dangerous. Not even by him."

"*Not even by him*?" Kamaal echoed. "He's done nothing but sacrifice and follow wherever you go for more than a decade, and that's what he'll keep doing until he knows you're free of this curse."

"I never wanted him to do that," Amar muttered.

"No, but *he* wants to. He does it because he loves you, because you're the only family he had for a very long time. And still, after everything, you talk about dying like it's nothing and it doesn't matter because you won't stay dead. But it's *not* nothing to him."

Aleida was not the recipient of Kamaal's words, but she flinched a little nonetheless. The sudden understanding brought with it a twinge of shame.

Kamaal stood, and his voice took on a gentler tone when he spoke again. "When you lose your memories, it doesn't only hurt you, Amar. In some ways I think it hurts him more. I don't know if he can bear for you to forget him again. These last few months were…" He trailed off, shaking his head. "I suppose I don't have any right to lecture you. After all, I let him go all those years ago, and I wasn't there for him the way I should have been. Let's both not make that same mistake again, yes? He's a better man than either of us deserve, and entirely irreplaceable."

He strode off in the same direction Mitul had gone, leaving Aleida and the others to sit beneath the weight of his words and the sobering realization that reuniting with Amar hadn't actually made their problems any simpler.

AMAR

NOT LONG AFTER KAMAAL LEFT, KESARI AND ALEIDA CRAWLED under their blankets to sleep, but Amar stayed up. He didn't feel right about the disagreement with Mitul and couldn't in good conscience go to bed like nothing had happened. So he waited, and when the minutes stretched on, he waited some more. How long of a break did Mitul need, anyway?

Guilt and stubbornness fought for control of his next action, though when it came right down to it, he knew exactly what he needed to do. He *had* been an ass, as Kamaal had so accurately put it, and now it was on him to apologize and make amends. That was the very least he could do after the undying loyalty Mitul had shown him these last ten years. Longer than that, even. He'd never been anything but a loyal friend from the day they met, when Mitul was still a child and Amar had fewer deaths behind him.

He'd thought he understood what he was putting Mitul through every time he died. Only now, with Kamaal's words shooting straight to his core, did he realize he didn't have any idea at all. He'd lost plenty of people over the centuries, and he knew well what it was like to be the one left behind when loved ones died. But to have someone exist in that awful in-between space the way he did, still there but simultaneously absent because he couldn't remember any part of their shared life—it must have been a terrible torture for Mitul.

He stood, making every effort to avoid meeting Lucian's gaze. The Spirit Tarja had been watching him for the last several minutes, as if waiting to see how long it would take him to finally do the right thing. Mercifully, he kept to himself whatever clever commentary he might have had and simply asked, "Care for a little light?"

Amar held his palm face up and conjured a glowing orb over it. "I've got my own now."

"Ah yes, I suppose you do. Well, good luck then."

Amar gave him a curt nod before setting off in the direction Mitul and Kamaal had gone.

He didn't have to go far to find them. They stood side by side, Mitul tucked under Kamaal's arm with a hand resting on the man's opposite hip. A gap in the forest canopy revealed a patch of starry sky, and Kamaal pointed to something up there, whispering in Mitul's ear as he did so. The musician laughed softly, and Amar paused for a moment to watch them. What a beautiful gift it was that they'd found each other again, after all these years. He'd have to remember to ask Mitul how it had happened.

When he took another step, a branch snapped beneath his feet, and both men turned at the sound. Kamaal gave Amar a quick glance and pressed a kiss to Mitul's temple. "I'll let you two talk," he said quietly. The smile he gave Amar when he walked by was one of friendly encouragement, and it eased some of the tension within Amar to know there would be no lingering misgivings between them.

He approached Mitul slowly, heart hammering with sentiment he didn't know how to express. He scuffed his toe over the mess of fallen leaves beneath his feet and found something hard—a rock or nut. He rolled it back and forth under his boot. Mitul waited with his arms crossed, still watching the stars.

"I'm sorry," Amar said at last. "I didn't mean to hurt your feelings or whatever."

"*Or whatever*?" Mitul repeated flatly.

Skies, he was off to a terrible start. The words were all wrong, as dry and hollow as an empty snail shell. But he didn't know how to offer more than that. "Shit, you know I'm not very good at this. Talking and feelings and all of that."

"A poor excuse, considering how much time you've had to learn the skill."

Amar pressed his lips together. He was right, and more importantly, he deserved for Amar to at least make the effort. So he tried again. "I really am sorry. I shouldn't have said what I did. It's not fair for me to make light of my own death when you're the one left to deal with the consequences every time. It must be…" He struggled to find the right descriptor. "Hard. Impossible."

Mitul gave a halfhearted shrug. "It's not so bad, really."

"Liar."

The man let out a gentle scoff. "Yes, all right. It's awful, and I hate it. But you know I'd do it all over again if I had to, don't you?"

Amar's chest warmed with something akin to a beam of sunshine bursting through storm clouds.

Almost immediately, the sound of his own gunshot in the guardhouse rang through his mind again. "You don't *have* to, though. I mean it. I can manage on my own."

"I think you've proven several times now that that's not true," Mitul replied with a hint of teasing. "Look what happened the last time you died and I wasn't around to tell you what was going on. You ended up trying to take over the country."

"I'm serious. You have Kamaal again, and years' worth of happiness to catch up on together. Stop worrying about me."

"You say it like it's so simple, like I can just wave the worry away whenever I want." He shifted his position to get a better look at Amar. "If it were me asking you to do the same, could you?"

"Oh, absolutely," Amar said with a smirk, but he didn't mean it, and they both knew it.

Mitul went back to staring at the stars, and they lapsed into a comfortable silence. It felt good, so simple and familiar that Amar could hardly believe he was ever capable of forgetting it. If there was any memory or feeling he could bottle up and carry in his pocket to pour out the next time he forgot his past, it would be this.

"What do you remember about the day we met?" Mitul asked after a little while. "You do remember it now, don't you? For a long time, I was the only one who did. I always regretted that I never knew your side of the story."

Amar did remember, not with perfect clarity, but with enough detail to recount the memory Mitul wanted. "It was in Jakhat. I found you playing near that big Tarja academy after I'd been wandering around without my memories all day. Hearing your music was the first time I'd really felt peaceful since I woke up."

"Really?"

He nodded. "I'd seen my own reflection by then and guessed I was about seventeen or eighteen, so I was impressed someone even younger than I was could play so well." He paused, recalling how he'd approached the scrawny boy with a secondhand saraj that was obviously too big for him. "I think I asked who taught you to play like that, assuming you were under the apprenticeship of some great musician, but you said you'd taught yourself."

"You didn't believe me," Mitul said wryly. "Called me a liar."

"Did I?"

"Oh yes, you were very suspicious. You hung around for days trying to prove I'd been lying—at least that's what I thought at that time. Maybe you were only there to listen to the music. It was a little frightening, to be honest."

"Sorry."

"No, it's all right. After that incident with the thieves, I figured you weren't so bad after all."

"Ah, the thieves! I do remember that."

Mitul gave him a wry smile. "They'd stolen from me before, you know. I was an easy target. Always came by on the days there were more people about and my earnings were a little better. But then you ran them down and made them give the money back. I wasn't so scared of you after that, but they certainly were. They never stole from me again."

"I did it because of the bread," Amar said, plucking the detail out of memory like a lost coin under a mattress, unnoticed for such a long time he hadn't missed it until now. But it was important.

"The bread?"

Did he really not remember? Amar could picture it as clearly as if it had happened yesterday. "I followed you one day. Maybe I was planning to steal from you myself, or maybe I wanted to catch you returning to some wealthy estate where your master teacher lived. I don't remember, but I watched you spend all your coin on an apple and a small loaf of bread, then you found a shop awning to sleep under. When you caught me skulking around, you waved me over and shared your bread."

Mitul cocked an eyebrow. "Not the apple?"

"I think you'd scarfed it all down by then."

"Hmm, probably. I was starving most days."

"I know. But you still shared with me—a stranger who hadn't been very kind to you."

"Well, you came around, didn't you?"

They'd been fast friends after that, and when people began to mistake them for brothers, they didn't bother to correct the assumption. They quarreled almost as much as real brothers did those first few years, but never enough to break the underlying devotion they had for one another.

All these years later, after everything they'd been through, that devotion was the same.

"Do you really think I'm making a mistake, going to Jakhat?" Amar asked.

"No, I don't. Of course I don't. It's a noble cause, and I'm proud of you for stepping up and taking responsibility. I understand why you have to go."

"But?"

The man shrugged. "But nothing, really. I'm just scared."

"Me, too."

"Good. That means you'll be careful, right? You're not going to be reckless, throw your life away without a care in the world."

"Of course not. I meant it, Mitul. I really am sorry. I don't want to do that to you again."

"I know."

"And you really don't have to come along."

"I want to," he said resolutely. "Kamaal, too. We've already talked about it. And honestly, it's not only because of you."

"Oh, really?"

"Really." He winked, eyes glinting mischievously. "It seems we have our minds set on being the heroes who will save Kavora."

"*Heroes!* Is that all?"

"I guess if you want to be more sentimental about it, we have a rather paternal urge to look after Kes and Aleida, too."

Amar raised an eyebrow. "Kesari I can understand, but Aleida? Honestly, I'm surprised she's still with you all. She was practically feral when we found her. I'd have expected her to go rogue a long time ago."

"She's not so bad," Mitul replied, that *paternal urge* he'd mentioned seeping through the fondness in his words. "She had to grow up too fast and hasn't had anyone looking after her for a very long time. For now, she seems willing to let us fill that role, and I do worry about what trouble she might get into if no one's around to steer her in the right direction."

Amar smirked as they headed back to where the others rested. "Well, look at you. Here I was worrying about how terribly lonely you must have been without me, but you found a husband *and* adopted a teenager since I've been gone."

"Oh, shut up. No one's gotten married yet."

"*Yet*," Amar repeated, and even though he couldn't see Mitul's face, he was sure the man was blushing.

"Stop looking at me like that." He shoved Amar in the arm. "Skies, I thought *I* was supposed to be the romantic one. Look, we've got a war to stop first, all right? You can get all weepy about my marriage vows later."

Amar grinned. With any luck, when this was over, they would all have the opportunity to do exactly that.

KESARI

KESARI FOUND SLEEP DIFFICULT THAT NIGHT, AND WHEN SHE WOKE up for the third time in the early hours of the morning, she gave up on the endeavor entirely. Her mind still buzzed with the exhilaration of finally having Amar back and the knowledge that this was in part due to her own efforts. The magic she'd used had worked, in spite of her lingering doubts, and now he was here, snoring beneath his blankets a few paces from where she rested. She smiled as she sat up and stretched.

"It must have been a good dream to have you grinning like that," Lucian said quietly from the pit where he hovered.

Kesari shuffled over to join him, dragging her blanket with her. "No dreams. I couldn't even sleep that well."

"We're still an hour or so from dawn. You should try again."

She shook her head. "I'm not really tired."

"Suit yourself. Are you going to tell me what you're so pleased about, then?"

She shrugged, trying to put words to the feeling. It was something bright and golden, the exact opposite of what she'd experienced every time her guilt whispered that she was a failure, a useless little girl whose magic could only ever bring hurt and ruin. She'd started to believe the opposite over the last several months, thin shreds of confidence knitting themselves together every time she healed a wound or used her magic to protect her friends. But this—this was so much more.

"I think I'm just really proud of myself. I mean, we practiced that spell so many times, and you said it would work. You all did. But I wasn't sure until Amar showed up here. Everyone helped, getting the journal to him and all. But *I* did it. I brought his memories back."

"You did," Lucian said with a slight chuckle.

A thought came to Kesari then, warm as an oversized coat in winter and sharp as the smell of peppermint. She had to swallow a knot in her throat to speak the words aloud. "I think Rajiv would be proud of me, too."

"Kes, he was *always* proud of you. You know that."

She did. He'd told her so many times.

"Confidence looks good on you," Lucian added quietly.

She nodded. It *felt* good, too. Maybe it wouldn't last forever, and maybe it wouldn't be constant. A life without mistakes was impossible, and she still took hers rather hard. But she'd done plenty of things right, too, hadn't she? That was good enough.

She was good enough.

She tilted her head back, peering past the trees to the starry sky above and picking out what constellations she could find there. She thought of home, and long summer nights with her family, where Dad taught them the Atrean names of the stars and all their stories only to have Mum correct him where the Kavoran tales were more interesting. A sudden longing pulled at her—a longing she hadn't felt for a very long time.

"I wish I was home," she whispered to the night.

Lucian let the words hang between them for a while, then said, "You can go back anytime you like. It's safer there. No war, and I doubt Valkyra's assassins would follow you all the way back to Atrea."

He had a point, and it did sound appealing. She could picture all her favorite things about Deveaural so vividly it hurt. Her mother's cooking, Navya's laughter as they raced through the streets, the salty smell of ocean air at the docks, Dad reading in his chair by the fire. All of it so perfectly comfortable, so perfectly *home.* And so very far away.

She'd been away for so long, and in her brief travels back, she hadn't ever been ready to stay. Now, she thought she might be. The idea of stability and being constantly surrounded by her family's love was a tide that pulled at her heart and drew her to peaceful shores, promising that this time, she could find safe harbor.

But she had a family here, too, and she loved them too much to leave them now when they still faced so many dangers and unknowns. If there was a chance she could help them any more than she already had, she needed to see this through to whatever end it might have.

"Soon," she said. "But not yet. Maybe after we get Amar to Jakhat and he finds a way to break his curse. Then I'll go home. For good this time."

"I hear Deveaural is in want of a new wizard," Lucian suggested.

"I'd never be able to replace Jameson. But it might be nice to open up a little healing house. Only, I wouldn't want to be called a wizard, or a witch, or anything like that."

"Sorceress?" He winked. "Priestess?"

"Oh, stop." She rolled her eyes in mock annoyance. "A lofty title's the last thing I need. Just Kesari will do."

"Wonderful. I'll have a sign made. 'Magical Healing Arts by Just Kesari.'"

She stifled a laugh. "We'll put you on there, too. 'Supervision by Lucian, Talking Flame.'"

"Oh, that'll really have them baffled. You'll have only the mad ones for customers."

They laughed and then lapsed into silence for a few minutes until Lucian spoke again.

"Amar asked me to go to Hayathu."

"He did?" she asked. "When?"

"We talked about it on the way here. He wanted me to leave as soon as possible, but I said I had to discuss it with you first. Apparently, King Bhajan and his council have decided to send more soldiers hunting for mesala. He wants me to warn the Sularans."

"We should," she replied quickly.

"Yes, but…well, I can get there a lot faster on my own."

The realization was a sharp twist in her gut. "Oh."

"If you don't want me to go—"

"No." Him staying wasn't an option. She couldn't let her own fear and selfishness get in the way of doing the right thing. If he didn't go, who would? No one else could get there as fast as him, and he might still bring the warning too late. Besides, she knew those fears were all but baseless now. For so long, Lucian had been her only tether to some semblance of strength and courage, a lifeline in the storms she felt surrounded by. But that was becoming less and less true by the day. She had the others now, and more importantly, she knew she could count on herself. Of course she wanted Lucian to stay. But she didn't *need* him the way she used to, and there was something freeing in that for both of them.

"You have to go," she said. "I'll be fine."

"I know you will. I'll hurry, and I'll meet you all in Jakhat later. Who knows? Maybe Saya will return with me."

Kesari brightened a little at that idea. "I'd like that."

They sat there enjoying their last quiet minutes together as the sun rose and the others slowly roused themselves. Amar was clearly anxious to get moving, but at Kamaal's insistence, he agreed to a quick breakfast. While they all sat and ate, he glanced pointedly at Lucian.

"Have you decided whether you're going?"

"Yes, yes, I'm going." At the others' curious expressions, he explained. "Amar has a message he wants delivered to the Sularans. But before I go, I thought I should share the brilliant idea I came up with last night."

He paused for dramatic effect, seeming to enjoy the deepening scowl on Amar's face and the exasperated look Kesari gave him. With a smirk, he continued. "As much as I can appreciate Amar's desire to approach the empress and plead his case, there are valid concerns about whether she'll even listen to him or simply put him to death for treason. Along with the rest of us, if we're not careful. I would very much like to avoid that, as I'm sure we all would."

"Yes, indeed," Mitul said, raising his cup to Lucian.

"Which means we need to give the empress every reason to hear you out from the start. I think I know how to do that."

"How?" Amar prompted, clearly growing impatient with Lucian's theatrics.

"We get someone to corroborate your story. Someone Empress Dashiva knows by reputation if not personally. A Tarja who was once a great teacher—so great, in fact, that she trained not only our dear friend Jameson, but also Nandini Kumar herself."

"Skies be damned," Aleida groaned. "You're talking about Tamaya Takhar."

"Ten jitaara to Aleida for the correct guess!" he said brightly. "Though I would have appreciated a little more enthusiasm. Something like, 'What a clever idea!' Or even, 'You're a genius, Lucian!'"

"It *is* a good idea," Mitul mused, turning to Amar. "She saw you die, and she was there when you came back to life. She could at least vouch for that part of your claim. It's the most unbelievable piece of the whole thing."

"A detour to Tarsi is going to cost us valuable time," Amar replied. "Though I suppose the timing won't matter if we get to Jakhat and Dashiva refuses to listen."

"It's going to be hard convincing her to come with us," Kesari said, recalling the stern old Tarja's stubbornness all too well. She'd pestered Tamaya for weeks before finally getting the help she sought, and even then, it wasn't exactly the sort of help she'd wanted.

"She likes a good puzzle," Lucian reminded them. "A challenge. Present your case that way, and she might agree."

"You don't seem too happy about this plan," Kamaal said to Aleida.

The young woman's face had remained pinched ever since she'd guessed who Lucian was talking about. She crossed her arms and leaned back with a sigh. "It's a fine plan, but she won't like seeing me again." She offered no further explanation, and they all let the matter drop.

"It's your choice, Amar," said Mitul. "What do you think?"

"I think that I really don't want to die again," he said after a few moments. "And I need Dashiva to believe me. That could be a lot easier if my explanations are backed by someone she trusts. We'll go to Tamaya first." He stood and fastened his cloak around his shoulders. "Come on, then. Let's get moving. We're already wasting time."

They made quick work of their preparations. Most of their things were already packed in the event a swift departure was needed, and after some debate, they opted to take the horses but leave the wagon behind. They still wanted to avoid the main roads as much as possible, and maneuvering the rugged forest trails would be a massive inconvenience with the wagon. Mitul would ride one horse, which he protested was unnecessary until everyone else flatly insisted. The other horse would carry their food, blankets, and additional supplies.

"You've got everything you need, then?" Lucian asked Kesari as she slung her pack onto her shoulders.

She nodded. "You should be on your way, too. Amar keeps looking at us like he's going to shout at you if you don't get moving soon."

"Oh, let him wait a few minutes. For a man who's lived centuries he certainly is impatient, isn't he?"

"Can you blame him?"

"No, but a little longer won't hurt anyone. I can fly quicker and farther than the fastest racing dragon. One of the advantages of not having a body that needs food and rest." He smirked. "Don't get into any trouble you can't get yourselves out of while I'm gone. I won't be around to save you all. Whatever will you do without my wit and heroics?"

"Oh, all right. Now you're just being obnoxious. Get out of here before I decide I never want you back."

He gasped. "You wouldn't!"

It was all a game, a little banter between friends to dull the ache of goodbye, but something about the truth in their exchange suddenly weighed against her chest like a stone. Maybe it was because they were going back to see Tamaya, and Lucian's departure now was a stark reminder of why she'd sought the old Tarja out in the first place—to put a permanent end to the Bond she and Lucian shared.

How could she have ever wanted something like that?

"Hey," he said softly, drifting a little closer when she didn't return his quip with one of her own. "You're all right. Breathe."

She did, her lungs filling with air to match the slow expansion of his flames. Her lips trembled with the effort of keeping her breaths steady. She wouldn't cry. Not now. "Go ahead," she said after a few more seconds. "I'll be fine. I promise. Say hello to Saya for me."

"Of course."

He began to drift away, and the fear that she would never see him again—or at least not for a long time—seized her so strongly that she had to call out to him. "Lucian, wait!"

He turned back around but remained where he was. "Yes?"

"I love you. You know that, right?"

He chuckled and kept drifting away. "Love you too, Kes. I'll see you soon."

AMAR

AMAR'S IMPATIENCE EASED GREATLY ONCE THE GROUP FINALLY SET off for Jakhat, and he quickly settled right back into the rhythm of a day on the road. They kept up a brisk and steady pace, though Kesari sometimes fell behind for a few minutes to perform some magic. When they stopped to eat and rest that afternoon, she explained that she was setting alarms similar to the ones she'd created around their campsite before. They'd only serve to alert them of anyone who might be coming up behind them, but that was better than nothing.

Before they set off again, Mitul waved Amar over. His saraj case was slung across his back, but he pulled it off now and laid it on the ground to open. Underneath the instrument lay something long bundled in several layers of fabric. Mitul pulled it free and began to unwrap it. "I almost forgot. You probably want this back."

Amar knew what it was even before it was fully uncovered, and his hand went to the empty sheath at his belt. Sunlight gleamed off the lotus-adorned hilt of his Shavhallan sword as the last wrappings fell away, and he took the blade back from Mitul with gratitude. "I was hoping one of you had picked this up."

"Well, we couldn't leave it there," the man said. "Especially not after finding out where it came from and how old it is. Do you have any idea how much that thing must be worth?"

Amar turned the blade over and took another moment to appreciate its familiar weight in his hands. The weapon had been with him through lifetimes and, in some ways, had become the thing he defined himself by, especially when he knew nothing else about himself. The sword told him he was a warrior, and for centuries, he'd thrown himself into one battle or another because he didn't know how to do much else.

But a warrior could also be a protector, and in many of his lives, that was exactly what he'd become. He'd found things worth protecting—*people* worth protecting. The sword was a good reminder of that, too.

He slid the blade into the empty sheath at his waist and gave Mitul a nod. "I'm sure you could have sold it for a hefty sum, but it's worth more than all the treasure in the world to me. Thank you."

"Of course. It's good to see it back where it belongs."

The next two days were relatively warm for the winter season, and their journey through the forest remained pleasant. Nights were cold but bearable next to the campfire, which burned hotter and longer than usual thanks to Kesari's magic. They took turns keeping watch by night, and by day, Kesari's alarms gave them some peace of mind that they wouldn't be caught completely off guard in an attack from behind. So far, they'd been lucky enough not to cross paths with anyone, and Amar hoped it would stay that way as long as possible.

On the third morning, he let Mitul, Kamaal, and Aleida go ahead while he fell back to talk to Kesari as she channeled her magic across their path. "Can you show me how to do that?"

"I guess so," she replied a bit hesitantly. "Lucian would be a better teacher, but I'll try."

They walked a little farther, and with the next alarm, she went through the procedure step by step, including some basic instructions for channeling altma effectively. Valkyra had already taught him this, but never so thoroughly. Mostly, she'd been impatient with his questions about his new power, though she had given him enough training to defend himself and perform a few basic attacks.

When Kesari guided him through setting the next alarm, he managed it successfully after only a few failed attempts, and she grinned at him in shared celebration of his accomplishment. "That was perfect! Nice work."

"What happens if one goes off?" he asked.

"I'll show you." She backtracked through the iridescent thread of altma, and a sudden tingling sensation shot up Amar's arm.

He gave a little yelp of surprise. It wasn't painful exactly, but it was certainly uncomfortable. "What was that?"

"Sorry," she replied. "Probably should have warned you. We needed something noticeable, but I didn't want them sending up any flares or making a lot of noise. You know, in case there are soldiers about, or whoever Valkyra's sent after us. These just send a little zap to whoever created them. Usually that's me."

"But since I made that one…"

"Exactly. Sorry." She recreated the magical alarm herself, then quickened her pace to match his so they could catch up to the others. "They won't last very long, maybe an hour at most. But that should give us decent warning to look out for anyone who might be after us."

"Smart."

She held her chin a little higher. "I thought so."

Amar let out a chuckle.

"What?" she asked.

"Nothing. I shouldn't be so surprised, after the way you handled yourself at the guardhouse. But before that, the last time I saw you, you were still…" He struggled to find the right word; the last thing he wanted was to offend her. "You're much more sure of yourself now. It's a nice change."

"Thanks. I like it, too."

Several minutes later, they paused again, and Amar set another alarm. Kesari watched, offering little guidance this time and nodding approvingly when he did it right. When they continued on, she pulled something from her pocket to show him—a folded sheet of paper scrawled with black ink.

"What's that?" he asked.

"A page from the Shavhallan records Saya took."

Amar frowned. "I thought you burned those."

"All but this. It talks about breaking a curse. I thought it might be helpful with yours. But there's something else here that Lucian and I always had a question about." She skimmed over the page as they walked and read a single line aloud. "*A Tarja must draw on the blood of their own body and the jhivan of their spirit to provide the power needed for an effective curse.*"

"What of it?"

"That word—*jhivan*. Lucian thought it must mean altma, and maybe you missed translating it from the original Shavhallan. But I don't remember you missing a translation anywhere else. Did this one slip through, or does it mean something else?"

Amar took the page from her and studied the line again. "I didn't miss it," he said, handing it back. "As far as I know, there's not a Kavoran word for it. Jhivan is something else. Connected to altma, but not altma itself."

"I'm not sure I understand."

He thought of the elaborate painting on Valmandi's palace ceiling, depicting three figures who circled each other amongst the clouds. "There are three elements of life or creation involved in using magic, right? Mind, body, and spirit. To channel altma, we have to balance these within ourselves, like you were showing me back there."

"That's right."

"A long time ago, Tarja theorized of a fourth element. Jhivan. I'm certainly no scholar, but my understanding is it was more significant than any of the other three, something that was woven between all of them. It was believed jhivan was the energy of life or creation itself."

A divot formed between Kesari's brows as she puzzled over this, and she glanced down at the paper again. "So what this is actually saying is that a Tarja has to draw on their blood…and their own *life* to create a curse?"

"That's a fair enough interpretation."

"But how does one even *do* that?"

"I don't know." He thought of Mahati's bones lying scattered in their cell, motionless while the rest of Shavhalla's skeletons came alive each night. He'd suspected then that she'd given her life to power the curse she'd laid upon the entire city, and this was only further confirmation of that suspicion. But he didn't know enough about magic to be certain. "Like I said, I'm no scholar, and the knowledge was probably lost after curses were outlawed."

Kesari folded the paper up and stuck it back in her pocket. She spoke so softly Amar was only half certain she was still talking to him. "I wish Lucian was here. He'd be able to make more sense of it than I can."

"You'll have plenty of time to ask him when he gets back. It's not a puzzle that needs to be solved today. Until this war is ended, breaking my curse is the least of my concerns."

Kesari nodded, but the way she gnawed at her lip told him she was still mulling it over. He left her to her thoughts when she stopped again to set the next alarm and kept walking until he'd caught up with the others. Mitul, Kamaal, and Aleida were exchanging jokes, and Aleida was finishing explaining one that apparently made a lot more sense in Visan than it did in Kavoran. It reminded Amar of a riddle he'd heard around the palace a few weeks back that Mitul might appreciate.

He waited for an opening in the conversation and started to tell it, but his words were immediately drowned out by the shout from behind them.

"Kesari!" Kamaal hissed. He spun around at the same instant Amar did.

A figure darted out from the trees behind them, charging straight at the girl, who still lagged some distance back. The person was large by any standard, but they absolutely dwarfed Kesari.

Aleida was already running to Kesari's aid, though Amar wasn't sure what she would do when she got there. Before she could reach her, before Amar could even draw his sword, fire streaked through the trees like a scythe cutting through grass.

The horses screamed in panic. Mitul's took off at a sprint, and the one Kamaal was leading reared up on its hind legs. It nearly came down on top of Amar in its efforts to flee. Kamaal tried to soothe the animal, and Amar looked back to the path, sword in hand.

Both Kesari and her attacker had disappeared from view behind a wall of flames.

KESARI

KESARI YELPED AT THE SHOCK THAT SHOT UP HER ARM, INDICATING one of her alarms had been set off. The only questions now were *which* alarm, and by whom.

She got both answers the second she spun around to see a man the size of a bear hurtling toward her.

He made a slash through the air with one arm, and heat warmed Kesari's back as flames formed a wall behind her. He'd cut her off from the others, and she hadn't seen whether he was alone or working with a larger group. Perhaps they were hoping to isolate each person and pick them off one by one.

She wasn't going to let that happen.

The man closed in, and Kesari channeled altma into her legs to dodge his attack. She threw herself sideways. A *whoosh* of air dragged through her hair and clothes as the man passed her by. She conjured a fireball in her palm. The man whirled back around to face her, and Kesari shot the fire directly at his torso.

He reacted quickly, throwing up both arms with a barrier shield between them. The flames fanned out harmlessly to either side of his body and vanished into the air. Kesari hurled another fireball, then another and another, each one bigger and more powerful than the last.

The man kept his shield up and walked forward, forcing Kesari to back up. She continued to hurl everything she could at him, until her heel caught on something behind her. Her magic faltered for a fraction of a second as she stumbled, and the man shot forward. His arm hooked her around the torso, and her back slammed against a tree with enough force to send pain ricocheting up her spine. A thick hand closed around her throat. Her feet dangled several inches above the ground.

The pain was a sharp distraction, but only for a moment. She let it sweep through her, acknowledging its presence without allowing it to overwhelm her focus. She engulfed her hand in flames once more and raised them to his wrist. He released her the moment he felt the heat.

She dropped, coughing. The instant her feet hit the ground, she channeled altma to propel herself up and over his head in an arcing twist.

When she landed, she was facing his back. He started to pivot, and she braced herself for whatever he might throw at her next. Her hands created the beginnings of another shielding barrier while she directed a second surge of altma through her feet and into the ground.

Flames sprung to life in the man's palms. He let them fly even as the ground gave way underneath his feet, causing him to stumble and sink up to his knees in dirt and rock. By the time the flames had burned through Kesari's barrier, she'd moved away, springing at her attacker before he could recover. She forced him to bend forward with magically strengthened arms, then pinned his wrists to the ground with two more barriers. Between that and the trench he'd sunk into, he was well contained, for now.

Her breath came out in hard pants, and she could feel her altma starting to slip. She wouldn't be able to maintain this much longer. Damn it, where were the others?

"Stop!" Amar cried out. "Don't kill him."

She hadn't planned to, but perhaps it was better if their assailant thought her capable of doing so. She glanced up through the waves of thick black hair that had fallen over her face and was relieved to see her friends all hurrying toward her. No one appeared to be hurt, and they weren't being actively pursued or attacked by anyone else. It seemed this man had been working alone.

Kesari took several deep breaths to settle herself as the others gathered around her. The wall of fire that had initially separated them was now extinguished, and though Mitul, Kamaal, and Aleida all appeared visibly shaken and confused, Amar's expression was one of complete calm. He'd drawn his sword, but it was lowered, the tip hovering above the ground.

"Well, Tarik," he said to the man, "you found me."

13

AMAR

TARIK GLARED UP AT AMAR WITH ENOUGH RAGE TO BURN A CITY, BUT beneath that fury was something else—something inquisitive. Amar had no difficulty imagining what the old guard's questions might be, but until he could ensure everyone's safety, such curiosity was a secondary concern.

"We have a lot to discuss," he said. "But first, I need to know if anyone else is with you."

Tarik opened his mouth, then snapped it shut again. Perhaps he'd decided it would be better not to say anything at all. That wouldn't do.

"Have any of your other alarms gone off?" he asked Kesari.

The girl shook her head with some hesitation. "I don't think so. I didn't feel anything, but I was a bit distracted."

"Who exactly are you people?" Tarik barked the question forcefully, like he hadn't been able to contain himself any longer despite his earlier resistance to communicating. That was a start, at least.

"My friends," Amar answered. Tarik's scowl deepened. An understandable response, given that these were the same people who'd attacked Amar at a Valmandi guardhouse three weeks prior. "I promise I'll explain once I know we're out of danger. Was anyone else with you?"

"If there was, I'd have been foolish to attack alone."

He'd take that as a no, then. Tentatively. "Good."

"*Good*? You should be glad to see me, or anyone else for that matter. After all, this was supposed to be a rescue mission, *Prince Savir*." He spat on the ground at Amar's feet, then redirected his ire at Kamaal. "And *you*—you've been a friend to King Bhajan and Queen Indira for years. I can only imagine a handful of reasons why you'd be here with *him*—none of them good. What do you have to say for yourself?"

"I maintain the upmost respect for the king and queen," Kamaal replied. "Once we all calm down, I'm sure we can talk things through and settle this."

Amar sighed. Talking things through was all well and good, and it didn't *seem* like anyone was with Tarik. But that didn't mean it was a good idea to sit here and wait, on the off chance anyone *was* nearby. Unfortunately, Tarik appeared unlikely to cooperate, and he was a much more dangerous foe while he still had his magic.

"Does anyone happen to have any daravak lying around?" Amar asked.

At this, the guard emitted a string of colorful insults Amar would have previously thought far beneath his sense of decorum.

"I think I still have some in my satchel," Aleida replied. "But the other horse ran off."

"He can't have gone far," Mitul said. "Come on. I'll help you look for him." He reached down to hoist Aleida up behind him, and they rode off to search for the missing animal.

Amar pressed the tip of his blade to the soft skin beneath Tarik's jaw, more to make a point than as an actual threat. It was effective enough to get the man to stop ranting for a few seconds. "I'll make you a bargain. A question for a question, honest answers only. I think we can both agree we owe each other that much."

"I owe you *nothing*, you lying bastard."

Amar lifted a brow. "I'm sorry to hear that. I suppose it might be easier if we part ways here." He injected a menacing note into his tone and slightly increased the pressure on his blade for added reinforcement. "Of course, I can't have you following us again. Kes, if you'd be so obliging."

The girl gave a curt nod like she knew exactly what he was talking about, but before she could take action, Tarik fell for their bluff. Or at least bought into it enough to decide he shouldn't test them. "Fine. But I get the first question."

"Fair enough." Amar pulled the blade away but did not sheathe it. A single drop of blood fell from the tip and onto the translucent barrier encasing Tarik's left hand. He watched it roll down and soak into the dirt.

"You're obviously not the real Prince Savir," Tarik said. "So who are you really?"

"Amar. At least, that's what I go by these days. Before that, I was dozens of different people in just as many lifetimes. My original identity was Prince Darshak Kaur of Shavhalla."

"Right," Tarik said with derision. "And I'm the King of Atrea. You're nothing but a con man. Playing the part of whoever you need to be to swindle your next mark. Is that it?"

Amar let out a huff. "If only it were that simple. But no, I'm afraid you're wrong there. I never meant to swindle anyone. When I came to the palace and met with the king and queen, I truly believed myself to be Prince Savir. I was just as deceived as the rest of you."

Tarik's eyes narrowed, and that questioning look grew more prominent. "What do you—"

Amar held up a hand. "It's my turn for a question. Is anyone else coming after us?"

"You already asked that."

"So I'm asking again, and this time, I want a clearer answer."

"There were others sent, but I don't know where they are. I was on my own, and as far as I know, no one else is nearby. They were still trying to pick up your trail closer to the city."

Amar frowned, though the news wasn't unexpected, and they were far enough from Valmandi now to ease his mind a little. But Bhajan would want Prince Savir found as soon as possible, no matter the circumstances of his sudden disappearance. What did they believe had happened to him, anyway?

"What did you mean when you said you were deceived?" Tarik asked.

That answer required more time and explanation than Amar could give right now. "It's a long story. I can share it in full later, but the quick version is this. Several months ago, I found myself in a strange place with no memory of who I was or how I'd gotten there. A powerful Spirit Tarja convinced me that I was Prince Savir and that she was my longtime caregiver. She said we were attacked on our way to Valmandi to reunite with my family and lay claim to my throne. You remember my pet dragon?"

Tarik nodded. "They found her locked inside a chest in your room. Buried under that mess you made before you left." He gave Amar a pointed look.

"A pity she didn't stay there," he muttered. "But that's her. A Spirit Tarja named Valkyra. You may know her better as Nandini Kumar."

"The former imperial advisor?"

"Yes. She used me to start this war. Magistrate Ashaya has been working closely with her. I didn't realize the truth until the battle with Jakhat, when my true memories came back to me." Not a full answer, but it would have to suffice for now. "My turn. What happened after I left?"

Tarik didn't respond immediately, and Kesari prodded him a little with her knee on his back. "Hey! He asked you a question." The role of cutthroat ruffian didn't fit her very well, but she was certainly putting her all into playing it.

"The king was outraged, as you can imagine," he said, "The queen was beside herself with worry. But they kept the news quiet. Only the advisors were told, and whoever Khatri sent looking for you. And of course, Magistrate Ashaya still has assassins hunting for your friends. I always thought he was taking that whole mess at the guardhouse a little too personally, but if you're telling the truth about his allegiance to the Spirit Tarja…who exactly *are* these friends of yours, anyway?" He scowled. "No, wait. Don't answer that yet. That's not my real question."

"You haven't even finished answering mine," Amar said.

"What more do you want me to say?"

Amar stared at him pointedly, waiting.

Tarik let out a frustrated groan before continuing. "At first, they thought you'd been taken hostage somehow. The queen *still* thinks that, or hopes it, because the alternative is that you ran away, and she can't bring herself to believe her beloved grandson would be so cruel. But when I told Bhajan how you'd left me in the forest and escaped, he didn't seem surprised. I assume that has something to do with the argument you two had."

"Something like that."

"That's my question then. Why *did* you run away? Aside from the fact that you suddenly realized you weren't the real Prince Savir." His eyes narrowed. "And I'm not saying I believe that excuse, by the way."

Of course he didn't. Tarik had been skeptical of him from the start. Why should that change now?

Before Amar could answer, Aleida and Mitul returned with the second horse. She handed the reins off to Kamaal and scurried over with a small bundle of cloth clutched in one hand. "I've got the daravak. Kes, you might want to stand over there."

The girl backed away from Tarik, her face taut with the concentrated effort of keeping him contained. The guard squirmed as Aleida approached but could not break free. "Is this really necessary?" he growled. "We were having such a good chat."

Amar couldn't tell whether he was being sarcastic or not, but regardless, he wasn't about to risk the man escaping or putting up another fight. "You'll take it, and then we'll strip you of your weapons until you can be more reasonable. You're coming with us. We'll finish this conversation on the move. You've already wasted more of our time than we can afford."

For a few seconds, it looked like he might attempt one last fight, but after a glance at Kesari and the blade in Amar's hand, he seemed to reconsider. Aleida unwrapped the bundle to reveal a few dried pieces of daravak, and she held one up to the guard's lips. He took it from her, chewed, swallowed, and opened his mouth to show that it had all been consumed.

A few seconds passed, and Amar gave Kesari a nod. The barriers around Tarik's wrists dissipated. He hoisted himself up and out of the trench where he'd been stuck. Amar watched, keeping his sword raised and ready to strike should the man try anything.

Kesari moved in to unburden him of his weapons—a sword, a pistol, and a few knives. She looked incredibly small next to his towering frame, but not once did she flinch or show even the tiniest trace of fear. If anything, Tarik looked a bit scared of her, watching her movements warily and keeping perfectly still all the while, as if any suspicious movement might incline the girl to attack him again.

She took all the weapons to their pack horse for storage, but not before Aleida plucked out the belt with Tarik's holstered pistol and cartridge pouch. She buckled it around her own waist, looking quite pleased with herself, and raised an eyebrow to Kamaal as if asking for his input. The artist shook his head but gave her a crooked little grin. Tarik scowled at them both.

"Let's go," Amar said. Aleida, Mitul, and Kamaal took the lead with the horses. Kesari hung back, flanking Tarik on the side opposite Amar. He was grateful for the backup. Even with Tarik disarmed and his magic blocked, he presented an unknown element of risk.

"So tell me," Tarik said once they'd fallen into a steady pace. "Why did you run?"

"Because talking to Bhajan didn't work," Amar said. "I didn't get a chance to explain *everything* to him, but he didn't even want to hear me out. That was the argument you heard. And then Valkyra found out what I knew, which meant she couldn't manipulate me anymore. She would have had me killed, so I trapped her and left to find my friends. We're on our way to Tarsi, then to Jakhat to speak with the empress."

Tarik let out a short bark of a laugh. "You must have a death wish if you think talking to the empress will do any good. It doesn't matter if you're the real Prince Savir or not; you're still a traitor as far as she's concerned."

Amar shrugged. This was true enough.

"You still haven't told me everything," Tarik said. "Why did you—"

Amar cut him off. "Now that we're moving again, I'm happy to explain in detail, I promise. But I have one last question, and you owe me another answer."

"Fine. Let's have it."

"Do you know how many people are looking for us right now?"

"Not exactly, but it's fewer than you might think. A few of Khatri's spies, whatever assassins Ashaya's already sent after your friends, and me. That's it. Like I said, the king wanted to keep your disappearance quiet. If word gets out, it will hinder the war effort." His frown darkened. "He needs you back."

"And you mean to take me back to him by any means necessary," Amar said with a wry smile.

"Yes."

"Well, I appreciate the honesty. I hope you'll change your mind by the time you've heard me out, though."

The man grunted. "Start talking."

It took Amar the rest of the afternoon to tell his story in full, especially with Tarik's many follow-up questions. He kept trying to poke holes in the information Amar had provided, and to be fair, there were enough dubious elements already to make it a rather implausible tale. The others filled in some of the gaps with their own perspectives, and hearing them verify Amar's claims seemed to help a little, especially where Kamaal was concerned. From his high position in the palace guard, Tarik had born witness to the artist's longstanding friendship with the king and queen. That respect for the royal family was something they shared, and though he'd expressed anger toward Kamaal before, he still seemed a little more inclined to listen to him than to any of the others.

Amar wrapped things up by explaining where they were going now and why. Tarik's expression grew more curious at the mention of Tamaya, and he was especially interested in the fact that she'd seen Amar come back to life herself after his body was carried to her doorstep months prior.

"I take it you're familiar with her?" Amar asked.

Tarik let out a little chuckle. "Any Tarja of my generation who trained at Jakhat's largest academy knows Tamaya Takhar. She was a formidable teacher."

"Do you trust her, then?"

Tarik considered this for a few moments. "I can see where you're going with this. I'm still not inclined to believe you, but if Tamaya were to validate your claims—"

"Whoa," Mitul called out softly, reining his horse to a stop and then shifting around in the saddle. "There's something up ahead. Maybe we should go another way."

"What is it?" Aleida pushed ahead in complete disregard of his warning. She inhaled a sharp gasp, and Kamaal went to put an arm around her shoulder. She shifted closer, leaning into his side as if finding security in his presence.

Amar exchanged a look with Tarik, and they strode past Kesari, between the two horses, and around Kamaal and Aleida to see what everyone was looking at. The view that greeted them was a brutal one—a small clearing that looked to have been the site of a skirmish. Half a dozen mangled bodies littered the ruined forest floor, some so disfigured it was difficult to tell that they were even human. Four of the dead wore the red uniforms of Valmandi soldiers, and two were dressed in Jakhat's green. Blood darkened their clothes and the ground beneath them, and their faces were twisted with whatever agony they'd experienced in their final moments. A trio of crows picked at the open stomach of the farthest corpse, unconcerned with the group of travellers who had stumbled upon their feast.

Amar's insides churned. He'd long since grown accustomed to the horrors of battle, but the emotional weight of human suffering never lessened. Especially not now, seeing *these* bodies. *This* was the cost of the war that had started because of Prince Savir's return. If he'd made different choices that day in the forest when Valkyra had attacked them all, if he'd found a way to defeat her instead of trading his life for his friends', would things have turned out differently? Could he have prevented this war somehow? Prevented these soldiers from dying?

A knot tightened in his throat, but he forced it down along with any further outward display of emotion. Crying for them would do nothing, and he owed it to them and their sacrifice to keep moving forward, to put an end to this before more of their comrades died. But first, there was something else he needed to do.

He stepped forward. "I'm going to bury them."

Tarik matched his strides. "I'll help you."

Kesari and Kamaal went with them. Mitul slipped down from the saddle and stayed with Aleida, speaking to her in gentle tones as she turned her back to the scene, head bowed in an attempt to hide her expression. Amar imagined this must be too close a reminder of the horrors she'd seen during the invasion of Vis, and he couldn't fault her for needing to step away.

They chose a spot at the edge of the clearing to lay the soldiers to rest. Kamaal said the trees above were a type that would flower beautifully in the spring. Kesari used her magic to dig out six graves, and Tarik helped Amar carry the dead over while Kamaal carved prayer symbols into a few carefully selected branches to be used as markers. They considered burning the two bodies in green uniforms, as was the funerary custom in Jakhat, but decided against it. The smoke and smell might attract attention, especially if other soldiers were still nearby.

Once the bodies were in the ground, Kesari covered them, and Kamaal placed a marker over each one. Together, they walked away from the site to rejoin Mitul and Aleida, but Amar lingered a few moments longer. Tarik remained with him.

"You never wanted this war," the old guard said.

"No, I didn't."

"I remember you telling the council and the king. Several times, in fact."

"I still went along with it, in the end," Amar said ruefully. "But I swear to you, I didn't know. If I had, I never would have let things go this far."

Tarik let out a long sigh. "You've put me in a tough spot, you know. I'm supposed to bring you back, but if what you're saying is true, I'm not sure that's the best option anymore. On the other hand, I have my orders, and it's not my place to contradict the king's decision."

Amar nodded. "Your loyalty is to Bhajan. I can appreciate that. But you're also responsible for his safety, aren't you? Your first job is to protect him. Does that include protecting him from himself?"

"Don't do that," Tarik muttered. "Don't twist words around to try and make my orders align with your goals."

"It was only a question."

"I think I've had enough of your questions for one day. Besides, if you tell the empress what's happened, she'll only have more reason to call the king a traitor. She'll throw all her power into ruining him."

"I'd like to hope she's smarter than that," Amar replied. "Half the country has sided with Valmandi, and Bhajan did what he thought was right based on the lies he was told. He and I might have different definitions of what's 'right' *now,* but I'd still like to see him come out of this as whole as possible."

Tarik inclined his head as if considering this but said nothing more.

"Come with us to Tamaya's at least," Amar said. "You can decide what to do then. I won't let you take me back to Valmandi, but if you want to return on your own, I won't stop you."

"I don't suppose you'll give my weapons back or stop dosing me with daravak, either."

"I can't risk that."

Tarik crossed his arms and squared his shoulders to Amar. "Fine. I'll come with you, for now. But you'd better not be lying to me."

Amar couldn't help smiling. He'd heard the guard make a similar threat before, and yet somehow, he was still standing, alive and capable of having a civil discussion with Tarik. That had to indicate there was at least some small level of trust between them.

Amar could work with that.

14

ALEIDA

THE TREES IN THIS PART OF THE VIHAARA FOREST DIDN'T LOOK familiar—not in any particular way, at least. But Aleida knew Tamaya Takhar's home was close. In fact, they'd probably arrive by sunset. Thus far, she'd managed not to dwell on her previous encounter with the old Tarja, but now the memories seeped to the forefront of her mind like a fog. The pained twist of the woman's face, the weight of Valkyra's body on her shoulder, the insult spat in her face.

Bloodthirsty heathen.

She was not looking forward to facing Tamaya again, but she still couldn't tell if that was because of her own guilt, or because of who Tamaya was and what she represented. The woman had trained Nandini Kumar herself, and the insult she'd hurled was a direct reflection of the disdain some Kavorans still held for Visans, a people they considered second-class simply because none were born blessed with the natural ability to channel altma.

It was so much easier to justify the invasion of an entire nation and the erasure of its people if they weren't considered fully human.

Aleida would be perfectly content to never see Tamaya or bigots like her ever again. But that still didn't justify her torturing the old woman.

Mitul noticed her brooding almost immediately, because of course he did; he always noticed things like that. He'd the decency to let her stew on her own for most of the morning, but when she fell several paces behind the others, he began to look back at her periodically, his smile warm but concerned. Eventually, he slipped out of the saddle and passed the reins to Kamaal. He lingered there a while, making a show of stretching his limbs after spending the last several hours on horseback, but Aleida knew he was waiting for her.

She made no effort to avoid the encounter. The pressure of her held-in confession only kept building, and if she didn't let it out on her own terms, Tamaya would tell everyone anyway. At least this way, Aleida could share her own perspective. Not that it would justify the worst of her actions.

Mitul fell into stride beside her but said nothing at first. They walked on like that for several minutes, their matched footsteps crunching the leaves underfoot in a steady rhythm. Finally, he said, "Are you going to make me ask?"

"Are you going to make me tell you?" Aleida retorted snidely. The reflexive harshness still came easier sometimes than a candid, more vulnerable response. Or maybe she just didn't want to acknowledge that she'd let her walls down enough to spill everything the moment he asked.

He shrugged, nonchalant. "No, not if you don't want to."

She pursed her lips and let a few more of her steps crunch before speaking. "I don't want to see Tamaya again."

"Again?" Mitul prodded gently.

"How do you think I found you all after we fought and Amar died?"

"I assumed Valkyra followed us, or at least figured out which way we were going. And you said you used your drawings to track us down."

"Yes, but first I talked to Tamaya." *Talked to.* She scoffed. Saying it like that made it sound so innocent. She dipped her head and stuffed her hands deep in her pockets, arms rigid. "I forced her to tell me where you'd gone."

"Oh."

He still didn't understand the full extent of what she'd done, and she needed him to. If this was why he finally rejected her, so be it. But it mattered that he hear the details from her, not from someone who hated her.

"I tortured her," she said, carefully articulating each word. "I attacked an old woman in her own home, and when she refused to tell me where you'd all gone, I used my magic to hurt her until she gave me answers."

He said nothing, and his silence scared her so much she could do nothing but keep talking to stave off the discomfort.

"She wasn't the only one. There were others. Jameson, for one. And more—half a dozen or so. I was doing it for Tyrus, but maybe I could have found another way. I didn't *have* to hurt them. It was just easier." She paused to suck in a deep breath, her eyes still fixed on the ground in front of her feet, leaves flattening beneath every step. "I'm not a good person, Mitul."

She waited, but the harsh sting of his reproach never came. She glanced over at him, not up at his face, but at the solid length of him still matching pace beside her. There was no extra tension in his limbs, no outward sign that he was shocked or repulsed by her actions. When she did dare meet his gaze, his eyes were as warm and welcoming as ever.

"No one really is, you know," he said. "All good or all bad."

She rolled her eyes, though she wasn't sure whether she was more annoyed with his answer or with herself for thinking he could ever respond with anything but understanding and acceptance.

Wasn't that what she'd wanted from him?

"I've upset you," he said.

"No," she muttered, her scowl deepening. But maybe he had. Maybe she wanted him to get mad, dole out some kind of punishment, react with the same level of disgust she harbored toward herself. It was what she deserved.

"What's that look for, then?"

"Shouldn't you be upset or something? You and Kamaal treat me like I'm fam—" She clamped her mouth shut to bite off the rest of the word. "Like I'm the same as the rest of you. But I was ready to kill you all before Shavhalla. I did a lot of things I'm not proud of. You weren't there. You don't know."

"I know that you loved your brother so much you were willing to do anything to save him." Mitul's voice remained as compassionate as ever. "And I know you wouldn't feel this bad about the mistakes you've made if you weren't a good person. I see that good in you every day, but you're only human. We all do things we're not proud of. It's what you do next and how you try to make amends that really matters."

"You mean I need to apologize to Tamaya." Aleida wrinkled her nose at the idea.

"Only you know what you really need, but that might be a start." He nudged his arm against hers and winked. "And for the record, you *are* family. Didn't you know that already?"

Her heart swelled with that same bittersweet ache that always came when she thought of family. Losing the one she'd been born into had been the hardest trial of her life, and she'd never intended on finding a new one. But they'd found her, and though it wasn't quite the same, it was more than she ever would have hoped for when she and Tyrus were orphans in a world that had taken everything from them.

She looped one arm through Mitul's. He patted her hand, and they trailed after the others along the sun-dappled path through the trees.

When they reached Tamaya's humble abode, daylight was fading, taking with it what little warmth the sun had given and leaving only the dark chill of winter behind. They were still some distance from the fence surrounding her home when the door opened, and the short old woman stepped out to watch their approach. Everything about her seemed to sag downward, from the limp twist of the disheveled bun on her head to the pull of her frown and the way her shoulders hunched forward. Aleida remembered her being small, but she hadn't been so shrunken the last time they'd met. Perhaps it was the cold, or perhaps simply her age overtaking her. In any case, her eyes were as bright and sharp as ever, and when Kesari raised a hand to her in greeting, her voice rang out clear across the distance between them.

"What trouble have you brought to my doorstep this time, girl? No more corpses, I hope." She nodded in Amar's direction. "I can see this one's still enjoying his resurrection."

"Hello, Tamaya," Kesari said. She stopped outside the low wooden gate and made a slight bow, as did the others. Aleida remained standing tall, even when Tamaya's scowl deepened upon seeing her. She might owe the old Tarja an apology, but she didn't owe respect to anyone who didn't respect her, and she wouldn't let Tamaya make her feel small or lesser now.

"What's *she* doing with you?" The old Tarja extended a bony finger toward Aleida.

Mitul's answer was immediate and assertive. "She's with us now. She's been a great help."

Tamaya clicked her tongue. "Oh, I'm sure she has, right after she and that little bitch dragon of hers ambushed me in my own home."

Tarik looked at Aleida like he'd just learned she liked to kick puppies. She half expected to see the same murderous indignation in the others' eyes, too, but she didn't find it. They were all staring at her, of course, but not like *that.* Not like anything, really. They simply waited.

She sighed and took a few steps closer, until she was near enough to lean over the gate, her hands resting on the rough wood. "I'm sorry," she said with genuine regret, looking Tamaya in the eye. "I shouldn't have done that. I was wrong to hurt you, and if there's anything I can do to make it right, I will. If you're not comfortable with me being here, I'll wait outside, but please don't punish them because they're with me. Talk to them. Help them."

Tamaya's head cocked to one side. "Hah! Straight to the point then. This isn't a courtesy call to pay your respects, is it?"

Amar looked a bit embarrassed. "Tamaya, if I—"

"No, no. I never expected it would be. But I'm out of the business, you know. I'm not taking any questions or magical mysteries or charity cases these days. Couldn't help much anyway, even if I wanted to. And I'm not in the mood for company, either, so you'd best be on your way."

"You're not at all curious?" Kesari called out even as the old woman started to turn away. "About Jameson, or whether we got Amar's memories back? Or what about me and Lucian? We found a way to break our Bond, you know."

At this, Tamaya paused, and the disapproval written on her expression was not unlike the look she'd had when she was pinned against the wall with Aleida looming over her. "I told you it was blasphemy. You shouldn't have done it."

"I didn't." Kesari lifted her chin proudly. "We learned how, but we didn't go through with it. I couldn't."

"Where is he then? Your Spirit Tarja."

"He's away, but only for a little while."

"You're still Bonded?" Her voice contained a note of suspicion.

"Yes. I swear." To prove her claim, she raised a hand and conjured flames around it, then snuffed them out a second later.

Some of the tension eased out of Tamaya's expression. "And did you find your peace, then?"

"In some ways. Not entirely. But I'm a lot closer than I was before."

Kesari had successfully grabbed Tamaya's attention, but it wasn't going to last if they couldn't give her a compelling reason to continue the conversation. Already, she was shifting back around toward the door.

"We came because we need your help to stop the war," Aleida blurted out.

"*My* help?" Tamaya barked a short laugh. "I told you already, I'm not much use to anyone these days."

"You are to us," Amar said. "Or you could be. The empress may not believe what we have to say, but she has reason to trust you."

Tamaya clicked her tongue and made a sour expression. "I haven't been in the empress' good graces since her fallout with Nandini Kumar. It didn't matter that *I* never did anything to break her trust personally—the fact that I trained the one who betrayed her was enough."

Maybe that was the key to getting the old woman to listen. "It's her fault all of this is happening in the first place," Aleida said. "Nandini, I mean. She's the one who really started this war."

"She's been dead for three years, girl. You'd think a Visan would know that better than anyone."

"She's a Spirit Tarja." Aleida cocked her head to the side and looked at the old woman pointedly. "How did you put it? My little bitch dragon?"

Tamaya's brows shot straight up as realization dawned on her. She surveyed the group for a few more seconds, chewing on her bottom lip. Then, with a wave of her hand, she beckoned them forward. "Well, come on then. I suppose we'd better sit down and have a talk after all."

AMAR

IT TOOK MORE THAN AN HOUR FOR AMAR TO TELL TAMAYA everything that had happened over the last few months, starting with the restoration of his memories and his journey to Shavhalla. The news of Jameson's death and the circumstances surrounding it did nothing to endear Aleida to her, but she seemed more furious at Valkyra than anyone else, and rightfully so. Throughout the telling of his tale, she vehemently denounced several of the Spirit Tarja's actions, sometimes punctuated by a stream of obscenities when she was particularly enraged.

When Amar finished speaking, Tamaya thumped the table with a fist. "I taught her better than that," she said somberly. "Loyalty to our country and its people—*that* was what she should have learned from me. Not this selfish hunger for power and revenge."

Despite her newfound personal connection to the conflict, the old woman was understandably reluctant to get directly involved. Convincing her that her input would be valuable wasn't difficult; despite the strain in her relationship with Dashiva, Tamaya agreed that there was still enough trust between them for the empress to believe her words.

Convincing her to accompany them to Jakhat was much harder. She insisted that a letter would suffice, but Amar had his own doubts about that, which he voiced adamantly. Mitul, Kamaal, and even Tarik backed him on this, but in the end, it was Kesari's pleadings that swayed the woman. Despite her outward gruffness, she seemed to have a soft spot for the young Tarja, especially now that she knew the girl hadn't given up her Bond with Lucian after all.

"I do have a niece in Jakhat," Tamaya mused, her words so quiet Amar was certain she must be talking to herself. "I suppose it wouldn't hurt to see her again, especially now. One last time." She sat up a little taller and gave Amar a nod. "You win. I'll go."

She spent the rest of the evening packing for their journey, muttering to herself all the while about what a travesty it was that an old woman couldn't be left alone in peace and quiet, and how unjust it was that she now had to get involved in a conflict she never wanted to be a part of. "Dragging a poor old woman out of retirement like this," she said to a pair of old boots as she knocked them together to remove layers of caked mud. "It's not right. Of course, it's all Nandini's fault. She ought to be ashamed of herself."

They spent the night there, and the following morning dawned cold but bright. Tarik finished readying himself to leave before anyone else, and Amar half expected him to return to Valmandi on his own, as per their agreement. Instead, he waited for them outside. He gave no explanation for why he'd decided to accompany them to Jakhat, but Amar didn't need one. He returned the guard's weapons, and Aleida begrudgingly started to hand back the pistol she'd taken.

"You go ahead and keep that," Tarik said. "It suits you. You know how to use it, right?"

Aleida nodded, tucking the gun back into her belt. "Thank you."

Once they set out, everyone made an effort to keep Tamaya as comfortable and content as possible. Complaints were still written clearly across her face, but the cold seemed to have stolen her voice. She sat atop the horse Mitul had been riding, huddled beneath several layers of blankets and looking a bit like a glowering owl with its feathers all puffed out.

Several unremarkable days passed, and Amar was grateful for the lack of excitement. They stuck to seldom-used trails and avoided the main road, which made for slower travel but also ensured they were less likely to run into anyone else. Even so, Amar missed Lucian and the added layer of safety that came from his scouting. The threat of Valkyra's assassins still loomed heavy in his thoughts, and he often insisted on taking the longer watches at night for his own peace of mind. If they were going to be ambushed in the dark, he wanted to make sure he was awake and ready to defend the others.

It was during one such watch, long past midnight, that Amar felt a prickling at the back of his neck. It came on suddenly, startling him back into alertness when he'd begun to doze off. They weren't far from Jakhat now, and two weeks of poor sleep and near endless walking were taking a toll. He rubbed his eyes and stretched his arms, annoyed with himself for nodding off. He couldn't do that again. It put the others at risk, and that defeated the whole purpose of him taking watch in the first place.

He stood and shook out his legs, searching the shadows of the trees for any signs of movement. Nothing appeared out of the ordinary, but the uneasy feeling didn't immediately subside, and he couldn't help wondering what terrible dangers might have crept up on them during his brief lapse in vigilance. He drew his sword slow and quiet, then strode into the trees away from the camp. Channeling his altma, he made a dim orb of light to illuminate his surroundings. When he sent it to drift a few paces ahead, a shadow slipped between a pair of tall mahoganies.

"Who's there?"

There was no answer. He raised the point of his sword and followed the light, hoping to discover some small animal scurrying through the underbrush. He kicked at a few of the nearby bushes in an attempt to scare out whatever might be hiding there. Nothing moved.

"Come out and show yourself!" he called, a little louder this time.

Still no response, but Amar didn't yet trust that everything was safe. He backed up, heading for camp but still watching the area where he'd seen movement. His shoulder blades hit something hard. The trunk of a tree, he thought—until the solid surface shifted against him.

He spun around and slashed with his blade. A voice cried out, but Amar's altma fizzled, and his magical light vanished before he could see the other person's face. His eyes were not adjusted to the sudden darkness that surrounded him. All he could make out were a few general shapes and shadows. One seemed closer than the rest, darting past him and around to his back. He followed as best as he could but reacted too slowly, too blindly.

"Mitul!" he called out in warning. "Kesar—*oof!*"

All the air rushed out of him with the sudden blow to his chest, and he doubled over, still swinging his sword wildly. It was all he could do, thanks to his own stupidity. He shouldn't have counted on being able to maintain the light he'd conjured. He had too little control over his magic for that.

Something flashed in front of him, a blaze of orange and yellow that illuminated the shadows. Amar's eyes stung from the heat, but he could see, and that was a welcome relief.

He launched himself at the closest attacker. She went down with a quick slash to the throat, and Amar turned his attention to the source of the light. Kesari and the others were up, fighting off their own group of assassins. One lunged at Tamaya with a raised dagger. Rather than fight back, the old woman cowered. An instant before the man fell on her, Aleida shot him in the back with the pistol Tarik had given her. The sharp *crack* reverberated through the stillness of the forest like thunder.

Before he could go to their aid, Amar caught movement in his peripherals. Something was headed right at him. He managed to duck before the blow landed, but another followed from the opposite direction. Someone seized his sword and wrenched it away. In the same instant, a second person stole the gun from his hip. The pair of assailants had moved so quickly they had to be channeling altma.

He could play at that, too. Jaw set, he reached for his own magic, hoping the strain of keeping it steady didn't show on his face. He didn't have as much control over it as he would have liked, but these two didn't know that. They might not even know he had magic.

"It's all right, Your Highness," the nearest one said. "Come with us. We'll keep you safe, escort you back to the palace." She had her hands raised in a placating gesture, but the sparks of altma still crackling in her palms were a clear threat. He *would* come with them, whether it was of his own free will or against it.

Amar watched her—watched them both—like they were a pair of cobras preparing to strike. None of them moved for the space of three heartbeats, and for an instant, Amar thought that maybe he could find a way out of this where they all walked away unharmed. Like with Tarik.

Then a cry came from the camp—something pained and guttural, like an animal wounded. A quick glance over his shoulder confirmed it was a fallen assassin and not one of his friends, but in that brief moment of distraction, the enemies he faced closed in. The man tackled him to the ground while the woman used her altma to form a net from the branches around them. It happened in a fraction of a second. The net was on top of him, and his struggles to free himself grew more and more futile.

A hand went to the base of his skull. He channeled his own altma there, trying to block out whatever they were doing to him, but it was too late. A bone-deep weariness settled in, and his body went limp.

It would be so much easier to sleep, let them carry him back to the palace and the soft, warm bed that awaited him there…

They began to drag him. He didn't know for how long, but he was fairly certain he lost consciousness a few times, despite his best efforts to stay awake. He would blink, and when he opened his eyes, the landscape had shifted.

Stay awake, stay awake, stay awake. He managed to maneuver his hand to his mouth and bit down on one of his fingers, hard enough that the pain cleared away some of the fog in his mind.

"Get off of him," a voice boomed. "Now."

Amar blinked drowsily, and when his vision came into focus, he saw Tarik standing a few paces off, sword drawn. He made no move to help Amar, nor to drive off the attackers. Time seemed frozen, perhaps because no one was moving, or perhaps because of the cottony haze stifling Amar's senses.

"Sir!" One of the attackers saluted Tarik. Guards, then, or soldiers. Probably specialists, given their fighting skills, but their deference to Tarik meant he outranked them.

"We've secured Prince Savir," the woman said. "Would you like to bring him back to the palace with us?"

Still fighting drowsiness, Amar watched in slow motion as Tarik sheathed his sword and gave the pair a nod.

What was he doing? It was like something out of a dream—a nightmare where Amar was frozen and unable to do anything but watch. After everything he'd seen and heard, Tarik was still choosing to follow the orders King Bhajan had given him. And why shouldn't he? His loyalty to the king ran longer and deeper than his loyalty to Amar.

But this wasn't about Amar. This was about the entire Kavoran empire and the civil war tearing it apart.

Had he been wrong about Tarik? Perhaps the man's goals and values were more aligned with King Bhajan's than Amar had presumed.

It is far too late for any of us to back down.

Whatever your life was before this, you are *the prince we need now, and this war has been a long time coming.*

Amar squirmed, spurred on by newfound panic. Tarik was going to drag him back to the palace after all. He'd only been waiting for the right opportunity, and this was it. They would take him back, and Valkyra would kill him, and whether by her words or the king's, Amar would be manipulated into playing prince once more. All so Bhajan could have his war and his long overdue justice, and in so doing give Valkyra the revenge and power she sought.

And his friends? They were a nuisance to her. They would have to be eliminated.

"Stop," he shouted. The word did not come out as loud or as strong as he'd intended. "Don't!"

Tarik ignored him, keeping his focus on the other two soldiers. "Who sent you out here?"

"The king," one replied. "He's been in a rage since His Highness disappeared. We were warned he might not come willingly, but—"

"And King Bhajan gave you the orders himself, did he?"

"Well, no, come to think of it. It was one of his advisors, the magistrate."

Tarik looked down at Amar, but his expression was unreadable. Amar made another attempt at channeling his altma. He could still sense it but didn't have the energy to *do* anything with it. Most of his focus was currently directed toward staying conscious.

"What about the dragon?" Tarik asked.

"What, the prince's pet?"

"Yes."

"Well, she's sort of taken a shine to the magistrate, but I don't see what difference that—"

His voice pitched high as an unseen force knocked him off his feet. He flew backward like a ragdoll, limbs splayed. Amar didn't see where he landed, but the sharp cracks told him he'd probably broken at least a couple of bones. An instant later, his companion met a similar fate.

Tarik bent and put his hands to the net of branches that trapped Amar. It snapped and fell away. Once freed, Amar gratefully took the guard's offered hand and rose to his feet. The world immediately began to spin and lurch.

"Whoa there, careful." Tarik placed a steadying hand on his shoulder.

"Mitul and the others—"

"They're fine. Kamaal was wounded, nothing too serious. Kesari's patching him up."

Amar looked to where the two attackers had landed in a heap at the base of a large tree. "Are they dead?"

"Only unconscious, probably a few bumps and bruises. They won't be coming after us again for a while, but once they've healed themselves, I expect they'll be right back at it. If you want them stopped permanently, you'll have to do it yourself. I won't kill a couple of good soldiers for following orders, but I won't stand in your way, either."

Amar considered the pair for a few minutes. Tarik was right—they'd likely come after them again. Maybe it was foolish to let them live, but he couldn't bring himself to kill them, either. The whole reason he was trying to end this war was to keep soldiers like them from dying. They weren't pawns to be sacrificed in pursuit of that goal.

"I won't kill them, but do you think you could make one of those nets from the branches like they had me in? It could keep them contained a while longer, buy us more time."

Tarik did as Amar had asked, then they made their way back to camp together. Still feeling incredibly fatigued, Amar held on to the bigger man's arm for support. "I really thought you were going to turn on me," he said.

Tarik grunted and gave him a wry half-smile. "I can't say I didn't consider it, even after we left Tamaya's. I still wonder if I should just do what Bhajan asked me to do, like I always have."

"So why haven't you?"

Tarik didn't answer right away, and when he did, there was a heavy sadness to his voice. "It's like you said. He needs protecting from himself. I hate that it's come to that, but here we are." He sighed. "And, I suppose that means I trust you. At least enough to let you try this, if you really think it will stop the war."

"Do *you* think it will work?"

"I don't know. I hope so. It will be better for us all if it does. But there are other forces at work here, as we've both seen with King Bhajan himself. Justice, vengeance, greed, pride, control—those are strong motivations. The people in power won't let go of them easily."

Amar couldn't argue with that.

Part II

The Family we Built

ALEIDA

ALEIDA STARED ACROSS THE MAYUKA RIVER TO THE CITY OF JAKHAT beyond, its roofs and terraces visible in the bright moonlight. She and her companions had traveled well into the night to reach it, and now, only a single bridge crossing stood between them and the city.

Unfortunately, that bridge was heavily patrolled by Jakhat soldiers, who were dutifully and thoroughly inspecting all who passed, whether they were coming or going.

"How do you want to do this?" Mitul asked Amar.

The man had been silently frowning at the bridge for a few minutes now, and none of them dared break from the cover of the forest until they knew how to proceed. Aleida had been under the impression that Amar already had a plan worked out, but now that they were here, he seemed stumped. Getting to Empress Dashiva might be more complicated than they'd anticipated.

"Prince Savir made a very public appearance here not too long ago," Amar said. "If any of those soldiers recognize me, they'll arrest us all, and who knows when or if I'll ever get to see the empress?"

"Maybe we can find a way around," Kesari said. "Cross the river somewhere else."

Mitul frowned at that. "The water will be freezing, and some of us can't swim."

"I could help you across," Aleida said. She was an excellent swimmer, and the cold water didn't frighten her as long as they had Kesari's magic to warm them up after.

Tamaya let out a disgruntled scoff. "You think you're the first fools who've thought about doing exactly that? They'll have soldiers patrolling the riverbank at least half a day's journey in either direction, and magical alarms to alert them of anyone trying to cross without inspection."

"Kes and Tarik could take care of those," Amar said, looking at each of them with absolute confidence.

Kesari scrunched her mouth to one side, seemingly unconvinced. "Well, we could try."

Tarik shook his head. "If we miss one, they'll spot us, and we'll look all the more suspicious for attempting to get around their security." He crossed his arms and leaned a little closer to Amar, speaking softly. "Maybe it wouldn't be so bad to let them catch us. Once they realize they've captured Prince Savir, they'll take you before the empress at some point. She'll be interested to know what you're doing here, at the very least."

"Maybe. But they could just as soon kill the rest of you on sight for conspiring with a traitor."

"I think they'll want to talk to us, too. Find out what we know, what we were doing with you."

"Maybe. But it's not guaranteed, and I can't put the rest of you at risk like that. Besides, I need to make sure I'm talking to Dashiva herself as soon as possible."

"Exactly," Tamaya said. "Why take the risk? A lot of the soldiers up there will be new conscripts, barely trained and under pressure waiting for a fight. At least let us make it to the palace before we throw ourselves into anyone's custody. We'll have a better chance with the palace guards than with a bunch of jittery recruits fresh out of basic training."

"So how do we get past them?" Kesari asked.

"I think I can talk them into letting us through," Kamaal said. "But Amar would need a disguise. A good one."

"Just rough him up a little," Aleida said. "Give him a head wound, cover half his face with a bloody bandage. Tear his clothes, rub a little more dirt on him. He was all clean and polished the last time he was here. They won't recognize him as Prince Savir if he looks like a sorry mess."

"And I don't already look like a sorry mess?" Amar asked with a smirk. "We've been on the road for weeks. None of us are exactly looking our best."

"Sure, but you could stand to be a little rougher. Make them uncomfortable. They don't look at you twice if they're uncomfortable with what they see." Something she knew all too well, after all the nights she and Tyrus had spent in dishevelment, huddled up together in alleys and under shop awnings. Most who passed simply winced and averted their eyes as quickly as possible.

Mitul found several fresh bandages in his pack. Kamaal dug out a small box of paints in little jars that he'd insisted on bringing along, as if he was sure he'd find an opportunity for a relaxing painting session somewhere along their journey. Aleida had teased him about it for a few days, and he raised an eyebrow at her now as if to ask how glad she was that he'd brought them along after all. She rolled her eyes in response but couldn't help grinning.

While Amar set about strategically damaging and dirtying his clothes, Kamaal mixed red and brown to paint carnage on the bandages. He tested it on Amar a few times, tying it in place and then removing it again to make adjustments and add more paint. It took far longer than was probably necessary, but Aleida could understand wanting to get the look right. Creating something was never a simple or careless process for an artist, even when the creation in question was a bloodstained rag for a fake injury.

Once it was finished, they secured it over Amar's head to cover his left eye. His hair was long enough to sweep down across his brow and partially obscure the other eye. Combined with the disgraceful state of his attire, the effect left him looking exactly the opposite of a prince. Hopefully that would be enough to get them across the bridge and into the city.

Only one way to find out.

The soldiers on the bridge watched their approach with stiff postures and wary eyes. Kamaal led the way with Tamaya riding one horse. Mitul led the second by the reins, and the others spread out to either side, keeping their hands in the open and easily visible. Aleida had seen soldiers in the city dozens of times before, but these ones made the back of her neck prickle. Something in the way they stood, the way they watched her, the way their fingers curled around their rifles. For a second, she was eleven years old again, watching dozens of people in those uniforms march into Libera.

"Stop there!" one of them called out when they were still several paces away. "State your names and business."

"Kamaal Ruman," the artist said. "I'm just returning home and bringing some of my family with me."

A few of the soldiers exchanged looks, and Aleida's palms began to sweat. What if they didn't believe Kamaal? What if they decided to arrest everyone until they could verify his story? What would they do when they *couldn't* verify the identities of his so-called family? She wasn't even Kavoran; she certainly didn't *look* like she could be a blood relative.

"It's not a good time for Jakhat's most highly esteemed citizens to be traveling," said the ranking officer. "There's a war on, you know."

Kamaal chuckled good naturedly. "Yes, so I've heard."

The officer remained stone-faced.

Kamaal sobered. "My apologies, sir. I certainly didn't mean to be dismissive of your warning. I understood the risks when I set out, and I never intended to be gone so long. But, as you said, there's a war on, and such things put into perspective what's most important. Like family."

The officer tilted his head a little. "Word 'round here is you ran off to Valmandi to throw your support behind Savir."

The knife-edge in his voice was an open accusation. Aleida tensed, but Kamaal remained perfectly unruffled.

"Is that so? What an unfortunate rumor. Thank you for letting me know what I'll need to correct once I'm back home."

The officer's eyes narrowed. "So you weren't in Valmandi?"

"Oh, I was. And I did see the king and queen, if that's your next question. I'm sure you've had reports about that."

The man nodded stiffly.

"For whatever my word is worth to you, I promise I didn't go there to give Prince Savir my support."

The officer's lips curled in a sneer, and though he looked like he wanted to spit at Kamaal's feet, he stopped short of actually doing so. "You can see how it looks, though, you going off to dine at the palace and all that."

"If I've personally offended you, I do apologize," Kamaal said. "I couldn't deny King Bhajan and Queen Indira's invitation without raising suspicion. We've been on good terms for such a long time, and my only priority was to get my family out of Valmandi and back here as quickly as possible. I didn't want to risk anything that might make their departure from the city more difficult."

"Your family?" the officer asked.

"As I said. My grandmother." He gestured to Tamaya, who'd thrown her hood over her eyes to avoid the slight chance she might be recognized. Then he motioned to Tarik, Amar, and Kesari in quick succession. "My cousin and his two children. And, of course, my apprentice." This last title was given to Aleida, and though it wasn't real, she couldn't help standing up a little straighter at the thought of it. How proud she would be if she truly were Kamaal's apprentice.

"And him?" The officer pointed at Mitul.

Kamaal blinked, panic flashing in his eyes for the barest flicker of a moment. Then he seized Mitul's hand with a beaming smile. "Oh goodness, where are my manners? I assumed you'd heard. This is my husband, Mitul Rama."

To his credit, Mitul played along with the charade beautifully, appearing only slightly flustered as he stepped closer to Kamaal, which could have been attributed to bashful romantic tenderness for all the soldiers knew. Aleida did her best to keep a straight face, but the corner of her mouth may have slipped upward just a little.

"I didn't know you were engaged," the officer said with a frown.

"It happened rather quickly, I admit. We eloped while we were in Valmandi. Didn't seem right to make a big scene, what with the war and all."

The man's shoulders relaxed a little, and he gave the supposed newlyweds a nod. "I can respect that. May the skies smile on your lives' entwinement."

"Thank you, that's very kind."

"All right, well go on, then. Over the bridge and home to Jakhat. And once you're there, stay put. No more unexpected trips to Valmandi or anywhere else. You're far safer here in the city."

"Of course. I trust we're in capable hands with soldiers like you and your subordinates here keeping watch."

Tamaya harrumphed loudly from the top of her horse, but Amar began coughing before any of the soldiers had time to take offense.

The officer wrinkled his nose as they passed, his gaze following Amar. "And get that boy to a healer quick as you can. He looks frightful."

Once they'd traipsed past the checkpoint and were safely on the other side of the river, Tamaya let loose the words she'd likely been holding back during the entire exchange. "What a sorry bunch of louts they were. And that officer—a complete buffoon. How many Valmandi spies have slipped past him, I wonder? I never would have let some famous ponce sweet-talk me into letting his whole family through without a full inspection. What kind of chickenshit training are they putting new recruits through these days?"

Kesari shrugged and looked up at her. "I guess we should be happy you weren't the one in charge of that checkpoint, then."

"Hmph. Indeed. I *never* would have been so lax, back in my day. That's the worst thing about getting old, you know—realizing you'll soon leave the world behind to a bunch of numbskulls like that."

She kept going, but Aleida didn't have the patience to listen to her spiteful prattling. She hung back and soon found herself lagging behind everyone else, trailing Mitul and Kamaal.

"So, your husband?" Mitul asked playfully, nudging his shoulder against Kamaal's.

"I had to say *something*," the artist replied. "I wasn't sure they'd let you in if you weren't family of some sort. *Husband* made the most sense."

"You said it awfully fast," he teased.

"Is that a problem?"

"No, I just…to be honest, I suppose I liked the idea."

"So did I." Kamaal laced their fingers together. "In fact, I think my only regret is that it's not true. Not yet, anyway."

"Are you..."

Kamaal shrugged. "Maybe. Though now is obviously not the best time. So, I suppose I'm asking if you'd be open to it—to me *really* asking, properly, when our current concerns aren't so pressing."

Mitul raised Kamaal's hand to his lips and kissed it. "Only if I don't ask you first."

Aleida marched past them. "You two are absolutely revolting," she said, and they both laughed. No doubt they'd be whispering more sweet nothings to each other once she was out of earshot.

She smiled to herself and shook her head. Their saccharine affection for each other was a bit much to witness sometimes, but she wouldn't have traded the pair of them for anything. They were a light in the storm, a constant reminder that even in the midst of loss and betrayal, war and turmoil, there was still room for love and for the joy created within that love.

It was the closest thing to god she still believed in, and realizing that brought a peace she hadn't experienced since she'd determined Artex and faith to be a sweet but hollow lie. Maybe her Visan religion didn't hold all the answers she'd once believed it did, but there was still a very real power in people and the connections that grew between them. That was a truth she could still hold dear.

AMAR

THEY MANAGED TO MAKE THEIR WAY THROUGH THE CITY WITHOUT incident, though Amar couldn't help noting the more somber air about the place compared to the last time he'd visited. Jakhat was never this quiet, even at night, but now the streets were deserted and all the doors and windows closed tight. Several of the homes had candles and flowers outside their doors, and in some cases artistic renderings of the dead these memorials paid tribute to. Fallen soldiers, every one of them, lost to Kavora's civil war.

No matter how he looked at it, there was no sense to any of it, no comfort he could take in knowing that at least if he ended the war, their sacrifices wouldn't have been for naught. Because that wasn't true. They'd been victims of a fight that never should have started in the first place. There was no righteous justice in any of this, no right or wrong side, no dignified heroism in death. It was *all* wrong, and he had to end it before Valkyra made things any worse than she already had.

He hated her. With every fiber of his being, he despised her. The feeling chewed a hole through his heart and filled it with poison. He glanced at Aleida walking tall beside him. Was that how she always felt? It must be. She had more reason to hate the Spirit Tarja than any of them. How did she stand it? How was she not yelling and throwing things and threatening to hit people all the time? That was what he wanted to do, and he had far more years of experience at controlling his temper than she did.

Not that he'd ever been particularly good at it.

They were getting closer to the palace now—close enough that it was time Amar shed his disguise. He pulled off the painted bandage and stuffed it into his pocket. After smoothing out his clothes and combing his hair back with his fingers, he asked Tarik, "Well, do I look anything like a prince again?"

The man grunted. "A very neglected one, I suppose. But that's my fault, abandoning my duty to look after you."

"How dare you?" Amar responded flatly. "I'll have to talk to the king about that, make sure he gives you a very stern lecture."

Tarik winced a little. "Please don't joke about such things. I'm going to have enough explaining to do as it is."

"Sorry. I'm terrible at jokes, especially when I'm nervous."

"What's there to be nervous about?"

Amar blinked. What *wasn't* there to be nervous about? Then he caught the slight upward turn of Tarik's mustache. "Oh. You're joking."

"Very astute, *Your Highness.*"

This time, it was his turn to wince. "Don't start calling me that now."

"I won't," Tarik replied. "But do you think *they* will?"

Amar shifted his attention to the palace gates ahead, where six guards armed with rifles watched them with increasingly incredulous looks. They were slower to react than the soldiers on the bridge, though to be fair, these guards likely recognized Amar from his previous visit to the palace. Thus, they had to experience the more complicated mental process of questioning what the hell Prince Savir was doing here—and looking like he'd just crawled out of the woods, no less.

"Stop where you are!" one called out.

Amar complied with the order, as did Tarik and his other companions behind them. "I need to speak with the empress," he said.

"Oh, I'll bet you do," the guard replied. "But I don't think she's in a mood to speak with you, you warmongering charlatan." She spit a glob of saliva a rather impressive distance to hit Amar square in the chest. Disgusting, but he supposed from their perspective, he deserved that.

"Warmongering charlatan," he murmured to Tarik. "I've been called worse."

"I've called you worse myself."

"Have you?"

"Not to your face."

"Well, thank you for that. I think."

"Stop whispering!" the guard shouted. "Disarm yourselves immediately. Try anything, and we shoot."

Amar had no doubt they meant it. All six rifles were now aimed at him, and given how seriously Dashiva was apt to take her own security, they must all be excellent marksmen. He obeyed without hesitation, as did the others. Swords, pistols, and daggers clattered to the ground in a heap.

"This is ridiculous!" Tamaya called out shrilly. "Don't you know who I am?"

"You're Tamaya Takhar," said the guard. "And you're now an accomplice to this traitor. Same goes for you." She jerked a nod at Kamaal. "I don't give a monkey's ass what your name or reputation is. You're all going straight to the cells until the empress decides what she wants done with you."

They closed in, and Amar kept a close eye on Tamaya to make sure she didn't do anything stupid in her frustration. She was clearly unhappy about being treated like a criminal, but fortunately, she seemed to have enough sense to submit to the arrest without a fight. Daravak was administered to all of them, and then a guard bound his hands so tight his wrists began to chafe almost instantly.

It wasn't exactly the warm reception Amar had hoped for, but he hadn't ever expected things to go that well, and he was content enough that he hadn't simply been shot on sight. At least they were here now, and getting somewhere, even if *somewhere* was only a cell. Dashiva would certainly be curious about why he'd shown up at her gates to turn himself in.

Cell or not, that curiosity could work to his benefit.

KESARI

THE CELL ON THE LOWER LEVELS OF THE IMPERIAL PALACE WAS AS cold and gray as one could expect such a place to be, but it wasn't entirely uncomfortable. Kesari used one foot to test the mattress on the floor and found it surprisingly cushioned. The washbasin and bar of soap were also a particularly nice touch. Two guards even brought in a cot and several extra blankets once Tamaya had thoroughly scolded them—a tirade that consisted of statements like, "How dare you make an old woman sleep on the floor?" and, "Your own grandmothers would be ashamed of you for treating me this way."

It was still a cell, but a rather hospitable one by any standard, and Kesari knew they had Tamaya to thank for that. She might now be considered a traitor thanks to her association with Amar, but she was still a retired Tarja commander of some renown. That earned her—and thus all of them—certain comforts that likely weren't given to all prisoners.

After the confrontation at the gates, the four men in their group had been dragged off elsewhere, but Kesari wasn't worried about them. Given Prince Savir's status and value as a hostage, they likely weren't faring any worse. With any luck, Amar would have a chance to speak to Empress Dashiva in the morning, and this whole thing could be cleared up quickly. What that might entail, Kesari had no idea, but for now, she could content herself with waiting. Sleeping would certainly help pass the time, but the night's excitement still had her buzzing with energy.

Unfortunately, her cellmates weren't particularly good company. Aleida had immediately claimed one of the mattresses on the floor and was now facing the wall sleeping soundly. Tamaya was fussing with the blankets on her cot and muttering to herself about what a disgrace this whole situation was, and how she should have stayed home where she belonged instead of gallivanting off to try and save the empire like some kind of hero half her age. Given the way things had played out so far, Kesari couldn't fault the old woman for being disgruntled.

If Lucian were here, Kesari could have at least talked to him. He always knew how to keep her entertained with a story or with a few quips about whatever situation they were in.

Skies, she missed him.

She sighed and rolled up her mattress to form a semi-comfortable seat against the wall. Tamaya gave her a sidelong glance and plopped down onto her cot, which let out a rather alarming creak. Hopefully, it wouldn't break in the night and put the woman in an even worse mood.

"A pity your Spirit Tarja isn't here," Tamaya said. "I'll bet he's useful in a crisis like this."

"He is."

"That's magic, though. Always useful, until you need it most and it's not around anymore. Almost makes you wish you never had it to begin with."

Clearly, they weren't talking about Lucian anymore.

"I don't know why they bothered to give me daravak at all," Tamaya went on. "I'm all spent. Couldn't channel altma now to save my own life."

"They don't know that," Kesari replied, propping her arms up on her knees. "To them, you're still the legendary Commander Takhar."

"Legendary? Hah! I'll have that inscribed on my memorial." She cackled a little at that, a thin, spidery noise that danced up Kesari's spine and chilled her bones. It was grim to speak of death so candidly, but perhaps that was the only way of coping when it loomed so near. A natural-born Tarja's altma faded away as they reached the end of their life, and the fact that Tamaya could no longer use her magic was a sure sign that death was close.

How strange must it be to know it was coming. There was no exactness in the timing, of course, but the idea of 'soon' was vexing enough. Did she fear death? Even now, did she grieve for herself and the life she would soon say goodbye to? Perhaps a little morbid humor was the only way to keep those darker thoughts at bay.

"You're still so young," she said, smiling at Kesari a little. "So far from death. But closer than most your age, eh?"

Kesari shrugged. It was the one part of her Bond she didn't like to think about—the one part she probably hadn't given enough thought to when she'd agreed to it in the first place. Sharing her life with Lucian meant she'd be extremely lucky to live as old as fifty. That had seemed so far off when she was just fourteen and at least twice as naive as she was now. Now, she'd seen death firsthand. She'd been the cause of death. It had only been a few years, but she had a much deeper respect for how precious every day was. All she had was this one life, however short it might be.

"What about her?" she asked, eager to shift the conversation away from herself but still as curious as ever about the workings of magic. "Aleida wasn't much older than me when she formed her Bond, and then it was severed against her will. Will her life still be cut short?"

Tamaya worried at her lower lip for a few moments before answering. "Hard to say for sure, but I don't think so. The early death comes from splitting one life between two souls over the course of many years. Her Bond was broken before it had a chance to take much from her. She'll have as long as any of us have in this world, as long as something else doesn't kill her."

That was good news. Aleida had lost enough already. Assuming she could carve out some happiness for herself once this was all over, it seemed only fair that she be able to stick around long enough to fully experience it.

"You'll be all right, girl," Tamaya said, the usual harsh grumble to her voice replaced by an unexpected softness. "Death comes for us all eventually, and a life full of magic can be an exceptional one, even if it ends sooner than we want it to."

Kesari nodded. Exceptional—that was certainly true. Whether for good or ill, her Bond with Lucian had set her down a transformative path. There had been pain along that road, but there had also been joy and growth. She and Rajiv had always talked about going off and having an adventure, and though he wasn't here to live it himself anymore, he would have loved that she was having one without him.

But adventures had to end sometime. Maybe it was just the fact that Lucian was gone and she was stuck in a cell feeling very lonely, but Kesari's heart ached once again with a deep and sudden longing for home. For her family.

Whatever time she had left, she wanted to spend it with the people she loved.

AMAR

AMAR FOUND HIMSELF ISOLATED IN A ROOM OF HIS OWN, THE accommodations decent enough despite the hostile welcome he and his friends had received. Such animosity was to be expected, given the circumstances, but he hoped the others weren't suffering any unnecessary cruelty because of their connection to him.

Hours passed. He tried to sleep but couldn't, so instead, he mentally rehearsed what he needed to tell the empress, pacing the floor of his cell until he thought he would go mad from the suspense of waiting. There were no windows, and it was impossible to tell exactly how much time had passed, though if he had to guess, it must be nearly morning. What was taking Dashiva so long? Even if it was the middle of the night, someone should have told her about his arrival. Did she simply not care, or was she trying to send a message about how unimportant she deemed him and his arrival to be?

Finally, the lock on his door clicked, but when it swung open, he froze. The person who had come to retrieve him was not the unfamiliar guard or soldier he'd expected to see there.

Instead, he found himself staring at the scarred face of General Avani Muraka, Jakhat's top Tarja military leader and secret ally to Valmandi.

"Well," she sneered, stepping into the room and closing the door behind her. "What a predicament you've found yourself in, little prince."

"It's good to see you again, general." Amar frantically pieced together memories of his last encounter with Muraka and recontextualized them with all he'd learned since. He and Ashaya had met with her secretly to convince her that he was the real Prince Savir and someone she owed her allegiance to. After that, he'd overheard a strange conversation between Valkyra and Ashaya.

At the time, he'd been so upset by Valkyra's suggestion that he would never recover his lost memories to give much regard to the rest of their exchange. But there had been something else—the magistrate telling Valkyra she might need to visit Muraka herself in order to really convince the woman to work with them. In doing so, Valkyra likely would have revealed who she truly was.

That was what had turned Muraka. Not Prince Savir's claim to the throne or Ashaya's logic, but the respect and loyalty she had for Nandini Kumar, former imperial advisor and the most powerful Tarja Kavora had seen in centuries.

The question now was, how much did she know? And how much did she suspect Amar knew?

"Is the empress ready to see me now?" he asked. The sooner he could talk to her, the better, and if that took him out of close quarters and a private conversation with Muraka, so much the better.

"She is," the general replied. "But you and I ought to have a little chat first, don't you think?"

"We don't want to keep her waiting."

"Oh, she'll be fine. Tell me, what brings you here all the way from Valmandi? Where's your little pet dragon?"

Amar felt like he was cornered in a game of samud, where any choice might be the wrong one. Her questions were meant to size him up, get a clearer picture of what he knew. Amar couldn't give away anything important, but he also needed to learn what *her* game was in order to get past her and finally see Dashiva.

The fact that she was asking about Valkyra in such terms meant she was unaware or at least unsure about whether he knew that she and the dragon had met.

"I left her behind," he said.

"And your business here?"

"Like I said, I need to talk to the empress. My business with her is my own. I'd like to keep it that way."

Muraka stepped closer, leaning forward slightly and lowering her voice. "You know where my loyalties lie, Your Highness. I only want to help. I fear you've made a severe miscalculation in coming here."

"And why is that?"

"The empress won't listen. Whatever you have to say, she's not going to believe you. She'll have you killed, and your friends, too. You're all traitors to the empire, as far as she's concerned."

That did put a chill in Amar's stomach, and he didn't do well enough to hide it, judging by the way Muraka's eyes brightened. She had hit on his worst fear. He'd put not only himself but all of his companions at risk by coming here.

And yet, he suspected the general was bluffing. Empress Dashiva would at least hear him out, if only to satisfy her own curiosity about his sudden arrival. Whether or not she believed him remained to be seen, but he'd taken every precaution he could in that regard.

"Let me help you," Muraka said. "I can get you out of here before anything goes wrong. All of you."

And there, that was it. She had played her hand. She wanted him out of the palace, not only to prevent him from talking to Dashiva, but also to get him back to Valmandi and under Valkyra's influence. She knew he wasn't the real Prince Savir—Valkyra must have told her that much. Once he'd run away, the Spirit Tarja would have reached out to any ally she had to try and track him down. Including Muraka.

She must also suspect that the best way to return him to Valkyra was to make him believe his friends' lives were in danger if they stayed here. Once they were outside the palace, she could kill him without raising suspicion, leave Jakhat with his body, and spin whatever tale she had to when he awoke to convince him to return to Valmandi. It would be messy, but there he could resume his role as puppet prince, and everything would continue mostly as before.

He wasn't fool enough to believe his friends would survive such a chain of events.

As far as she knew, he still believed her to be an ally. For now, he might have to play along. She wasn't going to let him out of her sight, and she certainly wouldn't be taking him to see Dashiva.

"You promise you can get my friends out of this alive?" he asked, ladling a hefty dose of hesitation into his voice.

"I promise. We can use the secret passages that run through the palace. Once I get you to safety, I'll come back for them."

Amar swallowed, allowing his eyes to wander and worrying at his bottom lip as if he were still considering his options. Then he nodded. "Maybe you're right. I didn't mean to drag them into this. I didn't think it would get this bad."

"Of course you didn't," Muraka said. "But it's going to be all right. Come quickly now. The longer the empress waits, the more impatient she'll get, and we want to be well on our way before she sends anyone looking for us."

Amar followed her out of the room and past the two guards standing watch in the hallway. They saw a few more as they walked, along with several servants going about their early morning duties. Amar took note of the route they were traveling; this was not a part of the palace he'd familiarized himself with during his last visit. After turning down several corridors and going up a couple flights of stairs, they came to an area he recognized, and he was able to get his bearings.

Muraka led him down an empty hall and pushed open a door. He followed her into a bedroom—hers, if the many decorative weapons, military commendations, and hunting trophies were any indication. A brass paperweight sat on a desk within easy reach, and Amar grabbed it while Muraka's back was turned. He held it in two hands behind his back. It had a nice heft to it, and now that they were alone…

She went to the corner of the room and moved aside a tall, broad-leafed plant growing out of a colorful pot. When she pressed her fingers to a seam in the wallpaper, a section of the wall slid away to reveal a dark passage behind. She motioned Amar forward. "This way."

He peered inside. "It's pitch black in there."

"Your magic?" Muraka waved her hand in a circle to indicate that he should channel a light for himself.

"Daravak."

"Ah. Here, then." She faced the darkness and raised her hand to channel her own altma.

He struck.

Muraka seemed to see the blow coming at the last moment and jerked back in response, but not quickly enough. The paperweight cracked hard against the side of her skull.

She swayed for a moment, then fell. Amar caught her and shifted her weight so his arms were hooked under hers. He dragged her backward into the tunnel and left her lying there in the dark. She was already groaning when he stepped over her body, and he made a quick exit from the room.

He was out of time. Getting to Dashiva was his only priority, and he thought he knew exactly where she'd be. The palace had a throne room for public audiences, of course, but Dashiva rarely sat there. Jasala handled most of the business brought before the court. If he was right—skies, let him be right—she'd want to see him somewhere more private, somewhere she felt most comfortable. The same room she'd been in when they first met, surrounded by plush cushions and the gold-framed paintings she loved.

Amar ran.

This was perhaps not the best decision, as it immediately drew the attention of everyone who could see him or hear his pounding footsteps. A finely dressed woman shrieked as he flew by her on the stairs. A servant shrunk back, trying to melt into the wall to avoid being trampled in his passing.

And then there were the guards. At least three began chasing him, and he had no doubt more were coming. Amar ignored all their cries to stop. If he could get to Dashiva, everything would work out. She'd asked to see him. She wanted to talk to him. She would listen, no matter the circumstances of his arrival.

The room was close—just a hallway and another turn around a corner, and he'd be there.

Something struck him hard in the back, and he went sprawling onto the marble floor with a groan.

"Seize him!" came a bellowed command. The words were entirely unnecessary, given that guards were already piling on top of him like a pack of wolves tearing into their meal. Amar fought back, clawing at legs and arms and anything he could get his hands on to try and free himself. One guard had a dagger in his boot, and he pulled it free.

Before he could brandish the weapon as a threat, a new voice called out, clear and authoritative—and angry.

"Stop this at once!"

AMAR

STRONG ARMS HAULED AMAR TO HIS FEET. HE STILL CLUTCHED THE dagger, but he didn't raise it. He didn't need to. Princess Jasala's order had been enough to immediately stop any threat to his safety.

She stood there with her head held high, somehow managing to appear as if she was looking down at Amar and the guards despite being shorter than them all. "What are you doing? Savir is a guest, and I will not have our guests treated so harshly."

"He's a prisoner, Your Highness."

Jasala shot the guard a withering look. "The two are not mutually exclusive."

"He was trying to run!"

"Run where? If he wanted to leave, he knows the way out, but I don't believe he was going that way."

"Well, no, Your Highness." The dagger was wrenched from Amar's hand. "But he still shouldn't be running about like he was."

This time, Jasala fixed her cold gaze on Amar. "No, he should not. General Muraka was supposed to be escorting him."

There was a pause, a few whispers, and then one of them said, "We haven't seen the general."

Jasala's eyes narrowed. Before Amar could answer the unasked question, she spoke again, her voice more tense. "Well, I'm sure he has some explanation for that, but it can wait. My mother grows impatient." She pointed to a pair of them. "You two can come with us. The rest of you, find General Muraka and bring her to me."

"Yes, Your Highness."

The guards flanked Amar as they walked the remaining distance to Dashiva's sitting room. It was exactly the one Amar had been trying to reach, the walls covered in dozens of paintings, including several he recognized as Kamaal's work. The empress herself stood in the doorway to the balcony, silhouetted against a fiery sunrise. "There you are. I was beginning to wonder what was taking you so long."

"It seems he ran into some trouble with the guards on his way here," Jasala said, motioning to the pair of them. "You may wait outside. Do not let anyone disturb us."

They departed, but the royals' personal bodyguards still lurked in the corners of the room, watching Amar intently and making very clear what could happen if he dared try anything.

Dashiva smoothed out her dress and lowered herself into a tall armchair. Jasala took up a position behind her and remained standing. Amar bowed, squaring his shoulders to them both as he straightened. "Thank you for seeing me, Your Imperial Majesty."

"Well, you certainly didn't leave me much choice, *Prince* Savir." Before, she might have tried to conceal the derision in her tone. Now she made no such efforts. "I'm going to have to execute you, of course, but before that, I'd like to know why you would be so stupid as to deliver yourself right into my hands. I always knew you were a charlatan, but I never took you for a fool."

"If I'm a charlatan, it wasn't intentional," Amar replied, "though I fear that does still make me a fool. I came here because I've made a terrible mistake—many terrible mistakes—and I would like to set them right. If you would graciously lend me your ear, I believe what I have to say will bring some clarity to the situation we find ourselves in."

Dashiva frowned. "A pretty way of saying you want to make excuses for this war you've started."

"Not excuses, Your Majesty. I accept my share of the burden of responsibility, and I'll do whatever I can to repair the damage done.

But that burden isn't mine alone."

"Go on, then. Say whatever it is you came here to say."

Amar hesitated. "It's a long story, and the pieces may not all seem connected until the end. Will you promise to hear me out until I'm finished?"

She sighed, settling back into her chair with her hands folded in her lap. "As long as we're not here all day, that's fine. Just get on with it."

Throughout his journey these last few weeks, Amar had done little else but consider the best way to share his tale with Dashiva, and it flowed out now with carefully rehearsed precision. He didn't start from the beginning six centuries ago when he was cursed, but rather with the part that was most directly connected to her own story: Valkyra's pursuit of him across Kavora and into Atrea, using Aleida as a pawn in her schemes. When he finally revealed that his immortality was the reason she had pursued him, Dashiva narrowed her eyes in skepticism but allowed him to continue.

Neither she nor Jasala spoke at all, and Amar tried not to read too much into their expressions. He worried about their response, of course, but the best thing he could do now was finish explaining how he'd come to play the role of Prince Savir and what he hoped to accomplish by coming here now.

"I truly never wanted a war, Your Majesty," he said in closing. "I told you as much during my previous stay here, and it was something I said to King Bhajan often. It's still true. My only purpose in coming to you was to urge you to end this conflict before any more of your people suffer."

Dashiva shifted forward in her chair and took a long drink from the chalice on a nearby table. When she was finished, she said, "And how exactly do you propose I do that? You had more sway in convincing Bhajan to surrender, but you failed. From what you've told me, he's determined to wage this war at any cost. He would refuse to surrender no matter the circumstances, and I will certainly not be surrendering to him, if that is what you're seeking."

Amar set his jaw and swallowed the angry retorts pressing against his teeth. He hadn't come here hoping Dashiva would surrender, but she was arguably the most powerful person in all of Kavora. Her apathetic demeanor and seeming unwillingness to use that power for good grated on him. Curse these monarchs and their foolish pride. They would see the entire empire burned to the ground before they deigned to admit any fault or error in judgment. But had he truly expected anything less, especially after his last conversation with Bhajan?

"Use me," he said. "You have me now, and I'm not going anywhere. You can say Prince Savir has given himself up, that I've come to realize you and Jasala are the true heirs to the throne and the rightful rulers of Kavora. You can even say I've admitted to being a fraud all along, have me executed, if you like." Mitul would hate that, but one death—and subsequent resurrection—was a trifling price to pay for peace. "Whatever you need to do. Use me, and end this before it gets any worse."

Dashiva gave him a thin-lipped smile, which made her look something like a cat who had cornered a mouse. "You put your life on the line so easily, false prince of Valmandi. What *should* we call you, now that we know you are not who you've claimed to be?"

"Amar."

She waited a few seconds, then asked, "And do you have a family name, Amar?"

He hesitated, but only for a moment. "Rama."

"Well, Amar Rama, you certainly do know how to spin an interesting tale."

She didn't believe him. "My companions can vouch for all I've told you," he said quickly. "Including Tamaya Takhar and Kamaal Ruman."

Dashiva waved a hand. "I'm sure, though it's clear enough already that you are not the same boy who came here four months ago. You carry yourself differently, for a start. More confidently. Some might even say more nobly, if you can appreciate the irony." She leaned forward, staring at him pointedly. "But you aren't a prince, either. You're *no one*."

"No one of renown, anyway," Jasala cut in, offering Amar a thin but kind smile. "Not as far as the politics are concerned."

"Even so, executing you would certainly send a message," Dashiva continued, "but if Bhajan is so determined to fight, he'll simply spin that execution to his advantage. He'd make a martyr out of you, and it would be easy. He could say you were always the real Prince Savir, and that we only coerced you into confessing otherwise."

She had a fair point.

"And if all you've said is true," Jasala added, "you'll come back to life again, won't you? How are we supposed to explain that?"

There was a knock outside, and Dashiva motioned for one of her men to answer it. Amar had forgotten any of the bodyguards were standing there until the man moved. He opened the door to reveal the same palace guards who had captured Amar in the hallway some time before.

"The princess asked us to bring General Muraka to her," one said hesitantly.

"Ah yes," said Jasala. "Show her in, please."

"Well, that's the problem, Your Highness. We haven't been able to find her."

Amar hadn't told them that part—not yet. He'd been so caught up with everything else that it had slipped his mind, and now both Dashiva and Jasala were looking to him for an explanation. He wasn't looking forward to providing one, given how bad the news was, but they needed to know everything.

"General Muraka tried to sneak me out of the palace once she learned I was here. I suspect she meant to kill me and drag me back to Valmandi. She's been passing information to them for months now." Best to get it out in the open straight away. "Valkyra—Nandini's doing, I'm afraid."

Jasala cast a worried look at her mother, but the empress simply took a breath and lifted her eyes to the ceiling. "Ah, now that makes perfect sense. The general always did look up to Nandini." She nodded to the eager young faces outside the door. "Send a search party after her. She is to be brought back here immediately, either of her own free will or against it, but alive. We'll need to question her."

She gestured to her bodyguard, who shut the door, and turned her attention back to Amar. "Well, you may be no one of renown, but you've certainly brought us an impressive amount of disturbing information to consider. I'm not sure whether I should thank you or curse you for the trouble."

"Both, I imagine."

She scoffed and ran her bony hands over her face, the first crack he'd ever seen in her carefully polished mask of royal refinement.

"If you're not going to execute me," Amar said, "what will you do?"

"A wonderful question," she sighed. "And one without an easy answer. For now, we'll want to corroborate your story, of course, which means we'll need to talk to your friends one by one." She looked to the bodyguard again. "Have Kamaal Ruman brought up next, then the guard from Valmandi. Oh, and the third man, too, I suppose—what was his name?"

"Mitul. Mitul Rama."

"Rama. Some relation of yours?"

Amar shrugged. "Adoptive, I suppose. He's known me longer than anyone else."

"Ah, good. Yes, bring all three up here. And take Amar back to his room. Have him watched. Carefully."

This last bit was directed at Amar as much as at the bodyguard. A warning, not that he needed one. Though much still remained to be seen when it came to the empress' next steps, for now, he was exactly where he wanted to be.

ALEIDA

ALEIDA HAD TRIED TO STAY OUT OF TAMAYA'S WAY DURING THE entirety of their journey to Jakhat. She'd given the old woman the apology she owed her, but that didn't mean they needed to be friends. Now, however, curiosity was getting the best of her, and when the guards returned Tamaya to their shared cell and took Kesari instead, Aleida decided to strike up a conversation.

"Where did you go?"

The old woman sat down on her cot. "To see the empress."

"And?" she prodded, eager for more information. It would likely be her turn before long, unless the empress thought a lowly Visan refugee like her too unimportant to speak to. She wasn't sure which outcome she should hope for. On the one hand, she could provide valuable corroboration for Nandini's role in this entire scheme, and a part of her wanted to face the woman who'd ordered the invasion of her homeland. On the other hand, she wasn't sure she was ready to confront that. She might never be…and she might never get another chance like this.

"What did she say to you?" she asked when Tamaya didn't answer her first inquiry.

"What do you think?" the woman replied grouchily. She tried to fluff a rather pathetic pillow without much success. "She asked about Amar. I answered as best as I could, told her what I've seen."

"And did she believe you?"

"As far as I could tell."

"Do you think she—"

"Listen, girl," Tamaya snapped. "I have had a very long day already. Several very long days, in fact, ever since you miscreants showed up on my doorstep again. I barely slept a wink all night, and all I could think about when I was talking with the empress was how much I wanted a nice, comfortable bed and a long nap. It seems I won't be getting my first wish, but I would like to *try* and get some rest on this rickety old thing. So please, I'm begging you, hush up and let me do that."

Aleida scowled. "Fine. You don't have to be rude about it."

Tamaya muttered something unintelligible as she rolled over on the cot to face the wall. Within a few minutes, her snores filled the room.

For what felt like hours, Aleida sat there, waiting for Kesari to come back, imagining what her own turn to speak with the empress would be like. Her mental picture of Dashiva was not a flattering one—never had been—but it occurred to her now that she didn't actually know what the woman looked like.

Obviously she couldn't be the green-skinned, fang-toothed figure of her imagination, like a child's monster come to life straight out of a story. But she still *felt* like that, sitting on her throne in some faraway land and ordering armored troops to take over Vis, kill anyone who resisted. Kill anyone who so much as *looked* like they might resist.

Aleida *despised* her.

The only reason she was even here was because she hated Valkyra more. That, and because this whole thing was important to Amar, and thus important to Mitul. She owed it to him, at least, to see this through and to help however she could. Even if it meant having a civil conversation with a woman who had destroyed her life.

When Kesari did come back, there was no time for Aleida to question her before guards whisked her away to meet with Dashiva herself. All she got was a quick look of reassurance and a few mumbled words of encouragement. "You'll be all right. She's not so bad."

Easy for Kesari to say. She hadn't endured everything Aleida had as a direct result of the empress' actions.

"Let's go!" a guard said sternly, motioning for Aleida to walk in front of him. She did, and he gave her directions through a twisting maze of white corridors lined with greenery that flowered in a way that shouldn't have been possible this long before spring. It must have taken at least a few Tarja to keep the palace looking the way it did, likely Tarja who were specialists in the growing and nurturing of plants, like Hasan.

Aleida felt a twinge of guilt at the thought. She hadn't written to the man or even spared him so much as a thought in months. She should have, especially with Tyrus' passing so recent. It wasn't quite the same, of course, but Hasan was perhaps the only other person alive who knew the specific pain of losing him.

The guard stopped in front of a painted white door and took a few seconds to give Aleida a quick pat down. She'd had nothing dangerous on her person since they stripped her of Tarik's pistol and a dagger, but she couldn't blame them for taking precautions. Once satisfied that she wasn't carrying anything harmful, he opened the door and motioned for her to go inside.

Aleida held her head high as she walked in, her gaze immediately drawn to the two women seated before her. One was fairly young, maybe ten years older than Aleida herself. She bore a striking resemblance to the older woman. They had the same aquiline nose, and each wore their long hair braided over one shoulder, the only difference being that one braid was raven black while the other was gray streaked with white. The younger woman gave Aleida a small smile, but the older one—the empress—regarded her with a flat, almost bored expression.

"Aleida Ceran, isn't it?" asked the princess.

Aleida quickly realized she was forgetting her manners. A righteous sense of indignation gave her pause for one more second, then she forced herself to bow to the ruler of Kavora and her heir. She took care to smooth away her grimace before rising. "Your Majesty."

"I expect it brings you no pleasure to be here, child of Artex," Empress Dashiva said.

She paused there, waiting for Aleida to answer, as if it actually mattered what she thought of this strange meeting. Well, at least they weren't going to pretend everything was beautiful and sunny. Aleida nodded curtly and clamped her hands together tight behind her waist.

The empress gave a small, lazy shrug. "I'd hoped to spare us both the discomfort of forcing you to speak with me, but your companions tell me you're very much caught in the center of all this."

Again, Aleida nodded.

"We'd appreciate you answering some questions for us," said Princess Jasala. Her voice had a gentler tone than Dashiva's, which only made Aleida more wary.

"I can do that."

"Good," the empress said. "Let's start with Nandini Kumar. Or rather, Valkyra, as she's chosen to call herself these days. Tell me how you met her."

Aleida recounted the story with as much detachment as possible, like she was describing someone else's life rather than her own. The details were more painful spoken aloud, all the ways Valkyra had been manipulating her excruciatingly obvious in hindsight. She wanted to grab her past self by the shoulders and shake her, stop her from making such terrible decisions. But she knew it wouldn't have done any good. Back then, she would have done anything to save Tyrus, and it was exactly that desperation that had pushed her to trust a strange Kavoran spirit with her life.

The empress was particularly curious about Valkyra's appearance—not the form she'd taken after their Bond was made, but the way she'd looked as a spirit upon first coming to Aleida, and again after their Bond was severed. Aleida gave as much detail as she could remember, right down to what she had been wearing. When the empress was satisfied with her answers, she moved on to asking about Amar's curse. She still seemed to have some lingering doubts about the veracity of his claims and wanted to know whether Aleida had ever actually witnessed one of his deaths and resurrections for herself. She hadn't, but she spoke about what evidence she'd seen of such occurrences, along with the fact that each cycle also caused him to lose his memories.

"This memory loss you speak of seems rather convenient," the empress said, "given all the havoc he's caused as Prince Savir. Such an easy excuse, allowing him to wash his hands of all responsibility and claim he didn't know any better because he couldn't remember who he really was."

Aleida scowled at this. "He came here, didn't he? How is that making excuses and not taking responsibility?" Her words came out much harsher than she'd intended, but she was tired, and she didn't want to be here talking to this woman. Still, she was better off playing sweet and docile than riling the empress with her poor attitude. "Forgive me, Your Majesty, but don't you think it would have been easier for him to run away and disappear? Leave Valmandi and Jakhat to sort this mess out on their own?"

"And leave Nandini to hunt him down wherever he goes?"

Aleida shrugged. "She'll do that anyway, and coming here, I expect she'll know exactly where he is before too long. I know it's hard to believe, but the memory loss is real, and it's cost him—all of us—more than you know. He shot Mitul because he didn't remember him. His oldest friend, and he almost killed him. He never would have done that if he hadn't lost his memories."

"Which one was that?" Dashiva murmured to Jasala.

"Kamaal's romantic partner," she replied. "The one Amar spoke of as an adoptive relation."

"Ah, yes. Well, I suppose you do make a fair point there."

Dashiva asked a few more questions after that, but nothing too difficult or invasive. She seemed generally uninterested in Aleida herself and was only concerned with her connection to Amar and Valkyra. Once they'd exhausted all the information she could provide on those fronts, the empress wrapped up the conversation quickly.

"Thank you for your cooperation. You've done well. You mentioned your brother is ill. I'd be happy to send one of my best healers to him. Perhaps there's something—"

"Don't bother," Aleida said sourly. "He died."

"Oh. How unfortunate."

They stared at each other awkwardly for a few seconds, Aleida's nails digging into her palms with how tightly she was clenching her fists. She wanted to scream at the empress. She offered her help with such an air of grandeur, like she was doing Aleida some great favor only to respond with apathetic niceties when she realized Tyrus was past the point of helping. Maybe she wasn't directly responsible for his illness, but she *was* the reason he'd had to spend his last years in some Kavoran house on the other side of Erythyr without their parents there to comfort him.

Her eyes burned with pent-up rage and grief, but before she could let any of it out, Jasala was at her side. The princess' light touch against her arm brought Aleida back to the moment at hand, and she blinked away the sting of tears.

"I'll escort you back now," said Jasala.

"Oh, just get the guards," Dashiva muttered, but Jasala ignored her, putting gentle pressure on Aleida's arm to guide her toward the door. They left the room, and the princess motioned to the two guards waiting outside to hang back a little when they started walking.

"I'm sure it can't have been easy for you to hold your tongue in there," the princess said. "I don't know what personal tragedies you've suffered as a result of my mother and Nandini's actions, but I'd like to apologize. Personally, and on behalf of the Kavoran Empire."

Aleida clamped her jaw shut to keep herself from saying anything impertinent. Apologies were about as useful to her as a boat full of holes. Jasala might mean well, but Aleida wasn't so naive as to hope the princess was sincere enough or informed enough to make meaningful reparations once she was Kavora's ruler.

Fortunately, Jasala seemed to catch on that she wasn't in the mood for talking. They walked the rest of the way in silence, their footsteps echoed by the guards' booted feet behind them. When they came to the room Aleida, Kes, and Tamaya had been locked up in, the princess stopped. "Thank you for sharing your information with us, Aleida Ceran. You've been a tremendous help."

A guard unlocked the door, and Jasala began to turn away. "Wait, Your Highness," Aleida said.

"Yes?"

"Do you think I could—instead of staying here, can you put me in with the others? I swear, I won't cause any trouble." She'd spent the last hour haunted by the family that had been taken from her. Right now, all she wanted was to be with the new family she'd built around herself since.

"I don't see why not," Jasala replied. "Follow me."

They walked down the hall to another room, and when the guard unlocked the door, Aleida needed no encouragement to enter. Tarik, Mitul, and Kamaal were all sitting on the floor, but Kamaal stood up as soon as he saw Aleida and pulled Mitul to his feet as well. The door shut, and both men looked at her expectantly.

"Is everything all right?" Mitul asked.

She shook her head, throat aching, soul weary. Without her having to say anything at all, they wrapped their arms around her. She squeezed them back as hard as she could, taking comfort in the safety of their embrace.

No, everything was *not* all right, but standing here with them, she was as close to all right as she could be for now. That was enough to get her through this day and the next and the one after that.

AMAR

AMAR WAS LEFT IN HIS ROOM ALONE FOR THE REST OF THAT DAY AND the next. His requests to see his friends—which became progressively less polite as the hours passed—were met only with silence. He tried not to worry too much about them, and he couldn't begrudge the empress whatever time she was taking to deliberate on all he'd told her. Still, his patience wore thinner and thinner with every lonely minute he was left without news.

When his door finally opened, he had half a mind to make a hostage of the person on the other side until he could get answers. He froze when he saw who was entering.

"Oh. Princess Jasala. I wasn't expecting you." Not that he was complaining. Surely she wouldn't have come here unless she had business with him, and she could certainly give him the answers he wanted.

"Hello, Amar. I'm sorry we've kept you waiting so long." She motioned for all but her personal bodyguard to stay outside and shut the door. "I have a few matters to discuss before you and your friends are released."

"You're letting us go?"

"I think so. Of course, there are some important stipulations you'll have to agree to, but that's what I'm here to explain." She sat on one of the cushions against the wall, motioning for Amar to do the same. He did, and she crossed her ankles, the fabric of her green dress fanning out to either side of her legs like palm fronds.

"My mother and I have decided it best that you keep up your facade as Prince Savir." It was the last thing Amar wanted to hear, but before he could protest, she held up a hand. "Now, don't look at me like that. I knew you wouldn't like it, but at least hear me out. It wasn't a decision we made lightly, and it's what we believe is truly best for the people of the empire."

Amar remained skeptical, but he waited for her to continue.

"We've been calling you a fraud and denouncing your claim to the throne from the beginning, but it hasn't made any difference. Tales of Prince Savir's return have been around for years, and everyone loves a good story. You brought that story to life. People clung to it, including King Bhajan. Many will hold on to it regardless of whether you want them to or not, especially if Bhajan himself won't admit the truth."

"Maybe he just needs another chance," Amar said. "I didn't get to explain as well as I wanted to. Now that he's had some time to process things, maybe he—"

"We cannot rest all our hopes on *maybes*. King Bhajan is a good man. I still believe that. I hope we can find a way to end this peacefully, but that only happens if we leave him no other options, and the best way to do that is for you to publicly ally yourself with us. As Prince Savir."

Amar's shoulders slumped. "I don't see what good it does for us to keep lying to everyone."

"More good than it does to tell the truth," Jasala replied. "You said you left Valmandi in a bit of a tumult. Your guard says the story going around is that you may have been kidnapped. If you start claiming you're not Prince Savir after all, Bhajan could accuse us of that kidnapping and then forcibly coercing you to deny your true identity."

"He could say the same about Prince Savir's sudden decision to side with you."

"True, but retaining the title makes the whole situation less suspect. It at least allows your followers to retain their support for you while also drawing their loyalties back to where they truly belong—with the empress."

"I don't want to keep pretending," Amar said.

Jasala tilted her head to one side. "But you will, if it's our best chance at a peaceful resolution to all this. That is, if you really meant what you said about having the best interests of the empire and its people in mind."

He sighed, unable to argue with that, though there was a significant logistical problem to consider. "I can't keep it up forever. I don't age. Eventually, people will realize something is wrong with me."

"You might not have to keep it up for long at all," said Jasala confidently. "Just long enough to get us through this mess. After that…to be honest, that's the least of my concerns right now. I'm sure we can find any number of solutions when the time comes."

A fair point. Amar gave a slight nod in agreement.

"Alternatively, and on a much darker note, you could admit that you were never the real prince, and we would execute you. We'd have to, there's no getting out of it. Treason of this level is a capital offense. My mother has half a mind to execute you anyway, if only to test your wilder claims."

"I suppose you'd execute anyone who helped me as well."

"There's a chance we could make some exceptions for the friends who came here with you. But the short answer is yes. King Bhajan and Queen Indira would certainly be considered traitors, along with most of their advisors and high-ranking military officers. By continuing as Prince Savir but renouncing your claim to the throne, you give us leeway to extend mercy, so long as Valmandi surrenders."

"We'd be backing Bhajan into a corner," Amar said. "That *could* force him to surrender, but it could just as easily strengthen his resolve to keep fighting."

"I think he's smart enough to make the right choice."

Amar wanted to believe that, too, but after the rage he'd seen in the king's eyes at the mere suggestion of ending this war, he couldn't be sure. "I don't know. This is personal for him. He believes the empress killed his daughter and grandson."

Jasala averted her gaze. "Yes, well, he has every right to hold a grudge for that."

Amar raised his eyebrows. "You're admitting it's true?"

She gave a barely perceptible nod. "My mother would have done anything to protect her legacy. For years, the throne was destined to be hers, until her brother finally produced an heir, erasing the future she'd been preparing for. She only told me the truth a few years ago—the lengths she went to in order to protect her claim, and mine."

"Does anyone else know?"

"Magistrate Ashaya, I expect, but only because Nandini would have told him. She was the one who hired the assassins, then disposed of them once the job was done. As far as I know, no one else alive can attest to what happened to the infant prince. My mother is…not fond of loose ends."

Amar leaned forward with his elbows on his knees and waited until she was looking him in the eye. "Why are you telling me this?"

Jasala sighed. "Because every day, I wish she'd chosen differently, but here we are. I can't change what happened then, but I can try to be a better ruler than she is, once my turn comes. And I believe you can help me with that."

"How?"

She raised her knees and draped her arms over the top of them, her fingers toying with the embroidered leaves on her gown. "You're not the first immortal to grace the halls of this palace."

This piqued Amar's interest. Someone else like him? He suddenly felt very arrogant for ever assuming he was the only one, but he'd never heard of anyone else afflicted with this curse.

"My ancestors passed down the legend of a Tarja advisor," Jasala continued. "Someone who served our family for generations. They always went by a different name and always claimed to be some relative of the previous advisor even though they were the same person. They'd disappear every few decades to reinvent themselves before returning, but the secret of their immortality was passed along from one ruler to the next. A curse, I believe, like yours, though in their case, it may have been self-inflicted."

Amar tried to remember all the imperial advisors he'd met during his previous stay at the palace. "Who is it?"

"Who *was* it," Jasala corrected him. "A legend now. No mention of them exists beyond the time of my great-great-grandfather."

Disappointment snaked its way into Amar's chest. For a few seconds, he'd had a glimmer of hope that he wasn't alone in bearing this curse. As caring as his friends were, there were certain things about him they could never understand. It might have been helpful to meet someone who knew what it meant to live hundreds of years with still no end in sight.

"I'm asking you to serve as my advisor," the princess said. "My mother has allowed me to choose a handful of people to add to our council, and I want you among them."

Amar didn't know what to say to that. He wasn't a politician, nor did he want to be one. These past few months had given him more than his fill of monarchical schemings. "Forgive me, Your Majesty, but I don't think that's a good idea."

"Why not? Think about it. Prince Savir allies himself with Jakhat and takes a spot on our council. It's not the throne, but it's still a high position of power. One even your staunchest supporters would appreciate."

"I'm not really a prince, remember?"

"You *were* a prince once, were you not?"

It took him a few moments to realize she was referring to Shavhalla and his status there. "That was a very long time ago."

"Yes, exactly. You have a unique perspective, Amar. The wisdom and experience of six centuries lives within you, and I would consider myself a fool not to take advantage of that."

"That's very flattering, Your Highness, but I don't feel very wise. Mostly the opposite, in fact."

Jasala flashed a sly grin. "And I would argue that might be a sign of your wisdom in and of itself. Only fools truly believe they know more than everyone else." She pushed herself up abruptly, then extended a hand to pull him up. Amar took it. "Think about it overnight," she said when he was standing in front of her. "Promise me you'll at least do that."

"I will," Amar agreed reluctantly. "But if I say no?"

"I won't force you to do anything against your will. If you really don't want to be Prince Savir or serve on the imperial council, I can try to figure out something else and get my mother to agree. Whatever you decide, I promise I'll do what I can to ensure your friends' safety."

"Thank you."

She gripped his hand a little tighter. "But I do hope you'll keep in mind what might be best for the empire. I truly believe this is the solution we need."

He said nothing in response to this. He could see her side of it, but doubts still lingered in the back of his mind, and he didn't want to rush into anything without thinking through it. "Can I see my friends now?"

Jasala nodded. "They should all be in the small dining hall by now. I do need to insist that you all stay here until after you've made a decision, but please consider yourselves guests rather than prisoners."

Guests who weren't allowed to leave were the same as prisoners, but Amar didn't say that.

As they walked together, he asked, "Whatever became of General Muraka? Has anyone found her?"

"Unfortunately not," she replied with a scowl. "We have people looking, of course, but she's clever. At this point, we'd be lucky to catch her. I assume she's headed to Valmandi to lend her services in person."

Amar agreed with this assessment. The best they could hope was that Muraka wouldn't be able to do half as much damage from the other side as she'd had the potential to do from within.

Jasala opened the door to a room with a long table. The smell of a delicious supper wafted out, and Amar waved when he saw his companions all seated, eating together and looking none the worse for wear after their ordeal.

"Amar!" Kamaal shouted, raising a glass in his direction.

Mitul waved him over, gesturing to the seat beside him at the low table. Amar took it, and when he glanced back to see whether Jasala was still there, she was nowhere to be found.

"Look at all this," Mitul said, patting him on the back with one hand and passing a basket of flatbread with the other. He gestured to the food laid out before them—practically a feast by all but the most prosperous standards. "You don't think all the prisoners get this kind of treatment, do you?"

"I think we've been upgraded to 'mandatory guest' status," Amar replied.

"If they keep feeding us like this, I wouldn't mind that one bit," Tamaya said, looking as cheerful as Amar had ever seen her with her plate piled high.

They talked amongst themselves while they ate, each recounting their individual conversations with the royal women of the palace. Amar listened intently, barely picking at the food on his plate. It seemed most of the questioning they'd endured had been civil enough, with the empress focused only on verifying Amar's claims and trying to discern whether any of them had reason to deceive her. They'd all come out of it unharmed and seemed in high spirits to be reunited—all except for Aleida, who sat across from Amar looking glum and only nibbling at a few bites of her meal.

He leaned forward to whisper to her while the others carried on. "She wasn't awful to you, was she?"

Aleida's frown deepened. "Not exactly. I mean, I'm always going to think she's awful, but she didn't do anything horrible to me specifically. At least not since we got here." She sighed and pushed her plate away. "How much longer do we have to stay here?"

"I don't know. Until tomorrow, at least." Until he could give Princess Jasala an answer, but he didn't want to make the others wait around any longer than they had to. "I'll try to get you all out of here as soon as possible."

Aleida sighed, but some of the tension in her shoulders seemed to leave with her exhale. "Sure. Thanks."

Kamaal raised his cup and tapped on it with his knife. It let out a ringing *clink clink*, and he beamed at all of them. "Attention, please, everyone. Now that we're all here and in better spirits with full bellies, Mitul and I have an announcement to make."

He paused for dramatic effect, which was promptly ruined by Tamaya shouting from the end of the table. "Oh, get on with it!"

"As you wish." He set his cup down, then clasped Mitul's hand atop the table. "We're engaged. Officially, as of this afternoon."

There were cheers and congratulations. Amar joined Tarik in banging his hands against the table to celebrate the announcement and raised a toast to the newly engaged couple. Even Tamaya was smiling, and Aleida seemed to perk up significantly. She leaned across the table to shove Mitul in the shoulder, unable to hide her grin. "You couldn't have told me earlier?"

He shrugged. "It was hard not to, but we wanted everyone to find out together."

She opened her mouth to say something else, then coughed, cleared her throat, and walked around to their side of the table. Her eyes were shining when she put her arms around both of their shoulders and pulled them in for a hug. She mumbled something to both of them, but Amar didn't know what it was until Mitul responded.

"We love you, too."

Amar waited until some of the celebration had died down and the congratulations were over. He didn't want to ruin the moment, and it was refreshing to have some good news in the midst of more sobering problems. But time was still a factor, and he needed help deciding what to do about Jasala's request. If anyone could provide that help, it was his oldest friend.

He leaned back and reached behind Mitul to tap Kamaal on the shoulder. "I'm so sorry to interrupt all this, but can I borrow him for a minute?"

"Of course," Kamaal said.

"You mind if we talk?" he asked Mitul, nodding to the far end of the room. A set of lattice screen doors led out to a balcony.

Mitul gave Kamaal a quick peck on the cheek and stood to follow Amar outside. The others carried on without them, passing the food around again to fill their plates with second helpings. Amar could still hear their muffled voices after he closed the doors.

Outside, the night air was cold and crisp, but it was early yet, and plenty of lights illuminated the city below. The fresh air felt especially good after two full days trapped inside a single room. He leaned over the balcony railing, hands clasped together. Mitul adopted the same pose beside him.

"Congratulations," Amar said, knocking his shoulder against Mitul's. "I'm really happy for you."

"Thank you," he replied, still glowing. "I know it was fast, but sitting in that room together, we both decided it didn't make sense to wait any longer. We've been waiting for each other long enough already."

"You certainly have."

"Anyway, the wedding won't be for a while yet. I want to do that properly, at least. Have all his friends and family there and give him the big party, all of that."

"And let's not forget how much *you* love a big party."

He laughed. "Yes, fine. It's what I want, too. So we'll wait. But it doesn't matter how long. The commitment's already there, and that feels…" He laughed again. "I don't even have the words to describe it. I'm just happy."

"As you should be." He let the silence linger there, reluctant to disrupt the joy of the moment.

"What's on your mind?" Mitul asked.

Amar hung his head, staring at his feet between the white marble rails. "You know, I thought coming here would simplify things. Force Valmandi to surrender, stop the war immediately—I don't know. Sounds stupid, doesn't it?"

"I'd call it hopeful, not stupid."

"That's a nice way of putting it." He let his eyes drift shut. "There are people out there suffering right now because of what I've done. Families who've lost someone to this war, soldiers freezing in their tents and tending to wounded comrades, orphaned children going to bed hungry. Six hundred years, and somehow I've ended up exactly like my father."

"Your father made war with no regard for the consequences," Mitul said. "He hurt people to serve his own pride and greed. You're nothing like him."

"The outcome is the same for the ones who suffer."

"Maybe, but the path leading to any outcome still matters very much."

Amar knew that was supposed to make him feel better, but it didn't. His path had been filled with war and violence for most of his very long life. "I just want to know how to fix it. How to *atone*. For my own crimes, and for his."

"I'm not sure you really *can* atone for someone else's actions."

Amar was about to argue this by repeating the words Mahati had spoken when cursing him. But when those words came to his mind, the memory of them still bright and clear, he realized something he hadn't before.

Your soul shall be bound to the physical world for as many lifetimes as it takes for you to atone for the atrocities of war.

There was no mention of his father anywhere within the stated conditions for breaking the curse.

He'd always assumed it was his father's wars he was supposed to atone for. After all, those had impacted Mahati directly, driving her to Shavhalla to seek vengeance. But the curse only mentioned the atrocities of war, not *his father's* wars.

Maybe Mitul was right. Trying to rectify every tragedy that had come from someone else's actions centuries prior would have been like trying to untangle a ball of yarn the length of the Mayuka River. Even trying to atone for the battles he'd fought during previous lifetimes would have been a challenge, and one he might still need to conquer. But not yet, not until he dealt with more immediate concerns. *This* war—the one he'd unintentionally started—this was the war he needed to atone for right now.

Whatever it took, he'd end it, then spend the rest of his days preserving peace any way he could. Maybe it wouldn't be enough to break his curse, but it might start balancing the scales against all the ruin he'd left in his wake through the years. It was certainly more on the right path than what he'd been doing.

First things first, though. He needed to figure out what to do about Jasala's request. Would playing along as Prince Savir make things better, or worse? He wasn't sure, but that was why he'd brought Mitul out here.

Amar lifted his head and looked over at his brother. "The princess came to talk with me today. She had some ideas she wants me to think over, a plan she hopes I'll agree to. I'm trying to figure out whether or not I should."

"Well, I can't choose for you, but maybe talking it through will help clear things up?"

Amar certainly hoped so. He told Mitul about Jasala's offer for him to join the imperial council as Prince Savir. As he restated all the same arguments she'd made to him, he found himself agreeing with her more and more, but there was one major concern that surpassed all others in his deliberations.

"I'd be living a lie," he said, then chuckled a little at himself. "Ironic, isn't it? Most of my life has been a lie because I didn't even know the truth of who I was, and now that I do know, a lie may be what's best for everyone anyway."

"It would be a lie of your choosing. Perhaps that's better in some ways?"

"And worse in others." He sighed. "What am I supposed to do?"

Mitul gave him a sidelong glance and a wry smile. "I can't tell you that."

Amar groaned. "Please, this once, can't you just give me the answer?"

"I don't know it."

"Sure you do. That's the one thing I've always been able to count on—you doing the right thing, even when I didn't think it was."

Mitul laughed, the sound starting out mirthful and then fading into something more somber as he shook his head. "Oh, Amar. I've made plenty of mistakes, trust me. No one gets through life always doing the right thing. The best we can hope is that our mistakes do the least amount of damage possible to everyone else, then try to learn from them and do better next time."

"Leaves a lot of potential for things to go wrong," Amar muttered.

"It does. I can't say I envy your position."

"Do you at least have any advice for me?"

He cocked an eyebrow. "I think Jasala has the right idea. We should all be asking *you* for advice, what with all that sage wisdom and experience living in your head."

"Doesn't feel like I've got much."

"You want my advice?" Mitul asked. "Trust yourself. It's *your* choice. You're the only one who can make it, but you've got to trust that you're capable of doing so. And maybe…" He trailed off, his gaze shifting back to the city lights beyond the palace.

"What?" Amar asked.

He sighed and said nothing for a few seconds, seeming to mull over his thoughts before speaking. "Maybe you shouldn't give so much weight to the fact that it's a lie."

Amar's brows furrowed. "I'm surprised to hear that, coming from you."

Mitul shrugged. "I'm not saying dishonesty is ideal, or that it doesn't have its own risks. But I don't think truth and lies are so starkly black and white, either. Lies can be useful tools. That's why people tell them so often, and not every lie has to be a bad thing. We treat them like they are because we hate the betrayal when we're on the receiving end. But a lie can be a shield as well as it can be a sword, if you're careful. And it doesn't have to last forever."

Amar frowned, but maybe he was right. How many times had they lied for each other, trying to protect each other, avoid starvation, or get out of some scrape? Of course, the stakes weren't quite so high back then—a stolen loaf of bread, make-believe fathers who would beat up any gang attempting to steal from them, a nonexistent grandmother on her deathbed to encourage extra generosity from their patrons. But this lie was far more complicated, and thus more dangerous.

"You'll make the right choice." Mitul nodded at the door, through which they could still hear the others chattering. "Whatever it is, I'm with you. We all are."

That, at least, Amar knew he could count on, and with Mitul's help in thinking through it all, he had his decision. As much as he wished for his days of pretending to end, his role as Prince Savir could still serve a greater purpose.

KESARI

KESARI AND HER COMPANIONS WERE ALL RELEASED FROM THE palace late the following morning after a final show of hospitality that came in the form of a delicious breakfast. All of them, that was, except for Amar, who would remain in the palace to maintain his facade as Prince Savir and serve as an imperial advisor, though he promised to slip away and come visit them when he could.

Tarik was staying behind as well. He'd been more than a little discontent with Amar's decision, and the two had discussed the issue in hushed but vehement tones through the entirety of breakfast. In the end, Tarik reluctantly agreed to continue serving as Prince Savir's personal guard, but only after Amar promised to give up the dishonest title at the first reasonable opportunity.

"Obviously I plan to," Amar had said rather indignantly, as if appalled that Tarik even thought he wanted to keep up the act forever. "That's why I came here in the first place. As soon as the time is right, I swear. And if there comes a point where you feel I've drawn things out too long, I expect you to tell me."

"Oh, I'll tell you," Tarik said, his face even more stone cold than usual. "I'll remove you by force if I have to."

Amar only chuckled at the threat. "Good. I'm glad we understand each other."

Jasala came to fetch him after breakfast. He bid everyone a quick goodbye, and they were quickly shuffled out of the room, down the hall, and through the palace doors without fanfare. The horses and supplies they'd brought with them were waiting in the courtyard outside, and the guards watched them until they were safely outside the gates and on their way down the sloping road to the city. Kamaal had offered them shelter at his place. He'd had a small guesthouse built on the same property as his studio for when his sister and her family visited, and everyone would fit comfortably there.

Tamaya complained that she'd had more than enough of their company and insisted on being taken to the home of her great-niece, who lived fairly close to the palace. "Might as well surprise them while I'm here," she said with a short little cackle. "Her husband's probably not going to like that, but what can he do? I'm family, and I'm ancient. He at least has the decency to show his elders respect."

As they followed Tamaya's directions to the house, Kesari noted how different the city felt compared to the last time she and Lucian had been here. Though no battles had taken place anywhere near Jakhat, the impact of the war was still clearly felt. There were far fewer people wandering the streets, and the lively market square she had once frequented was now eerily quiet as vendors and buyers conducted their business in lower voices.

The house Tamaya's niece lived in was large enough to give the impression that the family was quite well-off. The old woman climbed down from the back of her horse with some assistance from Kamaal and made her way to the front door, which was promptly answered by a young woman carrying a baby. Another child peered out from behind her legs and let out a squeal of delight when she saw Tamaya. She ran to throw her arms around her waist, and Tamaya hugged her back tight. The man who appeared in the doorway behind them looked distinctly less pleased, but he graciously invited her inside nonetheless.

Tamaya paused in the doorway and waved to her former travelling companions. "I'd say it's been a pleasure, but…well, good riddance, and good luck with whatever trouble you're getting yourself into next." She squinted, leaning forward a little. "Where is that girl? Kesari?"

"Right here." She took a few steps forward so Tamaya could see her better.

"There, good girl. You tell that Spirit Tarja of yours to look after you, all right? You both look after each other. And don't you dare take it for granted, your Bond, your magic. Never again."

"Never again. I promise."

Tamaya allowed the child holding her hand to drag her inside. The door shut with a snap. Kesari and the others turned back to the road and continued their journey through the city.

Kamaal was clearly excited to return home. He led the way, fingers interlocked with Mitul's, chattering about how nice it would be to sleep in his own bed again. He was already making plans to replace all the plants he'd given away when he left. "Of course, I'd love to have that beautiful laceleaf back," he said as they approached the brightly painted floral walls of his studio home. "But I could probably get a smaller one from Dahvi's shop, and—"

His words ended with a sharp gasp, and Kesari leaned to one side to see past his broad shoulders. The front door wasn't shut all the way, and it made a hollow *thunk* against the doorframe as it swung forward on its hinges and then back again.

Kamaal didn't move. Mitul leaned over to whisper something to him, but he didn't respond. Aleida was the first to step forward and push the door wide open, revealing the damage within. Tables and chairs had been upended, drawers ripped out and shelves torn from the walls. Papers, books, and art supplies lay scattered on the floor like windblown leaves in autumn, and what few of Kamaal's beloved plants still remained had been dumped from their pots to shrivel and die in sickly greenish-brown heaps.

"Your paintings—they're all gone," Aleida said.

"I gave some away," Kamaal said in flat, defeated voice as he stepped over the threshold. "Stored a few elsewhere. But yes. The rest are gone."

Aleida's hands balled into fists. "Someone stole them!"

"They probably hoped to sell them," Mitul said. "And given the state of the place, maybe they thought you had a secret stash of coin somewhere." He took Kamaal's hand again and raised it to his lips. "I'm sorry, my love."

The artist sighed and swept his curls back from his brow. "Well, it's certainly not the warm welcome I wanted to give you all, but maybe the guest house is in better shape." The statement was bereft of all his usual cheer, and the halfhearted smile he offered was a poor imitation of the real thing.

They traipsed around back to inspect the guest house, where they found an even worse mess. Kamaal froze in place once he was was through the doorway, staring at all his belongings strewn across the floor. Mitul hissed a curse under his breath and gave his partner a concerned look.

"We'll get it cleaned up," Aleida said softly. "And I'll bet Kesari can use her magic to fix a lot of what's broken."

"Absolutely," Kesari said. "We'll have everything ship-shape in no time."

Kamaal nodded absently, and Mitul righted an upturned footstool so the artist could sit and catch his breath for a moment.

The rest of them got straight to work. Kesari gathered whatever broken pieces she could find, everything from shelves to plant pots to kitchenware, and mended what she could. Kamaal directed her to ensure what wasn't missing went back where it belonged. Mitul and Aleida gathered and organized all the little things that had been scattered, then swept the floors and wiped down various surfaces.

When they had the place in decent shape, they returned to the studio to repeat the process. Kamaal still appeared shaken by the invasion of his home, and Kesari sometimes had to repeat a question to pull him out of his thoughts. Mitul began to hum a few tunes while he worked, and this seemed to cheer Kamaal up a bit. By late afternoon, he was even smiling a little again.

While tidying up a few blank rolls of canvas, Aleida pulled something out that had been lying underneath. She brought it over to Kamaal. "Look what I found."

He gently took the small painting from her. "Looks like they didn't take everything after all."

Kesari peered around his shoulder to get a look. The painting had clearly been stepped on or smashed. Its wooden frame was cracked, and the canvas had a tear about a finger's width in the center. The scene upon it depicted ocean waves breaking against jagged seaside cliffs. Looking at it, Kesari recalled the cliffs they'd seen from the deck of the *Vindicator* on their way to Shavhalla.

"Is that Vis?"

Aleida nodded. "It's home."

Kamaal passed the painting back to her. "You keep it. Not the best gift, I know, all torn up like that, but—"

She took it from him reverently and cradled it against her chest. "I love it, and I'm honored. Thank you."

They kept working, and between the four of them, the task went quickly enough. Kamaal sent Kesari and Aleida out with some coin and a list of ingredients for supper while he and Mitul finished up the studio. By the time they returned, the place was looking much better, and Kamaal's laughter came easily as he and Mitul began cooking together.

Kesari went with Aleida to change out of her dirty clothes and get settled in the guest house. As they were finishing up, Aleida said, "Hey, Kes? Can I get your help with something?"

"Sure. What is it?"

"It's for them." She looked out the window toward the studio. "Kavorans have engagement parties, right? We did in Vis, but I'm not sure what the custom is here."

"I think they do. My mum talks about an engagement party she and my dad had with her family, before they moved to Atrea."

"So Mitul and Kamaal should have one, right?"

"I don't see why not."

Aleida's eyes flitted around the room nervously, and she fidgeted with the hem of her tunic. "I thought we could put it together, make it a surprise. They ought to have something good, you know, after this and all the things they've been through. Or would that be silly, do you think?"

Kesari grinned, her imagination already sparkling with glee at the idea and the reaction she expected they'd have. "It's not silly, it's wonderful. How can I help?"

AMAR

"ARE YOU READY?" PRINCESS JASALA ASKED AMAR.

They stood outside the room where the Kavoran imperial council held their meetings. A large room, judging by the size of the polished double doors. Bigger than the council chambers in Valmandi. Amar felt he belonged here even less than he had there, if such a thing were possible.

That lack of confidence wouldn't do. A little nervousness was to be expected, but a prince should have some self-assurance in whatever room he walked into, and he was still supposed to be Prince Savir.

Necessary though it might be, the lie still curled uncomfortably in his stomach, cold and oil-slick.

Jasala's warm fingers brushed lightly against his arm. "Ready?" she asked again.

Amar forced his shoulders into a more relaxed position. "Yes."

She nodded to the guards on either side of the door, and they pulled them open to reveal a room that was even more expansive than Amar had anticipated. It had a heavier and more somber look than the rest of the palace, decorated with dark wood and fabric dyed in shades of deep green. Full bookshelves lined one wall, and a large window was central in another. In front of this sat a high-backed chair with gilded accents and a velvet cushion. Empress Dashiva sat there at the head of a table trimmed in furs and more green fabric. More than a dozen individuals occupied the remaining seats, all watching Amar's entrance with great interest.

Jasala gestured to a pair of empty places near the empress. Amar pulled out a chair for the princess before taking a seat himself, a small detail they'd planned in advance. It was important for him to endear himself to the rest of the council as quickly as possible, or at least to ease some of the animosity they held for him. No easy feat, considering his position as their enemy mere days ago. They were watching his every move, and he needed every advantage he could find, no matter how small or seemingly insignificant.

He could almost hear his own heartbeat in the silence that followed. Seconds passed, and at last, a long-haired man opposite him spoke. "I suppose I'll be the first to ask, then. What in the name of all the gods in Erythyr is *he* doing here?"

"My daughter will explain," the empress said coolly. There was something brittle in the way she looked at Jasala, but if this meant anything to the princess, she did not let it show.

The young woman stood with her hands resting on the table's surface, her expression serene as she scanned the faces of all in the room. "Savir came to us of his own free will. He wishes to lay aside all claim to the throne and to provide whatever support he can in resolving our conflict."

Several whispers and curious glances followed this statement. One of the advisors spoke up over the others. "If he's given up his claim, Valmandi should have surrendered already."

"Yes, they should have," Jasala agreed. "Unfortunately, Savir and King Bhajan disagreed on that point, and thus, he came to us. Savir wants peace, as do we all, but it's no secret that the king has long held his own quiet resentment toward my mother. This war has allowed him to try and exact revenge for misplaced grievances. The fact that he is not amenable to surrender is no surprise, but having Savir on our side removes the clearest justification others have had in siding with Valmandi. Perhaps King Bhajan will see reason, once his allies begin to leave him."

"That's all well and good," said the long-haired man. "But what is Savir doing here, in this very room? Is he not your prisoner? If we were to execute him like the traitor he is, we could make an example of him and perhaps force the king into submission."

Jasala gave the man a tight smile. "You don't know the king very well if you think that will subdue him rather than simply fan the flames of his resolve." She nodded to Amar. "I've invited Savir here as one of my advisors. I believe his insight will prove extremely valuable, and his willingness to serve is a reassuring step toward proving his loyalty."

This caused another buzz of murmured conversations around the table, much livelier and longer than the last. Jasala didn't so much as glance at Amar, but he thought he could see the tiniest hint of a smirk on her lips, almost as if she enjoyed stirring the council up like this.

The long-haired man spoke up again. "And what is to be the *official* position on Savir's relation to Her Imperial Majesty?"

Empress Dashiva cleared her throat, and the room went quiet. "Our official position has always been that Savir has no claim to the imperial throne. If he wishes to call himself the son of the late Emperor Akraja, I will neither endorse nor argue that, so long as he does not use his supposed lineage to try and seize power." Her gaze cut over to him, sharp and pointed. "Savir is to make a public announcement renouncing his claim and will pledge his loyalty to myself and Princess Jasala before the High Magistrate and the Divine Priestess. I want it done first thing tomorrow."

"I have no problem with that," Amar replied. "The sooner, the better."

"I'll make the necessary arrangements," said a woman at the far end of the table, frantically scribbling notes on a sheet of paper.

"Make a spectacle of it," the empress said. "I want as many witnesses there as you can pack into the temple grounds, and be sure to spread the word once it's finished. To King Bhajan and his allies in particular. He may not be dissuaded from his current path, but perhaps the more sensible among his supporters will reevaluate their loyalties."

"We can only hope," said another advisor. "In the meantime, we should consider how to best use Savir's new allegiance to our greatest advantage."

"I'm still not convinced we should accept his allegiance," said another, narrowing his eyes at Amar. "Shouldn't we still be considering execution?"

Jasala took over the conversation from there. She had a ready answer for this and every other concern raised by her advisors. Empress Dashiva said nothing, drinking from a large chalice and occasionally nodding in support of whatever Jasala had said.

When the conversation died down, the empress spoke up. "Perhaps we'd all feel a little more reassured of Savir's loyalty if he could give us some proof that he's truly set aside any loyalty to King Bhajan and Valmandi."

Amar sat up a little straighter. He'd suspected this was coming. Still, he couldn't help feeling conflicted about divulging the secrets and strategies of a man who'd treated him like a beloved grandson. Bhajan was stubborn, yes, and dead set on exacting vengeance for the crimes committed against his family. Amar didn't want him to suffer further, but he couldn't let the entire empire suffer, either.

"I do have some information about Valmandi's plans," he said. "It's a few weeks old by now, but I believe much of it is still relevant. My hope is that this information can be used to force Valmandi to surrender with minimal loss of life."

"That is my hope as well," said Jasala. "Please, tell us what you know."

He started with General Muraka's secret support of Valmandi and her scheme to depose the empress in an attack from within. The council seemed much more willing to believe him once the empress added that Muraka had attempted to escape the palace with Amar in tow and was still nowhere to be found. Unfortunately, Amar could provide few details about the planned takeover. With the general gone, it seemed far less likely to succeed, and he hoped Bhajan wouldn't follow through with it. Still, the possibility couldn't be ruled out entirely. The advisors made plans to find and weed out any other conspirators who may have been involved, but Muraka remained the most important missing piece.

Next up for discussion was Jakhat's new control over the southern farmlands. As Amar had expected, Jakhat had faced little resistance from Valmandi, thus securing for themselves enough food to feed their armies and the citizenry for an entire year if necessary. Maintaining reliable supply lines was still a challenge, but one they seemed confident they could manage.

When Amar explained that Valmandi hoped to retake the area, the council laughed him off—until he told them of the many new Tarja they'd added to their ranks in the aftermath of battle. Many of those soldiers would be inefficient as they were still learning to use and control their magic, but with some basic training, they would nevertheless bolster the ranks of Valmandi's Tarja army, and that was before further strengthening their power with mesala harvested from the Sular Desert. Amar also shared how scholars were studying curses to be used as a potential weapon against Jakhat. This earned him several more rounds of laughter, but Princess Jasala quickly cut them off.

"Unlikely though it may seem," she said, "it's at least worth looking into. Or have you already forgotten the message we received last month? Our informant told us then that academy scholars were working on something powerful and secret. It's likely it was this, is it not?"

"Even if it's true, they're foolish to pursue such an endeavor," said a man whose laughter had been amongst the loudest in the room. "All knowledge of curses was rooted out centuries ago. No one who has studied them since has had any success, and the few who claimed to come close were destroyed by their efforts or arrested and punished before they could be. They're wasting their time. We need not fear this threat."

"Not *this* threat, perhaps," the empress said. "But I am concerned about their growing stores of mesala. Their Tarja army has always been greater than ours, and if strengthened further, Bhajan may think himself powerful enough to secure a victory." She drummed her fingers against the table. "Send more troops to the south, and have our spies focus on discovering what exactly Valmandi's scholars are studying."

She started to rise, indicating that the meeting was about to end. Amar knew he shouldn't speak up now when he was still on such precarious footing here, but he couldn't help himself. "What about the Sularans?"

Dashiva looked down at him with a frown. "What about them?"

"My apologies for speaking out of turn, Your Majesty, but shouldn't something be done to stop Valmandi from trespassing on their lands and stealing mesala?"

"That sounds like a problem for the Sularans."

"But if we—"

"We're finished here," Dashiva said flatly, her nostrils flaring. "If you have a matter to bring before the council, you are welcome to submit a proposal for our next meeting. Until then, I think you've taken up quite enough of our time and resources, don't you, Savir?"

Amar pressed his lips together and didn't dare say anything more.

KESARI

As was to be expected, Prince Savir's public relinquishment of all claim to the imperial throne sent shockwaves through the city and beyond. Once the initial surprise of it had passed, a lighter and more hopeful feeling seemed to settle in. The timing seemed fitting, with winter coming to an end and spring right around the corner. Shops stayed open later, the streets were busier, children went back to wandering their old haunts with friends, and adults talked of the peace that was surely soon to come. Empress Dashiva had called on King Bhajan to surrender, promising that there would be no further punishment so long as there were no further attacks. Though additional troops were marching to the southern farmlands, these measures were largely viewed as a precaution. Even the increased presence of soldiers patrolling the streets could not curb the general feeling of optimism. Kesari found herself abuzz with it, too.

The next week was one of the most peaceful she'd experienced in a very long time, and she relished the simple comforts of life. The beds in Kamaal's guesthouse were incredibly luxurious, or at least they felt that way after so many nights camping outdoors. She slept in late as often as she could, and mornings brought hot breakfasts and lively conversations with some of the people she loved best in all the world.

There were warm blankets to curl up under, songs to listen to when Mitul played his saraj for them, and books to read that took her on fantastical adventures. During the day, her only concerns and responsibilities involved helping out with a few chores and working with Aleida to plan Mitul and Kamaal's surprise engagement party.

The only thing that could have made life any better would have been to have Lucian back.

She was in the garden reading late one afternoon when he found her. A low voice called out, slightly broken up by an underlying crackle. "Hello, Kes!"

She was so startled she nearly dropped her book, and her first thought was that she must be mistaken. It couldn't be him.

She stood and looked in the direction of the voice anyway, and her heart soared. Lucian flew over Kamaal's fence and danced circles around her like an autumn leaf caught in a whirlwind. "Lucian!" she said with a laugh. "You're back!"

He came to a stop hovering in front of her face, a dark, jagged grin flickering deep within his flames. "Did you miss me?"

"Of course! How did you know where to find us?"

"I figured there weren't too many places in Jakhat you could be. I also considered checking the palace dungeons, but in an effort to be less cynical, I thought we'd try here first."

"We?" she asked.

Lucian's grin widened, and he spun around to face the street. "Yes, *we*."

She caught sight of a tall figure walking toward them from some distance down the street. Two, actually, but Kesari's eyes were immediately drawn by the familiar loping strides of one, whose long hair was bound up in a ponytail that swung between strong shoulders.

The sly snicker Lucian let out was all the confirmation she needed. She tossed her book aside and started running. "Saya!"

Her friend met her halfway, and they collided in a tight embrace, both laughing. "You're here!" Kesari said. "How? Why? I wasn't expecting—"

"You'll have to stop crushing me if you want your questions answered," Saya said, pulling away and taking a step back. "There, that's better. Have you gotten taller? You look taller."

"I don't think so," Kesari said. The person accompanying Saya stopped behind her, and she got a better look at him. "Hello, Hazim."

Saya's oldest brother maintained a stoic expression but offered a small nod in greeting.

Now she was even more curious. "I wasn't sure you'd come back at all after Lucian brought his news. Certainly not so soon, or with company."

"I came as fast as I could," Saya said. "But not for Amar—or at least, not only for him. Hazim and I are here as ambassadors for our people."

Kesari raised her eyebrows. "Really?"

"My mother and the council sent us to negotiate with the empress." Saya's expression darkened. "Things haven't been going well back home. Lucian's warning was appreciated, but there's only so much we can do on our own."

"So you're going to ask Jakhat for help?"

"Yes. Our people have never had much trust for Empress Dashiva or the Kavoran empire as a whole—"

"With good reason," Hazim growled.

"True. But Valmandi is going to ruin us if they keep up these raids. We need allies. The enemy of our enemy, if necessary."

"What can we do to help?" Kesari asked.

"I'm not sure yet. For now, we just need a place to stay until we can gather more information."

"You're staying here, of course," Mitul said, stepping past Kesari to give Saya a hug. "It's good to see you again, my friend."

Saya patted him solidly on the back. "You, too. Where's that partner of yours?"

"Betrothed now, actually."

"Is that so?" Saya's brows lifted. "Congratulations."

"Thank you. He's inside getting supper ready. Come on. I'm sure you're both hungry, and I think we can provide some of that information you're looking for."

AMAR

AMAR SAT ON THE ENTRYWAY STEPS OUTSIDE THE IMPERIAL PALACE, fussing with the signet ring around his little finger while he waited for Saya. He'd put it in his pocket earlier only to pull it back out again, and he still wasn't sure he should wear it. The crest marked him a member of Valmandi's royal family, so in one sense, it could be viewed as a symbol of loyalty to King Bhajan—something that wouldn't earn him any favor here. On the other hand, everyone knew Savir to be Bhajan's grandson, so there was really no sense in pretending there wasn't some tie there. However small, the ring gave some legitimacy to his falsified identity, and he needed to maintain that.

He sighed, twisting the ring back into position, and stood up.

"Is that them?" Tarik asked from a few steps behind him.

Amar watched as two figures came into view, walking over the rise of the hill the palace stood on. He jogged down the steps, waving to Saya as he descended. They met at the bottom, clasping hands and pulling each other in for an embrace. Her hand was firm and solid against his back, and when she pulled away, she looked him over with an appraising gaze.

"The fancy clothes suit you," she said, "but you need a haircut."

Amar laughed. "It hasn't exactly been high among my priorities."

He looked to the young man standing beside her, solidly built and nearly as tall as Tarik. His eyes were the exact same shade of gold as Saya's, and he bore an obvious resemblance to some of their younger brothers, who Amar had met in Hayathu several months before. "You must be Hazim," he said.

The young man nodded. "How much longer until the meeting?"

Straight to business, though Amar could understand his desire to move things along. "Soon. Come with me. I'll show you inside."

They followed him back up the stairs, where Tarik was still waiting. Amar introduced them to the guard as they made their way into the palace and toward the council hall.

"Thank you for arranging this so quickly," Saya said as they walked. "I didn't expect we'd be seen for another week at least."

"It was no trouble," Amar said. Not exactly true, but she didn't need to know that. Princess Jasala had been perfectly willing to receive the Sularan delegates and let them present their case before the council. The empress, while not completely resistant, had been apathetic, questioning why they should waste precious time on a Sularan matter. Jasala's insistence was all it took to get her to relent, which was something to be grateful for, but Amar still worried about how the other advisors would receive Saya's request.

"I'm so sorry about Zefar," he said to both of them.

Hazim merely huffed and rolled his eyes in response, but Saya nodded solemnly. "He probably didn't deserve any of your sympathy, but—"

"But *you* do. I'm sorry."

"Thank you."

They stopped in front of the doors to where the council met. "I wish we had more time to catch up, but I really don't want to keep them waiting."

"We'll have plenty of time later."

Amar hoped that was true, though he found matters here were keeping him almost as busy as he'd been in Valmandi, and the empress seemed intent on watching him closely. He'd only managed to visit the others once in the nearly two weeks he'd been here.

"Wait here," he said. "I'll come get you when it's time."

He entered the room, where the rest of the imperial advisors were already seated and waiting. Jasala was there too, and she gave him a warm smile as he sat down in his usual place beside her. She leaned over to whisper to him. "They're here?"

"In the hall waiting."

"Good. We can start with them."

Empress Dashiva joined them a few minutes later, and with that, the meeting began. One of the advisors started to give an update on the search for General Muraka—still unsuccessful, given that she wasn't locked up in a cell—but Jasala cut him off. "I'm sorry, but I'd actually like to start with another matter. We have guests. They've traveled a long way to speak with us, and I believe we may be able to help each other. Savir, would you please invite them in?"

He rose from his chair, went to the doors, and pushed them open far enough to peer out into the hall. He beckoned Saya and Hazim inside, and they entered with their heads held high. Jasala motioned for them to go to the far end of the table, where they remained standing as Amar returned to his seat.

Jasala introduced them. "May I present Saya hás Seda and Hazim hás Seda, children of Masahi Seda of the Sularan tribes."

"Sularan royalty," Amar heard one advisor whisper to another.

Saya would have cringed if she'd heard them; Sularans voted for their leaders and found the practice of hereditary monarchy rather archaic. Although relatives of prior Sularan leaders were often elected by later generations, that was certainly not always the case, and there was no official passing down of power from parent to child. Still, as the eldest children of the current masahi, Saya and Hazim were important figures, and perhaps esteemed to be of even higher standing by Kavoran perceptions than they were by their own.

Empress Dashiva leaned forward in her chair, laying one hand on the table. "I take it you've come here with concerns about Valmandi encroaching on your territory."

"Yes, Your Majesty," Saya replied. "Despite our previous agreements, they continue to strip the land of mesala, threatening the balance of life in the desert and thus our people's survival. Every day, Valmandi soldiers push deeper into our lands. We have fought them off, threatened them, even killed them when we had to, though we take no pleasure in it."

Hazim made a low sound in the back of his throat, and Amar got the distinct impression that he actually didn't mind killing a few Kavoran poachers who'd dared to cross his path. He took half a step forward to stand in direct alignment with Saya.

"We've secured our borders as best we can on our own," he said, his deep voice making him sound much older than he was. "But the desert is vast and our numbers are few."

"Your help would be most welcome," Saya said. "Though our motives may differ, our goal is the same: to stop Valmandi's army from acquiring any more mesala."

One advisor was quick to jump in. "We are in the middle of our own war with Valmandi, as I'm sure you've noticed. United though our goals may be, we can't afford to send any of our own people to patrol your borders. As you said, the desert is vast, and such an endeavor would require resources we cannot spare."

"We can't afford *not* to help them," said Jasala. "If Savir is right about what Valmandi is planning, their Tarja forces pose a serious threat."

"That threat will be of no consequence once Bhajan surrenders. And at that point, Valmandi's armies will have no reason to raid the desert."

"*If* Bhajan surrenders," another advisor remarked. "We can't be sure that he will."

"He'd be a fool not to."

"And yet here we are, more than a week since Savir arrived and we've heard no word from Valmandi whatsoever. They've had plenty of time to receive the news and send back a response."

"Enough! That kind of fearmongering isn't going to help anyone."

"*Fearmongering*? I'm only being realistic."

From there, the room dissolved into a cacophony of heated arguments. Princess Jasala sat back in her chair, and both she and the empress remained silent through it all, watching, listening, and occasionally exchanging a knowing look with one another. Amar didn't dare jump into the fray himself, but he did cast a glance in Saya's direction. She met his gaze and rolled her eyes, shoulders tense and hands clasped behind her back.

After a few minutes, Dashiva cut them off with a few sharp handclaps. "Let's all try to be civil in front of our guests. I'd like to hear a little more from them." She gestured to Saya and Hazim. "Please, continue."

"We are only asking you to honor the agreement you've had with our people for decades," Saya said, her voice taking on a harder tone. "For years, you've ignored it, refusing to enforce existing trade agreements and punish the individuals who violate them. Now your apathy threatens us both, and still your advisors debate whether it is wiser to do nothing than to take action."

Hazim crossed his arms. "One begins to wonder if you're biding your time, waiting for us to grow weak so you can come in and claim our lands for yourself."

At this, the advisor across from Amar stood and slammed his palm against the table. "How dare you! These accusations—"

"Enough!" said Jasala, casting a sharp look at the man. Once he'd returned to his seat, she shifted her attention back to the Sularans. "I understand your concerns, but I can assure you we have no desire to claim the desert as our own. Nor any other lands, for that matter. On behalf of the Kavoran Empire, I offer my sincerest apologies that we have failed to honor our past agreements with your people."

Empress Dashiva's eyes narrowed a little at this, but she nodded stiffly in agreement.

The princess went on. "You're right. Valmandi's actions threaten us both, and we'd do well to work together. I propose that we send a contingent of soldiers to aid the Sularans in securing their borders."

A few of the advisors were quick to voice their agreement, but most stayed quiet, looking to Dashiva and waiting to see which way she would go. She said nothing, her expression unreadable except for the grim line of her mouth.

"Shall we put it to a vote?" Jasala asked. This caught Amar off guard. Monarchs were not expected to invite their council to vote on any subject, but none of the other advisors looked particularly surprised by the princess' statement. Was this something she did regularly?

"There's no need," Dashiva said. "We will send our soldiers. Not Tarja, though; I want them here to defend the city if Bhajan decides to continue this foolishness."

"It shall be done, Your Majesty," said a woman Amar assumed to be one of the military advisors.

"Saya, Hazim, you may wait outside while we finish here. Arrangements will be made to send the soldiers back home with you."

"Thank you, Your Majesty." Saya bowed, then followed Hazim out of the room into the hall.

From there, the conversation moved to discussing the specifics of increasing the city's defenses to protect against whatever Valmandi might still be planning. Jasala leaned over to Amar and whispered. "Would you go out and see if your Sularan friend is willing to meet with me after I'm finished here? I'd love to talk to her one on one."

"What should I tell her it's about?"

"Oh, just some ideas I've had about the future of our empire."

That piqued Amar's curiosity, but now was not the time for questions. He slipped quietly from the room while the meeting continued.

He found Saya and Hazim standing in the hall, whispering to each other rather heatedly in Sularan. Saya held up a hand when she saw Amar coming, and they both looked at him expectantly.

"Everything all right?" he asked.

"You tell us," Hazim snapped. "Can we trust them?"

Saya sighed. "He thinks coming here was a waste of time, and that they're just going to find some way to take advantage of us."

"A fair concern, given your history with them," Amar said. "But this is something Jasala wants, and I do think she's more trustworthy than her mother. More sincere, too. And for whatever it's worth, I have her ear and her attention. I'll do all I can to make sure they uphold their agreement and do right by your people."

Hazim looked like he wanted to throw some other retort in Amar's face, but Saya put a hand on his arm and spoke first. "We don't have to trust them—not completely. But we do need them. And we can trust Amar."

Hazim's entire body remained tense. "I hope this doesn't end with us worse off than we were before." He stalked down the hall a few paces and sat with his back against the wall.

"He's angry," Saya said. "And scared. He didn't even want to come, but my mother thought it would be good for him."

"It shouldn't have come to this," Amar said. "I apologize for my part in the troubles your people are facing."

"Your part." Saya tilted her head to one side. "If you've had any part, Valkyra is to blame for it. Besides, our friction with Kavora was building long before this war began."

She wasn't wrong, but that didn't completely assuage Amar's sense of personal responsibility.

"The princess asked if she could see you after this. She wants to talk."

Saya's brows drew together. "What, just the two of us?"

"Yes."

"Why?"

"Some ideas she's had, I guess. It's a good thing, Saya. Or at least, I think it could be." He lowered his voice a little to make sure the guards standing nearby couldn't hear them. "She's not like the empress. Not so concerned with power and legacy, I guess. They don't always see eye to eye, and I get the sense there are things Jasala would change, if she could. Things she *will* change, once she's in charge."

"What things?"

Amar shrugged. "Hard to say. I believe she wants to have better relations with your people, for a start. She also mentioned the future of the empire, whatever that means."

"Hm. Well, I guess it wouldn't hurt to talk some more, try and get on her good side. All right, you can tell her I'll meet with her."

KESARI

KESARI WAS HAPPY TO SEE SAYA RETURN FROM HER VISIT TO THE palace in decidedly better spirits than when she'd left that morning. Even Hazim didn't look quite as sullen as before, and the updates they provided sounded promising. Hazim would be returning to the desert in the morning with the soldiers the empress had agreed to send, but Saya had opted to remain behind. This was partly to ensure that Jakhat's leaders kept their word and partly to strengthen diplomatic relations between the Sularans and the Kavorans.

Over the next several days, Kesari, Aleida, and Lucian worked to plan and prepare their secret engagement party for Mitul and Kamaal. Saya enthusiastically joined in, though her frequent visits to the palace often kept her occupied with other matters. Princess Jasala seemed to have taken a particular interest in Sularan society and government and had requested that Saya educate her on these topics in-depth.

"I'm not really sure what to make of it all," the young warrior remarked one night as they were all were cleaning up supper. "Sometimes it seems like she's only curious, but other times, it's like…" Her brow furrowed, and she trailed off, shaking her head.

"Like what?" Kesari asked.

"I don't know. Like maybe she wants to learn from the things my people have done for centuries, even implement them here."

"What do you mean? What things?"

"Our government, I guess. The way everyone has a voice in choosing who leads us, the rules we live by. No royalty or nobility."

"That can't really be what she's planning," Lucian said skeptically. "This war has been destabilizing enough. Imagine the turmoil if she were to ask all the nobles in the empire to give up their power."

"It's a nice idea though, isn't it?" Kamaal said. "Letting the people have more say in the choices that impact them."

"Nice ideas aren't always feasible, no matter how much we might want them to be."

Saya put the last of the dishes in one of Kamaal's cupboards. "I could be wrong, anyway. For all I know, she's got some nefarious plan to use this information against us and do the same thing Kavorans have always done. Conquer, take over, erase whoever and whatever was there before."

"You don't really believe that or you wouldn't be telling her anything," Aleida said. Quieter, she added, "I wouldn't, if it were me."

"No, I guess I don't *really* believe that." Saya jabbed a finger at Mitul. "This is all your fault, you know. I fully blame you for turning me into such an optimist."

His eyes widened innocently. "Me? What did I do?"

"Two years ago, I wouldn't have trusted any Kavoran I crossed paths with. Then I join up with you and Amar, and you've got your music and your charm and your shining view of the world. Amar helps with my *haseph* even though he worries it's a bad idea. We travel across Kavora together, and I have to accept that you're not all the villains I thought you were. Now here we are, and I'm talking to the next Kavoran empress, trusting that it will only help my people instead of hurt them."

Mitul chuckled. "Well, I suppose I owe you an apology, then. I'm sorry for infecting you with my…what was it? My shining view of the world?"

"Don't bother," she said. "Erythyr might be a better place if we all had a little more of that."

The following morning after breakfast, Kesari, Lucian, and Aleida made plans to track down some more materials for party decorations. They'd been putting these together for several days now, hiding their creations in various nooks and crannies in the guesthouse so that nothing was left out in the open for Mitul or Kamaal to see when they happened to come by. The day that had been chosen for the party was two weeks away, but Aleida insisted they still didn't have enough lanterns to realize her vision, and they'd run out of paper. Again.

"Where are you all off to today, then?" Kamaal asked, setting up an easel and canvas.

"Oh, just…out," Kesari replied, cringing at how obviously suspicious she sounded. She could hardly blame Aleida for the glare she shot her.

"Hm. You three have been going *out* a lot lately. And Saya, when she's around."

Mitul descended from the upstairs loft. "And whispering things behind our backs. Let's not forget that."

"Ah yes, the whispering. You know, we're starting to wonder if you might be hiding something."

"And so what if we are?" Aleida said, marching to the door where Lucian already hovered. "Come on, Kes. Let's go see what kind of trouble we can get ourselves into."

"Have fun," Kamaal said with a wave. "And bring back some dried chilis for supper tonight, will you? Wait a minute, I'll get you the coin to pay for it."

"That's all right, I've got it," Aleida called back.

"Be safe," Mitul said as the door swung shut behind them. "Love you!"

Aleida exchanged a quick glance with Kesari and stuffed her hands into her pockets with a huff, but she couldn't quite hide the slight tug of a smile at her lips. It was such a simple exchange, but it reminded Kesari so much of routine conversations with her parents. A familiar ache throbbed inside her chest, and she wondered what they were doing right now, and whether they were thinking of her, too.

She was soon distracted from these thoughts by Aleida, who ran through a list of things they still needed to do to get ready. The food situation was her biggest concern, and there were several invitations to be delivered. She lamented again what a shame it was that Kamaal's sister wouldn't be able to attend, and Kesari offered all the usual reassurances that the party was nevertheless a kind gesture worth following through on. If they wanted to do something different to celebrate later on, they could do so whenever they chose. In the meantime, neither of them were going to be upset by a quiet little surprise gathering with people who loved them.

They found a shop selling a variety of art supplies and bought the paper they needed. Aleida also purchased a few new sticks of charcoal for her sketchbook. A bakery nearby sold beautifully decorated desserts, and they went inside to see how much it might cost to have some small honey cakes made for the party. The expense was well beyond what they'd expected, even accounting for how the war had impacted food supply and prices. They tried to barter back and forth for a few minutes, but when it became clear they weren't getting anywhere, they headed off to pick up the chilis Kamaal had requested.

Their route took them through the same neighborhood where Tamaya's great-niece lived, and Kesari remembered that she'd been meaning to stop by and check on the old woman. When she mentioned this, Aleida scoffed and asked, "What for?"

"I sort of feel bad," Kesari replied, "dragging her all the way out here and then leaving her on someone else's doorstep."

"She *asked* to be left there," Aleida reminded her. "She's probably fine. Terrorizing that poor family and complaining about every damn thing she can think of."

"Maybe we should check on *them*, then." She wasn't sure what good that would do, but she felt some obligation to follow up with Tamaya and make sure everything was all right.

"Couldn't hurt," Lucian agreed.

"You two go ahead," Aleida said. "She wouldn't want to see me anyway, and I don't really feel like seeing her."

"All right. Meet you back at the house?"

"Sure. I'll grab those chilis and try to put a few more lanterns together."

They parted ways, and Kesari and Lucian went looking for the house Tamaya's niece lived in. Kesari described the place, and Lucian made quick work of finding it, searching the streets from high up above and then returning to give her directions. A few minutes later, she knocked on the front door, and after a brief shuffling from inside, the niece answered.

"Hello," Kesari said. "You might not remember me, but I was with the group that brought your aunt Tamaya here."

"Yes, I remember."

"I wanted to see how she's doing. Could I talk to her for a few minutes?"

"You haven't heard?" The woman's brows furrowed, and she tilted her head to one side. "I suppose we should have notified you somehow, but…well, it happened so fast, and we didn't think you were particularly close. I'm sorry."

"Oh, that's all right. Did she go back home, then?"

"No." A child's shout caused her to peer back over her shoulder for a moment, and she lowered her voice before continuing. "She passed last week. Like I said, it was quite sudden. Peaceful though. She just didn't wake up one morning."

Kesari's head felt suddenly empty, and all she could think to say was, "Oh."

A child shouted from inside the house again, and the woman began to close the door. "I'm so sorry, but I really have to go. There's a little memorial around that side of the house if you want to pay your respects. Stay as long as you like."

The door shut with a dull *thunk*, and Kesari stood there staring at it for several long seconds. The world around her felt slow and muffled, like she was trying to run underwater and going nowhere. She went around the corner of the house where the woman had pointed. Nestled in a small alcove lay a ceramic panel painted with Tamaya's name and a candle that had long since burned out. A few other trinkets were scattered around, along with some wilting flowers.

Kesari knelt in front of the memorial and ran her fingers across Tamaya's name. The moment didn't seem real, more like something out of a dream.

"Kes?" Lucian said, drifting down to hover in front of her face.

"I just saw her," she replied, her own voice sounding hollow in her ears. "She told me that you and I should look out for each other, and not to take my magic for granted. Then she walked into that house like…like nothing was wrong." She wrapped her arms around her stomach. "She was *just* here."

"Her altma had been fading for a long time," Lucian said. "It must have been months since she could use her magic."

Kesari recalled all the times Tamaya had complained about that very thing. It was an organic progression for all natural-born Tarja nearing the end of their life; their ability to channel altma faded as their souls began to lose connection with the physical world.

Lucian drifted lower, casting Tamaya's memorial in a soft, orange glow. "She had to have known it was only a matter of time."

"So quickly, though? I didn't realize it would be like that."

A lump formed in her throat, and before she could stop them, hot tears welled up to blur her vision. At first, she tried to fight them, unsure of why she was even crying. She hadn't known Tamaya particularly well, and though the old woman had helped her, she'd also been rather unpleasant about it. The end of any life was a sad thing, but this felt more personal. A deeper sort of sorrow.

"I'm sorry, Kes," said Lucian. "I didn't realize the two of you had grown so close while I was away."

She wiped at her tears with the back of her hand, but more kept coming. "It's not that."

So what was it, then? Why couldn't she stop crying? Where was this sudden sense of heartbreak coming from?

She hugged her knees tight against her body. Lucian began to grow and shrink ever so slightly in a gentle rhythm. Though he didn't say it, Kesari could hear his voice in her head, the same mantra he'd always repeated during her worst moments until she found some semblance of control again. *Breathe, Kes. You're all right. Just breathe.*

She did, and when she was ready, she spoke.

"Will it be like that when I…when *we*…"

"No," Lucian said, mercifully cutting in before she could finish the sentence. "We won't be alone, for starters. My life is bound to yours. I won't go until you do, and you'll have my magic right up to the end."

The end. It suddenly seemed so soon. For everyone, even old ladies who had good, long lives and then died in their sleep. But Kesari had no hope of living that long. Mitul and Kamaal weren't so far from the age she hoped to be before her own time came, and they'd barely found their way back to each other. If that were her, finding someone she wanted to spend the rest of her life with in her forties or even her thirties, would it feel like enough time?

Did it *ever* feel like enough time, for anyone?

"It's so *short*."

"What is?"

"Life," she said. "*My* life."

Lucian's eyes flickered out completely, only for a moment. "It is," he rasped, and the gentle crackles in his voice were sharper and more broken than ever. "I'm sorry, Kes. That's my fault."

"No, I didn't mean—I'd never blame you for that, you know. Please don't feel guilty." She put her palms out underneath him, wishing she could hug him. "It was my choice to make, and I don't regret it. Not for a second."

"You did."

"For a little while. Not anymore. Never again." She sighed. "It's just that...well, I think I want to go home. I miss my family. Skies, I miss them *terribly*, and I've already been away from them for so long. I keep thinking that's where I should be."

A small grin returned to Lucian's flames. "We can go home anytime you like."

He said it like it was the easiest thing in the world, and that brought fresh tears to Kesari's eyes.

"Hey, what's the matter?" Lucian asked. "It's a good thing, isn't it? Your family will be so happy to have you back."

"Yes, but *they're* my family, too." She threw her arm out and pointed back toward the road in the general direction of Kamaal's studio. "Saya and Mitul and Amar, Aleida and Kamaal. I don't know how to say goodbye. I don't *want* to."

"Oh, Kes." He drifted closer, his heat warming her cheeks. "Do you have any idea how special it is that you've found so many people to love in this world? So many people who love *you*?"

She choked out a soft, "I know."

"Goodbye doesn't have to be forever, you know. And it doesn't have to come until you're ready."

"I don't think I'll ever be ready." She wiped at her tears again. "But I have to be. This is what I need to do."

"Do you want to tell the others?"

"Soon, but not yet. We have to stay for the party, obviously. Aleida will kill us if we don't."

"You're probably right about that. But after?"

"After," Kesari said, and despite the ache still lingering in her chest, there was something bright there, too. "Then we'll go home. To stay, this time."

28

ALEDIA

THERE WAS ONLY A WEEK LEFT TO PREPARE FOR THE ENGAGEMENT party, and Aleida was finally beginning to feel as if the whole thing was coming together. Decorations were finished, a few guests had offered to bring food, and all that remained was to deliver a final invitation.

She set out to do so, enjoying the warmth of spring coming into its own as the last traces of winter faded away. Kesari and Lucian joined her, talking through some of the preparations that still needed to be made for their journey home, and Aleida tried not to be too distracted by the swell of emotions this brought up. She'd come to enjoy the younger girl's company these past few months. The two of them were very different, but Kesari was easy to get along with and in some ways reminded Aleida of her brother. She would miss her when she was gone, and she couldn't help feeling a small twinge of jealously that Kesari had a home and a family to return to.

She reached into her pocket for the names and location Amar had written down for her. Avita and Dahvi, a couple who had been friends with Kamaal and Mitul for more than a decade. They lived in one of the wealthier neighborhoods near the palace—somewhere Aleida got the immediate sense she was not supposed to be. Soldiers patrolling the area gave a questioning look, but they didn't focus on her for too long. Her obvious Visan features still made her appear somewhat out of place, but these days, when the Kavorans had made enemies of each other, Visans seemed to draw far less suspicion than before.

She glanced up at the palace overlooking the city and wondered again how much longer it would take for this conflict to resolve. What was King Bhajan waiting for? Prince Savir's renouncement of any claim to the throne should have ended all of this. The fact that it hadn't put her on edge. What strings was Valkyra pulling behind the scenes? What power did she still have, even without Amar as her puppet?

Thinking about it too much put her in a sour mood, and she was trying very hard not to let her thoughts wander to such dark places when she had so little power to change the situation. She focused on leading the way to deliver her invitation. It took some effort to decipher Amar's rough descriptions, but they finally found the couple's home.

The woman who answered the door was roughly the same age as Kamaal and Mitul. When asked, she confirmed that she was Avita, and she seemed delighted when Aleida handed her the invitation and explained what it was for. She asked if she could bring anything, and Aleida said that wasn't necessary, but in typical Kavoran fashion, she insisted. They spent another five minutes talking about desserts, at which point the woman urged Aleida and Kesari to try some of the biscuits she and Dahvi had made the day before. They both left the house with smiles and full bellies.

"I like her," Kesari commented brightly as they wound their way back through the streets in the direction from which they'd come. "Nice lady."

Aleida nodded, though this was unsurprising, considering Avita was friends with two of the best people she knew.

"It's all done then, right?" Kesari asked. "All that's left is to decorate the day of the party."

"And get rid of Mitul and Kamaal for a while so we can surprise them." This was the part she was less certain about. "I mean, they definitely know something's going on, right? It's going to be hard to *really* surprise them."

Kesari shrugged. "That's not so important, is it? It's more about showing them how happy we are for them and celebrating with them."

"Right," she said with a sigh, appreciative of the reminder. "I want everything to be perfect, you know? It's not much, only a stupid party, but after everything they've done for me, this seems like the least I can do for them."

"And they'll love it. It's not stupid at all."

They were nearing a main road that split off in two directions, one leading up the nearby hillside to the palace. A few dozen people had gathered in the center of the street, all facing the same direction, and a hubbub of voices filled the air. It was not a happy sound. The skin at the back of Aleida's neck prickled.

"What do you think's going on there?" Kesari asked.

"I can go have a look, if you want to wait here," Lucian replied.

But Aleida didn't want to wait, and she continued on while Kesari hesitated a few seconds behind her. Something was moving beyond the crowd. She could see glimpses of it between their heads, sometimes rising above them for a second. A dark shape, almost liquid in its movements, but she couldn't figure out what it was.

"Aleida, wait," Lucian warned. "We don't know—" He made a sharp, sputtering hiss. "Skies, what *is* that?" Without waiting for an answer, he shot ahead, and Aleida and Kesari exchanged a glance before hurrying after him.

They managed to squeeze in between a few of the onlookers, filling in a gap toward the front of the group. Once there, they could see why no one was moving forward any farther. A line of Jakhat soldiers in green blocked the street, brandishing bayoneted rifles in clear warning that no one was to come any closer. Beyond them, three more soldiers knelt in a huddle, palms pressed to the ground. These were Tarja, judging by their posture and the strange magic they seemed to be summoning.

"What is that?" Kesari asked, echoing Lucian's earlier question. "What are they doing?"

Aleida shook her head, unsure what to make of the dark tendrils that writhed and coiled in the air above and around the three Tarja. It was inky black but faded at the edges, with smaller particles forming a thin mist around the main portions. The Tarja appeared to be working together to control it, rising from the ground in unison and then spreading their arms wide. As they did, the blackness grew as if being drawn up from the ground.

"It's the same over on Jasmine Street," someone behind Aleida whispered. "Soldiers blocking the road to the palace, Tarja working some kind of shadow magic."

"Still no idea what they're doing?" another voice asked.

"They're not saying. Told us all to leave but didn't seem too bothered when some stuck around."

"Maybe it's a drill?" Kesari suggested, casting a sidelong glance at Aleida. "Some training exercise?"

"Maybe," she said. The prickling at the back of her neck remained, and she had the sudden urge to turn her gaze skyward. There was nothing there against the clear blue sky—nothing except for Lucian drifting down to hover between them.

"Come on," he said. "We should get going."

"Wait," Kesari replied. "I've never seen magic like that before. Look how coordinated they are, working together like that. What *are* they doing, exactly?"

"Shadow magic. Smoke and illusions, mostly, but it can be a good carrier for other things."

"Like what?"

He ignored the question. "We need to leave. I don't like the way those soldiers are acting."

Aleida didn't like soldiers in general, but when she glanced back at the line of them before her, she could see what Lucian meant. Their postures were tense, hands wrapped tight around their rifles as if ready to put them to use at any second. Their eyes darted across the crowd with all the vigilance of guards watching prisoners during a transport, just waiting for something to go wrong. They looked far too agitated for this to be a simple training exercise.

"Let's go," she said, nudging Kesari in the arm. The girl let out a heavy sigh but didn't protest further. Aleida pivoted, seeking a path back through the crowd, which had doubled in size since their arrival. Before she could begin to shuffle her way out, a high-pitched shriek came from some distance behind her. She looked back.

Several of the onlookers pointed up toward the palace. A streaking red light rose high above the ivory towers and their golden domes, brilliant against the blue morning sky. It scattered in a ring of sparks, a loud boom echoing in its wake. The chattering of the crowd intensified, but it was the cry from one of the Tarja behind the soldiers that caught Aleida's attention.

"Blades!"

The metallic slide of steel rang sharp in her ears as the three Tarja drew their weapons. The dark tendrils around them were still growing, faster now, and spreading wider, reaching higher. In unison, the Tarja sliced deep gouges into their own palms. They held them out, allowing the blood to drip down as if feeding the shadows rising from the ground beneath them.

"Skies," Kesari hissed beside her. "They can't be—! Lucian?"

"I think they are."

"What?" Aleida asked, mesmerized by the sight of the dark tendrils weaving together, now forming more of a blanket than individual strands.

"They're casting a curse," Kesari said.

That couldn't be. Curses were outlawed, all knowledge of their creation eradicated. Impossible.

And yet…

"Let's go!" Lucian snapped, and this time, there was no hesitation. Aleida squeezed between bodies as she made her way through the crowd, glancing back occasionally to make sure Kesari was still close. Behind them, three voices spoke in unison as the darkness completely enveloped the Tarja.

"With the blood of our bodies, we lay this curse upon the imperial palace of Jakhat and all within its walls. A mist of poison shall engulf the palace, killing all who breathe it in, and it shall not disperse until Empress Dashiva falls."

There were a few nervous laughs from onlookers, but several were quick to do as Aleida and Kesari had, leaving the scene as fast as possible. When the black cloud started to move, panic rippled through the crowd, and people began to leave in earnest. Aleida broke into a run with them, glancing over her shoulder to see Kesari hot on her heels, and beyond that, something terrifying.

The dark cloud spread, not only up the hill toward the palace, but outward, through the streets and into the city. In seconds, the soldiers who'd held back the crowd were swallowed up, but their screams and choking coughs cut through the cries of those fleeing. Everyone ran, their terror spurring them on more urgently now. Some pounded on doors, pleading to be allowed entrance, while others simply tried to force their way inside. In both cases, they often disappeared inside the dark cloud before managing to find shelter and safety.

Aleida forced her own legs to run faster, then paused to reach back and grab Kesari by the wrist so they wouldn't get separated. She wasn't as fast as Aleida, but it didn't matter anyway. Another glance told her the darkness was faster than either of them. Already, it was engulfing more people. Seconds later, their cries of pain rang out as they breathed in the poison promised by the curse.

"This way!" Lucian called. He'd veered off down a side street, and Aleida followed him with Kesari still in tow. Good—this was good. The buildings to either side would offer them some cover, and if they could make it to the other side, maybe they'd be safe.

She plunged ahead, emerging into a wider street, another main artery of the city. The noise and chaos here was even worse than where they started. Someone jostled her as they ran by, and she nearly fell. When she looked around to get her bearings, she caught a glimpse of the palace up on the hill, its white towers almost completely hidden behind the darkness still coming toward them.

They hadn't escaped it at all.

"Keep running!" she shouted, pulling at Kesari's arm again.

The girl remained firmly planted, wrenching her wrist free of Aleida's grasp. "We can't outrun it."

"We have to! It can't keep spreading forever. If we get far enough—"

Kesari wasn't listening to her. Her hands moved in purposeful sweeps over and around her head, and something translucent began to shimmer around them. A barrier.

Aleida took a step back, looking between the dark, encroaching mist and people still fleeing up the street behind her. A barrier might not work, and what if Kesari couldn't maintain it?

Aleida could still run, trust her fate to herself instead of leaving it in someone else's hands. But Kes was right, and if she couldn't outrun it—

She stepped closer to the other girl, only a hands' width left between them. The barrier was expanding, but the dark cloud was closing in fast. Kesari had shut her eyes, focusing only on forming the barrier.

Aleida wanted to scream, urge her to hurry, work faster, but she didn't dare do or say anything that would break her concentration. She glanced to one side. The darkness was so close now that she could have taken three strides and touched it. Her heartbeat reverberated through her chest like thunder.

This was it. She was either going to live or die here, and it all depended on Kesari's magic.

The dark cloud swept in. Aleida held her breath, eyes wide open, ready to be swallowed up.

It never happened. The mist swirled around the invisible sphere surrounding them like smoke against glass, dispersing out to either side when it couldn't penetrate the barrier. Aleida's gaze snapped back to Kesari. Her eyes were open again, and she exhaled slowly as she watched the darkness outside their little bubble of safety.

"Good work, Kes," Lucian said. "Can you hold it?"

"For now," she replied.

That didn't sound good. Aleida's mind was still reeling from the panic and chaos of the last few minutes, but she could easily recall the words spoken as the Tarja cast their curse. It would last until Empress Dashiva had fallen, and it was meant to engulf the palace, not the city. The Tarja creating it probably hadn't intended to be caught in the poisonous fog. Something must have gone wrong.

"They were wearing Jakhat uniforms," she said. She'd only made that connection now, but Jakhat soldiers never should have attacked the palace at all.

"Uniforms are easy enough to come by," Lucian said. "Only Valmandi would know enough to even dare attempt a curse. Fools."

Aleida's thoughts spun around this information for a few seconds, but some warning voice in the back of her mind screamed for attention. She wasn't thinking clearly, and none of this mattered right now. "We need to find our way out of this darkness. Kes, can you walk and keep up that barrier at the same time?"

"Yes," she said resolutely. "Lead the way, but go slow."

Aleida faced south, the direction they'd been running in their attempt to escape the curse. Lucian made himself a little bigger and pressed against the front of the barrier to illuminate their path. The mist was like a fog, thick and cloudy. His light couldn't permeate it very far, but what they did see was grim.

Several bodies lay in the street, limbs twisted where they'd fallen, many of them clinging to each other. None had been spared, not even the animals. A dog and a few chickens lay limp in her path, and she skirted past them to walk by the tiny legs of two small children, their mother slumped over their bodies as if she'd been trying to shield them from the darkness.

Tears burned at her eyes, and Kesari let out a choked little sound behind her. For a moment, the barrier shrunk inward and the mist pressed closer, a sign of the girl's wavering focus. Aleida stopped, waiting for her to regain control.

"How could they do this?" she asked in a shaky voice.

The barrier sucked in even closer. Aleida leaned back to avoid being caught outside it, and she wrapped Kesari's hand in hers, hoping to soothe her.

"I know," Lucian said gently. "It's terrible, and you can mourn them later. Right now, we need to focus on getting the two of you out of here. Can you do that?"

Kes nodded, set her jaw, and pushed her free hand out. The barrier expanded to a more comfortable size.

"That's it," said Lucian. "Just look straight ahead. Focus on the back of Aleida's head. She'll lead us through. Don't look at anything else."

Aleida faced forward again, keeping hold of Kesari's hand. "Ready?"

"Ready."

They walked on. Aleida took care in choosing their path, trying to avoid getting too close to any of the bodies so Kesari wouldn't trip over them. It was a slow process, and Aleida found herself thinking more and more about the streets of Libera after the invasion. She and Tyrus had wandered through the wreckage hand in hand, startled by every clatter or cry. Kesari's hand began to feel smaller in hers, like Tyrus' had been then, and she had the same urge to pull off her scarf and tie it around the younger girl's eyes so she wouldn't have to see the devastation.

Minutes passed, or maybe hours. She couldn't tell. The bodies grew fewer the farther they went—perhaps some had managed to outrun the curse and escape after all. Still, the darkness remained, cloudy and roiling against the barrier.

Aleida looked up, hoping to see the sky or sun somewhere up beyond the mist. She didn't, but something *was* moving up there, its shadow barely visible at the very edge of Lucian's glow. A bird, maybe. But that didn't make sense. No living thing caught in the mist should have been able to survive—she'd seen enough proof of that already.

She stopped to watch it soar smoothly overhead. A long tail trailed behind its wings. A dragon.

A *white* dragon.

No living thing could survive this, but Valkyra was not alive, and surely she would want to inspect this unexpected outcome of her endeavors.

Kesari squeezed her hand. "Why did we stop?"

Aleida barely heard her. She was still watching the space above her head. The flying creature flapped its wings once and wheeled back around, circling lower. Aleida knew what she would see even before it landed on a window ledge mere paces away.

Valkyra's eyes locked onto hers, and she gave that same demure little smile Aleida had come to know and hate. Kesari mumbled something behind her, but the barrier did not waver. If anything, it seemed to grow.

"She can't hurt you." Kesari squeezed her hand again.

"I know." But that knowledge did nothing to cool the heat rushing through her blood. She wasn't worried about Valkyra hurting her. Instead, she seethed with the knowledge that, once again, the dragon was *right there*, and Aleida could do nothing about it. Her smile was a taunting reminder of all the ways she'd failed, of all the power Valkyra still held. And the bodies around them were cruel evidence of the damage she was still capable of causing.

The dragon spread her wings and launched herself into the air. Aleida clenched a fist as she watched her go, then realized she was clutching Kesari's fingers far too tightly in her other hand. She loosened her grip and faced forward again. There was nothing she could do about Valkyra right now. *Nothing*, and as much as that angered her, it was out of her control. She would just have to live with it.

"Come on," she said and took another step forward. "We have to keep going. Kamaal and Mitul must be worried sick by now."

She prayed the mist hadn't reached them, too.

AMAR

FOR WHAT MUST HAVE BEEN THE HUNDREDTH TIME IN THE PAST week alone, Amar wondered if coming to Jakhat had truly been the best choice after all, or if perhaps he would have been better off staying in Valmandi until he managed to convince Bhajan to surrender. The imperial councilors seemed passionately fond of arguing with one another in an effort to gain the empress' praise and attention—a rare thing, especially these days. They reminded him of a pack of starving dogs fighting for scraps, though in some cases, he thought the dogs probably would have been better behaved. The current argument closely resembled one they'd had the day before and centered around what was to be done about King Bhajan. He had yet to officially respond to the news of Savir joining with Jakhat, and while there had been no more news of additional attacks or skirmishes between patrolling soldiers, there had also been no indication of surrender.

Amar had urged them all to bide their time, but some argued that they should increase pressure on Bhajan, perhaps even go so far as to lay siege to Valmandi until he yielded. Even Dashiva and Jasala were split on this issue, with Jasala recently confiding in Amar that her mother was looking to execute Bhajan for treason if he didn't call off this fight by the end of the month. It would be a bold move, and one that could cause half the citizenry to resent the throne. But she made a fair argument about not wanting to seem weak by allowing the king to continue without repercussions when he no longer had any cause to fight.

Amar rubbed at his temples in an attempt to ease the headache that was forming. One of the more long-winded advisors was still rattling on about the optics of attacking Valmandi outright when a long shriek sounded outside. It was perhaps the only thing that could have silenced him so quickly, and soon they were all hurrying to the windows to see what was going on.

"Skies above—what is that?"

Amar stood on his toes to look over the heads and shoulders of those in front of him. The windows had been shut to keep out the morning chill, but through the glass he could see something very large and very dark sweeping up the hillside toward them. It was obviously magic—there was no other reasonable explanation—but he'd never seen anything quite like it. Shadow magic was usually confined to a much smaller area, meant for tricks and illusions and perhaps the odd stealth job. This was much more—something that would have taken several Tarja to conjure in a carefully coordinated strike.

His blood went cold at that thought.

For a moment, the darkness seemed to falter and slow. Instead of flowing only up, it swept out from every direction, including back down and out into the city. Then it was upon them, swallowing up the palace, pressing against the windows, and engulfing everything in shadow.

From the darkness, several disembodied voices spoke in echoing unison. "With the blood of our bodies, we lay this curse upon the imperial palace of Jakhat and all within its walls. A mist of poison shall engulf the palace, killing all who breathe it in, and it shall not disperse until Empress Dashiva falls."

The panic of the imperial council echoed through the room as everyone began talking at once. Amar's heart dropped to the bottom of his stomach. A curse. It shouldn't have been possible. Valmandi never had all of the records Saya brought from Shavhalla, yet they'd found some way to create a curse. Now, they were using it to attack the palace.

That was why Bhajan hadn't surrendered yet. He knew he still had the upper hand, and he'd woven the empress' downfall right into his plan. If the mist really was poisonous, then they were all trapped here in the dark. At least until Dashiva was dead.

Valmandi was going through with their plan to take over the palace—and the empire.

Amar channeled his altma to light the room even as someone screamed. His racing pulse and frantic thoughts made it hard to control the magic, and the light flickered several times before fading out entirely. One of the other Tarja advisors seemed to have caught on to the idea, however, and an orb of bright white light rose to the ceiling.

Amar searched the room for Dashiva. His eyes landed on a body sprawled facedown on the floor, blood spilling out from underneath it. He didn't let his gaze linger long enough to puzzle out who it was. Not the empress or Jasala, and that was all that mattered.

More cries rang out as the other advisors spotted the body. They ran to the door, nearly tripping over each other in their haste to escape. Amar was jostled this way and that, but he stood firm, eyes searching. Someone else was in the room with them—perhaps several someones.

A glimpse of movement caught his attention, opposite the direction everyone else was running. A blade glinted and slashed. The Tarja advisor's light went out as blood spilled from her body.

"Guards! Help!"

Shouts echoed each other as everyone repeated the cry, but the guards outside the council hall were already trying to get in. Thuds and muffled voices came from the other side. They couldn't break through, nor could the horde of advisors push their way out.

"Empress!" Amar called out. "Princess! Where are you?"

He tried to pick out their voices amongst the other cries, but to no avail. Perhaps they were dead already. Perhaps they were both too afraid to answer in case the assassins found them first.

He channeled his altma again. This time, the light held. It was a small, dim thing, but in its illumination, he spotted the same agile figure as before, a dagger gripped tight in each hand. Across the room was a second person. Taller, bulkier. Someone he knew.

Amar didn't have to ask himself how General Muraka had managed to infiltrate the palace unseen. She knew all the secret passages. He'd seen her use them twice before. Now, she stalked toward Empress Dashiva with purposeful strides, hand outstretched.

The second, smaller assassin was moving toward Jasala.

Amar considered his options for a split second, but the choice was easy—one of the easiest he'd ever made.

He channeled his altma and attacked. The light died as he put all his focus and energy into the lightning that burst from his palm. Blue tendrils crackled in the space between himself and one of the attackers, then the room went pitch black.

There was a sharp cry, a *thud* as a body hit the ground, a woman's stifled sob.

In the opposite corner of the room came a pained gasp, a wet squelch, and another *thud.* Amar knew she had fallen even before the darkness began to recede. He had made his choice, let one die so he could save the other.

The conditions for breaking the curse had been met. Empress Dashiva was dead.

AMAR

AMAR WASTED NO TIME IN PUTTING HIMSELF BETWEEN MURAKA AND Jasala.

The mist outside recoiled and dispersed, flooding the room with sunlight once more. Amar pulled the daggers from the fallen assassin's grip and whirled around to face the general.

"You," she hissed, pulling a small throwing knife from her belt. More glinted there, and Amar could already see where this was going. Before she could attack, he flung one of his daggers, channeling his altma to guide it.

Muraka deflected it with her own magic as easily as if it were a child's toy.

Her upper lip curled in a sneer. She raised her hands, and Amar braced himself for whatever was to come. Behind him, Jasala let out a faint whimper. He tried to make a barrier like Kesari had shown him, but he wasn't going to be fast enough. Wasn't going to be strong enough—not to face off against one of the most powerful Tarja warriors in all of Kavora.

But Muraka did not direct her attack at him. Instead, she turned on the advisors all huddled together at the door. Knives went from her belt to her hand and across the room faster than Amar's eyes could track. The panicked cries that had begun to die down intensified once again.

Some of them scattered, but Muraka's aim was deadly. Amar channeled his altma to strike her with lightning. She spared a moment to put up a barrier and continued her onslaught.

The doors to the room flew open, and guards rushed in with weapons drawn. Tarik led the charge. He staggered once as a blade struck him in the side, then continued on, flames swirling around his hands and then shooting outward. Muraka shifted her barrier to block them. Her blades depleted, she began using objects from around the room as projectiles.

A part of Amar wanted to stay and see the fight finished, but his first priority was Jasala. "Tarik!" he called out. "Help me!"

Without waiting for a response, he lifted the princess up by the arm. "We have to hurry. Can you run?"

She nodded shakily, pupils dilated with shock, and he half-dragged her to the door.

"I'm here!" Tarik said from close behind. "I've got your back."

They stepped over bodies and ran out the doors. More corpses lay in the hallway—guards and soldiers, mostly, but also a few servants and other palace habitants. Everywhere Amar looked, crimson spattered the once-pristine white halls. Obviously, the rest of the palace was no more secure than the council chambers. There went his plan to find a safe room for Jasala to hide out in until this was over.

"Where are we going?" Tarik asked, his voice raspy.

"Anywhere but here," Amar said. He kept running, still towing a breathless Jasala along with him.

A woman stepped out from an alcove with her sword raised. She wore the green uniform of a Jakhat soldier, but that didn't stop her from attacking the princess. Tarik lobbed a fireball at her arm before she could get too close, and she went down screaming.

"She was one of ours," Amar said.

"If she was, she's a turncoat," Tarik replied. "Could have been one of Valmandi's soldiers in Jakhat's uniform. That's how they attacked the rest of us out here."

They reached the central staircase and started down. "We'll go to Kamaal's," Amar said. It was the best thing he could think of.

"The studio?" Tarik wheezed. "It's not exactly a fortress."

Amar scoffed. If he had access to a safe fortress right now, he'd count it a miracle. As it was, he would have to make do with his friends, an artist's studio, and the hope that no enemies would think to look for the princess in the city. "Kes and Saya are there. They can help us protect her. And you need a healer."

"Oh, piss off. I'll be fine."

He certainly didn't sound fine, but at least he hadn't lost his cantankerous edge.

Jasala was about to run through the front doors of the palace, but Amar pulled her back. "Wait!" He spared a few moments to strip a nearby soldier of his rifle and cloak. After checking the rifle to make sure it was loaded, he draped the cloak over Jasala, pulling the hood forward as far as it would go to hide her face.

Her cheeks were wet with tears, but she nodded resolutely when he looked her in the eye. "I'm all right. Let's go."

She pushed the door open and immediately let out a gasp, staggering forward like a wounded animal. For a moment, Amar feared she'd been shot by some unseen foe. Then he saw what had caused her reaction, and he nearly fell to his knees himself.

Everyone was dead. *Everyone.*

He should have expected it. That was what the curse had been—a poisonous mist that would kill any who breathed it in. It had surrounded the palace, and anyone caught outside would have succumbed. There were at least a few dozen human bodies in the courtyard alone, along with several birds, a few dogs, and a horse.

How far did this go? How wide was the darkness' reach?

Tarik walked past them with wide eyes, one arm wrapped around his stomach. The sleeve and everything beneath it were dark and wet. The fact that he was still on his feet was miraculous, and Amar knew he must be channeling altma to keep himself upright.

"How could he do this?" Tarik whispered. "King Bhajan—he would *never*. I didn't think…" He shook his head.

"We need to get you to Kesari," Amar said. He had half a mind to try healing Tarik himself right here and now, but he had no idea where to begin and didn't want to make things worse.

The guard acted as if he hadn't heard. He took two steps down the stone stairs, then stopped and sat down, shoulders hunched. "He would never," he said again. "It can't have been his idea."

"He at least approved it," Jasala said. "That's worse."

Tarik reached up to grab Amar's hand, eyes glassy, fingers warm and slick. "You know him. He's a *good* man. He wouldn't have."

"You have to get up." Amar tugged at his arm with both hands. "We can't stay. Your wound—"

"My wound," Tarik scoffed. "My *death*, more like."

"Stop that!" Amar snapped, furious that the guard wasn't even going to try and fight for his own life. "It's not very far. Come on, get up!"

Tarik didn't move. "You go. I'm staying here."

"I'm not leaving you!" He couldn't, not when Tarik had done everything in his power to protect Amar time and time again.

"Don't be stubborn." He pointed to Jasala. "Get her out of here. I've done my part. You're on your own now." He pulled his arm away from the wound in his side, and blood pooled out onto his lap.

The sight of it brought to Amar's mind memories of hundreds of comrades killed in dozens of battles throughout his many past lifetimes. A burning spread behind his eyes, and he forced down a lump like hot coal in his throat.

"Might see you later," Tarik said, curling in on himself even more. "Might try to find Bhajan, once I'm a spirit."

"It's too far," Amar said. "You'll fade before you reach him."

"Still, have to try." His voice was growing weaker. He lifted his gaze to Jasala. "He's not a monster. Don't let this ruin our chance at peace."

She pressed her lips together and said nothing.

Voices sounded from somewhere in the distance, and footsteps echoed from around the other side of the palace.

"Go," Tarik said. "Leave me."

Amar didn't want to, but the guard was right. Getting Jasala to safety was most important, and right now, there were too many enemies in the palace to know who they could trust. She was already moving, descending the stairs two at a time.

"I'm sorry," Amar whispered to Tarik.

"It's been an honor to serve you, Your Highness."

He slumped onto his side and went still.

KESARI

KESARI FELT HER STRENGTH WANING WITH EVERY PASSING MINUTE as she fought to maintain the barrier shielding her and Aleida from the poisonous mist. She forced herself to take one more step, then another, and another. It helped not to look at the dead bodies all around them, but that couldn't stop her from thinking about them, and if she wasn't careful, those thoughts would overwhelm her. Rather than trying to push her emotions away—a futile endeavor—she held them alongside her concentration on her magic. As tragic as the situation was, the knowledge of what could happen to herself and Aleida kept her motivated and focused. She wouldn't let the two of them end up like those poor souls.

When she was almost certain she could go on no further, the darkness suddenly began to give way, and the sun shone bright above them once more.

"Did we finally make it out?" she asked.

"That, or the curse was broken," Lucian replied.

Aleida frowned. "But that would mean Empress Dashiva is dead."

"Maybe it was a defective curse. Which seems highly likely, considering how it backfired."

Backfired. Kesari shuddered. That was the perfect word to describe what had happened. But *why*? What had gone so wrong to cause this?

Unless it had been intentional from the start, but she didn't think that was the case either. Curses had to be specific, their terms spoken aloud and sealed with a binding of blood and jhivan by the ones casting it. If the Tarja had wanted to attack the city, they wouldn't have targeted the palace alone when speaking their curse.

Those questions could wait, though. Cautiously, Kesari released her altma. The barrier slipped away, and she inhaled the fresh air, still half expecting to drop dead. She almost laughed aloud when she didn't.

Aleida started walking, and Kesari hurried to catch up. She knew where they were headed—and why they were in such a hurry—even before Aleida asked. "Do you think everyone else is—?"

"They're fine," she said. She refused to believe otherwise. Judging by the lack of dead bodies in the street ahead, the mist hadn't spread this far, and they still had some distance to go before they reached Kamaal's studio. Still, she wouldn't rest easy until she saw for herself.

With the darkness gone, people began to exit the buildings where they'd taken shelter. The farther they walked, the more crowded the streets grew until it seemed like everyone in the city was outside, talking to each other and trying to figure out what was going on. Minutes later, soldiers appeared, urging everyone to head back inside and stay there until further notice. Kesari and Aleida were stopped by one passing patrol and had to explain that they were on their way home before they were allowed to pass.

They came around the bend to the street where Kamaal lived and found it deserted of all but a squad of soldiers hurrying in the opposite direction. Aleida ran to the door and flung it open with Kesari close behind. They were immediately swallowed up in a tangle of arms and bodies as Saya, Mitul, and Kamaal all came to embrace them.

"Oh, you're all right!" Kamaal said. "We were so worried."

"Us too," said Aleida.

Mitul took a step back and looked them over from head to toe. "You're not hurt at all? You're both shaking. Aleida, your face is so pale."

"We're fine," Kesari said, but her voice came out high and tremulous. Her own and her friends' survival had been her only concern until now. Knowing they were safe opened the floodgates to the panic she'd managed to keep in check thus far. Her lungs suddenly felt too small to hold the air her body needed, her chest too tight to let her heart beat a normal rhythm.

"Come sit down, both of you." Kamaal ushered them to a couple of chairs near the window. "I'll make some tea. You look like you could use it."

"Do you know what happened out there?" Saya asked. "All we could see was the palace. It disappeared in a black cloud all of the sudden."

"You weren't there," Kesari said, simultaneously relieved and worried for Amar, who most certainly would have been inside the palace during the attack.

"No, I was already on my way here when it happened. People are saying there was a magical attack in the streets as well."

Kesari, Lucian, and Aleida shared what they'd witnessed while Kamaal made their tea. The others' faces darkened as they listened to the grim tale, and Mitul kept looking out the window toward the palace. Kesari knew he must be worried about Amar, too.

"It was her," Aleida said. "Valkyra. We saw her."

Mitul gave her an alarmed look. "Did she see you?"

Aleida nodded and said nothing more, frowning down at her shaking hands wrapped around her cup. Until now, Kesari had allowed her to do most of the talking, content to sip her tea and ease her own nerves. She took over the telling of their story now.

"She watched us for a little while. She looked…"

"Proud," Aleida finished quietly.

"Wretched bitch," Lucian muttered.

Saya tilted her head back and said something vulgar in Sularan. "I never should have brought those records from Shavhalla. Amar was right. Why didn't I listen to him?"

"You couldn't have known," Mitul said. "This isn't your fault."

She sighed. "Fault or not, the outcome is the same. We've had our problems with the Kavorans for years, but I never wanted to see them suffer like *this*."

Lucian drifted a little closer to the warrior. "They did this to themselves, Saya. I don't think anyone wanted this, but they chose to tamper with magic they didn't fully understand, and it went wrong."

Why, though? Kesari was still trying to puzzle that part out. A single Tarja was capable of creating a curse, and they'd had at least three working together in unison. Likely more, given that the dark cloud had swept in from so many directions. The red flare they'd seen could have been used to coordinate others, signaling them when it was time to begin. Which meant they would have had more than enough power to channel the altma required for a curse, even if it was still a new and unpracticed skill. And they may well have been using mesala to further amplify their magic.

Had it simply been *too much* power? Or was there something more at play?

A sudden noise at the door made her jump. Kamaal had barred it shut, but someone was trying to force their way in. Kesari conjured a ball of fire in her palms, ready to hurl it at whoever was outside. Kamaal gave her a look as he went to the door, and she realized her reaction was probably more than was warranted, a result of fear and heightened sensitivity after what she'd experienced. She let the flames die down but kept a wary eye on the door as he opened it.

Two figures hurried inside. One was Amar, and Mitul immediately went to embrace him. "What are you doing here? We thought you were in the palace. I worried that—"

He stopped short when the second person lowered the hood of their cloak. Kamaal started to bow to Princess Jasala, but she raised a hand to stop him and made a bow herself. "Please, the honor is mine. I'm sorry to intrude like this, but we needed somewhere to go, and Amar thought this was the safest place I could be."

Kesari exchanged a look with Saya, who frowned deeply. Things must be very dire at the palace indeed for the princess to be safer here than she was within its walls and guarded by those sworn to protect her.

Kesari stood, offering her chair to Jasala, who took it graciously.

"Can I get you anything?" Kamaal asked. "Tea? Food?"

"Don't trouble yourself. A quiet place to rest and gather my thoughts is more than adequate for now."

"What happened?" Mitul asked.

"You saw the darkness," Amar said, peering out the window to scan the street. "A curse. Killed anyone who breathed it in. Covered the palace and some of the inner city. There must be hundreds dead."

"Yes, we know. Kesari and Aleida got caught in it."

Amar spared a glance back at them before returning his gaze to the window. "And you survived?"

"Kes made a barrier," Lucian explained. "What else happened at the palace? Why did you bring Her Highness here?"

Amar gave a brief summary of the attack in the council chambers. The news that Dashiva was dead came as a shock, even though Kesari had known that might be a possibility. With everything else that seemed to have gone wrong, she'd hoped the curse had faded because of some malfunction, not because its conditions for breaking had actually been fulfilled.

He described how the palace guards had been overwhelmed and slain in a covert attack. "Some of Valmandi's soldiers must have infiltrated the palace. And Muraka could have had others ready to turn. She'd been working with Valmandi to orchestrate this for months, but when she fled the palace, I didn't think she still had the means to execute her plan."

"None of us did," said Jasala. "And I certainly didn't think Bhajan would go through with it—not now."

Amar finally pulled his focus away from the window, seemingly content that they hadn't been seen or followed. "Tarik helped us get out. But he was wounded, knew he was going to die. We had to leave him."

"Skies, I'm sorry, Amar," Mitul said. "He was a good man."

"I just don't understand why he would do this," Amar said. "King Bhajan, I mean. I thought he was a good man, too. This is...monstrous."

"If it makes things easier, we don't think the curse was intended to kill so many innocent civilians," Lucian said.

Amar huffed. "No. Just anyone who worked near the palace. The guards and advisors and servants trying to do their jobs. They didn't deserve this." His brows furrowed. "But you're saying the curse went wrong somehow?"

"How can you know that?" Jasala asked.

"The way it was spoken," Lucian said. "We heard the Tarja casting it. They only meant to surround the *palace* in darkness and poison, and for a little while, it looked like they were successful. Then it started to spread, worked its way back into the city."

Why had it gone wrong, though?

The answer didn't really matter, of course; understanding why wasn't going to bring back all the people who had died. But Kesari had always been profoundly curious about magic and how it all worked, and something about this nagged at her.

"They never should have experimented with something so dangerous," Lucian hissed angrily. "There were too many unknown variables. Foolish, reckless."

Unknown variables meant missing information.

Perhaps information they never would have had access to because it was part of the Shavhallan records they'd never seen. The part that had been burned once Zefar turned it over to Saya.

And the single page Kesari had torn out, hoping it would be useful in finding a way to break Amar's curse.

While the others continued talking, she slipped away, heading outside and around to the guesthouse behind Kamaal's studio. Lucian hovered faithfully behind, and by the time she reached the door, Saya was tagging along, too.

"What are we doing?" Lucian asked as she began to rummage through the room looking for all of her things. She'd taken the liberty of unpacking most of them once they arrived, and in the intervening weeks, they had spread to every corner of the room she and Saya shared.

She stuck her hands into the pockets of a pair of trousers. "I'm looking for…oh, here it is!" Triumphantly, she held aloft the torn page she'd been searching for. It was quite crinkled and worn by now, much of the writing smudged but still legible. She spread it out and scanned the page until she found the part she was looking for, checking to make sure it was the same as she remembered.

"Look at this," she said, pointing to the familiar line on the page and reading it aloud. "*A Tarja must draw on the blood of their own body and the jhivan of their spirit to provide the power needed for an effective curse.*"

Saya frowned. "I don't understand."

"They didn't draw from the right power source," Kesari said. She made a slicing gesture across her palm. "They got the blood part right. They cut into their own skin and said the correct words—*with the blood of our bodies.* But jhivan—they never said it. They never used it to channel their altma and power the curse."

"I'm sorry," Lucian said. "I think I'm still missing something."

"I always wanted to ask Amar what that word meant, and I did, while you were gone." She was practically buzzing with the excitement of solving this riddle and being able to share it with him. "Jhivan isn't altma, it's something else. The energy of life, something woven through all three of the other elements we try to balance when we use our magic. Mind, body, spirit, and connecting them all, *life*. Jhivan."

"It's almost like a Bond," Lucian muttered.

"What do you mean?"

"You get to channel altma through me, and I get to share your life. A Bond isn't a curse, exactly, but it lasts in a way other types of magic don't, and it's broken when the living partner dies. Maybe that's jhivan—the same energy that fuels a curse."

All of this talk about their Bond and he was missing the point. "Yes, but don't you see? They didn't say that part. They missed it. They didn't know, because they never saw *this*." She waved the paper in front of him.

Lucian began to mumble the words the Tarja in the city had spoken. "*With the blood of our bodies, we lay this curse*…Kes, you could be right."

She smiled, but that smile quickly died away as she realized once more that it didn't matter. Solving this puzzle was meaningless. And as far as she could tell, there wasn't even anything in it that would help Amar.

"You're right," said Saya, her voice quiet and heavy. "That must have been the missing piece."

"Possibly," Lucian said. "There's no way to test our theory—not safely, anyway."

"What do you think, though? You're the expert among us."

Lucian was quiet for a few seconds, then said, "Yes. I believe Kesari's right. If a skilled enough Tarja were to test this out, perhaps using mesala to amplify their power, I suspect it would work. They could create a curse."

The weight of that realization settled over them with a somber silence. For five centuries, curses had been nonexistent. Now, they might be coming back, and the final detail needed to make them successful was right here on a scrap of paper in Kesari's hands. How long before someone figured out that information on their own? How many more 'experiments' gone awry before curses fully returned to Erythyr?

"Burn it," Saya said, nodding to the page. "Destroy it, and we *never* speak of this to anyone."

"I don't know if that will be enough," Kesari said.

"Maybe not, but it's all we have control over right now. I made a mistake bringing that information out of Shavhalla, and Zefar made a mistake in trading it to Valmandi. I can't stop what's already been done, but I can at least do this. Please, Kes, burn it."

That was all the prompting she needed. She lit a spark with her fingertips and watched as the paper ignited and curled and burnt away to ashes.

AMAR

THE SOLDIERS PATROLLING JAKHAT MAINTAINED A STRICT CURFEW for the remainder of the day, forcing everyone to remain indoors until further notice. Princess Jasala was understandably eager to return to the palace and attend to the numerous duties and responsibilities that awaited her as the new empress of Kavora, but Amar convinced her to wait long enough to send Lucian first. He was gone for a couple of hours, by which time it was growing dark, but he brought back a wealth of valuable information.

"They've got General Muraka locked up in the dungeons," he said. "Dosed with daravak and looking pretty beat up."

Jasala's shoulders seemed to slacken a little at this news. "They were unsuccessful in taking the palace then, she and her conspirators?"

"Correct. The empress' body has been moved to her chambers. Discreetly, it seems. Only a handful of people know she's dead, or that you're missing. They're very worried, though. Someone named Taj appears to be running things in your absence."

Jasala gave a small smile at this. "One of my hand-picked advisors. Good. He's loyal, level-headed. What of the others who helped Muraka?"

"They're interviewing everyone, rounding up those suspected of treason and anyone who can't verify that they're actually enlisted with

Jakhat's military. No one's been executed, but the cells are certainly filling up. Not only in the palace, but throughout the city."

Jasala turned to Amar. "I really need to get back. Will you take me?"

"That may not be the best idea," Lucian cut in. "Amar, there's talk going around the palace that you were involved, that this was Valmandi's plan to put Prince Savir on the throne all along. They're looking for you."

As upsetting as this was, Amar wasn't surprised. Most of the advisors who could have vouched for his efforts to defend the princess against Muraka were dead, and those who weren't may have been too panicked to make much sense of whatever they'd witnessed in that room. Despite the loyalty he'd pledged to the empress and her heir, he hadn't had enough time to earn the council's trust, nor anyone else's. Their suspicions of him were understandable.

"I'll take you," he told Jasala. "But we'll have to go quietly, and we'll be breaking their curfew. I don't dare hand you over to the first soldiers we come across and blindly trust that they'll get you back safely."

"Nor would I want you to."

"We'll come, too," Kesari said. "Lucian can scout ahead for a safe path, make sure we don't run into any soldiers."

Saya stepped forward. "You have my bow and my blades at your service as well, Your Highness."

"Thank you," the princess said.

They waited a few more hours until night had fully settled over the city. Mitul, Kamaal, and Aleida wished them all good luck and sent them out onto the streets. Lucian led them to a shadowed alleyway, and they waited there while he went ahead to determine their next best route.

They continued this way through the city for some time, stopping to wait in some hidden place while soldiers passed them by and proceeding only when Lucian indicated it was safe to do so. It made for a slow journey, and the palace felt farther away than it ever had before, but Amar didn't dare take any chances. The country had been destabilized enough as it was. If something happened to Jasala, things would get significantly worse.

They came to a more heavily patrolled area, and Lucian warned it might be a while before he made it back. He left them in an alley between two empty shops, and Amar sent Saya to one end and Kesari to the other to keep watch while he and Jasala waited in the center.

After a few minutes, she spoke to him in a whisper. "There's something I've been wanting to ask you, Amar."

He almost shut down the conversation; this didn't seem the time or place. But they'd probably be here a while longer, and it might not hurt to hear her out. "All right."

"Why me?" she asked. "You could have saved my mother. You *should* have—she's the empress. So why me, and not her?"

The question surprised him. Did she really not know? Did she not understand how easy the choice had been, how obviously right to save her and let Dashiva die?

He didn't quite know how to explain it in a way that wouldn't sound cruel, but he'd been honest with her so far. There was no reason to lie now.

"I know she was your mother, Your Highness," he whispered, "but she was terrible. Anyone with sense and a decent understanding of you both could see that you would make a better ruler."

Jasala said nothing for a few seconds, and Amar couldn't make out her expression in the dark. Perhaps she was angry that he'd spoken ill of the late empress, and perhaps there had been a more tactful way to put it. But he needed her to understand why he didn't regret his decision, why he would do it all the same again if he had the chance.

"My mother was strong," Jasala said. "She brought peace to Kavora."

"Only after continuing a tradition of war and conquest. I know you haven't forgotten Vis so easily. Before that, she killed Prince Savir to secure her throne and her legacy. And Saya was right about the agreements dishonored between the Sularans and your people. I see only conflict and suffering in those choices—at least for those on the other side. The peace you speak of is an illusion."

"And you think I will be different?"

"Yes," he replied easily. "You have honor, integrity. You care about people."

"Your assessment of my character could very well be wrong."

Amar smirked. Was she trying to convince him that he'd chosen poorly? "Perhaps. I've certainly been around long enough to see those in power disappoint their subjects repeatedly. But I've also seen enough good in the world to hope for something better."

"Something better," she repeated inquisitively.

He nodded. "I didn't see it in your mother, but I think I see it in you. If you prove me wrong, well, I'll still be glad I took the chance."

She went quiet again for a while, and when she spoke next, Amar thought he could hear a tremor in her voice. "She should have lived. I'm not ready."

Amar reached out gently until his fingertips found hers. She clasped his hand, and he squeezed once before dropping it. "You're ready enough. That's all you need. You'll figure the rest out as you go." It was something Valkyra had told him, and as much as he hated the source of the advice, it felt applicable here.

"With your help?" she asked.

"With whatever help I can offer," he agreed. "If you still want me for an advisor, you have me."

They waited for a few more minutes before Lucian returned. Their path forward required absolute silence so as not to alert any passing patrols. It took them another hour to reach the road leading up to the palace, at which point there was nothing to do but finally make their presence known.

Amar led the way with Jasala right behind, Kesari and Saya flanking each side. The guards assigned to that area surrounded them immediately and would have arrested Amar if Jasala had not spoken up and told them to stop. They were surprised when she spoke, clearly not expecting to find her in a soldier's cloak being escorted though the streets of the city in the middle of the night. She bid a pair of soldiers to lead Saya, Kesari, and Lucian back home so they wouldn't be stopped by any patrols, then ordered a carriage be brought for her and Amar.

Only when they were safely enclosed within it and shielded from outside view did Jasala finally allow herself to cry, tears running down her cheeks in shining rivulets. Her shoulders trembled, but she made no sound, and by the time they reached the palace's front doors, she had dried her face and composed herself perfectly once more.

AMAR

AMAR DIDN'T SLEEP THAT NIGHT. JASALA REQUESTED THAT HE STAY with her while she saw to the many tasks requiring her attention, and who was he to refuse her? They started by speaking to one of the advisors, Taj, who regarded Amar with great suspicion and seemed eager to sweep the princess away from him. He quickly changed tack once Jasala snapped at him that they had no time for such misgivings and told of how Amar had saved her life.

"My apologies, Savir," the man said with a contrite bow. "It seems we should be thanking you, but you have to understand—Valmandi's attack has thrown us all into a panic. We wanted answers, and the most logical explanation seemed…well…"

"I understand," Amar said.

"As valid as that initial concern may have been, it ends now," said Jasala. "No one wants answers more than me, but they have to be the *right* answers. Otherwise, we're wasting our time. Wouldn't you agree, Taj?"

"Of course, Your Highness."

"Good. Tell me everything you know and all that's happened here since the attack."

He did, bringing her quickly up to speed on the current state of affairs. Half of the advisors serving on the imperial council were dead, including some of the members Jasala herself had appointed. At least two of those positions required immediate replacement, and Jasala wasted no time in naming suitable candidates and ordering that offers be extended to them.

"Yes, I *know* it's the middle of the night," she said in response to the uncertain looks of the messengers she'd given these instructions to. "Wake them up! We obviously have a crisis to manage here, and I need all the help I can get."

Next, Taj informed them that General Muraka was safely in custody and being interrogated by some of the finest investigators Jakhat had. So far, that questioning had yielded nothing they didn't already know or suspect. She admitted to working under orders from King Bhajan and had confirmed that the cloud of poison was Valmandi's attempt at a curse. She also acknowledged that it was never supposed to spread through the city but, according to Taj, "she didn't seem particularly disappointed when she heard that news."

"I'm not surprised," Jasala said, wrinkling her nose. "The woman's always had a nasty streak."

"What would you like us to do with her, Your Highness?"

Jasala considered this for a few moments. "Savir, do you have any reason to believe she has additional information we need?"

"She may," Amar said, "though I sincerely doubt she'd tell us."

She turned to Taj. "Have the investigator finish questioning her, then find a few Tarja willing to assist with her punishment in the morning. I don't want her coming back as a Spirit Tarja."

"You mean to kill her then?" the advisor asked.

"Yes. It seems we'll be holding a funeral, a coronation, and an execution all in one day."

He lifted his brows at this, but said only, "Yes, Your Highness." Then he shuffled away to the cells to relay her instructions.

The princess went to a nearby window and looked out over the city below. Most of the buildings were dark, though several lights could still be seen bobbing through the streets as soldiers went about their duties. Amar went to stand beside her.

"Big day tomorrow," he said. "But you're right to get through it all at once, I think."

Her shoulders relaxed a little. "I needed to hear that. My mother would be absolutely *livid* about not being honored properly."

By longstanding Kavoran tradition, a new ruler could not be crowned until the old one was properly laid to rest. Typically, this involved a two-day period of mourning, but in the middle of a war and after such an outright declaration of hostilities still to come, they didn't have that luxury. Jasala needed to take her throne as soon as possible and fill the void left by Valmandi's attack. They could not afford to appear weak or wounded. Not now.

"Your mother's not here having to make the hard decisions," he reminded her. "You are."

She kneaded the tension in her brow with long fingers. "I honestly don't know whether she'd be proud of me or disappointed by the way I've handled things today. I keep wanting to ask, and then I remember I can't. How foolish is that?"

"It's not. Not at all." He should know; he'd lost enough people to be very familiar with the feeling she was describing.

"She didn't like most of my ideas, you know. She always thought I was too soft and tolerant. Now we've been attacked in our home, and the last thing we need is soft, but here I am. The only option."

"The *best* option. Besides, I've seen nothing but strength from you today in handling all this."

"Well, that makes one of us," she said shakily. "Skies, I'm so exhausted I could collapse right here and sleep for days."

Amar smiled. "I think you can spare a few hours. Rest might do you some good."

She closed her eyes for a moment, then shook her head and turned away from the window. "Not yet. Let's get through tonight, and then tomorrow, and maybe sometime after that, I can rest a while."

The next morning dawned with a funeral pyre in front of Jakhat's oldest temple, a beautiful building that had been kept up immaculately over the years and where all of Kavora's rulers traditionally had their final rites performed. Smoke rose to fill the pink and orange sky, and Amar stood beside Jasala before the crowd that had gathered to pay their last respects.

Once the pyre had burned away, Dashiva's remains were cleared and put into an urn, which was then ceremoniously passed on to Jasala. She rode back to the palace in a carriage to change out of her simple, white mourning attire into something more suitable for her coronation. This also took place at the temple, with Jasala crowned by the High Magistrate and the Tarja priestess of greatest seniority. It was a quick and somber affair without much fanfare, unlike most coronations past. The citizens bowed to Jasala and she bowed back, and when it was over, the crowd dispersed with quiet murmurings.

Then came the execution, which was to be a public spectacle, given the nature of Muraka's crimes and her position in Jakhat's military. Amar suspected the turnout exceeded even that for Jasala's coronation. The location had been specifically appointed for such events, though it had not been used for some time. A raised stone platform stood in an open area colloquially known as Widowmaker's Square. Amar vaguely recalled that he and Mitul had performed here a few times after they first met, until another musician told them the place was haunted and that to sing there was to invite evil into one's life. Amar had never believed in such superstitions, but Mitul had still been young enough to be rather terrified by the notion.

Amar did sense a sort of eerie feel about the place now, but he suspected that had more to do with what was coming than it was about any ghosts of the past. He didn't care to watch the execution, but it would have been notable for him not to make an appearance. He escorted Jasala to the seat that had been placed for her, allowing himself to be seen by the crowd. Then he left her to the care of her guards and the attention of her other advisors, slipping away to a quieter alcove off to the side of a nearby shop.

A wagon pulled up beside the new empress' carriage, looking rather small and drab. Half a dozen Tarja soldiers immediately surrounded it. They roughly hauled Muraka out from the back, her head covered in a dark hood and her hands bound tight in front of her.

The crowd jeered and booed as she was led to the stone platform. Some threw rocks but were quickly stopped by soldiers, presumably so that none of the projectiles would hit the Tarja escorting her. Muraka herself was eliciting no sympathy from anyone, nor did she deserve it.

She may not have been solely responsible for yesterday's attack, but she was certainly the face of it now, and it was likely that most of the onlookers knew someone who'd died from that curse.

Amar crossed his arms and scuffed his boot across the cobblestone. Executions were always such an unpleasant affair, but this one had been unavoidable. He watched as the disgraced general was shoved roughly up onto the platform. The executioner, clad in robes of red and white, stepped forward to pull off Muraka's hood. This drew more angry shouts from the crowd, but Amar only scowled. She had clearly been beaten extensively, her face a mass of dark bruises and bloody cuts, new wounds open over old scars. She looked defeated, her confidence reduced to resignation as she stood before this mass of fury and hatred with slumped shoulders and downcast eyes.

"Looks like she had a bad night," said a low voice to Amar's left.

He turned to see Tarik's spirit there. "What are you doing here? I thought you were going to try and reach Bhajan."

He shrugged. "You were right. It's too far. I wouldn't make it before I faded, and even if I did, I don't think I'd know what to say to him." His pale blue form was already fuzzy at the edges, the details of his face blurred.

"You don't want to make a Bond with anyone?" Amar asked. "Live on a while longer?"

"I've lived long enough. My time's over, and I died fighting to protect someone, as it should be. Don't see the point in lingering."

The executioner began to call out Muraka's crimes, pausing after every one to let the crowd's response die down enough that he could continue.

"I did want to see this, though." Tarik gestured to the scene before them. "I always thought these Jakhat executions were so barbaric, but I get it now. It's kind of cathartic, isn't it?"

Amar couldn't quite bring himself to agree, but he did understand what Tarik was saying. There was no real justice for something like yesterday's attack, but if this was the closest they were going to get, he could see why people might want it.

"You know Bhajan's going to have to face the executioner, too."

Tarik let out a faint sigh and crossed his arms. "That's up to the new empress, I guess. And maybe you. She listens to you."

"I can't talk her out of it. It's not my place, wouldn't be right."

"And you think killing him is going to make things right?"

"Not entirely, but it would be fair."

"Fair." The guard scoffed at the word.

"Hundreds of people are dead, Tarik. Either Bhajan ordered that attack himself, or he sanctioned it. He can't escape blame, even if he didn't intend for things to be this bad. Such is the burden of power, is it not?"

"And what about *your* burden?" Tarik asked. "Your responsibility in all of this? What price do you pay for all the lives lost in this war you started?"

Amar ran a hand over his face. He had no good response to that. So far, he hadn't had to sacrifice much at all—not compared to so many others.

They both shifted their attention back to Muraka. The Tarja who had brought her forward now stood in a semi-circle behind her, hands outstretched as the executioner closed in. Amar had seen enough Tarja executions to know they were draining her of whatever altma remained within her and would continue doing so until she died. It was what should have happened to Nandini Kumar, an assurance against the executed remaining in the world as a Spirit Tarja.

The executioner pressed a hand against Muraka's chest, directly over her heart. The watching crowd fell so still that Amar could hear nothing but the flags hung throughout the square rippling in the breeze. Muraka's eyes fluttered closed, and as she swayed and sagged, the executioner caught her with his free hand and lowered her gently down. He stayed there with her, palm still pressed to her heart, for at least a minute more, making sure her heart had truly stopped for good.

"And that's that," Tarik muttered. "A skilled warrior dead, caught with the wrong allegiances in the wrong place, wrong time. You know, if that attack had come before you left Valmandi, she might have been called a hero, and we'd be riding into Jakhat triumphant to put the rightful heir on the throne."

"You never believed I was the rightful heir," Amar said.

"I did, for a short time. Bhajan did."

The crowd began to disperse, and guards escorted Jasala back to her carriage. Amar had ridden with her, and when she scanned the crowd, he knew it was his face she was searching for.

"What do you want me to do about Bhajan?" he asked. "What is it that you think I *can* do?"

"He's lost his way," Tarik said, "but I have to believe he's still the same good man I knew and served most of my life. He wouldn't have wanted all those people dead."

"I know that."

"Then save him. Please. Whatever that looks like."

"Tarik, I'm sorry, I don't think—"

"I'm not asking you to withhold justice or spare him of all consequence. But surely there's a middle ground somewhere." He reached out as if to grab Amar's sleeve, but his semi-translucent hand went right through it. "I can't protect him anymore," he said in a lower voice. "That was all I was ever supposed to do, until he asked me to protect you instead. Just tell me you'll try, in honor of whatever service I was to you. Please."

"You have my word," Amar said. "I'll try."

"Thank you."

Jasala leaned out of her carriage window, still waiting for him. Amar turned back to Tarik. "You should come with me. You could talk to Jasala yourself, make a case for showing mercy to Bhajan."

He shook his head. "It would look like begging, coming from me. No, I think I'm done with this city. I certainly don't want it to be the last thing I see before I leave this world entirely." He cocked his head thoughtfully. "I'll head north, find somewhere quiet in the mountains with lots of trees and birds."

"That sounds perfect," Amar said, and it did. He suddenly felt very old and very tired, the weight of centuries bearing down on his spirit full force in a way he didn't often sense. How much longer would it be before his own soul finally found its way to the afterlife?

Not yet. He still had too much to do, too much to atone for.

"Goodbye, Tarik," he said. "Thank you for everything, and I'm sorry."

"There's nothing to be sorry for," he said. Then he walked around the corner and was gone.

Part III

The Bond Between Two Souls

ALEIDA

ALEIDA LOOKED AT THE COLORFUL PAPER FLOWERS AND LANTERNS she and Kesari had spent hours making, and instead of feeling excitement and joy, she wanted to cry. Everything had been ruined, and the decorations were now useless because there wasn't going to be a party. How could there be when the entire city was in mourning? It wouldn't be proper.

That only upset her even more, because what kind of terrible person thought about something as silly as a party when hundreds of people were dead?

It was never *just* a silly party though. It was a celebration of something beautiful and happy and pure. Maybe she should have known better than to count on that. After all, experience had shown her repeatedly that happiness was only something to be ripped away, and that made her want to cry, too.

Mostly out of spite, she held all her tears in and began smashing the stupid decorations instead.

"What are you doing?"

She stopped, her foot raised and poised to come down on a pale-yellow lantern. She turned to see a wide-eyed Kesari standing in the doorway with Saya and Lucian behind her. Her face instantly grew hot.

She felt like a child caught in the middle of a tantrum. "I—sorry. I figured…well, we don't really need them anymore, do we?"

"Why not?" Kesari asked. "Did something happen?"

"No, but we can't really have a party now."

Kes frowned. "Oh. Right. Bad timing, I guess."

"What do you mean?" Lucian asked. "Because of the attack?"

Aleida nodded.

He snorted, his flames curling and a few sparks flying free. "Well, that's silly. Something bad happened, and that means we're not allowed to celebrate anything good that might be happening, too?"

"Doesn't it seem a little inappropriate?"

"Oh, I don't know. To be honest, I've never cared much about society's standards for what was appropriate and what wasn't. So long as you're not hurting anyone, that is. Love seems at least as worthy of recognition as tragedy, and frankly, we could all use a little joy right now."

"That's true," Saya said, and Kesari nodded in agreement.

Lucian drifted closer to Aleida, hovering in front of her at eye level. "We don't have to do it, of course, but it would be a shame to let all this effort and planning go to waste. It was your idea, though. What feels right to *you*?"

Aleida considered this for a while, surveying the damage she'd managed to do in only a few minutes. Many of the decorations she and Kesari had put together were crumpled, but most seemed salvageable. She could easily imagine what they'd look like draped from the ceiling in the studio, and she could picture the joyful looks on Mitul and Kamaal's faces when they saw them. The mere idea of it warmed her. She was doing this for *them*, and regardless of whatever else was happening, they deserved a night of happiness and recognition.

Perhaps joy and grief could coexist. Perhaps there was room to celebrate love and commitment even in the midst of grief.

"I think I still want to do it," she said. "It feels right."

"Agreed," said Saya, offering a smile. "Come on. I'll help you get these cleaned up."

Two days passed in quiet solemnity as the city collectively mourned those killed in the attack. On the third day, funeral pyres burned, filling the sky with gray smoke and a distinctive smell. Kamaal and Mitul made the rounds to visit friends who had lost loved ones, and Aleida went with them in a show of support. It was a somber affair, and by the time they arrived back home, she only wanted to sleep off the melancholy feeling that had come from witnessing so much pain and devastation.

The following morning, Kesari and Lucian began to prepare for their long journey home. They wouldn't leave for a few more days still, not until after the party, but Kesari seemed eager to have everything ready. She talked about her family and the things she was looking forward to telling them and doing with them when she got home. Aleida tried not to think too much about the impending goodbye. It already hurt more than she'd expected, even after Kesari promised she'd come back to Kavora to visit them all soon, perhaps even bringing her family with her.

That got Aleida thinking about what she would do once Valkyra was no longer a threat. She'd never really considered it since Tyrus had died. Perhaps she'd go back to Chatanda, at least for a little while. She wanted to see where her brother had been laid to rest and pay her respects properly. But that wasn't home; it never had been. As much as she appreciated Hasan, she'd never really let herself get attached to him or to Chatanda itself.

She didn't have a *place* to call home anymore, but she did have people. Two people, specifically. But they were about to be newlyweds and might not appreciate her loitering around. Not that they'd ever tell her to leave but…well, she didn't feel right about staying, either. She'd spent so long on her own, always finding a way to get by without asking for anyone else's help. She knew she could count on Mitul and Kamaal for anything, but the idea of relying on them felt uncomfortable, almost shameful.

Maybe she'd find her own place here in Jakhat, close enough to Mitul and Kamaal that she wouldn't have to deal with another painful goodbye, but where she could still thrive in her own independence. She could work, build a new life for herself. Doing what, she had no idea, but she'd have to make a living somehow.

It was strange to imagine a future where she settled down somewhere, her days playing out peacefully until she grew old. She'd had so little peace since the invasion of Vis, she could hardly even remember what it felt like. Even so, she wanted that for herself, however she managed to come by it.

The following evening, Amar came by to check on them. Kamaal invited him to stay for dinner and he was happy to do so. Before they sat down to eat, he pulled Aleida aside, out of earshot from Mitul and Kamaal.

"I've found a couple of people who are willing to come and play some music for the party," he said. "Is that all right, or did you have something else planned already?"

The fact that he'd simply assumed it was still happening made her smile. It felt like a reassurance that she'd made the right choice in deciding to go through with it after all. "That will be perfect."

He glanced over to where the two men were cooking together, dancing around each other as they moved about their task with gentle touches and occasional laughter. "I should be thanking you. They deserve all the joy in the world. It's a beautiful thing you're doing for them."

She blushed a little at the compliment. Kamaal called out that supper was ready, and they all squeezed together around the low table.

As they passed the food around and ate, Amar gave them a few updates about his work at the palace and developments that had occurred since the attack. The Tarja scholars they'd consulted agreed that the curse Valmandi had attempted must have gone awry, and the deaths of so many had likely been unintentional. Several more accomplices to General Muraka's plan had been caught, giving them a clearer picture of how the events of that day had been planned and executed.

Unfortunately, that understanding was of little help in preventing what was coming next. Scouts had reported that Valmandi's army was now marching to Jakhat and would likely be outside their gates in less than a week. It was, however, a much smaller army than it would have been a month prior. Several of King Bhajan's allies had abandoned him in recent weeks. Still, he refused to surrender, and Empress Jasala had been consulting with her military officers and strategists every waking hour to determine their best options for defending the city.

"Does Valmandi even have the numbers to mount such an offensive?" Saya asked. "Jakhat's army must be far larger at this point."

"It is," Amar said, "but many of them are still stationed in the south, defending the farmlands there. Valmandi's Tarja have always had better training, and they have a large supply of mesala. The attack on the palace was a clear demonstration of their power, and we can't rule out the possibility that they'll use a curse again. Right now, that's our biggest concern."

Kamaal raised an eyebrow. "Surely after all the damage it caused last time, King Bhajan wouldn't dare give those orders."

"I wish I could believe that, but he's obviously not the same man we both thought we knew."

"Do you think he even knows?" Mitul asked. "The curse went wrong, but he might not realize the full extent of what that means."

"He must have received word by now," Amar said. "And still, he marches his troops here. They've shown no sign of turning back. Jasala has half a mind to send the full force of her army out to crush them before they can even come close to attacking the city."

"Hundreds would die," Lucian said. "Lives that shouldn't be lost, on either side. Those soldiers don't have much choice but to follow the orders they're given. It's not their fault the king has gone mad."

"Not mad," Amar said. "He's relentless and angry, and maybe that's worse. I thought that perhaps with Dashiva dead, he'd stop. But he seems fully determined to destroy all traces of her legacy."

"It's Valkyra," Aleida said. "That's what she wanted, isn't it? She had some personal vendetta against Dashiva."

"So it would seem."

"She's probably manipulating Bhajan the same way she did you and me and all of her other puppets. Maybe she's not talking to him directly, but she still has Ashaya to do her bidding, and that might be enough."

Amar sighed. "You're probably right. Any brilliant ideas on how to stop her?"

"Not unless she's dead." She cut into a piece of chicken rather aggressively with her knife.

The others kept talking, but Aleida hardly paid attention. A familiar rage roiled inside her. It was one thing to manipulate a desperate girl into chasing a miracle and losing her chance to say goodbye to the only living family she had left. It was another thing entirely to orchestrate a civil war that had left thousands dead. But Valkyra had never cared about the suffering of others. The invasion of Vis had been proof of that long before this war started.

She needed to die—permanently this time—and Aleida would do everything in her power to ensure she met the fate she deserved.

AMAR

AMAR STAYED AT KAMAAL'S LONG AFTER HE SHOULD HAVE, RELUCTANT to leave the comfort of his friends' company. It grew quite late before he even considered returning to the palace, and once that thought entered his mind, all he could think about was how heavy things felt there, the constant pressure to offer up whatever wisdom and experience he supposedly possessed in order to help with some impending crisis. There were so many of those lately, and he was exhausted. Another hour slipped away, then two, and when Kamaal offered to let him sleep on the small chaise in the guesthouse, he accepted happily.

The weight of his responsibilities roused him before dawn. He slipped out quietly, not wanting to wake anyone else, and made his way back to the palace. The guards let him pass without fuss; he was a well-known face here now, and word of how he'd saved Empress Jasala had spread. If anyone still questioned his motives or loyalties, they did not say so aloud anymore.

He went to his room to wash and change his clothes. There, he was informed by one of the servants that the empress had asked to see him as soon as he returned. When he expressed concern about waking her, they told him she was already up. She'd likely been awake all night—again.

He found her in one of the sitting rooms in a mostly unused wing of the palace. He'd come to know her habits a little better over the last few weeks, and this particular room seemed to be a place where she came when she wanted peace and quiet. It was here that Amar had played samud with her during his first visit to the palace, when he was her cousin Prince Savir and they were still getting acquainted. Now the samud board sat untouched, except for the single piece Jasala held between her fingers, her thumb running circles over the polished wood.

She lounged in an armchair below a tall window, watching the sunrise with her legs tucked up beneath her. A heavy embroidered robe draped over her nightclothes and skimmed the floor. Amar took this as a positive sign; she had at least made some attempt to sleep last night. Still, when she shifted around to face him and offered a small, weary smile, he knew it hadn't been enough. The creams and powders she wore to enhance her appearance hadn't yet been reapplied for the day, making the dark shadows beneath her eyes more apparent than ever.

"There you are," she said. "How are your friends doing?"

"As well as anyone can be, given all that's happened." He sat down in a nearby chair and leaned forward with his elbows on his knees. "You should get some sleep, Your Majesty. Wearing yourself out isn't going to help anything."

"It seems like nothing I do is helping anything." She sighed and opened her hand to let the samud piece lay flat against her palm. It was a settler, one of the most numerous pieces in the game, but also the weakest, and often sacrificed in the process of trying to gain ground against one's opponent. When Amar had played samud against Jasala, she'd often avoided such sacrifices, opting for more drawn-out strategies that put her stronger pieces at risk but saved her settlers. On a few occasions, she'd managed to end the game with all of them still on the board.

Unfortunately, real war was more complex than a game of samud, and plenty of innocents had already been sacrificed in this one.

"I need your wisdom, Amar. And your advice."

"On what?"

"King Bhajan. It seems we'll have to fight his army, and my military leaders have all finally come to a consensus on a strategy that should prevent as much death as possible. At least, on our side."

Amar winced a little at that caveat, but he understood the desire to prioritize their own soldiers' lives ahead of Valmandi's. As much as he saw both sides as being part of the same whole, that wasn't actually the case, not currently. The empress had a duty to all her people, including those currently marching behind Bhajan's banners, but right now, she had a particular responsibility to those who'd remained loyal to her.

"What will they do about Valmandi's Tarja?" Amar asked. "We can't let them perform another curse."

"No, we can't. In past battles, our soldiers have been able to use daravak to disable many of their Tarja. We're hoping to use a similar strategy here, though it will prove far more difficult given how many of them we expect to face."

Amar remembered the strategy she was talking about. That disabling of Valmandi's Tarja had forced him to lead a contingent of reinforcements into battle, right before his true memories were restored. It could work again, though he wasn't sure how far or how quickly the daravak could be dispersed.

"I'm confident in our plan, and I'm almost certain of our victory," Jasala said. "But afterward, when the dust settles and I have to deal with Bhajan…I don't know what to do."

"What are the options?" Amar wanted to know what she was even considering before he offered any of the supposed wisdom she sought from him.

"Kill him, obviously. Queen Indira, too, as well as any of his top advisors and military leaders. That would be the most straightforward. Make an example of them all, do it in public, have some big trial to expose all their crimes. I can see the benefits of such an act."

Amar could, too, but speaking them aloud might help her weigh them against her other choices. "And what are those benefits?"

"They'd all get the punishment many would say they rightly deserve, and I'd be perceived as a strong leader who won't tolerate defiance. Ideally, no one would dare to rise up and challenge my rule again." She sighed. "Of course, it could backfire, and some might call me a tyrant, become outraged enough to take up arms. Maybe not now, but eventually, like Bhajan did. All those years letting his anger over his daughter's death fester. I worry that an execution throws us right back into that same cycle of hatred and vengeance. And, given the way he was manipulated and deceived, I'm not sure executing him would be entirely just."

"Most people aren't even aware of that part," Amar said. "And sharing that information could make things worse."

"I agree. But it puts Bhajan's actions in a new perspective, doesn't it?"

Amar nodded. "I'm not sure he would have done any of this if it weren't for those deceptions."

"Exactly."

"Another option?"

"I could make sure he's killed in battle," she said hesitantly. "That's likely what my mother would have done, and I can see the benefits of that, too. It would be cleaner. He'd be gone, and I could offer condolences to his family and his supporters, then wash my hands of the whole affair. But it's underhanded, and I'd like to think I'm better than that." She closed her fingers around the samud piece. "Maybe that's just my naivety and inexperience."

"You're not naive, Your Majesty. You *are* better than that."

"I try, though I fear the weight of ruling might slowly wear away at my morals, as it seems to have done for so many before me." She looked him in the eye, her expression grave. "You'd tell me if you ever saw that happen, wouldn't you?"

"I promise."

"Good." She went back to staring out the window. "The last option is harder, but it has some advantages, too. I could let Bhajan live."

Amar didn't quite know what to make of the fact that she was even considering this. Tarik would have been pleased, and he could easily recall the man's sincerity as he urged Amar to find some way to spare Bhajan. Perhaps this was how, but he still wasn't sure Bhajan *deserved* sparing.

Then again, who was he to decide what anyone deserved?

"People might see that as a weakness," he said.

"There would still be some severe consequences, of course. But yes, many people will view anything short of execution as a lenience he doesn't deserve. It might have been different if his curse hadn't killed so many. Or perhaps even if he surrendered. But marching his army here, insisting on another battle—these are not actions I can take lightly."

"What other consequences can you give him?" Amar asked. Whatever they were, they needed to be significant enough to show that justice was being served, even if it was in an unconventional manner.

"I'd strip him of his crown and his title, for starters. There would be no more kings and queens in Valmandi, and the region would fall directly under my rule, like every other province in the country. I'd also take him prisoner, and he would spend the rest of his life behind bars."

"And Queen Indira?"

Jasala shook her head. "It's unclear what role she's played in all of this, but I can't allow her to remain free and serve as a potential rallying point for those who still want their monarchs in Valmandi. She can share a cell with her husband, if she wishes, or she can remain a guest in this palace. A closely monitored guest."

"A hostage," Amar said.

"Yes."

"It sounds like a lot of effort on your part. And a lot of uncertainty." He could almost hear Tarik chiding him for the statement; he was not making a very good case for sparing Bhajan's life, and he'd told the old guard he would try. Still, he had a duty to advise Jasala, and that included helping her see every potential consequence of her choices. "What are the benefits?"

She stood and walked over to the samud board, placing the settler piece back in its designated starting position. "A selfish one, first. By letting Bhajan live, I don't have to kill a man I thought of as a friend and mentor, and I don't have to leave his wife a widow when she was never anything but kind to me. They always treated me so well when I would visit Valmandi. Queen Indira was the one who taught me to play samud."

Amar remembered fondly the mornings he'd spent playing with the queen himself as she tried to get to know her grandson. She'd always been kind to him, too. Like Jasala, he hated the idea of her suffering, but how much could one person's suffering really factor into this decision when there were so many victims of King Bhajan's actions?

Not his actions alone, Amar reminded himself. But even this did not change the fact that he had ultimately given the orders, or at the very least, allowed those orders to be given in his name.

"I'm sorry, Your Majesty, but I don't think you get to be selfish in this decision. Is there any other reason to spare him?"

Jasala picked up another samud piece, larger and arguably stronger than any of the others, though it still had certain weaknesses. The monarch. "I don't want to be an empress who keeps her power by killing all voices of dissent. Obviously, Bhajan has gone well past that point, but even so, half the country was willing to follow him and restore his version of right and wrong. As I said, I don't want that same half stewing in their anger once this is over."

"What *do* you want, then?" Amar asked.

"I want us to heal." She set the samud piece down and pivoted to face him. "I want us to be a unified nation once more. As much as I want to avoid seeming weak, there's a part of me that hopes letting Bhajan live could be a first step toward that reunification and healing."

Amar could see the wisdom and value in that, though the more cynical part of him wondered if her hopes were misplaced.

"Besides," Jasala added, "he could still prove useful. That usefulness dies with him if he's executed."

"Useful how?"

"In making sure that the people who still trust him are willing to accept the changes I want to make over the next several years."

Changes. There was a certain heaviness to the way she said the word that gave Amar a little thrill. He wasn't entirely sure whether it was worry or inspiration.

"The time has come sooner than I expected," she went on, "but I always knew that when I became empress, I'd like to do things differently. Not everyone is going to welcome that, and I may very well need Bhajan's help in better understanding his subjects and the people of influence in Valmandi, if only so I can better convince them to give new ideas a chance."

"Would you care to share any of those new ideas?"

"Absolutely, but not until we get through the current crisis. All I can tell you for now is that it would mean giving up a lot of my own power in favor of sharing it with others. I'd like to see my subjects have more say in the decisions that impact their lives."

Amar suddenly understood very clearly why Jasala had been spending so much time with Saya. "You mean to govern your people the way the Sularans do."

"Something like that. Eventually. It will take time, and we have our own unique needs and challenges to consider. But someday, I'd like to get to a point where I'm not the sole person in charge of making the big decisions." She raised an eyebrow. "Like what to do with King Bhajan, for example. You still haven't told me which way you think I should go, and I did ask for your advice."

Amar chuckled a little. "That you did."

"Well?"

He shrugged. "If Bhajan hadn't attacked the city, and if he were coming here to surrender instead of fight, allowing him to live would be the more evident choice. It makes sense, for all the reasons you gave, and I agree that he could be useful."

Jasala tilted her head to one side. "But?"

"But he's done a lot of harm. Many would call for his execution, and you would be fully within your rights to kill him. No one could justifiably say he didn't bring it upon himself."

Her shoulders sagged a little. "So you think I *should* execute him."

"I think the decision is yours, Your Majesty," Amar said. "I can't make it for you. I also think there's strength in showing restraint and looking ahead to the future rather than destroying the tools you have simply because they hurt you."

Jasala threw her hands up. "Skies, can you stop being cryptic and give me the answer?"

He chuckled a little, remembering so recently when he'd asked Mitul the same thing—to give him the answer rather than letting him figure it out for himself. He told her the same thing his friend had then. "I don't know it."

"Then what use are you to me as an advisor?" she said with a little laugh, then sighed. "Obviously I don't mean that. There are plenty of people who would tell me exactly what they think I should do, and I could have gone to any one of them for advice. I asked you because I wanted your insight to help me make my decision, and you've given it. Thank you."

Amar got the sense he was being dismissed. He bowed and went to the door, but paused there for a moment. "Whatever you decide," he told Jasala, "I know it will be what you believe best for this country and its people. You have my trust, whatever that's worth."

She smiled. "It's worth everything."

ALEIDA

ALEIDA WOKE EARLY THE MORNING OF THE PARTY, HER MIND immediately abuzz with the anticipation of what was to come. She washed and dressed in her best outfit, then braided her hair and twisted it up into a low bun. By the time she was finished, Saya and Kesari had awoken, too, and Kamaal was knocking on the door to let them know breakfast was ready.

The morning passed in much the same way as so many of their previous mornings, with good food, friendly conversation, and easy cooperation as they went about doing some household chores together. Saya helped Kesari pack up the last of her things for the journey home—she and Lucian planned to leave first thing the next morning—and Aleida found ways to pass the time until the final party preparations could begin.

She sat on a chair in Kamaal's studio that afternoon, humming to herself while she drew in the sketchbook he'd given her. He was working on a new painting himself—a portrait of a child wearing a crown of colorful flowers. It was coming along nicely, and she enjoyed watching him work, asking him questions and trying to soak up whatever knowledge he had to give her. Sometimes he asked her opinion, and while she'd initially hesitated to give it, he'd sought it enough times and with enough earnestness that she realized he did truly want to know, and she offered it more freely now. He didn't always take her ideas or suggestions, but his explanations for why he did or didn't were informative. Even if it was something as simple as, "That doesn't quite feel right."

Skies, she still couldn't believe this was her life sometimes, sitting in the studio of her lifelong idol and learning from him directly. Her hands might not work the way they used to, but she was making art with them nonetheless, and Kamaal's experience and encouragement was invaluable in that process.

"You're in a good mood today," Mitul remarked from his seat near the window, where he sat replacing the strings of his saraj. "What is that song you're humming? I think I've heard it before."

"An old Visan work song," she said. "My father used to whistle it when we went out on the fishing boat. I don't actually know any of the words."

Mitul finished tuning the instrument and plucked out a few notes of the song. She nodded at him approvingly.

The front door opened, and Saya walked in with Lucian hovering over her shoulder. He gave Aleida a sly wink as he passed, and she went back to her sketching, trying to look casual.

"Mitul, Kamaal," Lucian said. "I need your help with something."

Kamaal wiped his paintbrush on a rag before setting it down and looked at the Spirit Tarja with great interest. "What is it?"

"Kesari's birthday is coming up, and I want to get her something before we leave."

Aleida perked up a little at the mention of this. It was new information to her, but apparently not to Saya. Lucian had volunteered to get Mitul and Kamaal out of the house so final preparations could be made for the party, but when Kesari had asked how he planned to do so, he'd mischievously told them all to leave that to him. It seemed he had his own surprise planned, though—an ulterior motive for volunteering for this particular job.

"Oh, that's a lovely idea!" Mitul said. "How can we help?"

"There's a shop not far from here. They have all kinds of magical books and artifacts. I thought I might get her something from there, but I'm honestly not sure what to pick. I could use your guidance." He extended a few tendrils of flame outward. "That, and I don't have hands to carry the money I'll need to purchase it. Or to carry the gift back. Or to wrap it up for her as a surprise. You get the point."

Kamaal laughed. "Hands, right. We have hands."

"What about Saya?" Mitul asked. "Her input could be useful, too."

"I've been asked to visit the empress this afternoon," she lied. "I'll have to leave in a few minutes, but that gives me enough time to keep Kes distracted so she doesn't tag along with all of you."

"I suppose we'd better get going, then," Mitul said. "Are you in a good place to stop working for now, my love?"

"As good as any. Let me wash these brushes, and we can be on our way."

"Oh, I can do that," Aleida said. "You two go on."

"You don't want to come along?"

She shook her head and held up her sketchbook. "No, I was going to finish this, then maybe take a nap. I didn't sleep very well last night." That last part was true, though that was only because she'd been too excited about today.

Kamaal went to the door and slipped on his shoes. "All right, then. We'll be back before supper. Have a good nap."

He followed the others outside, and Aleida watched out the window as Saya made a show of returning to the guesthouse to 'distract' Kesari. Mitul and Kamaal walked down the street hand in hand, and once they'd disappeared from view, Kesari and Saya came outside. Aleida caught their gaze through the window, and they grinned back at her.

Time to get to work.

By sunset, everything was in place and ready for Mitul and Kamaal's return. The studio floor had been cleared to allow room for dancing, and Amar was showing the pair of musicians he'd invited where they could play. Flowers and magically illuminated lanterns hung from the ceiling so thickly Aleida couldn't even see its surface through all the lights and colors, the soft glow creating a cozy atmosphere that seemed to radiate warmth and bliss. Everyone who entered remarked on how beautiful it was, and Aleida's heart swelled with pride at each compliment.

Only half of the guests they'd invited had actually shown up, which was still better than she had expected, given the events of the last week. These included Avita and her wife, Dhavi, who brought some of the sweet biscuits Aleida and Kesari had previously sampled at their home. Other guests brought food as well, items that could be easily shared amongst a group. It all sat on a table draped with yellow fabric along the far wall, along with a few bottles of wine that would be opened to toast the happy couple once they arrived.

Aleida stood at the window with Kesari while their guests talked and mingled. Lucian should be bringing the two men home any minute now, and her breath caught every time a pair of figures walked by. Finally, she spotted them, faintly illuminated in Lucian's orange light.

"They're coming!" Kesari said, and she and Aleida drew back from the window to gather with everyone else in the center of the room.

A hush fell as they all waited for the door to open. Aleida clasped her hands tightly together in front of her lips and rocked up on her toes, barely able to contain her anticipation. Laughter came from the other side of the door. When it finally swung open, everyone began to clap and cheer, and the musicians started up a lively tune as Mitul and Kamaal walked in.

Aleida smiled as she took in their reactions. Mitul's eyes immediately went to the decorations hanging from the ceiling, his mouth falling slightly open. Kamaal flashed a wide grin, and he set a wrapped parcel down on a nearby shelf before approaching the group. "What's all this?" he asked with a laugh.

"An engagement party!" Kesari announced.

"For us? How wonderful! Look at this place! I didn't know it could look this good."

"It's incredible," Mitul said, his voice low and perhaps still a little stunned. "Whose idea was this?"

Aleida heard her name spoken by several people at the same time, and she could feel them all staring at her even as she ducked her head to hide her reddening cheeks. Mitul wrapped an arm around her shoulder and squeezed, pulling her into his side for a quick hug. He whispered in her ear. "You have no idea how much this means. Thank you."

"It's nothing too fancy," she replied. "You deserve more, but this was—"

He cut her off. "Shhh, don't undervalue what you've done here. It's perfect."

She slipped away to let him greet everyone who'd come to offer their congratulations and well-wishes.

Lucian floated over to her with his usual jagged grin. "Mission accomplished. You really transformed this place."

"Thanks for keeping them away so long," she replied. "We barely got the last of it set up before you returned."

"Oh, I can be very good at distractions and lengthy fool's errands when the need arises. I led them from one end of the city to the other and back again, hunting for the perfect gift. If I do say so myself, I put on a very convincing act of indecisiveness, even though I already knew exactly what I wanted to get from the beginning." He let out a little cackle. "I think they were both quite irritated with me by the time we got back to the first shop to purchase the very first thing I'd shown them."

She laughed, certain he'd planned all of that on purpose for his own amusement.

"What did you find for her?" Aleida nodded to where Kesari stood eating with Saya across the room.

"Something special," he said with a wink. "Actually, would you be so kind as to go and pack it with the rest of her belongings? I want it to be a surprise."

"Sure." Aleida went to grab the parcel Kamaal had brought in and turned it over in her hands on her way to the guest house. A book, if she had to bet money on it, or a box with something of similar weight inside. She resisted the urge to give it a good shake in case it was anything fragile.

With the gift safely tucked away in Kesari's packed bag, Aleida rejoined the party inside the studio. The musicians were playing a lively melody, and most of the guests had begun to dance. With very little urging from Kesari, Aleida joined in, allowing herself to forget all troubles for a little while and enjoy the music. She danced with Kamaal and then with Mitul, then in a group with Saya and Kes while Lucian wove loops between and around them. They took it upon themselves to drag Amar onto the dance floor, which he protested with all the grumpiness of a curmudgeonly old man before finally relenting. By the time the party slowed down and the first guests began to leave, it was nearly midnight, and Aleida's entire body was as empty of energy as her heart was full of joy.

She collapsed onto a chair beside the open window to let the breeze cool her off. The faster, more upbeat songs of earlier in the night had given way to some slower numbers, and a few remaining couples swayed gently across the dance floor. Mitul and Kamaal were among them, and Aleida let out a sigh of satisfaction as she watched them, their eyes bright and smiles warm as they held each other close.

The night had turned out to be everything she'd wanted and hoped for, and though she knew it was impossible, she desperately wished it could last forever. Though life had so often shown her it was full of storms, she contented herself with basking in the glow of this warm, cloudless night for as long as it lasted and took comfort in the knowledge that whatever might come, she had shelter. She had home and people who loved her, and that was enough to help her weather anything.

AMAR

AMAR'S EYELIDS WERE GROWING HEAVY, BUT HE COULDN'T BRING himself to move from the comfortable chair he'd found in a corner of the studio. All of Kamaal and Mitul's extra guests had gone home for the night, including the musicians Amar had invited. None of the others had gone to bed yet. Kesari sat with Lucian and Saya on the opposite side of the room, conjuring simple illusions with her magic that shimmered in the air between them. They talked and laughed in hushed tones, and Amar smiled at the contrast between this scene and the memory of the young Tarja he'd first met who was too afraid to use her magic.

Beneath the loft stairs, Mitul sat with his saraj propped across his knees, fingers strumming a soft, gentle melody while he sang quietly. The words and the tune were unrecognizable, but as Amar listened, he wondered if Mitul had written the song specifically for Kamaal.

My love is the sound of midnight laughter,
Shared dreams and secrets whispered in the dark.
My love is the dreams we'll build together.
A life shared now
And into forever.

My love is a vibrant painting on canvas,
A chorus finally put to the right song.
I wish to be the brush in your hand forever,
Finish our masterpiece,
Sing our melodies.

My love is a promise I've longed to speak,
A vow I will hold in my heart forever.
My love is the starlight hanging over my path,
A guide in the night,
My light in the dark.

He kept playing even after he ran out of words, and Kamaal leaned over to rest his head on Mitul's shoulder. Whatever fate or destiny had led them back to each other, Amar was grateful for it. After everything Mitul had sacrificed for him, he was entitled to this happiness and so much more.

Which made what Amar had to do next all the more difficult.

He was glad they'd all had a chance to experience this night together, something pure and good before the heartache that would likely follow. As much as he hated the idea of putting them through such heartache, it was necessary, and whatever the coming days brought, they'd get through it. They had each other. Even though Kes was leaving, she had Lucian, and she was going home to her family, who could provide all the love and support she might need.

He sighed and forced his eyes open, rubbing at them in an attempt to drive away his fatigue. A few long stretches helped, and he walked outside to where he'd seen the top of Aleida's head through the window. She was looking at the stars but glanced over as he approached and moved aside a little so he could sit on the bench with her.

They didn't say anything to each other, and Amar joined her in gazing up at the night sky. It was easier this way, looking at the stars and pretending for a moment that everything was right with the world—that Valmandi's army wasn't coming, and Jakhat's soldiers hadn't marched out of the city only yesterday to meet them, and there wouldn't be hundreds of people killed in battle in another day or two.

Amar had one last idea on how to stop all of that, and though he doubted it would even work, he had to try. For that, he needed Aleida's help.

She broke the silence before he could. "The musicians you brought were great. Everyone seemed to like them."

"I'm glad I could contribute." He glanced over at her. "Mitul and Kamaal had a good time. You did a great job with all of it. I know it meant a lot to them."

She let her eyes drift shut, inhaling and then letting out a slow breath. "They mean a lot to me," she said quietly.

"I know." He let out a little snort and gently nudged her arm. "Look at us, two friends at a party. Hard to believe you hunted me down and killed me less than a year ago."

She cocked an eyebrow. "It hasn't even been a year? Damn. It feels like a lifetime."

"Oh, it has been. *Two* lifetimes, from my perspective."

She scoffed. "You're lucky you're immortal. You have a habit of attracting trouble. The fatal kind."

He huffed. Oh, how right she was. And now, he was about to go deliberately hunting for more.

"I have a favor to ask you," he said. "It's a big one. You're not going to like it, but I wouldn't be asking if it weren't important. And it's for a greater good—something we both want."

She stopped looking at the stars and leaned forward, shifting her body to face him. "And what is it we both want?"

"Valkyra gone. Revenge, if you want to call it that."

Her eyes narrowed a little. "All right, I'm listening. What's the favor?"

"My curse. As long as I carry it, Valkyra will have the same immortality I do, and that will always give her some power to do harm. But I have an idea. If I'm right, it could be enough to break the curse, stop the battle that's coming, and get rid of Valkyra all at once."

"How?"

"First thing in the morning, I'm riding out to meet Valmandi's army. I need to talk to King Bhajan one more time, try to convince him to surrender and send his army home."

"And you think you'll be successful this time? Hasn't he proven that he's beyond being reasoned with?"

"I need to try." No, that wasn't good enough. "I *have* to make this work. It's the only way we get to peace without another fight, and I believe it's a key part of my atonement for this war."

"Which is the condition for breaking your curse."

"Yes," he said. "But there's another part. It's more complicated, and that's what I need your help with. If it works, Valkyra will be gone."

He described his plan in detail, including reviewing all the steps he'd already taken to put it in place. As he'd predicted, she didn't like it. Her eyes widened when he explained what her role would be, and when he finished, she shook her head vehemently.

"I *can't.* Amar, *you* can't. Or you shouldn't." She glanced over her shoulder and through the window behind them. "The others—Mitul! Think of how that would affect him."

"I know," Amar said. "Believe me, he's been my biggest consideration in all of this. But I know he'll understand, eventually, and as much as I hate to say it, the benefits outweigh whatever pain this might cause him."

She shook her head again but didn't argue the point. Her shoulders slumped as she leaned back against the wall and folded her arms around herself. "What if you're wrong?"

"Then I'm wrong, and nothing changes, no harm done. But if I'm *right*—skies, don't you understand what that means? Valkyra would be *gone.* She'd never be able to manipulate anyone again the way she did you and I. I know you want that."

"Of course I want that, but..." She tucked in her lower lip and scowled down at her feet. "What if he hates me? I couldn't stand that. I need him—him and Kamaal both. They're all I have."

"They could never hate you, Aleida. You're family—family they chose, and they're not the kind of people to walk away from that just because they're upset about something you did. Besides, they know you. They know what this means to you. They'll understand."

She still looked uncertain, eyebrows drawn and mouth pinched.

Amar reached into his jacket and pulled out several envelopes. "I wrote him a letter to explain. There's no room in it for him to blame you, and he wouldn't anyway. But once he reads it, he'll understand why it had to be this way."

"Then why not tell him?"

"Because he'd try to talk me out of it, and he's probably the only person that could."

"And I'm really the only person you could think of to do *this*?" she said bitterly.

"You're the person I trust most to see it through," he said. "Kesari's too gentle. She wants to take care of everyone, and besides that, she's going home. I can't ask her to stay and get further wrapped up in this. I thought about asking Saya, but there's a good chance she'd say I'm an idiot and then go telling Mitul everything. She's more loyal to him than she is to me, and for good reason. Kamaal would be the same."

Aleida swore under her breath. "All right, I get it. It has to be me."

"It has to be you."

She stayed quiet for a while longer, and Amar let her take the time she needed to consider. At last, she said, "I'll do it. For Vis. For Tyrus."

"For Tyrus," he echoed.

A weight seemed to lift from his chest, and he rifled through the envelopes until he found the one with her name on it. "Here. Do me a favor and don't read it until after."

"You can't tell me what it says now?"

He tucked the rest of the letters back into his jacket. "What would be the fun in that?"

"None of this is fun," she grumbled.

"No, it's not. But I appreciate it all the same. Thank you, truly." He stood up to leave her with her thoughts. Perhaps he spotted a wet glimmer in her eyes as he turned away, but there was nothing he could think of to say that would make any of this easier.

Even so, he didn't regret asking her. It needed to be done, and she better than anyone could understand why.

KESARI

DESPITE HOW LATE SHE'D GONE TO SLEEP THE PREVIOUS NIGHT, Kesari rose at dawn, eager to begin her journey home. There was an undercurrent of sadness, of course; she hated to say goodbye to her friends. But as Lucian had reminded her several times over the last couple of weeks, it didn't have to be a permanent farewell. She planned to return to Kavora to visit someday, maybe with her family. Her mother was Kavoran and had often talked about visiting home, but traveling so far with young children was surely a daunting task. Now that Kesari and Navya were both older, perhaps a family trip to Kavora could be arranged.

She changed into fresh clothes and put on her boots and cloak. Aleida was no longer in her bed, but Saya was. She stirred and awoke as Kesari went about her morning preparations.

"You're leaving already?" she asked sleepily.

"I'm up. Thought we might as well get an early start."

"Come here, then." She sat up and stretched her arms, waving Kesari over with her hands.

Kesari bent to hug her, blinking away the sting of tears in her eyes. "I'll miss you. Thank you for showing me how to be brave."

Saya squeezed her shoulders tight. "We'll see each other again. May the sun warm your path and lead you safely home."

Kesari pulled back and wiped her eyes with her thumbs. "And you, whenever you leave for home."

"Soon," Saya replied, flopping back down on the bed. "But not yet. I'm still so tired from last night, I think I could sleep for a week."

Kesari laughed and lifted her pack onto her shoulders. "Sleep, then. Have good dreams."

"Goodbye, Saya," Lucian said. "Until we meet again."

"Until we meet again." She gave a little wave as they walked out the guest house door, and Kesari swallowed the knot in her throat when it closed behind them.

She walked from the guest house and was surprised to find Aleida there, waiting at the gate with her satchel slung over one shoulder. When Kesari and Lucian approached, she jumped a little.

"Oh—Kes! Lucian. You're up early."

"I couldn't sleep any longer. I figured we might as well get started. It's a long road home."

She waited a few moments for Aleida to volunteer the reason for her own early morning start, but nothing came.

"Well, I guess I'd better go in and say goodbye to those two." She jerked a thumb over her shoulder to the studio.

"No, wait!" Aleida said quickly, and she reached for Kesari's sleeve as if to physically hold her back, stopping halfway there and then freezing. She drew her hand back sharply and wrapped it around the edge of the gate.

"You're acting awfully suspicious this morning, aren't you?" Lucian said, floating a little closer to her and eyeing her bag meaningfully. "Almost looks like you're running off somewhere."

Her eyes widened for a moment, but then she glared at him. He grinned back, clearly pleased to have struck on something.

Before he could comment further, Aleida stood up straighter and looked toward the road, where the *clip clop* sound of hooves was drawing closer.

Amar rode up on a horse with a second one tethered to its saddle. His gaze slipped right over Aleida with little interest, but he frowned when he saw Kesari and Lucian. "What are you two doing up?"

"Why does everyone keep asking that?" Lucian muttered to Kesari as he returned to hover over her shoulder. "It's morning. The sun is shining, the day has begun. But we're not allowed to wake up and get moving?"

"I wasn't expecting to see you, that's all." He cast a questioning look at Aleida, but she immediately averted her eyes.

"All right, clearly something is going on here," Lucian said. "Would either of you care to tell us what that is, or should I go get the others so we can all play a little guessing game?"

He moved in that direction, and they both immediately snapped at him to stop. This, of course, only prompted a crackling little snicker, but he remained where he was.

"Well?" Kesari asked, now equally curious. She'd been eager to get going, but this was amusing enough to make her linger.

Aleida shrugged, and Amar let out a sigh as he patted his horse's neck. "There's something I need to do, and I've asked Aleida to help me."

"Well, that's a vague answer," Lucian said. "More hints for our guessing game, I think."

"Please stop," Amar said flatly. "You can't tell the others—I mean it. If you're so curious, I can explain more on the way out of the city. That's where you're headed, right?"

Kesari nodded. "Yes, but I wanted to say goodbye to them first."

Amar slid down from his saddle and handed the reins to Aleida. He reached into one of the saddlebags, pulled out a few envelopes, and handed one of them over to her. It had Mitul's name scrawled across the front in black ink. "Would you settle for writing them a note on the back of this?"

Kesari frowned. It didn't feel right, leaving with nothing more than a note, but the agitation in Amar's voice and body language indicated how important this was to him. She trusted that, even if she didn't yet know why. She also got the sense that whatever this was about, he might be in trouble, and she couldn't let him and Aleida go off on their own until she knew what they were up against.

"Very well," she said reluctantly. "Give me something to write with."

Aleida quickly dug a pouch of art supplies from her pack and passed

Kesari a stick of charcoal. She wrote a few lines to Mitul and Kamaal on the blank side of the envelope, then passed it back to Amar. He stacked it with the others and went to the door of the studio. For a few seconds, he hesitated there, looking down at the letters. Then he bent, slid them under the door, and swiftly turned away.

"Shall we?" he asked, returning to the horses.

Kesari gave Lucian a little shrug. "We're ready," said the Spirit Tarja.

Rather than mounting the horses, Amar and Aleida led them by the reins on foot, and they all set off together through the streets of Jakhat. Kesari paused for a moment to look back at Kamaal's studio with its yellow walls and colorful floral mural. She silently vowed to herself that this would not be the last time she saw it.

Lucian bobbed in front of them like a soap bubble caught in the wind. "Come on, then, you two. Talk. I think the suspense could actually kill me if I wasn't already dead."

"It was your idea," Aleida grumbled to Amar. "You tell it."

"I'm going to talk to King Bhajan," he said. "Give him one last chance to be reasonable before he sends his army to slaughter."

"Oh," Kesari said. She wasn't sure what she'd expected, but that seemed rather straightforward. "Do you really think that will work?"

"It has to," he replied resolutely. "I'm also hoping that if I can convince him to surrender, I will have satisfied the conditions of my curse."

Kesari grinned. A mission to break his curse sounded much more interesting.

"I thought the curse required you to atone for your father's wars," Lucian said.

"I thought so too, at first. Or I assumed. But it was never specified. I'm just supposed to atone for war, whatever that means. What better way to do that than to end the one I started?" He shrugged. "It might not be enough. But even if it's not, I have to try. For everyone's sake."

"A noble undertaking," Lucian said, then shifted his gaze to Aleida. "But why does he need *you*?"

She glanced at Amar with raised eyebrows but kept her mouth firmly shut.

"Valkyra will probably be lurking around somewhere," Amar said.

"And I need to talk to Bhajan without her interfering. Aleida's coming along to provide a distraction."

Kesari's eyes widened. "That sounds risky. Are you sure you're up for that? Maybe you should have asked Saya to come. We could still go back and—"

"No," Amar insisted. When she gave him an inquisitive look, he added, "She needs to stay and continue advocating for her own people. I can't disrupt that."

A fair enough reason, Kesari supposed, but there were others he could have gone to for help. "I understand why you didn't want to tell Mitul and Kamaal," she said. "They would have tried to talk you both out of it, or tried to come along, and it's probably more danger than you wanted to put them in. But you could have asked me, you know." It almost hurt, the fact that he hadn't come to her. Did he still see her as a weak, scared little girl who couldn't defend herself, let alone anyone else?

"I didn't want to ruin your plans," he said, the explanation quick and easy—not an excuse, but the truth. "You're going home. Your family's waiting for you. This isn't your problem."

"*You're* my family," Kesari said. "I care about your problems, and if there's something Lucian and I can do, we want to help."

He said nothing for a few seconds, then shook his head. "You don't have to."

That was neither a refusal nor a denial that they could be useful. "I know that. I said we *want* to help. We could work with Aleida to distract Valkyra."

"That might actually be helpful," Aleida muttered.

Amar shot her a look, but she only shrugged in response.

"It's out of your way," he said.

"Not really," Lucian replied. "We have to head south anyway, same as you. It might delay us for a little while, but not enough to make much difference. In fact, we might have an easier time getting past whatever soldiers are around if we're with you instead of on our own."

"That's true," Kesari said. "Come on, Amar. We can help, you know we can. We're coming along, and you can put us to use however you need. It's good to have a Tarja around in tricky situations, you know."

"Kes, *I'm* a Tarja."

She scrunched her mouth over to one side. "Well…"

"Not a very good one," Lucian said.

Aleida let out a snort of laughter.

"You're all absolutely heartless," Amar grumbled, but the corner of his mouth raised in a small half-smile. "Fine, then. Come along if you must, but if you change your mind at any point, feel free to leave. I won't hold it against you."

Kesari flashed a quick grin at Lucian. This was good, and it felt right. One last adventure before they really said goodbye to Kavora and returned home. With any luck, she'd help to leave the place better off than it was today.

AMAR

ONCE THEY LEFT CITY, AMAR AND HIS FRIENDS MOUNTED UP AND SET off through the forest heading south. Kesari and Aleida rode double on one of the horses while Amar took the other. They rode all through that morning and into the afternoon, pushing the horses as hard as they could without overtiring them. Based on the latest scout reports, Amar expected they could reach Valmandi's military encampment by evening, and then the more complicated part of their mission would begin.

He grew more and more grateful for Kesari and Lucian's decision to join them with each passing hour. Guilty, too—he really hadn't wanted to interrupt their plans to return home, nor did he have any desire to put them in any danger. But he appreciated their help nonetheless. With Lucian scouting ahead, they were mostly able to avoid detection by Jakhat's military patrols. Additionally, Amar was sure Kes and Lucian would be of great service when it came to actually getting close enough to speak to Bhajan.

More worrisome was what came after, but that was why Aleida was here. He hadn't exactly been lying when he said he might need someone to distract Valkyra, but that certainly wasn't the only reason he'd asked Aleida to join him. As helpful as she might be, having Kesari along could complicate things.

He debated telling her his plan in full, but she'd hate it even more than Aleida did, and she probably wouldn't see the same benefits of going along with it. Knowing what was coming, leaving her in the dark felt almost cruel, but the alternative wasn't any better. She might not be able to talk him out of this the same way Mitul could have, nor would she put as much effort into doing so. But the dread of knowing what was coming might be worse, in some ways. He didn't want that hanging over her.

He still had her letter inside his jacket. When they stopped for a quick break that afternoon to stretch their legs and eat something, he gave it to her.

"Oh, I get one, too?" she said and immediately went to open it.

Amar put a hand over hers to stop her. "Save it. For after."

"After what?"

"I don't know. After today, after you're already gone and on your way home."

"All right. Mysterious, but that's fine." She opened her pack to tuck the letter inside and cocked her head to the side, pulling out a rectangular parcel wrapped in red paper. "What's this?"

"A gift," Lucian said.

"From you?"

He winked. "Maybe. Save that, too. Your birthday's coming up."

She narrowed her eyes suspiciously. "Hmm. Another mystery. Fine. Keep me in suspense, then."

They finished the lunch Amar had packed, which wasn't enough as he'd only planned for two, but he discreetly gave most of his portion to Kes and Aleida. Then they continued on their way, avoiding the positions Amar had marked on a map to show where Jakhat's army waited to ambush Valmandi in their final push to the city.

He wasn't sure any ambush would be very successful, and he'd told Jasala as much in private. Valkyra could scout the area from the sky as easily as Lucian could, and whether she was communicating with Bhajan directly at this point or simply relaying information through Ashaya, the result was the same. Jakhat's army didn't have the element of surprise any more than Valmandi's did. Still, they had the numbers, and with their troops in position, surrounding Valmandi's army from all sides would be simple enough.

Which could only mean that Bhajan was continuing this war in complete foolishness and pride, or he had some other trick up his sleeve. Another curse, perhaps, after they'd learned from the mistakes made in using the first one. Amar hated to think of what devastation that might bring, even if it didn't go exactly according to plan. *Especially* if it didn't go according to plan.

When the sun went down, Amar, Kesari, and Aleida stopped to wait while Lucian made a discreet flight through Valmandi's camp. It wasn't far now, and they'd be better off going the rest of the way on foot. He was gone for about an hour, and when he returned, he gave them a detailed description of the place. With those instructions, Amar drew a diagram on a page in Aleida's sketchbook, marking out where King Bhajan's tent stood as well as possible routes they could take to get there.

"Did you see the king?" he asked Lucian.

"He's in his tent."

"Alone?"

"He was when I left. He seemed restless, though, pacing around and muttering to himself. Someone brought supper but he hadn't touched it. He's clearly under a lot of stress."

As he should be. Amar was almost glad to hear it. Perhaps with the right push, the right influence, Bhajan could be talked out of this madness.

"What about Valkyra?" Aleida asked. "Did you see her?"

"She's with Ashaya, right there, in the center of the camp not far from Bhajan's tent."

Amar moved the pencil around until he received an affirmative response from Lucian and marked the spot on his diagram.

"They were talking to some of the military officers," Lucian continued. "Pointing out where Jakhat's soldiers are waiting and working on a strategy to get rid of the most troublesome groups. It was a little tense. Honestly, the whole camp seemed tense."

"What do you mean?" Amar asked.

"Well, obviously I wouldn't be expecting a celebration or anything, but it was eerily quiet. Gloomy. I even heard a few mutterings about soldiers deserting. Small groups every night since they started marching, apparently. There are extra guards posted all around the encampment."

"To keep people from leaving," Amar said. It wasn't the first time he'd seen it in all his years as a soldier, and given the predicament Valmandi's troops found themselves in, some desertion was to be expected. "That's going to make it a lot harder for us to get *in*, too."

Aleida shook her head. "Getting in is as easy as getting yourself caught by those guards. Bhajan will want to talk to you, won't he? He'll be too curious not to."

Amar agreed with that assessment, but such a plan had its own risks. "We can't get to Bhajan without going through the rest of the camp first. Valkyra and Ashaya will find out we're there before we even get a chance to talk to him." His original plan had been to sneak his way through the camp, but that was looking more and more foolish the longer he studied the diagram and considered his options. There were simply too many people to get past unseen. Maybe if he had one of their uniforms, though…

"We could draw them out," Aleida said. "Or at least draw *her* out. We could wait until late at night, and once most of them are asleep, Lucian could make sure Valkyra spots him hovering around camp." She shifted her gaze to look at the Spirit Tarja. "You wouldn't want to make it too obvious, of course, just enough to draw her interest. But then, once you have it, you leave the camp, and she'll follow."

"You can't guarantee that," Lucian said.

"No, but I'd certainly bet every coin I have on it," Aleida replied confidently. "She'll want to know what you're doing there, and she'll worry that we might be close, plotting something to disrupt her plans again."

Again. Amar smiled ruefully at that and was inclined to agree with Aleida. Valkyra certainly loved her schemes, and every time he and his friends had managed to throw one off track, even temporarily, she'd reacted with more emotion than he'd ever seen from her otherwise. She wouldn't want to risk such a disruption again when she was so close to getting what she presumably wanted: not simply war, chaos, or power, but a complete destruction of the legacy Empress Dashiva had so carefully built, both with and without Nandini at her side.

"And then what?" Kesari asked. "If Lucian leads her to us, I could probably trap her and keep her contained for a while. But if Ashaya comes with her, that's going to be more difficult."

"He wouldn't be able to keep up," Lucian said. "If she wants to follow me, she'll have to leave him behind."

"Which means he'll likely still be in the camp when I go talk to Bhajan," Amar said. That could certainly bring its own challenges, but he felt confident enough to handle those as they came. "That's fine. We can't possibly prepare for everything with so many unknown factors, but this gives us a good start."

"Agreed," Aleida said.

Amar looked between Kesari and Lucian. "A lot of this is riding on you, but if you want to turn back, my offer still stands. You don't have to do this. You can keep going, head home."

Kesari shook her head, and Lucian grinned at Amar. "You'd obviously be doomed without us, and no one wants that. Skies, what were you planning to do if we *hadn't* come along?"

"Pose as a couple of soldiers," Amar said. "Sneak in and figure it out as we went."

"And you were willing to go along with this?" Lucian asked Aleida.

She shrugged. "We would have made it work."

"Oh yes, I suppose at that point there would have been no choice. Either make it work or die trying. *He* can afford to die, but you certainly can't."

He continued muttering about how reckless they both were and how fortunate it was that he and Kes had discovered what they were up to this morning. Amar exchanged a somber, knowing look with Aleida. She frowned back at him.

Make it work, or die trying. That wasn't actually too far off.

ALEIDA

ALEIDA BLEW HOT AIR INTO HER HANDS AS SHE PACED BACK AND forth across a small stretch of grass between the trees, trying to stay warm. Amar was there in the forest's shadows somewhere, hidden from her view. When she walked back in the other direction, she could see Kesari standing at the edge of a small clearing, scanning the sky for any sign of Lucian coming back, though he couldn't have left more than ten minutes ago.

They'd drawn a little closer to Valmandi's camp—close enough to watch the smoke from campfires rising into the night sky, shrouding the stars in hazy gray. Most had burned out now, hours later, and the sky was clear, illuminated by more stars than Aleida could count and a moon that was nearly full. Kesari was watching for Lucian, but when Aleida looked to the sky, she watched for the glow of moonlight off white feathers.

While she paced, she thought of Mitul and Kamaal, what they were doing, what they must be thinking. They would have found Amar's letters by now, and they'd be wondering why Kesari had left without a word. They might be feeling sad, betrayed. They must have questions—questions Aleida would have to answer once this was over.

She didn't know whether she hoped more that Amar's plan would be successful, or that it wouldn't.

They waited, and Aleida continued pacing for what felt like hours, dreading what was to come and yet wishing it would happen already so she could escape the long anticipation. Better for *something* to happen than nothing at all.

Finally, Kesari pointed at the sky and said, "Here he comes."

Lucian streaked through the dark like a shooting star that had fallen a little too close to land, trailing orange flames like a tail. Aleida watched the emptiness behind him and saw only stars at first. Maybe he'd failed. Maybe Valkyra hadn't taken the bait and followed.

Lucian dropped down to where Kesari waited and stopped abruptly in front of her. "She's coming," he said. "She was right behind me until a minute ago."

"Did she go back to camp?" Kesari asked.

"I don't know."

Aleida knew. There was no way Valkyra would have simply given up the chase and gone back—not until she at least saw what she'd come out here to see. She was simply trying to avoid being caught.

Aleida spun in a slow circle, scanning the trees for any sign of movement, listening carefully to every sound. At first, there was nothing. She was too well hidden, too practiced at lurking in shadows and observing, eavesdropping. But then—there, what was that? A glimpse of something pale in the blackness, high up in the branches of a tree.

Aleida walked toward it while Kesari and Lucian continued to whisper behind her. She tried not to look directly at it, tried to appear as if she was still simply pacing. Then, when she was sure she was close enough, she looked up.

Valkyra stared down at her for half a second, then shot away from the branch and into the forest.

"She's here!" Aleida called as she ran after the dragon. "Come on!"

She didn't wait to see if they followed, and she didn't dare look back, but after a few seconds, she heard Kesari's voice behind her. "Lucian, fly up and watch from there!"

A good idea. For now, it seemed Valkyra was hoping to lose them in the forest. If she flew up into the open sky, she could get away easily, but not if Lucian was there watching, ready to pinpoint for them exactly where she was so Kesari could bring her down. Here in the trees, she was a much harder target.

Aleida kept up with her easily at first. They both had to duck and weave around trunks and branches, and despite Valkyra's smaller size, she seemed to have as much trouble as Aleida did, navigating the forest in the dark. But Aleida soon became winded, and Valkyra steadily increased her lead.

Where was Kes? They needed to catch the dragon before she slipped away, and their window of opportunity was closing fast.

"She's getting away!" Aleida's shouts were desperate, ragged things. "Kes, hurry!"

Valkyra's tail twisted around another trunk, and Aleida nearly ran straight into the tree. She stumbled, cursing, sure the dragon was about to escape for good.

Kesari suddenly surged past her, propelled forward by altma and moving so fast Aleida could feel a rush of air as she went by.

Aleida recovered her balance and sprinted after her. Forced to navigate by sound more than sight, she lagged behind. Branches cracked, Kesari shouted something to Lucian, and the forest ahead was suddenly illuminated with a fiery glow. In its light, Aleida could see the silhouettes of Kesari and Valkyra—flapping wings and outstretched arms.

She ran faster, fighting the sharp burn in her lungs and side as her body begged for more air. Kesari sent a barrier to close around Valkyra, but the dragon dodged it and wheeled around sharply—

Straight for Aleida.

She leapt, hands reaching, grasping at feathers and clawed legs. When she seized hold of something, she pulled it tight to her body, wrapping her arms around it as she came down hard on the ground.

Rocks and brush scraped against her shins and knees. Claws and teeth bit into her arms, thighs, neck, stomach. She didn't let go, didn't care about the pain. A frenzied laugh bubbled up from her chest and burst from her lips. She squeezed Valkyra tighter, pinning her wings and all her thrashing appendages with her larger, stronger limbs.

"I got you," she growled. "I got you, you bitch. You're not going anywhere."

Valkyra shrieked and managed to nose her way up through a gap in

Aleida's arm. She bit down hard on her shoulder and yanked back, tearing flesh. Aleida howled with laughter to smother the scream that wanted to break free.

Then Kesari was there, pulling at Aleida's arms and urging her to let go. A barrier pressed up against the inside of her arms and legs, and she realized Kes was trapping Valkyra inside. She let go, backed away, and the barrier closed fully around the dragon, a small sphere only slightly larger than she was. She clawed at it, beat herself against it, opened her mouth in a shriek they couldn't hear. And finally, when all of this proved futile and Kesari's magic held, she settled down to glare at them through the translucent orb.

With the excitement of the chase quickly fading, Aleida fell backward onto the ground to catch her breath. The sharp stings of her injuries suddenly seemed no laughing matter, but she still couldn't help smiling. She'd caught Valkyra. Finally, they had her trapped, unable to spin her spidery webs or scheme and plot anyone's demise. And Valkyra *hated* it. Perhaps she was finally getting some small taste of the helplessness she'd left Aleida with when she'd severed their Bond.

"Let me take a look at your wounds," Kesari said.

Aleida shook her head and sat up. "I'll be fine. You need to focus on keeping her contained."

"That won't be a problem. I still have some mesala from the Sularans, and I took some while we were chasing after her. I can handle a simple barrier while I work on healing you."

"You're certain? We can't let her escape."

"I promise. I know how important this is. She's not going anywhere."

Aleida arched a brow, but if Kesari said she could handle it, then she trusted her. And she really was starting to feel a lot of pain, especially in her shoulder. "All right, then. Go ahead."

"Try to relax."

Aleida realized then how badly she was shaking, and she forced herself to slow down her breathing. She flinched a little when Kesari put her fingers against her skin, but once the magic started flowing over her wounds, she relaxed into those touches and the cooling relief they brought.

"What do you want to do with her?" Kesari asked while she worked.

"Me? Why am I deciding?"

"You and Amar had this all planned out before we got involved. And besides that, don't you think it *should* be your choice? That's the whole reason you joined up with us, isn't it? To stop her."

Aleida inhaled sharply as Kesari's hand brushed over a wound on her thigh. The girl apologized, and some relief from the pain immediately followed as it was healed. The heavy ache in Aleida's chest, however, was going nowhere and only seemed to intensify when she looked at Valkyra.

"I wish we could kill her," she said. "Erase her spirit from existence and be done with her forever."

"That would certainly make everyone's life much simpler," Lucian said. "But until Amar breaks his curse and dies himself, it's not an option."

"I know that," she growled back. "I said I *wish* we could. She's a menace."

"No one's arguing that."

She stared at Valkyra, and the dragon stared back at her. This was all Aleida had wanted for so long, but it didn't feel any different. She still worried about what Valkyra could do. She still feared that she'd escape, and that her captivity was only temporary.

"Short of killing her, the best thing would be to lock her up somewhere she'll never be free, but I don't see how we do that, either. You can't keep that barrier going forever, and there's some risk of escape no matter how contained she is."

"You're right," Kesari said gently. "But for now, she *is* contained. So what do we need to do with her for now?"

Aleida thought about it. There was a chance that following through with the rest of Amar's plan could put an end to Valkyra forever. Amar would have made his way to Valmandi's camp the moment she appeared, and he might already be talking to Bhajan now. Lucian was supposed to check in on him at some point, and then they could decide the best way to proceed.

If Amar convinced Bhajan to surrender, Aleida needed to be there for what came after, and keeping Kesari and Lucian around could still be useful. She certainly didn't want them leaving until they did find a more long-term solution for Valkyra.

"It's up to Amar now," she said. "We'll have to wait for word from him before we decide anything."

"All right," Kesari said, backing away from Aleida and standing up. "Lucian, do you want to fly over to the camp and keep an eye on things from his end? You can come back and give us an update once you know more."

"Can you manage things here on your own until I get back?"

"Yes. Don't worry about us."

"All right, then. I'll be back soon." He shrunk himself down to the size of an ember and drifted away into the dark.

Once he was gone, Kesari spoke to Aleida. "Any chance you could try and get some sleep for a few hours while I keep an eye on her?" She nodded to Valkyra. "It will help with the rest of your healing, and we're just going to be sitting here waiting, anyway."

Aleida stood up, shaking her head. "There's no way I'm sleeping while she's around. If we have to wait, so be it, but I'm staying awake."

She knew Kesari had the situation handled, and maybe her body really could use the rest. But she wouldn't have been able to relax enough to sleep with Valkyra so close, nor did she want to give the Spirit Tarja any ideas that they'd let their guard down. She took up a position against a nearby tree and settled in for the long hours of the night that lay ahead of them.

AMAR

LEAVING HIS FRIENDS TO FEND FOR THEMSELVES AGAINST VALKYRA hadn't been easy for Amar, but he trusted them to be able to handle the situation while he focused on his own task. Now, he stood near the edge of the road where Valmandi's army had made their camp, unarmed and readying himself to approach. Aleida had spoken true in suggesting that the fastest way to see Bhajan was to get himself caught, and with Valkyra now gone, he should be able to count on speaking to the king without interruption, at least for a little while.

He waited a few more seconds, until he saw a pair of soldiers on patrol approaching. Then he stepped out of the trees and onto the road, hands raised over his head.

They spotted him immediately and closed in. "Hey! Stop right there! State your name and business here."

Amar stopped, flinching a little as their bayonets swung dangerously close to his face and neck. "My business is with the king," he said. "My name is Savir Akraja Jai Sharma, and I'd appreciate it if you could take me to see my grandfather."

One of the soldiers started to laugh, but his companion shot him a look, and he went quiet. They leaned in closer, studying his face in the moonlight with narrowed eyes. "You ever seen the prince up close,

Raam?" one asked.

"Not this close," Raam replied. "Only from a distance back in Valmandi. He sure does look like him, though."

"If you reach into my breast pocket," Amar said, "you'll find a signet ring with the royal crest. And of course, King Bhajan can vouch for my identity, if you take me to him."

"We're not taking you anywhere until we know who you are."

The other soldier searched his pocket, and when he pulled his hand free, he held the ring flat on his palm so they could both examine it.

"It's genuine, don't you think?"

The man called Raam picked up the ring to study it, and his frown deepened. "Go fetch Edha and a dose of daravak. Tell her it's important, but don't speak to anyone else or mention what you've seen. Understood?"

"Yessir."

"Hurry back."

The soldier hurried off to the camp while Raam kept his rifle trained on Amar. Amar interlaced his fingers behind his head and waited. Several minutes later, the soldier returned with another in tow, presumably Edha. She wore the emblem of a Tarja soldier on her lapel, and she looked none too happy about being dragged out of bed this time of night.

"Who's this?" she said gruffly, barely looking at Amar.

"That's what we need your help figuring out," Raam replied. He held his hand out. "Daravak?"

The other soldier placed a small bundle in his palm, and Edha kept her distance as it was opened. A sizeable chunk of the dried fungus was removed and held up to Amar's mouth. He ate it willingly, chewing, swallowing, and then opening wide to show that he'd actually gotten it down. They all waited a few seconds, and when nothing happened, Raam shrugged. "Well, if it's an illusion, he's not creating it himself."

Edha approached with her hands behind her back, jaw tense as she peered into his eyes. "Prince Savir, is it?"

"Yes. I'd like to speak to my grandfather."

"Oh, I'll bet you would. What I'm wondering is why we should let you. Even if you are the prince, you're just another one of Jakhat's lapdogs now, aren't you? For all we know, you only came here to kill the king or some other such trickery, and we can't risk that."

Amar managed not to roll his eyes with impatience. He couldn't blame them for being suspicious, but he didn't have time for this nonsense. "Fine," he said. "I'm sure the king will be glad to know you were so thorough and diligent in keeping him from seeing me. It's not like he has any pressing questions for me, or concerns related to how I went missing in the first place."

"It's for his own protection," she snapped.

"Are you saying that you three plus whatever guards are stationed outside his tent aren't capable of protecting him? Even when I'm unarmed and clearly unable to channel altma?"

Edha glared at him but seemed to be considering this. "Have you searched him?" she asked the other two soldiers.

"Not thoroughly," Raam admitted.

"Get to it then, and make him strip down. I don't want us missing anything."

Without further prompting, Amar stripped naked and the soldiers went through all of his clothes thoroughly. Once they were satisfied he wasn't concealing anything dangerous, they returned his clothing, and he dressed again as quickly as he could. "Well, that was fun, wasn't it?" he remarked glibly. "*Now* will you take me to my grandfather?"

"Fine," Edha said. "Raam, give him your cloak."

He did, and Amar threw it over his shoulders with the hood pulled up.

"Keep your head down," she ordered. "Don't talk to anyone or draw attention to yourself in any way, understood? We don't need your arrival stirring up any speculation and drama."

"Trust me, that's the last thing I want."

"Good. Follow me." She headed toward the camp. Amar and the other two soldiers followed.

He did as he'd been told and kept his head down, looking only at Edha's boots in front of him. He didn't even dare glance around the encampment, not wanting to be identified by any soldiers who might have recognized him from his time in Valmandi. The camp was quiet this late at night, though he could still hear the crackle of a few fires and a handful of voices speaking in hushed tones. No one seemed too concerned about the small group passing through their midst.

Finally, they stopped, and Amar lifted his head far enough to see the bottom of a large tent. He recognized it immediately. He and Bhajan had stayed in this same tent together before the battle near Valmandi, and like then, there were a pair of guards posted outside now. Edha motioned them aside and spoke to them quietly for a few minutes. Afterward, they came to get a look at Amar for themselves. They said nothing but exchanged surprised glances with one another. Amar couldn't remember their names but knew their faces, and they knew his. They motioned Edha forward, and she ducked inside the tent with one of the guards, presumably to inform King Bhajan of what was happening.

When they finally returned, it was to usher him inside. The king stood in the center of the tent, but it took Amar a moment to verify that it was truly him. Bhajan's face was gaunter than he remembered, his hair and beard longer and more disheveled than he ever would have let them become at the palace. He looked thin, like he hadn't been eating, and there were deep shadows beneath his red-rimmed eyes. In short, he looked far beyond his sixty-five years, whereas before, Amar might have guessed him to be much younger.

"Hello, Your Majesty." He started to bow, but before he could finish the gesture, Bhajan took a few strides toward him, ignoring the protests of his guards to stay back, and wrapped his arms around Amar in a fierce hug.

Amar stood still, not reciprocating the embrace but not pulling back, either. Bhajan's shoulders shook a little as he let out a half-strangled noise that sounded like a sob. This was certainly not the greeting Amar had expected, and judging by the dark looks cast their way, it wasn't what the soldiers had expected, either.

"Savir," the king muttered. He pulled away, leaving his hands on Amar's shoulders as he looked him up and down, his eyes bright and wide. "Skies, Savir, is it really you? Have you truly come back to us?"

Amar opted to redirect the conversation rather than answer the question. "We need to talk." He meant to tell Bhajan the truth—he had to. But he couldn't do that with others still here listening to it all.

"Of course, of course," Bhajan said. "I'm just so happy to see you.

Please, sit down." He strode over to a small table nearby and pulled the single chair out for Amar. "You look well. I was so worried. Did they treat you all right? Tell me everything."

"I will, I promise. But the things I need to tell you are for your ears only. I know I have no right to ask for your trust, but—"

The king turned to his soldiers without hesitation. "Leave us."

"I really don't think that's a good idea, Your Majesty," Edha said.

Bhajan's fist came down on the table so hard it shook. "I gave you an order! Leave us! Now!"

The fury in his tone was something Amar had only seen a few other times before, most notably when he'd suggested they stop fighting for the imperial throne. This time, there was something more erratic beneath that anger. This was not the same Bhajan he'd known in Valmandi. Which made the situation Amar had stepped into all the more precarious.

Edha set her jaw and gave him one last warning glare before bowing to the king. "As you wish, Your Majesty." She and the other guard marched stiffly out of the tent.

Bhajan swept his hair back where it had fallen in front of his face. His expression settled, and his body stilled in some semblance of composure, but Amar sensed that composure teetered on a knife's edge. Again, the king motioned for him to sit. "Can I get you a drink?" he asked. "We only have water, or some sohra that tastes like piss. Take your pick."

"Water's fine," he replied, taking the chair.

Bhajan poured some from a brass pitcher and handed Amar a cup, then went to the bed to sit. "What happened to you?" he asked. "You and I talked, and then you were gone. Start from there."

Amar took a deep breath. "I'm going to have to start a lot earlier than that, and what I have to say is going to be difficult for you to hear. It's the same thing I tried to tell you when we last spoke, but this time, I need you to hear me out until I'm finished." He leaned forward, holding Bhajan's gaze intently. "Please, I'm begging you. It's the whole reason I came here. You and I may be able to save hundreds of lives, but you *have* to listen to me."

"That's all I want, Savir." His eyes shone a little too brightly to be a trick of the firelight, and his voice was rough. "I'm sorry I didn't listen to you last time. I've thought about our conversation every day since you left. I shouldn't have been so harsh with you."

That was a good start. "It's all right," Amar replied, not because it really was, but because it was a way to repair the bridge they'd need to cross in order to make any of this work.

"Go on," Bhajan said. "I'm listening. I'll listen to it all, beginning to end, whatever you have to say to me."

"Good."

He wanted to believe him. He could only hope the king wouldn't change his mind when he realized Amar wasn't actually the grandson he'd loved and missed for so many years.

AMAR

TRUE TO HIS WORD, BHAJAN LISTENED TO AMAR'S TALE PATIENTLY, AND when it was finished, he drained his cup and stood to fill it again. This time, he poured from another pitcher—probably the one that held sohra. He brought it back with him and offered some to Amar, which he refused.

Bhajan drained that cup and poured another, but rather than drinking, he simply swirled the liquid inside as he stared down into it. Amar resisted the urge to say anything more, though he wished he could peek inside Bhajan's head to know what he was thinking.

At last, the king said, "I almost wish I could believe you were making it all up. But you're not, are you?"

"No. What would I have to gain by doing so?"

"That's the thing I keep getting stuck on."

"Really?" Amar asked, raising an eyebrow. "I would have thought it was the part about my immortality." That had always been the most difficult piece for others to swallow when he told them his story.

"It is rather strange, to be sure. But it does actually make sense, and it's not unheard of. I believe Jakhat used to boast an advisor who claimed to be immortal. Of course, that always seemed like a myth spun to elevate their own status and grandiosity, but that's not the only reason I believe you."

"What, then?"

"Because you've answered some of the questions we've been pondering for months. You spoke of the records that Sularan mercenary gave us. Our scholars discovered several references to immortality, though they were puzzled as to why those references were there. I suppose now we know."

Amar stiffened a little at the mention of Valmandi's scholars and curses. He hadn't yet broached that topic with Bhajan. In truth, he'd almost forgotten that the man sitting before him now—the same grandfatherly man who had treated him with so much kindness—was responsible for a curse that had killed hundreds of innocent people.

"And the other questions I've answered for you?" he asked.

"Tarik," Bhajan replied with a sad smile. "There were so many nights I wondered what had happened to him, and why he never completed the mission I sent him on. He was supposed to bring you back, but he disappeared, like you had. Then General Muraka and some of our spies confirmed that he was *with* you, as an ally. He stood by your side in support while you pledged allegiance to Dashiva, and that made me question his loyalty when he'd never given me cause to do so before. Now, I realize he was only doing what he thought was right. Like he always did."

"He was loyal to you to the very end, Your Majesty. He always believed you would do the right thing, and he hated that you'd been manipulated and deceived. The very last conversation we had was about his concern for you."

"Loyal to the very end," Bhajan said. "Even after my actions led to his death."

Amar had no good response for that, though he appreciated Bhajan's recognition of this fact. Guilt was generally a useless emotion, unless it motivated one to change their behavior, and in this case, Amar hoped Bhajan's guilt might give him a little extra nudge in the right direction.

The most difficult obstacle he'd had to face in coming here was now behind them. Bhajan had listened, and he saw the truth in the information Amar had provided, but there were still plenty of challenges to come. They would have to be navigated carefully.

The king reached forward to place his cup on the table between them, hanging his head. When he looked at Amar again, his eyes were hollow. "My grandson is truly dead, then, isn't he? He has been, all this time. And Priyani—oh, my dear, sweet daughter." His voice broke, and he cleared his throat. "Dashiva took them both away from me for a throne and a crown."

"Yes, Your Majesty," Amar said gently. "You were right. All these years, you were right. I'm sorry."

Bhajan put his hands in his face and wept silently. Amar let him, saying nothing and fighting back his own emotion. What a tragic tale this had all turned out to be. A mother and her infant son dead, a father and grandfather having his hopes restored and then dashed again after he'd already broken himself against the cliffs of vengeance. Amar hated his part in it, even if it had been unintentional. Now, he wanted nothing more than to atone for his mistakes and ensure that Valkyra received the justice she deserved.

Soon. But not yet.

"I'm sorry, Your Majesty," he said again. "There are so many things I wish I could have done differently to prevent the suffering this war has caused. But I can't go back, and neither can you. All I want to do now is repair the damage as best as I can, set things right again. I came here because I hope that's what you want, too."

"It's too late for that." The king's shoulders sagged lower. "We're here now, aren't we? We've committed treason. There's no way out except to see it through. I have to. For my daughter, for my grandson." Quieter, he added, "For myself."

"Haven't you done that already? Dashiva is dead. You made sure of that." He didn't quite manage to hold back the twist of anger in his voice, thinking of what that had cost the rest of the city.

"You think I'm a monster," Bhajan said. "So many innocent people died because of the attack I ordered. Tarik, too."

"You didn't *have* to use a curse. You had no idea what you were doing, and—"

"It wasn't meant to be like that. You have to understand." He sounded almost desperate for Amar to believe him. "Ashaya promised it would work."

Which meant Valkyra was the one putting such assurances in his mouth to pass along.

"We only meant to attack the palace," he went on. "We needed to buy enough time for our assassins and soldiers to take over. Many of them were caught in the curse as it spread through the inner parts of the city. We lost a lot of people, too, if that's any consolation."

"It's not!" Amar clenched his jaw, fighting hard not to scream at the man. "Ashaya might have been the one to bring the idea forward, but you're the king. You're responsible for all who serve under you, and you acted so foolishly. I know you to be a wiser man. You never should have attempted such an attack, especially using a curse." He wasn't trying to be cruel, but he needed Bhajan to understand what he'd done and take responsibility.

The king didn't argue with him. "I know. You're right. I *am* a monster, Sav—Amar. It was you who showed me that. Even when you thought the throne was yours, you advocated for peace. By contrast, I was ruthless, selfish. I regret it—all of it. But how could I have known? I thought I was doing the right thing."

"I know that," Amar said with a sigh, and he *did* know. He'd thought he was doing the right thing, too, before he had better information. It was the same for Bhajan. Now that they both knew better, they could make better choices. "Tarik begged me to find some way to save you. I can't promise that your life will be spared, but I think I have a way to save you from causing any further damage and carrying the guilt that would bring."

"How?"

"You need to surrender. Send your soldiers home, then you return to Jakhat with me. As a prisoner."

Bhajan's mouth pressed into a hard line as he considered this. "To be executed?"

"Perhaps. It's an option Empress Jasala is considering, but not the only option. If you give yourself up, she may have more reason to spare you."

"From her perspective, I don't see how I deserve to be spared."

"You don't," Amar said. It was true, and there was no point in pretending otherwise. "But you may still be useful. Jasala is wise enough to consider that in making her decision."

"And she would simply spare those who followed me? Surely it can't be that easy."

"She wants the same thing we both do. Peace. With as little upheaval as possible. Those who followed you did so in good faith. There must be consequences, but I'm hopeful that you'll be the only one who has to pay them. As is your burden as king."

"So it is," Bhajan said quietly.

When he said nothing more, Amar gave another gentle reminder. "It's either this, or you throw away the lives of hundreds of soldiers who will follow you into battle. There is no victory to be had here. Whatever retribution you were seeking, we're past that now."

"I know. I was thinking of Indira. How much this will break her heart." He sighed. "She didn't want me to come, you know. Tried to talk me out of it hundreds of times, begged me to surrender. I should have listened to her. I should have done a lot of things differently."

"Then do things differently now," Amar said.

Bhajan swallowed and rubbed his palms against his knees as he leaned back. "I'll do it. Of course I'll do it. First thing in the morning, I'll summon my generals and tell them. They'll lead our troops home, and I'll go with you, back to Jakhat and whatever awaits me there."

Amar's body relaxed a little as he released some of the tension he'd been holding on to for months. This wasn't over yet, but it would be soon. He wished Tarik were still here to see it. He would have been glad to know that he was right. As misguided as Bhajan had been, there was still some good in him.

"What about Nandini?" the king asked. "And Magistrate Ashaya. Given the lengths they've gone to, I don't suppose they'll be content to simply let this all go."

"My friends should have Valkyra trapped for the time being," Amar said. "I'll figure out a more permanent solution when I have the chance."

"If I might interrupt here…"

The new voice that spoke was one Amar knew well, but it made King Bhajan jump and reach for the sword at his bedside. Amar put a hand on his arm and gave him a reassuring look as Lucian extracted himself from a hanging lantern. The Spirit Tarja grew to his usual size and came to hover over Amar's shoulder.

"I apologize for the intrusion, Your Majesty," he said. "I have a message for Amar. And for you, I suppose. My name is Lucian, by the way."

"He's the one who's Bonded to my friend Kesari," Amar explained.

Bhajan sat back down but kept his sheathed sword across his lap. "What message do you bring for us?"

"As Amar was saying, his friends do indeed have Nandini trapped for the time being. Kesari is using her magic to contain her, and she's taken some mesala to enhance her power. I expect she'll be able to maintain that barrier for several hours more—long enough for you to send your troops home and ride with us to Jakhat."

"Good," Amar said. It wasn't a long-term solution, but if he was right, if he could break his curse by the end of all this, they wouldn't need any other solution. "As for Ashaya, that decision is yours, Your Majesty. At the very least, I think you should keep an eye on him."

"What I should do is have him arrested," Bhajan growled. He stood, walked to the tent entrance, and called out instructions to a guard. "Wake Magistrate Ashaya and bring him to me at once."

"The captain went to speak with him a couple hours ago," the guard replied. "She meant to bring him back here, but they haven't—"

"Why did she go to him?" Bhajan asked tersely.

The guard hesitated. "She said she was worried. You know, with Prince Savir showing up here so sudden. Said she wasn't qualified to deal with all this. I think she wanted to make sure everything was safe."

"Find them both. Now."

"Yes, Your Majesty."

The king grumbled curses under his breath, and Amar exchanged a look with Lucian. The grim expression in the flames matched his own worries.

Ashaya was a snake. If he hadn't come running straight here once he knew Amar was talking to the king, it was because he'd slithered off somewhere to wait for a more opportune moment to strike.

KESARI

KESARI KEPT VIGIL ALL THROUGH THE NIGHT, WATCHING THE SLOW drift of the stars overhead and channeling her altma continuously to maintain Valkyra's barrier. Despite her earlier protests, Aleida had finally surrendered to Kesari's urgings that she get some rest, though she dozed fitfully and startled awake every half hour or so. Her eyes would always go instantly to the white dragon, as if she needed to check and make sure she was still there, and then she would nod off again.

Lucian returned before the sun had fully risen. Aleida was awake the second he appeared, and he spoke to them in a hushed voice. "Come closer, and turn your backs. I don't want her reading your lips and figuring out what we're discussing."

They huddled together with their backs to Valkyra, though Kesari and Aleida both glanced at her often.

"Amar's talked the king into surrendering," Lucian said. "He's meeting with his generals now. They'll be packing up camp and returning home to Valmandi soon."

"That's great!" Kesari replied, but Lucian didn't look quite so thrilled. "What's the problem?"

"Ashaya has gone missing. They're searching all over for him, but the last anyone saw of him was hours ago."

"Maybe he got scared and ran off," she suggested.

"Or maybe he's looking for *her*." Aleida motioned in Valkyra's direction. "Trying to find some way to shift things in their favor."

"That's what we're afraid of," Lucian said. "We need to get Bhajan safely back to the city so he can formally surrender to the empress. And we need to keep Valkyra contained at least until then." He gave Kesari a questioning look.

"I'll be fine," she replied. She was tired, but not unbearably so. The mesala had worn off a while ago, but she still had another dose in her pouch from the Sularans. Even without it, she could manage for a while.

"Bhajan's refusing to take any of his own people with him as protection," Lucian continued. "He doesn't trust they'll be spared punishment as traitors. Which means it's up to us to escort him safely. If Ashaya or anyone else attacks, they could kill the king and then blame it on Amar or Jakhat."

"She'd love that," Aleida said, glaring at Valkyra. "Anything to stir up more conflict."

"I'm afraid so. Bhajan's death would leave Queen Indira ruling Valmandi, mourning her husband's suspicious and untimely passing. She'd have every reason to keep the fight going, and allies would rally around her cry for justice. Kes, I know how badly you want to go home, but—"

"Obviously we're not leaving now," she said. "The king has to get to Jakhat, and we can't leave our friends to protect him on their own while Ashaya is still out there."

"I thought you might say that." He smiled at her fondly. "Amar and Bhajan are going to meet us outside the camp. We'll need to retrieve the horses, and by the time we get there, they should be ready."

"Let's go, then," Aleida said, and she set off through the trees in the direction they'd left their mounts. Kesari waved her hand, and the barrier holding Valkyra drifted over to float in front of her while she walked.

"Are you sure you're holding up all right?" Lucian asked.

She nodded. "A little sleepy, but I can take a nap when this is over."

"Be careful not to overexert yourself," he warned. "You remember how exhausted you were the last time you channeled this much altma using mesala?"

"Oh, this isn't *nearly* that much, and you know it. We were running for our lives then, and I was trying to win a fight, keep us hidden, and heal Mitul before he—" She shook her head at the memory. It was still hard to think about him being in such a dire state. "This is so much simpler by comparison. I'll be fine, stop worrying."

"Asking me to stop worrying about you is like asking the sun to stop shining, you know," he muttered.

She rolled her eyes. "I swear, you're more sentimental than my mum sometimes."

"You love it."

She chuckled, but it morphed into a wistful sigh. "Skies, I miss her. I wonder if I can talk her into making some of her chicken soup when I get back. I always loved that stuff."

"Kes, I'm sure you can talk her into *anything* when you get back, she'll be so happy to see you."

Her smile widened with the thought of it.

They reached the horses and mounted up. The sun was now halfway over the horizon, and by the time they rode the short distance to the encampment, it was fully visible in the sky. A few soldiers watched them curiously as they approached, but most were so preoccupied with their duties that they paid them no mind. They were busy packing up tents and supplies, then loading them onto the wagons that had followed their march from Valmandi. Kesari overheard several pieces of conversation about the surrender and the end of the war. As far as she could tell, everyone was relieved to be going home. A little confused by the sudden change, perhaps, but not enough to protest it. Many of them were even laughing and joking with one another—a stark contrast to the picture Lucian had painted when he'd described the camp's atmosphere as gloomy.

Amar and another man—presumably King Bhajan—met them at the edge of the camp, already on horseback. A few soldiers were with them, each with a messenger bird on their arm or in a cage. Most were pigeons, but there were a few larger birds as well—strixes with dark, haunting eyes. Vis had been known to breed and train them to deliver messages, and since the invasion, there were far fewer trained strixes in the world than there once had been.

"Your family had a strix, right?" Kesari asked Aleida, watching the birds as they were set loose.

"Yes. Feros, we called him."

"What happened to him?"

"I don't know. My brother loved him a lot more than I did. I only saw him once after Tyrus died, and that was months ago." She shielded her eyes with one hand as she watched the birds fly. "Wherever he is, I hope he's happy and eating lots of rabbits."

"Where are they off to?" Lucian asked as they drew up beside the two men.

"To Jakhat, mostly," Amar replied. "And Valmandi. The rest are headed to the other provinces throughout Kavora, all bearing official declarations of surrender signed by His Majesty."

"Some will be shot down before they reach their destination," the king said grimly. "But I wanted to ensure everyone knows, in case I don't reach the palace to surrender myself to the empress in person."

"You don't need to worry about that," Amar said. "Kesari is one of the greatest Tarja I've ever had the privilege of knowing, and Aleida and Lucian both have a keen eye for danger. We'll keep you safe, I promise."

Bhajan gave them all a slight bow. His gaze shifted to Valkyra, sitting upright inside her barrier with her silky tail curled around her legs. "So that's Nandini Kumar?"

Amar nodded. "Or Valkyra, as she's been calling herself."

Bhajan tilted his head a little as he considered her. "I remember you being so much more imposing, but it seems you're capable of causing as much damage in this form as you were when you still lived. Whatever your fate may be after this, I pray it's exactly what you deserve." He tugged on the reins to turn his horse away and face north, toward Jakhat. "Come. I'm anxious to get through this day, or whatever might be left of it for me."

Kesari frowned at Lucian. Was the king expecting to die if he went to Jakhat? That made sense, she supposed. What surprised her was that, despite knowing he might be executed, he was still choosing to surrender himself. Whatever Amar had said or done to convince him must have been powerful.

She nudged her horse into a trot and followed the others, towing Valkyra along beside her. Amar directed them into positions he thought would be most suitable for their journey, with himself leading and Aleida riding alongside the king. Kesari and Valkyra brought up the rear, and Lucian performed his usual task of scouting the road ahead and behind for any signs of danger. Rather than sticking to the more heavily forested areas, they took the main road this time. They were less concerned about running into Jakhat's waiting troops and, in fact, Amar pointed out that it might be helpful to cross their path as they could provide extra protection in escorting Bhajan to the city.

For about half an hour, they rode in silence, their journey uneventful. Kesari patted the small pouch in her pocket to make sure what remained of her mesala was still there, in case she needed it later. There wasn't much left, but with any luck, she wouldn't need it at all.

As they were clearing the tree line to enter a large swath of empty land, Lucian shot toward them from the thick stretch of forest on the opposite side. "They're here!" he shouted. "They're coming! Get ready!"

Amar reached down for his rifle, and Aleida pulled her pistol from the belt at her hip. Kesari checked behind her and, seeing no signs of danger there, guided her horse into position on King Bhajan's exposed side, readying herself for whatever was coming.

They're here. Not *he's* here—not Ashaya alone. And they no longer had cause to fear being spotted by Jakhat's soldiers.

So who was it?

There was movement in the trees, and a growing rumble of hooves. In a sudden surge, they appeared from the forest like blood from a fresh cut. A man in dirty white robes led the charge, and behind him rode at least two dozen soldiers in red.

Ashaya hadn't run off on his own. He'd taken some of Valmandi's army with him, and the odds were now very much stacked against Kesari and her friends.

Inside her barrier, Valkyra looked as smug as a cat toying with a mouse.

Lucian came to a sudden stop at Kesari's side. "You might want to take the rest of that mesala now."

She fumbled for it in her pocket and tipped the pouch back to swallow the remaining powder in one gulp. Some of it got stuck in her throat on the way down, and she coughed a little as her connection to altma sharpened. Everything around her came into vivid focus, and she felt a charged sort of link between herself and the altma in all living things throughout the forest. The concentration she'd had to put into Valkyra's barrier was an easy thing now, and almost as reflexive as breathing.

The soldiers kept coming. Amar took aim, let them get a little closer, and fired.

His shot ricocheted harmlessly off a barrier in front of Ashaya, creating a shimmering ripple that fanned out all the way down the line of soldiers on both sides. The man's white robes billowed out behind him as he continued the charge. "Tarja, attack!"

Kesari raised a barrier in front of herself and her friends as a magical onslaught bombarded them. It held strong against a barrage of incoming flames, rocks, lightning, sharpened branches, chunks of ice, and more. Valkyra beat her wings against the sphere imprisoning her, as if she hoped to escape in the midst of Kesari's distraction. It didn't work. Kesari had everything under control. She could keep these defenses up all day if she had to—or at least as long as the mesala lasted.

"Kes!"

She heard Lucian's warning at the exact same instant she felt her horse twist and fall beneath her. The animal let out a hair-raising scream as roots and branches wrapped around its legs dragged it down. The weight of it crushed Kesari's left leg and pinned her to the ground. She cried out in pain and fought to keep both barriers up, but it was too late. The one shielding her and the others slipped out of her control, but she did manage to keep Valkyra contained.

Roots creaked and snapped, and Kesari's hip scraped on stone as the horse was dragged back. Her bones crunched against the jagged rocks beneath her, and she stifled a scream. When she glanced back, she saw dozens of writhing roots and branches reaching up from a chasm in the ground. It instantly reminded her of the hole Ashaya had risen from the last time they faced each other. Now, he was looking straight at her, his hands twisting in front of him as the roots kept pulling.

She was going to be dragged in if she didn't do something, but first, she needed to protect her friends.

Shifting her attention away from the pain and panic, Kesari revived the barrier shielding them from another frontal attack. She pushed it out as far as she could around and above them, then used her magic to strengthen the muscles in her arms. With a grunt, she lifted the horse off of herself. Aleida grabbed her by the shoulders of her tunic to drag her free, but there was nothing to be done for the poor horse. The slithering roots wrapped around its neck and squeezed as they continued dragging the animal. It screamed again and then fell suddenly, eerily still before disappearing into the ground. Kesari shuddered, half from the fear she'd seen in its eyes and half from her own pain.

Another shot rang out. Amar had reloaded and fired again. This time, there was a cry from the other side. Not Ashaya, but one of the other soldiers.

"Your leg's broken," Lucian said. "You need to heal it."

She knew he was right, but keeping Valkyra contained remained a priority. The dragon watched through the barrier even now, eyes glinting with the hope of escape, waiting for Kesari to make one wrong move.

"I don't know if I can do that and keep her trapped at the same time."

"Try," Lucian said.

She did, but it was too much, even with the mesala aiding her. The pain was a distraction. She couldn't keep both barriers going and heal herself at the same time. She was only willing to sacrifice one of those things right now, and it wasn't the barriers. Her own comfort would have to wait.

The barrage of magical attacks continued. Amar had positioned his horse right next to the king's as if attempting to shield him with his own body. He fired another shot, and a second Valmandi soldier fell. This was followed by more shouts, with several of their attackers pointing and reining their horses around.

Kesari looked to see what had them all so riled up. She might have whooped with joy at the sight if she weren't using all her energy to fight her own pain and protect her friends.

A few dozen soldiers in green uniforms had emerged into the clearing. They lined up in rows with their rifles raised, and an officer called out for Valmandi's soldiers to surrender. Several of them looked at each other in serious consideration of this offer.

"What are you doing, you fools?" Ashaya shouted at them. "Attack now!"

It only took two of them bravely charging forward to make the rest follow. Gunshots sounded from Jakhat's end of the clearing, though the sound was far more muffled than Kesari would have expected.

She watched a few of the riders slump in their saddles. The whole world around them seemed to tilt back and forth. Her vision blurred. The pain swam through her head like a shark, devouring all thoughts and all her focus.

The barrier. She needed to keep Valkyra's barrier up.

Ashaya's hand flew out suddenly. Something shot from it with the speed of an expertly thrown knife, though the object was bigger than that. It sailed right through where Kesari's defenses should have stopped it, straight toward King Bhajan still on his horse.

Amar was there in an instant, a quick maneuver placing his own mount between Bhajan's and the magistrate. He managed to stop the attack meant for the king—not with his magic or his sword, but with his entire body.

The object Ashaya had launched struck him in the torso and came out his back as a solid, bloody lump. Even through Kesari's muffled senses, the squelching noise resonated with sickening clarity. Bhajan's horse bucked and bolted away with the king still in tow. But Amar—

Amar slid from his saddle and hit the ground, where he lay still and quiet except for the uneven sound of his wet, ragged breaths.

ALEIDA

AMAR WAS DYING. NOT IN THE WAY HE HAD PLANNED OR HOPED, BUT dying all the same. This was exactly why Aleida had come with him, and now, she had her own mission to complete.

The first obvious threat was Ashaya. He'd let his barrier down, presumably to put all his strength into attacking the king. Recognizing an opportunity, Aleida wasted no time in dispatching him. He saw her coming, but not soon enough to register the gun in her hands or do anything about it.

To him, to Valkyra, she had always been little more than a nuisance, and pulling that trigger to prove them both wrong filled her with more satisfaction than it should have.

The bullet struck him square in the chest. Before he could recover enough to heal or protect himself, she sprang up, drew her dagger, and plunged it into Ashaya's neck. She pulled the weapon free only to bring it back down. It was a brutal, inelegant thing, and she tasted bile in the back of her throat as blood sprayed across her face again and again and again. When she was quite certain he was dead, she sheathed the weapon and dug through the pockets of his bloodied robes.

"Keep Valkyra contained!" she called to Kesari.

"She's got her," Lucian replied. "I hope you're looking for more mesala in those pockets. Otherwise, she's going to pass out, Valkyra will escape, and Amar will die."

Aleida huffed in response. One of those things needed to happen, but she didn't like the sound of the other two. She searched frantically. Damned robes. There was so much cloth, and whenever she thought she felt something useful, she would reach inside a pocket only to discover lumps or folds of more fabric.

At last, her hand closed around a small vial. Pulling it free revealed a dusky blue powder inside, and she held it aloft for her companions to see. "Is this it?"

"Yes!" Lucian said. "Hurry, bring it over."

Aleida uncorked the vial and brought it to Kesari. "Are you sure it's safe to take this much? Will it even make a difference?"

"We have to try something," Lucian replied.

Kesari shook the vial over her open mouth until it was half empty, then swallowed. Her eyes went wide and she inhaled a gasp. The barrier containing Valkyra expanded suddenly to enclose the three of them, Ashaya's body, and a still-barely-breathing Amar.

Valkyra shot up, wings unfurled, but she didn't have a chance to enjoy her freedom for even a second. The same roots and branches Ashaya had unearthed shot into the air with a wooden *snap*. They hooked around her wings and yanked her back down, meeting more roots that twisted into a cage around her.

She screeched and immediately began clawing at her enclosure. When that didn't work, she gnawed at the wood with her teeth, which forced her to stay mostly quiet. Aleida couldn't help smirking a little as she watched her. She might chew her way free eventually, but it was going to take a while.

"Ah, that's better," Kesari sighed. "Now I can focus on this." She put a hand against her injured leg and stared at it in concentration.

Aleida looked outside the barrier to the soldiers still battling. She searched for King Bhajan but couldn't see him. If he died, would all of this be for nothing?

No, that couldn't be. He'd signed an agreement to surrender and had sent it out to all corners of Kavora. Surely that was enough. It *had* to be enough. The war was already over, and Amar had achieved what he'd set out to do.

All that remained to complete his atonement was for him to pay the final price.

Sacrifice, redemption, justice, whatever you want to call it. It's something I have to do, Aleida. And I need you there to make sure it happens.

Kesari bent her leg back and forth a few times, feeling along the bone with her fingertips to make sure it was healed. Apparently satisfied with the results, she began to move over to Amar, and Aleida scrambled to beat her there. His eyes were closed, but blood continued to spill from his wound, and the pulse at his neck still beat faintly.

When Kesari reached a hand out to him, Aleida grabbed her by the wrist. "I can't let you heal him."

The girl wrenched her arm free and reached forward again. "I have to! He's dying. He'll forget everything again."

Yes, he would. And Mitul would be devastated, but she'd known that from the moment she agreed to go along with this.

Why not tell him?

Because he'd try to talk me out of it, and he's probably the only person that could.

Kesari already had her hands against Amar's skin, and the wound began to close from the inside. Not knowing what else to do, Aleida drew her dagger again and raised it over Amar's throat.

Kesari threw one hand out toward the pit Ashaya had dug up, and before Aleida could strike, two dirty roots coiled around her arms.

"What the hell are you doing?" Lucian shouted at her. "Drop the blade!"

Aleida wrapped her fingers even tighter around the hilt. "This was what he wanted!" she cried out. "I can explain."

It has to be you.

I'll do it. For Vis. For Tyrus.

"Explain after I've saved him." Kesari placed her hands over Amar's wound once more.

"No, stop!" Aleida threw herself against her restraints, her feet scrabbling for purchase against the ground. Her efforts were to no avail. "He *wanted* to die! It was part of the plan from the beginning. He meant for this to happen. Please, just trust me and *listen.*"

For a few seconds, she wasn't sure Kesari *would* trust her. After all, why should she? Aleida had once been the enemy, and despite all the connections she'd built with the others over these last several months, there must be some part of them that wondered if she was fully trustworthy. It would have been so easy to falsely claim this was what Amar had wanted when he couldn't speak for himself. Hadn't Valkyra shown them all how easily someone could be manipulated?

Besides that, asking Kesari not to help someone in need was like asking water to stop being wet. That was part of why Amar hadn't gone to her for her help in the first place.

Kesari's too gentle. She wants to take care of everyone.

"I swear this is what he wanted," Aleida said again. She stopped fighting and dropped the dagger, hoping that would be enough to earn Kesari's trust and gain her attention. "This is how he breaks his curse. This is how he atones. By convincing Bhajan to surrender so the war ends, and then…"

The girl's eyes flickered between Amar and Aleida, and she pulled her hands away from his chest. "And then *dying*?"

"Yes. He meant to poison himself once we turned Bhajan over to the empress. I was supposed to make sure no one tried to save him, maybe even…put him out of his misery if things got too bad." She let her gaze drift back to the dagger below her, then to Valkyra in her cage of roots. "If he's right and this does break his curse, *she'll* get her justice, too."

Kesari's brow furrowed for a moment as she puzzled over this. Then her eyes grew large. "If his curse is broken, he'll actually die. Permanently."

Aleida nodded. "And so will she."

Valkyra said nothing in response to this, but the sound of her chewing at her cage ceased. She sat rigid and upright, her eyes fixed intently on Amar.

Kesari put her hand against his forehead, but instead of channeling her altma, she simply brushed the hair away from his brow and combed her fingers lightly through it. "Oh, Amar," she whispered. "I hope you're wrong, but if this is really what you wanted..."

The roots around Aleida's wrists slipped away, and she picked up her dagger with trembling hands. Her stomach churned, and for a few moments, all she could think about was how horrified and disgusted Mitul would be when he learned what she'd done.

But do it she must. She'd promised.

Kesari turned away and pressed her face into her bent knees. Aleida let out a cry and plunged the dagger into Amar's neck. His muscles twitched, blood spurting from the wound. Aleida backed away and retched as she fought the urge to throw up. After a few seconds, he went still.

"He's gone," Lucian said gently.

Kesari lifted her head, and together, they all watched Valkyra. A Spirit Tarja who wasn't Bonded retained their human appearance, and that was the appearance Valkyra had taken when she'd severed her Bond with Aleida. Would she revert back to that spiritual form before fading away, or would the dragon body she'd adopted simply disappear?

Seconds passed, and nothing changed. Valkyra remained exactly as she had been, and with every breath Aleida took, her hope dimmed. The seconds soon became minutes, until finally, there could be no denying it.

Amar's plan had failed. His curse remained unbroken, his Bond to Valkyra still intact.

The dragon seemed to realize this in the same instant as Aleida. Her lips curled back in a cruel smile, revealing teeth as sharp as needles. She let out a soft, ringing laugh, her tail lashing back and forth behind her.

"Foolish girls. I was never going to die so easily."

45

KESARI

KESARI CHECKED AMAR'S PULSE, REACHING OUT WITH HER ALTMA TO try and sense whatever she might have missed before. But there was nothing. He'd died.

Valkyra had not.

She should have. They shared a life. The only explanation was that Amar's curse remained in effect, and thus his life had not truly ended—not permanently. Kesari was as elated by this realization as she was dismayed, if only for her friends' sake. Valkyra's destruction had been important enough to Amar that he'd sacrificed his own life and convinced Aleida to help him. Still, the Spirit Tarja lived on, and that sacrifice would go to waste.

Beyond the sphere of Kesari's barrier, the sounds of battle were dying down. She didn't dare look to see how either side was faring. She couldn't worry about that right now. An idea was beginning to form in her mind, and she needed to concentrate. There might still be some way to salvage Amar's plan.

As long as Valkyra lived, there would be no end to her schemes and the damage she might cause. And she would live for as long as Amar did. They needed to find some way to neutralize the threat she posed, but Kesari didn't know how to kill a Spirit Tarja when their living partner couldn't die. The next best thing was to keep her trapped, but as she'd proven already, she had allies. There might be others like Ashaya and Muraka who'd pledged their allegiance to her, and as long as those people remained willing to serve her, her escape would always be a possibility.

But maybe there was some way to prevent that. To keep her trapped forever, powerless, immobile, and incapable of communicating with anyone.

To do so would require a powerful type of magic—something that could last for centuries, if needed. A curse.

Kesari had seen a curse backfire to kill hundreds. She'd seen a cursed man and a cursed city. There was no reason to believe that a spirit couldn't be cursed, too. She could hardly believe she was even considering it, but with the mesala enhancing her magical prowess and the information from the Shavhallan records clear in her mind, maybe she could pull it off.

Was it worth the risk?

That answer was simple: no, probably not. But something in her needed to try. For the sake of her friends and all Valkyra had cost them.

For half a second, the memory of the clocktower in Deveaural flashed through her mind, but she didn't let herself dwell on it. She needed all the confidence she could muster to make this work.

Besides, she was not that girl anymore.

"Lucian, I'm about to do something very, very stupid."

"Are you now?" he said with a wicked grin. "That sounds exciting. Go on, then. Whatever it is, I'm sure you can handle it."

His unshakable belief in her was all the extra push she needed. She went to retrieve the dagger Aleida had discarded. Upon returning to Amar's side, she grabbed his hand and slipped off the signet ring that marked Prince Savir a member of the Valmandi royal family.

"What are you going to do?" Aleida asked.

Kesari ignored her, probably for many of the same reasons Amar hadn't told any of them about his plan. She didn't want to be talked out of it.

She drew the blade across her palm, wincing a little as blood seeped from the wound. A sticky wetness coated the ring she clutched in her injured hand as she dropped the dagger.

"Kes?" Aleida asked again.

Kesari looked at Lucian. His dark eyes were more intent than ever as he looked from her wound to Valkyra and then back to her again.

He knew. "Do it."

She let the barrier fall away. The soldiers around them began to approach. Kesari closed her eyes, focused on her breath, and reached for the connection to her altma. It was vivid and sharp, clearer than ever thanks to the mesala. The interwoven threads linking her mind, body, and spirit were in perfect harmony. She held them in her mind, then reached deeper, to the one thing that joined them all.

Herself. Her own life. Jhivan.

But it wasn't just hers. There was another energy there, intertwined, but not alive. Or at least, not fully. Weaker, and dependent on her life for its own.

Lucian. Their Bond.

She inhaled deeply and opened her eyes, letting her field of vision narrow until she saw only Valkyra. Then she spoke the words needed to create a curse.

"Nandini Kumar, by the blood of my body and the life within me, I curse your spirit to remain Bonded to Amar and trapped within the physical form of this ring until his life ends and both of your souls are released from this world."

Instantly, there was a change within her as the energy required to fuel the curse gathered in her body. Some of it came from the altma she always channeled when using her magic, but the rest was different. Hotter. Sharper.

The curse built up pressure like a volcano, all heat and energy that threatened to engulf not only her but everyone around her. The control she had over it was a brittle thing, and it would shatter if she could not tame it. She struggled to keep it contained and intact while still giving it the power it needed to form.

Valkyra screamed and beat at her cage with her wings. A red glow emanated in the space between her and Kesari, and her dragon form seemed to deteriorate. The edges melted away, like smoke trailing from a stick of burning incense. It separated from her and flowed to Kesari—to the signet ring that still lay in her open palm.

This was working.

Even so, she could sense her control wavering as the curse pulled more and more energy from her body. Her limbs trembled, her stomach twisted with nausea, and even the mesala she'd used to strengthen her powers couldn't stave off the fatigue that threatened to crush her.

It was too much. The curse was draining not only her altma but her jhivan, too—her very *life*.

Even as she swallowed the fear that came with the thought, she felt a sharp tug within her. It wasn't the pull of her own jhivan. Rather, it seemed to come from Lucian's energy interwoven with hers. The sensation was wrong, like something inside was being torn. She focused her control there, terrified that if she didn't hold on to Lucian, he might slip away from her completely.

He drifted into her field of vision and hovered there in front of her face. "You have to let me go, Kes."

"What?"

"This curse is taking your life. Even if you were to stop it now, it might *still* take your life. The power is too much."

She glanced past him to Valkyra. The dragon's screams were fading, and Kesari could see the trees through her semi-translucent form. "It's almost finished. I just need to hold it a little while longer." Her own voice sounded hollow and weak.

"And if you can't?" The fact that he was questioning her abilities now when he had only ever encouraged her was a clear sign that the situation was becoming dire. "I won't have you sacrificing yourself for this. Please, use the energy from our Bond."

"What will happen to you?"

"You'll have to let me go."

Suddenly, she understood. The curse was overpowering her because the source of energy she was drawing from was split, one part tied to another powerful magic—her Bond with Lucian. If she let go of that, she could finish the curse, but Lucian would no longer be Bonded to her. He would fade, and she would lose her magic forever.

She would lose *him* forever.

Tears burned her eyes and blurred her vision. Her hold on her magic wavered under the instability of her emotion, and she fought to regain control. "No, you can't."

"I want to."

"But I need you."

"Oh, Kes, you haven't needed me for a long time. It's been my greatest privilege to be at your side, but this is *your* life. I had mine already. My days in this world are such a small price to pay if it means stopping Valkyra and giving you a chance to live a long, happy life."

"I *do* have a happy life," Kesari said. "Because of you. What would I do without you?"

He smiled. "You'll figure it out. You always do."

The curse lurched and buckled, threatening to slip away completely. Valkyra's body seemed to be growing more solid again while Kesari only grew weaker. The harsh red light flared for a moment before dying back down.

This might kill her, and then Lucian would be dead anyway. They all might be.

She choked back a sob and reached for the jhivan that was threaded with Lucian's soul. It took conscious effort to redirect that energy from their Bond to the curse, but after a few seconds, she managed it, and then it began to flow as freely as a stream released from behind a dam.

The magic that had felt so beyond her control suddenly fell into perfect harmony. The red glow of the curse flashed brighter and held its intensity. A surge of magic pulled at Kesari's hair and clothes, whipping them against her skin. Valkyra's cries ended abruptly. Her wings faded away completely, then her tail, body, and head. A white trail of smoke flowed from her cage to the ring in Kesari's hand, which briefly became very hot and heavy before returning to its normal weight and temperature.

She was locked away forever, trapped in this powerless vessel until Amar's life and hers finally ended, whenever that might be.

Kesari swayed, her connection to altma disappearing as rapidly as the mesala had sharpened it. Lucian still hovered in front of her, but he was fading fast. She cupped her hands beneath him like that would be enough to hold on to him, to keep him here with her.

It wasn't.

Tears flowed freely down her cheeks. Lucian drew in closer, his dark eyes staring straight into hers, heatless flames brushing against the tip of her nose. "I am so proud of you, my brave, brave friend."

"Wait," she pleaded. "Don't go." She could barely make out his face anymore.

"Love you, Kes. Farewell."

"I love you, too. You know that, right? I love you. I'm sorry."

There was no answer, and she wasn't even sure he'd lasted long enough to hear her. The space where he'd been mere moments ago was empty.

Kesari slumped forward on top of her knees, wrapped her arms around herself, and wept.

46

AMAR

HE WOKE IN A LUXURIOUS, SUNLIT ROOM, CLAD IN SOFT FABRICS AND nestled against an array of plush pillows. He couldn't remember how he'd gotten there, which was mildly disturbing. More disturbing was the fact that he couldn't remember *anything.* Not his history, or where he was from, or even his own name.

A panic started to rise within him at this realization, but he breathed through it. Perhaps with patience and observation, he could figure out what was wrong.

He let his eyes drift around the room. There were three young women in it with him. One was a broad-shouldered Sularan. She sat against the door like she was guarding it, her arms crossed and her expression stony. A second young woman sat at the end of his bed, pale-skinned and with sharp blue eyes that watched him intently.

He couldn't see much of the third person. She lay in another bed on the opposite side of the room, curled up with her back to him. She looked smaller than the other two, and her thick, black hair led him to assume she was Kavoran.

"Oh good, you're back," said the Sularan. She rose from her chair and strode over to him as he sat up.

"Where am I?" he asked. "Who are you?"

She sighed and exchanged a look with the other young woman. "I can see why Mitul didn't want to be here for this." She tossed something onto the bed—a book, its cover weathered with age. "I'm Saya, that's Aleida, the girl on the bed is Kesari. Your name's Amar, but I'm guessing you don't remember that."

He frowned. How did she know?

"The journal should help," she went on, nodding to the book. "It's yours. Kes said there might even still be enough magic in it to help bring your memories back, but we won't know for sure until it happens. If it happens at all. For now, you're under strict orders to stay here."

"Orders from who?" he snapped.

"Empress Jasala, for starters. She'll probably come by later to see how you're doing."

Empress Jasala—did that mean he was in the imperial palace? Why? And what could the empress possibly want with him?

"More importantly," Saya went on, "*I'm* going to be making sure you stay here, and you'd really rather not test me."

"I wouldn't, if I were you," Aleida said.

"Even if you do manage to get past me, there are guards outside this room who have orders to keep you contained."

"Why would I try escaping?" he asked, even though he'd already been looking for a way to do exactly that. "I'm pretty comfortable here." Also true, but a lavish cage was still a cage.

"Because that's what you do," Saya said. "You come back to life, you don't remember anything, you get scared and angry, and then you try to run. I've seen it before."

Most of what she'd said, he could follow, but there was one part—"What do you mean, I 'come back to life'?"

"Read the journal. I'll have them bring you some breakfast. You're hungry, right?"

He nodded as he picked up the leatherbound book. Aleida watched him open it, then went back to the book in her own lap. She was drawing something, and for several minutes, the soft scratch of her charcoal and the rustle of turning pages were the only sounds in the room.

It took him the entire morning to get through the book, mostly because he kept rereading the pieces he found most confusing or unbelievable, which was most of it. There were several drawings in the back with notes referencing various people and places described in the journal, including the three individuals now in the room with him. He wondered if Aleida had drawn them, or someone else. Perhaps Kamaal Ruman, who was featured prominently in the later entries.

Finishing the journal left him with more questions than answers, but before he had time to ask any of them, there was a gentle knock at the door. Saya opened it to reveal a young woman in a long, colorful dress. The headpiece she wore marked her as royalty, and Saya and Aleida both bowed slightly as she entered with a personal guard.

"Would you please give us some privacy?" the woman asked.

"Of course, Your Majesty," Saya replied. "Do you mind if Kesari stays? She hasn't woken up yet, and I don't want to disturb her."

"That's fine, let her rest. The poor girl's been through such an ordeal." The woman—who Amar presumed was Empress Jasala—looked at Kesari with pity as Saya and Aleida slipped out of the room.

"Amar," the empress said. "How are you feeling?"

He realized he should probably show a greater level of respect and quickly rose from the bed so he could bow to her. "I'm well, Your Majesty. Thank you for your concern."

She smiled. "So formal. You have no idea what you're doing here, do you?"

"I'm afraid not." They were on good terms, he knew from the journal, though it felt surreal to imagine himself as one of her advisors. As for how close they might have been, that was harder to determine.

She clasped her hands together in front of her, her gaze darting briefly to the game table against the wall. "Would you like to play samud?"

It was almost laughable, the idea of playing a game when he had so many more pressing concerns. But who was he to reject an invitation from the ruler of the empire? "I would be honored," he said and followed her to the table.

She took the first move, and they went back and forth a few times before she spoke again. "You really don't remember anything, do you? The Amar I played against before would have recognized what I was doing by now." She easily took two of his pieces off the board.

"Maybe so," he said. "I'm a little distracted. Your Majesty will have to forgive me if I'm not playing as well as you're used to."

The empress chuckled. "Oh, I can imagine how distracted you must be. How confused."

She seemed so lighthearted—more than the ruler of a country at war should be. "Forgive me, Your Majesty, but don't you have other matters to attend to? I can't imagine playing samud with me is of much importance when you're dealing with a civil war." He winced a little as he said the words, fully aware of his part in starting that war, if the journal was to be believed.

She claimed another of his pieces. "Didn't Saya tell you? Perhaps she didn't have time."

"Tell me what?"

"The war is over, Amar. Valmandi's forces have gone home, King Bhajan surrendered himself to me yesterday afternoon, Magistrate Ashaya is dead, and Nandini Kumar is no longer a threat. All of that is thanks to you and your friends."

Amar scowled. "I don't remember."

"I know. I hope you will soon. You've been a wonderful advisor so far, but rebuilding this country to be what I've always dreamed it could be will take a lot of work. I need all your years of wisdom and experience now more than ever."

The war over, King Bhajan surrendered, Valkyra defeated—it was all so much. His mind was still reeling from the parts he'd read—a tale he was still questioning, even though it appeared to have been written by his own hand. How was he supposed to advise the empress of anything when he couldn't even remember his own history?

Jasala reached forward and laid her fingers over his. "It's all right. You don't need to worry about any of that right now. Let's focus on this, all right? A game. Games are easy. Even if you lose, the stakes are low. We can worry about higher stakes later."

Amar released a breath. He could do that. Setting his questions aside, he considered the board and made his move.

By the time Empress Jasala left, Amar had beaten her in two games of samud while she'd won three. They'd taken lunch together in that same room, and Amar let himself forget all his troubles for a while. Saya returned as soon as the empress left, but said that Aleida had gone back to Kamaal's studio to update him and Mitul.

"Why isn't Mitul here?" he asked. The man's name had been mentioned several times in his journal, always as a friend he could trust and someone who'd been with him longer than the others. A brother.

"He's angry with you," Saya said. "He couldn't bear to see you and not have you remember him again."

"Oh. Why is he so angry?"

She sighed. "Because you ran off to risk everything without telling us what you were planning. I understand why you did it, and he does too, but it still hurts to be the ones left behind. More so for him."

"I'm sure I had a reason for it," Amar mumbled, but that didn't completely ease the sting of guilt in his chest.

"Of course you did. For what it's worth, I think you did the right thing. But the letters, Amar—that was a knife to the gut for him."

"Letters? What letters?"

She didn't answer. She was sitting on the edge of Kesari's bed now, rubbing the girl's shoulder as she stirred and rolled over. "Hey there, Kes. How are you feeling?"

"Not good," she whispered. "Like a pumpkin with its insides all scraped out."

"That's awful, I'm sorry. Can I get you anything?"

"Water?"

"Right here." She helped Kesari sit up and drink. The girl looked haggard, her eyes puffy and red-rimmed, her lips dry, her hair tangled. Amar recognized her as the girl in some of the drawings he'd seen, but she looked wrong now with her bright eyes dimmed and her cheerful smile gone.

What had happened to her? What had been his part in it? And where was the fiery Spirit Tarja that was supposed to be Bonded to her? He had so many questions, but she didn't seem to be in any state to answer them.

"Amar, you're up," she said. "What day is it? How long was I out?"

"He woke up this morning," Saya said. "It's only been a day."

Kesari nodded. "You gave him the journal?"

"Yes. He's read it."

Her gaze slid to him. "And do you remember?"

He shook his head, and her shoulders slumped a little.

"Not *yet*," Saya said. "It hasn't been that long, though. It could still happen."

"If it doesn't happen soon, we should find another Tarja healer who can help him. I can explain the process to them." She sounded uncertain, and that brought back the same feeling of panic Amar had experienced upon waking up in a strange place this morning.

What if he never got his memories back?

"Why can't you do it again?" he asked, holding the book aloft. "It worked before, right? You put your magic into this, and—"

Saya gave him a sharp and furious look. "Don't."

"It's all right," Kesari said. "I wish I could, but…Lucian's gone."

She said it with such finality, and Amar realized he wasn't simply away temporarily. Which meant the girl no longer had access to her magic. "You severed your Bond? Why?"

"That's enough!" Saya said forcefully. "I'm sorry, but your questions will have to wait."

"That's not fair! I need to—"

"None of this is fair! Leave it alone. Give the magic some time to work, and you might remember the answers to most of the questions you have."

Kesari said nothing, but her eyes were vacant, and a few tears had slipped down her cheeks.

Saya put a hand over hers and spoke gently. "Kes, you need to eat something. It will help you regain your strength. Do you think you can manage that?"

She nodded. "Can we go? I don't want to be in here right now."

"Of course. Come on." Saya helped her stand and gave her an arm for support. They left, and Amar heard the Sularan giving strict instructions to the guards to keep an eye on him. One of them stepped into the room to do exactly that. Amar glared at him, to no effect, and finally gave up. He picked up the journal and read it again, but nothing new happened. His memories remained as inaccessible to him as before.

Supper came and went, night fell, and with nothing left to do, Amar went to sleep, ending his day in frustration and disappointment.

His dreams were vivid and tumultuous, and he tossed and turned all night as he drifted in and out of sleep. He saw battles in some of those dreams, people he could name, a city in ruins, a curse spoken in a flash of red light. Each awakening brought the feeling that what he'd dreamed had been real, and in his sleepy haze, it finally occurred to him that maybe these images *were* real.

When he next woke, it was in a cold sweat with a gasp. But he remembered. He remembered everything, right up until the point where he'd put himself in front of King Bhajan to protect him from Ashaya's attack, and Aleida had argued with Kesari to let her kill him.

He was glad she'd put him out of his misery, but the fact that he was still here meant his plan hadn't worked after all. His curse remained unbroken, and Valkyra—

"Amar?" came a whisper from the other side of the room, and he looked over to see that Kes had returned. She lay on her side, staring at him in the dark with wide, round eyes.

"It worked," he said. "I have my memories again."

"Good. I was worried there wouldn't still be enough magic in the journal to make you remember."

He recalled what she'd said earlier, about Lucian being gone, and his heart clenched. "Something terrible happened after I died, didn't it?"

She sat up and pushed herself back against the wall, pulling her blanket up over her knees and hugging them close to her chest. He sat up too, hanging his legs over the side of the bed and waiting patiently for her to answer. Whatever it was, it must be difficult to talk about, and he didn't want to rush her.

"You died," she said after a long pause. "Aleida said it was what you wanted all along. You thought you were breaking your curse, and if you died, then Valkyra would die with you."

"That was the plan," Amar said. "That was why I didn't ask you to come in the first place. I didn't want you trying to save me."

"You could have told me that."

"And you would have listened?"

She sighed. "Maybe not. It was hard, watching Aleida kill you."

"I never meant for you to get tied up in it," he said apologetically. "But your help was very much needed, in the end. I might not have been able to speak to Bhajan at all if it weren't for you." Which only made him regret all the more that she'd suffered some terrible consequence for providing that help.

"I'm glad I was there. Even with the way things ended up, I wouldn't change that."

She told him the rest—their realization that Amar's death hadn't brought the results he'd wanted, her decision to curse Valkyra and lock her soul inside his ring. Her voice wavered a little when she spoke of the curse stealing her life and Lucian's solution to that problem. In the end, they had been successful, but Lucian was gone, and so was Kesari's magic.

It was a sacrifice Amar had never anticipated either of them making, and it was only because he'd misjudged what was necessary to break his own curse that they'd been led to take such measures. He'd found a way to end the war, but that came with a cost, and rather than paying the price himself, his friends had.

"I'm so sorry, Kes. I know how much your magic meant to you. And Lucian, of course."

"Don't be sorry." She wiped at her tears with the back of her hand. "He was the best friend I ever could have asked for, and he was always willing to do anything for me. I may not have my magic anymore, but I do have my life back. All of it. I'm going to live to be a hundred, and I'm going to make the most of every single day. That's what Lucian wanted."

"I'm sure it is," Amar said. "What about Valkyra?" He'd already checked his fingers for the signet ring Kesari had tethered her spirit to, but it wasn't there.

"The curse will hold," Kesari said with certainty. "I did it right. She'll be trapped in that ring forever, unless you do manage to actually die, and then her spirit will leave this world with yours. A permanent end to her would have been better, but I didn't know how to make that happen. This was the next best thing."

"It's a fitting punishment," Amar said. "She'll hate being trapped and powerless for so long. My only worry is what happens if I die and forget again, lose the ring or throw it away. I'd feel better knowing there was some sure way to keep track of it."

"Well, for now, Aleida, Mitul, Kamaal, and Jasala all know about it. They can make sure you hold on to it, even if you do die again. It would be better if you just stayed alive, of course, but you seem to attract danger more than anyone I've ever heard of."

He chuckled. "I'll do my best. Where is it now?"

"Aleida insisted on holding on to it until you got your memories back."

"Good." He'd take it back from her as soon as he saw her again. It was his burden to carry, not hers. She'd spent enough time under the weight of Valkyra's torment already. It was high time she found some peace, and maybe she finally could, now that the Spirit Tarja was locked away where she could harm no one.

"So Valkyra's no longer a threat, and you might be the only person alive who knows how to create a curse safely."

"There's nothing safe about it," she said. "Even when you know how to do it correctly. That knowledge will die with me, if I can help it. Empress Jasala pressed me a little to share the information, but when I refused, she let it go."

"As she should have," Amar said. He'd definitely be advising her not to pursue such knowledge. If the last few weeks had proven anything, it was that the cost of that power was too high, the results too unpredictable. He suspected Valmandi had learned that lesson when their own curse backfired, and as long as the practice remained a punishable offense, it would fade back into obscurity and myth with time.

"I'm sorry about your curse," Kesari said. "It was a good idea, ending the war to atone for your part in it and then paying some price by sacrificing yourself. It should have worked."

Amar shrugged. "It almost seems too easy, though, doesn't it? Dying as a way to earn redemption and just leaving behind all the problems I created."

"I guess so."

He smiled as a better idea took shape in his mind. "You know, I think I've been going about it all wrong. I'm done chasing a way to break my curse, at least for now. I'm immortal, and that hasn't been easy, but maybe it can be a blessing, if I make it one."

"How do you mean?"

"I've spent so much time looking for the answers I thought I needed, being selfish about my problems when there are so many people around me who have problems of their own. Bigger problems than mine, especially after this war. Maybe I need to stop worrying about myself and look around a little more. Really focus on changing things for the better."

He had so many ideas already, and his position on Jasala's council gave him the power to see those ideas through. Even if those grander plans didn't work out and he spent the rest of his days simply hauling lumber to rebuild houses or tending to a farmer's orchards, that was what he would do. That was what he wanted.

He grinned at Kesari again and winked. "Six hundred years, I've been alive. Think of all the good I could do if I live another six hundred."

Part IV

To Those Who Remain

ALEIDA

ALEIDA,

I want you to know how much I appreciate you for seeing this through with me, and I'm sorry for putting you in what I know is a very difficult position. Mitul has become your family as much as he is mine, and I sympathize with how it must feel to keep him in the dark on this. I also know that you and I both understand better than anyone what it feels like to be under Valkyra's influence. The stakes are too high. We can't allow her schemes to continue, and I thank you for your willingness to do what's necessary, even if it ends up hurting someone we both love. He'll understand, in time. He'll forgive you. Still, I'm sorry for asking you to betray his trust.

I sincerely hope that by the time you're reading this, Valkyra is gone, and we're both free of her. Wherever life takes you now, I hope you find some peace in this world. I hope you're able to unload whatever burdens still lay heavy on your heart. I know those burdens, too. Not in the same way, perhaps—every loss is a little different. But they all hurt. I hope you can find healing, whatever that may look like.

Give our favorite musician a hug for me.

Amar

Aleida folded up the letter and stuck it back inside her satchel. She'd read it a few times now, and it brought on a mixture of feelings she wasn't quite sure how to deal with yet. Part of her was frustrated with

Amar for asking her to do something that hadn't even worked in the end, though she was angrier with herself for agreeing to it. She hadn't been able to look Mitul in the eye since coming back to Jakhat, and he seemed to be doing his best to avoid her, too.

"Give him some time," Kamaal said when he brought her supper out to the guesthouse—something she'd requested to avoid the discomfort of a shared meal. "He's hurt, and he hasn't even had a chance to talk to Amar about it yet."

"I just wish he could understand."

"He does, but sometimes that's not enough to stop the hurt."

"Is he going to be mad at me forever?" She couldn't bear it if that were the case.

"Of course not," Kamaal said with a little pat on her back. "Come now, don't you know him at all? He's terrible at staying angry for very long."

He left, and Aleida picked at her food alone, then went to bed.

The following morning, she was awakened by a rather insistent knock on the door, and when she opened it, her heart dropped. "Mitul!" He avoided meeting her gaze, but he was here, and that had to be a good sign.

"I'm going up to the palace to visit Amar," he said. "I wondered if you might like to come."

His voice was flat, but she took the gesture as a well-meaning one all the same, the first step toward mending bridges. "Sure. Let me get cleaned up a little. I'll be right out."

She hurried to dress and comb her hair, half afraid he would change his mind and leave her there. She was glad when she found him outside, still waiting.

They walked to the palace wordlessly, Aleida not daring to speak until Mitul was comfortable doing so. It wasn't a long walk, but it certainly felt that way with the awkwardness hanging between them. She never thought she could possibly be relieved to enter the imperial palace, but that was exactly what she felt as the guards led them down the winding halls to Amar's room. At least then, the silence would end, and whatever Mitul needed to say to them both would finally come out.

Amar and Kesari were both up when they entered the room, eating breakfast together and talking in hushed voices. Aleida was pleased to see that Kesari's complexion had brightened, and some of the lively spark in her eyes had returned. She still looked too tired, but after the ordeal she'd been through, that was to be expected.

"Mitul!" Amar said, standing up from the table and taking a few strides toward the man.

"Oh good," Mitul said. "You remember me."

"I do now."

The man's jaw remained set tight. He reached into his pocket and pulled out a sheet of paper, which had been folded over several times. With more force than was necessary, he thrust it against Amar's chest. "A letter?" he said disdainfully. "You run off to risk your life, and you leave me with a *letter*? Is that all I'm worth to you?"

"Of course not." Amar grabbed the paper before it could fall, and Mitul stepped back with crossed arms. "Like I explained, I didn't want you trying to talk me out of it."

"Because you knew it was a reckless, foolish idea."

"Because I knew you wouldn't have let me go."

"And since when have I been able to stop you from doing *anything* you set your mind to? You would have gone anyway, and I would have hated it, but leaving like *that*, sneaking away without a word—that's not fair. You should have told me." He glanced briefly at Aleida with these words, and she wilted under their implication.

"I thought it would be easier," Amar said.

"Easier for you, maybe."

"For both of us," he snapped.

"And what would have happened if you'd actually died? You robbed me of any chance to say goodbye."

"I said it in the letter," Amar said tersely.

"Yes, but *I* didn't! Skies, you can be so dense sometimes." He sighed, and some of the anger in his face smoothed away. "I thought you were gone, Amar. For good this time."

"I'm sorry. I didn't know how else to go through with it. If you'd told me not to do it, I would have listened."

Mitul stood there for a few seconds, opened his mouth to speak, and then clamped it shut. He uncrossed his arms and reached forward to put both hands on Amar's shoulders. "I'm just happy you're all right.

But you'd better not do something like that ever again—not without telling me."

"I won't."

"And you," Mitul said, turning to Aleida. "I suppose he swore you to secrecy, did he?"

She hung her head. "I'm sorry."

"No, I understand. What you all went through couldn't have been easy. I wasn't ready to hear it before, but I am now, if you still want to share."

Aleida couldn't speak for the others, but she certainly wanted to talk about it, at least with him. Amar requested a couple more breakfast trays for his guests, and then they all sat and talked as the morning passed by. Kesari remained mostly silent, fidgeting with the hem of her shirt and looking very much like she might start crying again at any moment. Telling the story was easier for Aleida; she'd come out of the situation with the one thing she'd wanted for months—Valkyra rendered powerless. Not erased from existence entirely, but she found her interminable containment an acceptable compromise.

"Do you have her with you?" Amar asked, and she knew instantly what he was talking about. She reached for the small bag tied to her belt, opened it, and dug through the assortment of coins inside until she found the signet ring that held Valkyra's spirit. As soon as she handed it over to him, she felt like she could breathe a little easier.

"I'll keep her close," Amar said. "Always. I won't lose her. You have my word."

"She can't hurt anyone anymore," Aleida said. "But it's a comfort to know she's in safe hands."

Afterward, their talk turned to what came next. Jasala had informed Amar that she wouldn't be executing King Bhajan and would instead sentence both him and Queen Indira to imprisonment in the imperial palace where she could keep a close eye on them both. So far, the king seemed supportive of Jasala's ideas to rebuild the empire and heal what damage the war had done, including by using his influence to broker peace between Jakhat and those who'd opposed the empress. Amar would be staying on the Jasala's council and hoped to be able to effect meaningful change in that position. When he said he wanted to abandon his quest to break his curse, Mitul looked surprised, but not in a bad way.

"Are you sure?" he asked.

"For now," Amar replied. "Searching for answers has gotten me killed more often than not, and it's caused my friends a lot of pain and sacrifice. I owe it to myself and the rest of you to try and honor *this* life, which wouldn't have been possible without all of you."

"I think that's a wonderful plan," Mitul said. "And what about you, Kes? Are you still planning to go home?"

She nodded. "Saya and I will leave in a few days. She's ready to go home, too. We'll travel together until we reach Hayathu, and then I'll go the rest of the way…on my own."

It seemed this realization had only now struck her, and Aleida tried to ease some of that sting. "Your family will be so happy to see you."

"I know. I'm eager to see them, too."

"I also need to leave," Aleida announced. "I want to visit Chatanda, let Hasan know I'm all right, see where Tyrus was laid to rest, and pay my respects."

"Do you want company?" Mitul asked gently.

She shook her head. "No. I think I need to go alone."

"All right. But don't stay away too long, if you can help it. You know you'll always have a home with Kamaal and I, as long as you want it."

"I know." She *did* want it. "I won't be gone for long, I promise."

"Good. Of course, you should all plan on coming back next spring for the wedding. We wouldn't dream of having it without any of you. Bring your family, Kes. All of you—bring whoever you want. We'll have a proper feast and a celebration that will be remembered in Jakhat for centuries."

"That sounds ambitious," Amar said.

Mitul shrugged. "No more ambitious than exploring the ruins of Shavhalla."

"Or bringing back someone's lost memories," Kesari added.

"Or making friends with the people you were trying to kill," Aleida said.

"All very true," Mitul said with a laugh. "Come on, Amar. Where's your sense of fun and spectacle? A big party will be simple after all this."

"So long as I don't have to be in charge of it."

"Of course not. But as my brother, I'll expect you to give a speech."

He leaned a little closer and winked at Aleida over the table. "A flattering one, otherwise we won't give you any cake."

Several days later, a boat took Aleida south down the Mayuka River from Jakhat, a journey which was fast and uneventful. Already, she felt homesick. Not for a place, but for people. She looked forward to returning to them.

When she disembarked, she followed familiar roads through newly planted fields and grain silos that had been emptied but would fill again. The last of the soldiers that had been occupying the region were marching home, and Aleida passed by several squads of them as she walked. She even saw one group made up of an equal mixture of soldiers in both red and green uniforms. The country was already beginning its healing, and though there were still many wounds that would require more time, this was an encouraging start.

She reached the edge of Hasan's apple orchard, the tree branches already in full bloom with tiny pink and white flowers. Hasan called out her name, and she spotted him waving to her from atop a ladder propped against one of the larger trees. She quickened her pace, and he hurried down to meet her.

"Aleida!" He threw his arms around her and squeezed tight. She hugged him back.

"Hello, Hasan."

"I've been so worried about you. You never wrote back, and then the war—I thought something terrible must have happened to you."

She didn't correct him. Something terrible *had* happened to her, but several beautiful things had happened as well. "I'm here now," she said. "Not for long, but I'm here, and I'm all right. I'm sorry for making you worry."

"I'm just glad to see you in one piece." He looked over her shoulder, shielding his eyes against the sun as he searched the sky.

Before he could ask the question, Aleida answered it. "Valkyra's not with me anymore. It's for the best, but I really don't want to talk about it."

"All right. We don't have to talk. But can I feed you at least? And I assume you'll want to visit your brother."

She nodded. "Yes, please."

"Come on, then. I'll take you to him."

He led her into the orchard, and at first, she thought they were taking a shortcut into town. There was a temple there and a small cemetery, always well cared for and blossoming with flowers in spring and summer. Instead, Hasan took her up a short rise to a hill overlooking his house and the surrounding orchard. There was a bench there, which Aleida had seen Tyrus sitting on the last time she'd visited. She could picture him there so easily now, a wide grin splitting his freckled face, his gray-blue eyes brightening with delight when he saw her.

They reached the bench, and Hasan pointed to a flat stone marker that had been set into the ground in front of it. The name *Tyrus Ceran* had been carved into the stone in both Kavoran and Visan letters, the latter of which Aleida could only read because her father had taught both of them to at least write their own names. Flowers bloomed all around the headstone, bigger and more vibrant than Aleida had seen yet this spring. Perhaps that was due to a little help from Hasan's magic.

"I couldn't bear to put him in the town cemetery," the man said quietly. "I thought he would have hated it there, and you too, if you ever came back to visit him."

Aleida knelt and ran her fingers over Tyrus' name, her sleeves brushing the delicate petals around it. She'd known he was gone for months now, of course, but seeing this made his death feel more real than it ever had before. Her vision blurred, and a few tears dropped onto the flowers. "It's perfect," she told Hasan. "You honored him well."

"So did you."

She shook her head, her guilt spilling out with her tears. "I left him."

"You fought for him. He knew that."

She sniffed and rose to sit on the bench. "I'd like to stay here a while, if that's okay."

"Of course. Take as long as you want. I'll have a warm bed and supper for you at the house whenever you're ready."

Once he was gone, Aleida let herself break down and cry like she hadn't done since she'd first received the news of his death. "I'm sorry, I'm sorry." She said it over and over again, wishing she could go back and change things, replaying all the choices she might have made differently.

"I hope you know that I loved you more than anything."

A low cry from above made her look up to see a familiar gray shadow in the branches. Feros looked down at her with round, black eyes. Had he shown up recently, or had he been there the whole time?

Once, that thought might have made her uneasy. Now, she took some comfort in it. She could imagine the strix sitting up there watching over her brother while he still lived, eating scraps from his palm and waiting for some message to deliver to Aleida. She could just as easily imagine him lingering there after Tyrus was gone, and the picture was a pitiful one. They'd never been friends, her and the strix, but they'd both been fond of Tyrus.

She raised her arm tentatively and spoke to him in a kinder voice than she'd ever used with him before. "Come on, Feros. Come and sit with me."

He fluttered down, not to her arm but to the opposite end of the bench, where he watched her closely, his head tilted in what she thought must be suspicion. She couldn't blame him for being wary of her. Moving slowly so as not to startle him, Aleida reached into her satchel and pulled out some of the dried fish she'd taken for her journey. She unwrapped it, pulled off a piece for Feros, and tossed it to him. He sniffed at it briefly before snatching it up and swallowing the whole thing in one go, then screeched at her for more.

"All right," she said with a slight chuckle. "I hear you. Come on, you'll have to take this one from me if you want it."

He seemed to have no issue with this, and after a few more bites, he had nestled against her side to eat every scrap she offered him. When she scratched at the ruff of gray feathers around his neck, he leaned into the gesture and closed his eyes contentedly.

Perhaps they could become friends after all.

She sat there a while longer, talking to Tyrus and telling him and Feros of all her adventures and her newfound family. She skipped nothing, not even the bad parts, and in telling the story, she found a little more compassion for herself. There was still so much she regretted, and maybe she would carry those regrets for the rest of her life, but she refused to let them be a burden anymore. They were lessons to learn from, not sticks to beat herself with forever.

Besides, she *had* fought for Tyrus, hadn't she? Even if she'd gone about it the wrong way sometimes, she had fought for his life out of love and concern, and maybe a little of her own selfishness. But mostly out of love.

There was nothing to regret about that.

KESARI

KESARI AND LUCIAN,

I don't have the words to express how grateful I am for everything you've done for me since we met, but I'll try anyway. You may have had your own reasons for taking me to Atrea, but then you stayed by my side to help me for the rest of this journey. When I became the enemy, you kept the others safe. In giving me my memories back, you saved me, and you will forever have my gratitude for that alone. It is an honor to call you both friends.

Kes, I'm so proud of the person I've seen you become over the last year. Of all the Tarja I've met in six centuries, there are none I'd rather have by my side than you. Your bravery and your inner strength are unmatched. Wherever you go, whatever you do, I know you'll be incredible. You already are. Please thank your family for letting me borrow your courage and your skill, and enjoy all the time you now have with them.

Lucian, I know I don't need to say it, but keep looking out for her.

May our souls meet again in the next life.

Amar

Kesari sat at the edge of the cliffs overlooking Hayathu's oasis settlement, rereading Amar's letter as the smell of campfire smoke began to drift through the air. Evening had come, and as far as birthdays went, this one had been decent enough. She'd played a few games with Saya's brothers and pretended it didn't hurt when the younger ones asked her to show them some magic like she had during her last visits. She'd put on a happy face when the Sularans cheered for her over dinner, wishing one of their voices was Lucian's. And she'd thanked Saya graciously for her gift—a necklace made of bone and onyx—and tried not to think of the wrapped package at the bottom of her pack.

With a sigh, she folded the letter back up and returned it to her pocket. Then she pulled out Lucian's gift.

She'd been so excited to open it when she first discovered it, but now that the time had come, she could hardly bear the thought of it. It was only a gift. She didn't know what she was so afraid of, but fear was the only word to describe the pit in her stomach and the racing of her pulse.

Saya found her there some time later, the package still unopened in her lap, her legs outstretched toward the edge of the cliff. "There you are," the warrior said, sitting down next to her. "I've been looking for you."

"Sorry. I didn't mean to disappear."

"That's fine. Are you going to open that? Do you want me to give you some privacy?"

Kesari shook her head quickly. "Stay. I don't think I can do it on my own."

"All right."

She turned the package over and hesitated another moment, then slid her fingers beneath the red paper. It came loose, and she pulled it away from the object inside. It was a book, its cover stamped with floral designs around the title.

The Bond Between Souls: Extraordinary Tarja and Spirit Tarja Pairs in Kavoran History.

There was a folded paper marker sticking out from the edge near the end of the book. Her throat tightened as she flipped to that page and saw the inscription written at the bottom of the last chapter. Lucian couldn't have written it himself, of course, but the words were his.

Here's to the day you and I end up in Volume II.

She could practically hear him saying it, his voice filled with his distinctive smug confidence. It broke her. She held the book against her and drew her legs up, leaning into Saya as the young woman wrapped an arm around her shoulders.

She'd meant what she said to Amar back in the palace. She wouldn't have changed anything, and she knew Lucian wouldn't have, either. But she missed him terribly, and she didn't think that feeling was ever going to go away.

She'd felt the same way about Rajiv. She still did, but somehow, she'd learned to live with it. She could learn to live with this hurt, too. But for now, maybe she needed to let it simply overtake her. If Lucian had taught her anything, it was that she couldn't run from her feelings any more than she could run from herself, but she was strong enough to handle them. Sobs shook her entire body, and she cried until she had nothing left.

Afterward, she and Saya descended the cliffs and made their beds under the open sky. They watched the stars appear one by one, Saya naming various Sularan constellations and speaking of the myths inspired by each one. Kesari stayed awake as long as she could, knowing the morning would bring another farewell she would never be truly ready for.

Being alone was not something Kesari was used to. She couldn't remember ever being truly alone for more than a few hours at a time, but that was exactly the position she found herself in once she left Hayathu to travel the rest of the way to Deveaural on her own. It was unsettling, and it only made the sting of Lucian's absence more obvious. He was gone, she'd left her other friends behind, and the world seemed a suddenly vast and ominous place without them.

After a few days, the solitude became more tolerable, though she was still excited to reach Malfram and spend a little time in civilization, even if everyone around her was a stranger. After a hot meal and a night in a rented room, she continued her journey, and a week later, the sprawling fields surrounding Deveaural came into view.

She stood on the hill overlooking them, gazing out across the city's buildings to the glittering sea beyond. Home had never looked so good, and the knowledge that she was here to stay made her weary feet light again.

She hurried down the hill and quickly found the roads that would lead her back to her family's house. Memories of conversations with Lucian came back to her clearly here, how she'd talked about opening a healer's shop somewhere in town, and how he'd smiled and said what an excellent idea that was. She'd have to make new plans now, but that was all right. She had time—more time than she'd believed she would ever have. Whatever she did, she would make him proud.

When she was close enough and couldn't bear to wait any longer, Kesari ran the rest of the way home, the wind stinging her eyes and whipping at her hair. Home, where the smell of freshly baked pie carried across the grass, wafting through an open window through which she could see her mum in the kitchen. Home, where Navya was talking to the chickens as she fed them, and her father was mending a fence for the goats. Home, with the sunlight gleaming off the roof of their house like gold, and it all looked so perfect that she felt her heart was about to burst.

Navya saw her first. She dropped the bucket she was holding and sprinted across the field, the tails of Rajiv's coat trailing behind her like wings. "Kesari! Mum, Dad, Kesari's home!"

She ran faster, so fast she felt like she was flying, and she didn't stop until she reached them. They wrapped her up in a tangle of hugs and laughter, warmth and safety.

Home. She was home.

AMAR

Mitul,

First, let me say that I'm sorry. I don't know if we'll see each other again. If everything works out the way it's meant to, then this is goodbye, and I know it's an inadequate one. A letter isn't enough, and you'll be angry I left without saying anything, and what I'm about to do will hurt you more than anyone else. But if I'd told you any of this before I left, you would have known something was wrong. You're the only person who could have talked me out of it, and it was too important to risk being talked out of, and too dangerous for you to come along. So here we are, with a stupid letter and a pitiful apology. I really am sorry, and I hope you'll forgive me someday. But you can't follow me this time.

You know all of what I'm about to say already, or at least I hope you do. In case you don't, I'll say it anyway. You've been the most loyal friend anyone could possibly ask for, and I thank you for all the love and support you've given me since we first met. Without you, I may never have known that I was cursed, let alone how to break it. You kept me on the right path when I was lost. You sacrificed so much for me. I don't think I ever properly thanked you for that. I'm not sure I truly can, but it means everything to me. Thank you, a thousand times over. No one has ever done more for me. No one has ever been so selfless.

It's time for you to be selfish now, Mitul. Marry Kamaal, grow old together, protect the joy you've found with each other, and live out the rest of your days making music and dancing and enjoying the company of those who love you. You deserve every happiness in the world.

Until we meet again, whether it be in this life or the next.

Your brother,

Amar

Amar gently folded up the letter, taking care not to rip the worn creases any farther, and slipped it back into his pocket. He'd held on to it for more than forty years, tucked away inside his journal. Including the journal itself, the Shavhallan sword in his closet, and the ring he wore on a chain around his neck, it was one of his most important possessions, and certainly his most sentimental. He'd be sad to see it lost to the flames, but it was a small loss, by comparison.

With a heavy sigh, he stood and went to the mirror, checking his appearance to make sure he looked presentable. His white funeral suit was immaculate, though the middle stretched a bit tighter around his stomach than it once had. He leaned in closer and combed his fingers through his hair, most of it turned gray now, but still as thick as ever. A neatly trimmed beard of the same color covered his jaw, hiding some of the wrinkles that were deepening around his mouth. The creases around his eyes and along his forehead were more prominent, but he wore them like a badge of honor. He'd earned them, after all.

He wasn't sure when the aging had started, or what exactly had caused it, though he did have some theories. He'd spent the last four decades in service to the Kavoran empire and its people, striving to help them recover and rebuild after the war, and afterward, to create as much peace, happiness, and prosperity as he could for all the people of Erythyr. Much of it was beyond his control, but he fought for what he could and lent his wisdom and experience where it was asked for—and sometimes where it wasn't.

It helped that Empress Jasala shared many of his goals, and with the support of many others, they'd slowly begun transforming the country into one where conflict was minimal and cooperation highly valued. The people of Kavora were given a louder voice to help with these changes, electing leaders who represented them to serve on Kavora's ruling council. Jasala remained empress, but the role held far less power than it once had, and that was exactly how she wanted it.

Somewhere along the way, the changes in Amar had started. Subtle at first—a filling out of his body to more adult proportions, a thicker beard, a few gray hairs. Eventually, the changes were undeniable. He was getting older. The curse, if not entirely broken, was break*ing*.

He thought he understood now what he hadn't before. To atone was more than simply sacrificing oneself or resolving an immediate crisis, though maybe that had been part of it. But he believed most of his atonement had come in the aftermath, in the rebuilding, in the daily hard work of mending bridges and healing wounds and trying to make the world a little better. Some of that work was fairly straightforward—ensuring Kavora kept its agreements with the Sularans and repairing some of the damage in those diplomatic relations. Other parts were much harder and more complicated, like restoring Vis as an independent nation and getting the council to agree to paying reparations.

There had been some backsliding, of course, and sometimes he found himself questioning whether he was still aging, or if that process had stopped. It always created a bit of a panic within him, and he would wonder if he was doing enough. Mitul had always reassured him that he was.

Where would he find that reassurance now?

He blinked back the sting in his eyes and took a deep breath, then slipped on his shoes and left his room in the palace. The carriage ride to the funerary grounds was a short one, and he managed to keep his composure throughout the trip.

When he stepped out of the carriage and saw Mitul's body on the pyre, keeping his composure became far more difficult.

He swallowed the knot in his throat and approached those gathered to pay their respects. He wasn't going to force himself through all the formalities of greeting them and thanking them for coming and saying how much it would have meant to Mitul that they were here. But he did at least want to greet a few of them, and he found their faces easily in the crowd.

Aleida was there at the front, her mouth tight and her eyes wet.

She'd taken Mitul's death harder than anyone, and she clung to Amar for several seconds when he embraced her. A few older children stood with her, orphans from the group home she'd started several years ago. She ran it with help from some other Visans who'd stayed in Jakhat rather than returning to their homeland. This allowed her to also focus on her artwork. Mitul and Kamaal had visited the group home often, always bringing gifts and songs and stories. The children loved them dearly and called them grandfathers. Their loss would be felt keenly, but they'd had a strong positive impact on those young lives.

Amar greeted Saya next. "Thank you for coming," he whispered. "I know your people must miss you." After her mother's passing a few years ago, she had been chosen as masahi, and her duties kept her very busy.

"They'll survive without me for a few weeks," she replied. "I only wish I could have been here sooner. There was so much I wish I could have told him."

"He knew," Amar said, offering her a gentle smile.

Finally, he went to Kesari. She'd come for Kamaal's funeral a few months prior, though she hadn't arrived in time to see him off. Still, she'd wanted to stay close and keep Mitul company, and she'd ended up living with him for a little while. Amar had been able to rest easier knowing she was looking after the man when he couldn't be around. She'd been the one to find Mitul a few days ago, still in his bed and looking like he was only sleeping.

It wasn't such a bad way to go, in the grand scheme of things. Amar could only hope he met such a peaceful end whenever his time finally came. Still, his heart ached when he looked at his dearest, oldest friend on that funeral pyre. Of all the losses he'd experienced in six centuries, this one hurt the most.

Mitul's body lay still, his wrinkled, knobby hands clasped atop his chest, his silvery hair draped over his shoulders and gleaming in the sun. His saraj lay beside him, ready to burn with him so he could take his songs into the afterlife. Amar didn't know whether he fully believed in such things, but he'd seen enough of spirits and magic to hope.

A few people approached the pyre and left their own offerings around Mitul. Aleida set a drawing beside his shoulder, and Kesari placed a flower from the garden he and Kamaal had grown behind the studio. Amar took the old, worn letter out of his pocket and stuck it carefully beneath Mitul's clasped hands.

It was tradition for a Tarja to light a Kavoran funeral pyre using magic, but Amar and Aleida had chosen to bend the rules of tradition today. At a nod from Amar, Kesari went to a nearby brazier and lit a torch. She carried it over and set the wood aflame. The fire spread quickly, and they all kept silent vigil over the body.

Amar felt Kesari's arm link through his as they watched the smoke rise. A few tears ran down his face and soaked into his beard, but despite his grief, he couldn't help smiling a little. This loss was heavy, but it was different from all he'd suffered before, and it marked a change that gave him some relief.

Mitul was gone, but eventually, Amar would follow. He wouldn't be left behind this time. He wouldn't have to carry this loss with him for centuries.

"Farewell, my brother," he whispered to the fire. "Until we meet again."

THE END

GLOSSARY

ALTMA – an energy source present in all living things which can be used by Tarja to fuel their magical abilities

ARTEX – the Visan deity, believed to be the creator of all things; sometimes referred to as 'the Artist'

BOND – a magical connection between a Spirit Tarja and a living person which grants the living partner the ability to channel altma at the expense of sharing the remainder of their natural lifespan with the Spirit Tarja

CHANNEL (ALTMA) – the act of drawing altma from one's surroundings and/or within oneself and using it to perform magical feats

CURSE – a specific branch of magic whose affects are longer lasting and more powerful than most types of magic; curses were outlawed in Erythyr several hundred years ago and much of the knowledge about them has been erased or forgotten

DARAVAK – a species of fungus native to Kavora which temporarily inhibits a Tarja's ability to channel altma

GHAYAT – a species of antelope-like creatures native to the Sular Desert that are an integral part of the ecosystem and the Sularan people's way of life

HASEPH – a rite of passage undertaken by all Sularan youth at age sixteen in which the participant is required to seek out and bring back to their tribe something of value so that they may become a full-fledged member of the tribe

JITAARA – The basic monetary unit of Kavora

JHIVAN – a word found in a set of ancient Shavhallan records believed by some to mean *altma* in Kavoran; *jhivan* is also sometimes referenced in myth as a fourth element of magic representing life itself

KANJIRA – a small handheld drum, typically a circular wooden frame covered on one side with a drumhead made from animal skin while the other side is left open

MASAHI – the highest-ranking member on a council of tribal leaders chosen to represent the Sularan people

MESALA – a species of plant native to the Sular Desert which is the main food source of the ghayat and whose flowers can enhance a Tarja's magical abilities; sometimes referred to as 'Sularan torches'

SARAJ – a Kavoran stringed instrument approximately one meter in length, which is versatile for a variety of musical styles and has a rich, reverberating sound

SAMUD – a strategy game favored among Kavoran nobility

SPIRIT TARJA – the spirit of a Tarja who died prematurely; this death causes the altma within them to tether their soul to the physical world either until the altma fades or until the Spirit Tarja forms a Bond with a living partner

TARJA – any person capable of channeling altma to perform magical feats; a Tarja may be born with the ability to use magic or, less commonly, may be someone who has gained those abilities by forming a Bond with a Spirit Tarja

CAST & NOTABLE FIGURES

Akraja Munar Sharma – deceased, former emperor of Kavora, father of Prince Savir, brother of Empress Dashiva

Aleida Ceran – a young Visan woman orphaned during Kavora's invasion of Vis, older sister to Tyrus, became a Tarja through her Bond with Valkyra

Amar – a Kavoran man cursed with immortality, currently believes himself to be Prince Savir, long-time friend of Mitul

Avani Muraka – an intimidating woman who serves as general of the imperial Tarja military forces

Bhajan Vora – king of the city of Valmandi within the Kavoran Empire, husband of Queen Indira, father of Princess Priyani, grandfather of Prince Savir

Chayani Sha – Advisor of Magic on the Valmandi Royal Council

Dashiva Sharma – reigning Empress of Kavora, younger sister of the late Emperor Akraja, mother of Princess Jasala

Dev Ashaya – Advisor of Law on the Valmandi royal council, formerly a member of Empress Dashiva's Imperial Council

Feros – a strix belonging to Aleida and Tyrus Ceran who often carried messages between them

Hasan Khurana – a Tarja healer and farmer who lives in Chatanda, former guardian of Tyrus and Aleida

Indira Vora – queen of the city of Valmandi within the Kavoran Empire, wife of King Bhajan, mother of Princess Priyani, grandmother of Prince Savir

JAMESON WEATHERFORD – deceased, an Atrean Tarja of great skill and renown, sometimes referred to by his formal title The Great and Honorable Wizard Jameson

JASALA SHARMA – official heir to the Kavoran imperial throne, daughter of Empress Dashiva, cousin of Prince Savir

KAMAAL RUMAN – a famous Kavoran painter, former parter of Mitul

KESARI EVES – an Atrean girl with Kavoran ancestry, sister of Rajiv and Navya, became a Tarja through her Bond with Lucian

KHAN – Advisor of War on the Valmandi Royal Council and commanding general of Valmandi's military

KHATRI – Advisor of Secrets on the Valmandi Royal Council

LUCIAN – Kesari's Spirit Tarja, takes the form of hovering flames and is typically about the size of an apple

MITUL RAMA – a middle-aged Kavoran musician, long-time friend of Amar, former partner of Kamaal

NANDINI KUMAR – deceased, former Tarja advisor to Empress Dashiva, now a Spirit Tarja who goes by the name Valkyra

NAVYA EVES – younger sister of Kesari and Rajiv

PRIYANI VORA SHARMA – deceased, former princess of Valmandi and empress of Kavora (through marriage to Emperor Akraja), daughter of King Bhajan and Queen Indira of Valmandi, mother of Prince Savir

RAJIV EVES – deceased, older brother of Kesari and Navya

SAVIR AKRAJA JAI SHARMA – son of Emperor Akraja and Princess Priyani, former heir to the Kavoran imperial throne, officially reported dead but believed to be alive by some

SAYA HÀS SEDA – a young Sularan woman completing her haseph, friend of Kesari, Mitul, and Amar

SEDA HÀS YUSANA – Masahi of the Sularan tribe in Hayathu, mother of Saya

TAMAYA TAKHAR – an elderly Tarja healer and former trainer in Jakhat's Tarja military, known for her great skill and knowledge

TARIK APTI – a stoic guard who has served the Valmandi monarchs for years, assigned to oversee Prince Savir's security

TYRUS CERAN – deceased, younger brother of Aleida

VALKYRA – Savir's Spirit Tarja (formerly Aleida's), takes the form of a small furred and feathered white dragon

VASU – Advisor of Diplomacy on the Valmandi Royal Council

ZEFAR HÀS YARATHA – a Sularan mercenary and an outcast among his tribe, Saya's former mentor

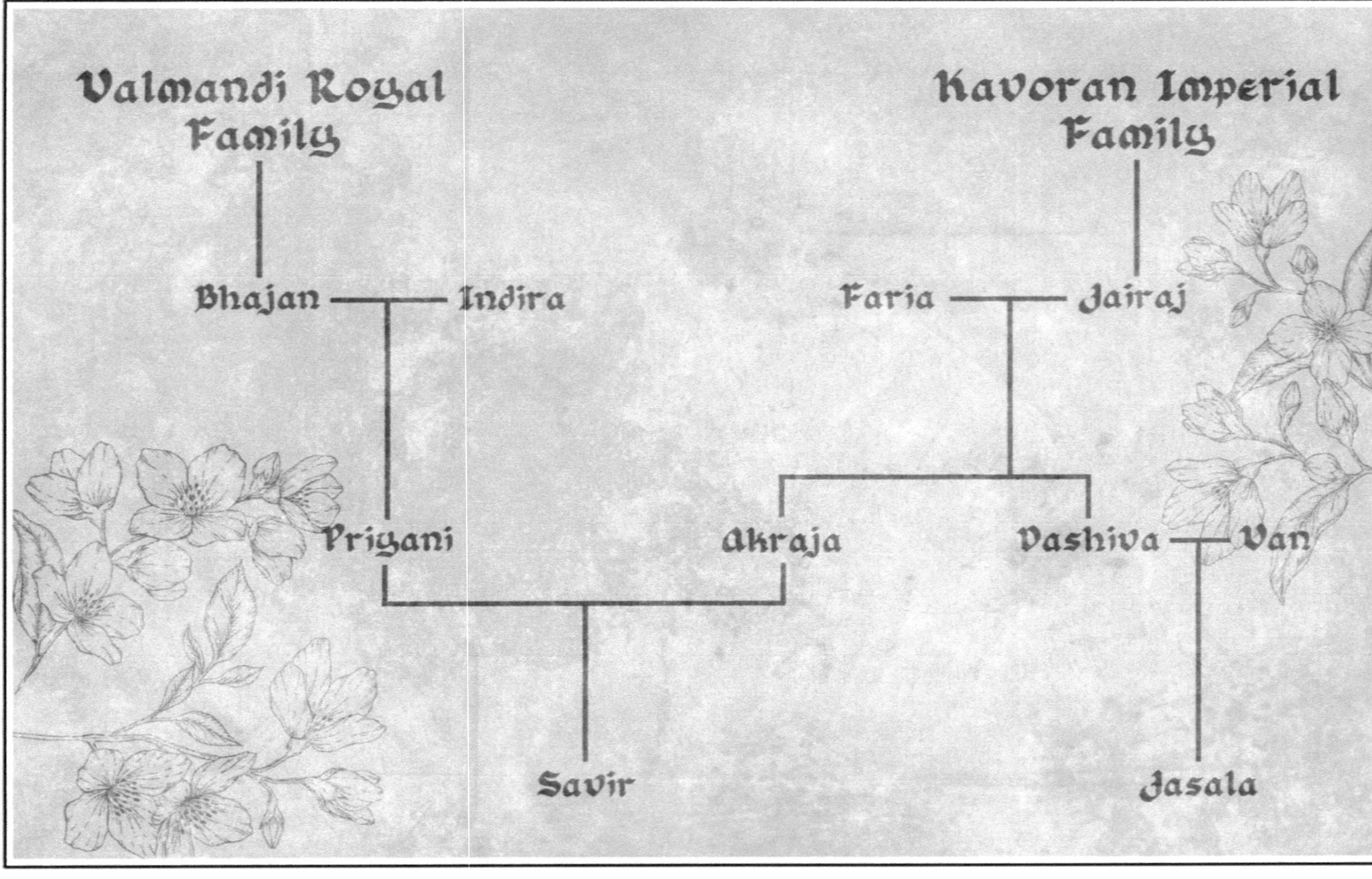
Valmandi Royal Family
Kavoran Imperial Family
Bhajan
Indira
Faria
Jairaj
Prigani
Akraja
Vashiva
Van
Savir
Jasala

DEAR READER

Thank you so much for taking the time to read this book. I hope you enjoyed it. Now that you're finished, please consider leaving an honest review. Reviews are especially important to indie authors and can help others make informed decisions about their reading experience, which allows the book to reach its target audience.

Follow me social media to stay up to date on my writing, and please feel free to reach out. Your questions and comments about the story and characters are always welcome and appreciated.

tahernandez.com
tahernandez@tahernandez.com
Twitter: @ta_hernandez5
Instagram: @ta_hernandez5
facebook.com/tahernandez05

ACKNOWLEDGEMENTS

Writing this series has been both a dream come true and a monumental challenge. Fortunately, I didn't have to go it alone, and I have so many people to thank for supporting me along the way.

My family has always been so encouraging of my writing and other creative endeavors. I appreciate you all for showing an interest in what I'm doing, for getting excited with me in my successes, and for picking me up when things are hard.

To Taylor, Michelle, Stephanie, Heather, Jordan, Megan, Sarah, Jenn, Chris, Mandy, Katarina, Alex, Bryanna, Cat, Becky, Catherine, Fem, and probably a dozen more people I'm not remembering right now (sorry!), thank you for your valuable input and for sharing your enthusiasm for the story and characters.

Last but not least, thank you, reader, for spending some time in the world of my imagination. Just the fact that you gave this story a chance means a lot, and the fact that you've stuck with the story and characters this long fills my heart with joy.

ABOUT THE AUTHOR

T. A. Hernandez is a science fiction and fantasy author and long-time fan of speculative fiction. She grew up with her nose habitually stuck in a book and her mind constantly wandering to make-believe worlds full of magic and adventure. She was first inspired to write after reading J. R. R. Tolkien's *The Lord of the Rings* many years ago and is now happily engaged in an exciting and lifelong quest to tell captivating stories.

She is a clinical social worker and the proud mother of two girls. She also enjoys drawing, reading, graphic design, playing video games, and making happy memories with her family and friends.

OTHER WORKS BY T. A. HERNANDEZ

THE CURSE OF SHAVHALLA TRILOGY

Tethered Spirits
Revenant Prince
Riven Empire (coming 2024)

THE SECRETS OF PEACE TRILOGY

Secrets of PEACE
Renegades of PEACE
Survivors of PEACE

OTHER STORIES

Whispers of Shadow and Starlight
Calico Thunder Rides Again

www.ingramcontent.com/pod-product-compliance
Lightning Source LLC
Chambersburg PA
CBHW020527310726
48979CB00014B/2243/J

9781734033038